Dragon Squadron

10 9 8 7 6 5 4 3 2 SECOND EDITION

ISBN-13: 978-1499374216   ISB-10: 1499374216

Printed in the United States of America
Cover design by L. M. Vitt
Book Design by L. M. Vitt

Dragon Squadron

Acknowledgments

This book, like my life, has been a process. It has not been easy and after all the times I had almost given up, I still push forward. There were many along the way that never given up on me and most of all, they made sure I had never given up on myself. My heart overflows with gratitude.

With that being stated I have to give special thanks to my son, my wonderful wife everyone that helped me make this book possible. Enjoy!

For Liz

Chapter 1

He nudged the throttle forward as he put the *Dragon's Heart* into a steep climb. Taking his WW II fighter to its limits, Conner's body gently pressed into his seat as he climbed; his attention centered on the altimeter as he waited. The indicator climbed past the red line several hundred feet, the engine sputtered and stalled. Noting the instrument, he cut back the throttle and leveled off into a gentle glide. As the small aircraft gently descended, the Allison V12 coughed and sputtered to life once again. Conner felt the pull of the propeller once again as he nosed the craft downward into a lazy spiral.

Amongst the floating mist of clouds, Connor felt most at home. His Curtis P40 Warhawk had been his favorite means of communing with the sky since his first combat training flight in the early 1940s. Its sleek lines of the fighter made it a formidable predator during the Second World War. The roar of the plane's V12 engine always kept his focus in the vast blue. In the cockpit of his plane, he could disconnect himself from the world and think about days long past.

He had purchased the airplane in which he had flown countless combat missions as part of the military. The *Dragon's Heart* had been his first and favorite in an extensive vintage aircraft collection. Over the years, many others had been acquired. Among them were a German BF 109 Messerschmitt, Japanese Mitsubishi A6M Zero, and other American planes such as a P51 Mustang, and a B17 Flying Fortress. Recently, an F4U Corsair had been added to the treasure trove of vintage war birds. Above all vintage and modern aircraft, his Warhawk was his most treasured.

Over the years, his crew had accomplished many modifications to the small fighter. A modified Allison V12 engine that produced close to an astonishing 2000 horsepower with a new five-bladed prop design and updated avionics were but a few of these improvements. She was faster than factory specifications and had a much greater range. The *Dragon's Heart* was quite the hotrod of the sky. She sported her original colors of tan and olive drab camouflage, as well as the winged tiger, a red angel *Lizzy*, and tiger's teeth that were synonymous with his famous unit.

Like his plane, Connor was far from the average. At first look, you would not suspect that he could be more than 25 years old. The wisdom in his eyes told a different story. He was not actually of the human race, but of the race of elves that had once been abundant during the time before time—during the age of magic. Anthriel had been the name given to him at birth. Older than any modern country or government, he was tall of stature and fluid in every movement, almost feline in nature. His face was not chiseled like most handsome men but had the look of sculpted porcelain that had been painted to give it a male quality like no other. Having no facial hair, as in all elves, he could be almost described as beautiful.

He had volunteered, being one of the last Riders, to stay behind with a handful of elves and dwarves to watch and protect mankind from the magic that had been hidden away and to protect mankind from mankind. The elves and dwarves made up his crew and staff. The rest of his race, along with the dwarves, had once again built great starships and returned to the heavens to continue learning what secrets the cosmos had to offer. They had destroyed the great elfin city, Atlantis, as well as hidden the dwarf city known as Shangri-La, deep within the earth before leaving the planet behind. The knowledge and power kept within these cities would be far too great for mankind to fathom, much less control.

Connor had blended in well and helped mankind as much as the limitations set forth by the Council of Elves and Dwarves would allow. From time to time, Conner would give human technology a nudge forward, helping the fortune of the stone city's inhabitants. At one point, he made the acquaintance of two brothers who had been in business together with a small bicycle shop on the east coast, giving them a few ideas. This started a series of discoveries that would change mankind forever. With patience and a little time, he had regained the ability to soar amongst the clouds and Wilbur and Orville became part of history.

Connor had been the Rider of his Skymate, a powerful emerald dragon. It had been well over a thousand years since he had danced in the clouds with Emorthra. The mighty dragon had been a strong and noble friend. With eyes, the color of jade and scales of deepest emerald green, Conner could never forget the image of his friend and comrade-in-arms for as long as he breathed.

A Skymate was a mystical winged beast that bonded with an elf or human and on rare occasion even the race of dwarves. These beasts have been dragons, griffins and even winged horses. It had been said that a bond between these beasts would go so far as the actual bonding of the two souls. Two minds, at times, would become one. The hearts and souls would feel the pain and joy of the other, even when miles apart. Riders and their Skymates were warriors and keepers of peace in the time before the human race dominated the planet. Riders were well respected by their peers and feared by their enemies. To be chosen by one of the noble beasts as its Skymate was an honor, as well as a great responsibility.

Connor was a warrior from another age. It was an age when men were few, and mystical beasts were plenty. There were no great winged beasts to share the sky in this era. Their memory had all but faded to legend. A fighter plane from the Second Great War was the closest he could come in these times of technology and science to that same sense of owning the sky. Now, only technology could help him touch the clouds. Flying with an open cockpit brought back fond memories of those times before mechanical workings. He could often imagine himself on the back of his emerald-scaled, fire-breathing friend.

In today's computerized world, keeping watch over mankind without being discovered became more challenging as mankind's technology advanced. Hiding his elfin ears had been the easy part. The difficulties brought about living in the twenty-first century AD had been his human identity. Elves lived as long as they were needed or were killed in battle. This did not work well for the government offices and census takers. To blend in better, every now and again he would have to disappear. He would be presumed dead, then in about ten or fifteen years, reappear, acquiring a new identity. Even this had become more difficult with the advent of Social Security, and all of the numbers that the governments used to oversee their citizens and collect their taxes.

Today, the spring time Wyoming sky beckoned him. On a backdrop of bright blue and fluffy white, he rolled his vintage fighter onto its right wing and pushed the nose into a slow and graceful dive. The controls were extremely responsive with the new addition of computer assisted flight controls. Swooping down like a raptor on unsuspecting prey, he rushed to the earth at speeds that exceeded 350 miles per hour. Pulling gently back on the stick, he leveled the agile craft just fifty feet from the ground and a split second from impact. Only with his elfin agility, calm and constitution could he handle the forces of the sudden stop in descent. No human, except for a trained Rider could even come close to this feat. He followed the terrain in nap-of-the-earth for several miles, before once again pointing the nose toward the clouds in a quick and steep climb. Adding a touch of spice to his climb, he put the craft into a slow, left-handed spiral.

It was a far cry from being in the saddle nestled on the shoulders of Emorthra, but the cockpit of his Warhawk had become his second home. He could never be one with this manmade, dwarf-modified warbird, but it is as close as he could get to dance with the sky as he did in the days of old. He could touch the billowy clouds, but the formed plastic and metal aircraft left him alone in the bright blue.

This was the first shakedown flight since the last overhaul of the *Dragon's Heart*. Computer boxes and electronic servo actuators replaced the steel cables, levers, arms and pulleys of the original flight controls. Along with a more agile craft, this also decreased weight. Less weight equaled more speed and greater range. With today's acrobatics, he was determined to put the controls through their paces or rip every rivet from the fuselage frame. So far, the Warhawk held together better than he possibly could have imagined.

The wind feathered Anthriel's long braided hair behind him as they danced among the clouds. With Emorthra's deep emerald scales beneath his saddle, he drank deeply from the cool, crisp, swirling mists of the deep blue sky. As one, Dragon and Rider cut through the billowing clouds like a sharp knife through fresh hot bread. Refreshed and exhilarated, they danced with the sky as their ballroom, the sun as their chandelier, and the wind to keep the time of their own music.

Conner felt himself go further back into his past. He fondly relished the day Emorthra chose him. In the hatchery where he stood as a young elfin boy, Anthriel marveled at all of the eggs lined up waiting to touch a rider. They were not organized but were in rows. Like monstrous Easter eggs, they were every color of the rainbow. Each one was nestled in soft elfin cloth and meticulously cared for by dragon and elf from the moment they had been laid.

On the day of his passage to adulthood, every elf was taken to the hatchery to see if he would be chosen. Anthriel was no exception. As many before him, he worried that he would not be chosen. Very few were called to be a Rider.

The elf was pulled away from his relished past by the flashing Marconi on his fuel indicator. The vision of the past which he had while performing such stunts made him uneasy. He did not like it when he could not focus totally on the task at hand. It had been a long time since he had had a waking dream. He was resolved to do some checking on it when he got back. A visit with the Skystone was in order.

The Skystone linked the elves and dwarves with the magic that was buried deep within the earth. It was used to keep watch over the magic itself, and was driven into the crust of the planet—put there by a volunteer of the race of dragons. The release of the magic would mean certain chaos and destruction for most of the mankind.

Running low on fuel, he knew that the test fight was near its end. It was time to head for home. Pleased with her performance, Connor could put the *Dragon's Heart* to rest, knowing that whatever stunt or maneuver Conner could imagine would be done without a moment's hesitation. He had full confidence in the machine's ability.

After a more than perfect landing, Connor taxied the *Dragon's Heart* into the massive hangar. Nestled in the seclusion of the Wyoming's Big Horn

Valley, the elfin and dwarf stronghold was away from the prying eyes of mankind and governments. Those who stayed behind liked it that way. The less contact they had with the public, the better. If this secret were to be discovered, life as mankind knew it would be distorted beyond their comprehension. Every belief that was held by the common people would not only be questioned but could possibly become instantly null and void.

The property had been in the possession of the fair folk long before the birth of the nation. Just outside the Native American reservations, it had been willed through fictitious names for generations to be a private sanctuary and kept up by a private trust fund. This fund was fueled by the large fortune amassed in the thousands of years by those who were left behind. Taxes were paid, and security kept.

The estate housed an airfield, hangar facilities, and a small farmhouse. The airfield and large hangar were the only things out of the ordinary to the naked eye in the Big Horn valley. The dwarves and elves took sanctuary below the surface in miles of great tunnels and halls that were carved painstakingly from the bones of the earth.

The P40 came to a stop just inside the door. Noticing the smile on Connor's face and as the head mechanic approached the plane, he directed other ground crews to their places. "Well, are ye finally happy now?" the balding dwarf shouted.

"Buck, you have once again outdone yourself!" Connor replied as he climbed out of the cockpit. The smile on the elf's face could not contain his excitement. It could only be compared to a child on a Christmas morning.

"As always, M' lad! You would be a fool to think anything less!"

"She is not a dragon, but her name suits her well, thanks to you."

"Now that all the bugs have been worked out, I can begin the refit on the *Griffin Claw*." Beaming with pride, Buck tossed a stubby thumb over his shoulder toward a B17 across the hangar.

The maintenance bays that housed the plethora of aircraft, ranging from antique biplanes to modern jets and a couple of helicopters, remained spotless. The high gloss epoxy floor was a wavy mirror image of what went on above it. It was as if it was perpetually covered with a thin layer of spring water. This cleanliness greatly contrasted Buck's grease-stained coveralls. The only thing that was orderly about the old dwarf's appearance was his beard. For fear of getting it caught, burned or tangled, he always kept his long whiskers neatly braided and tied several times just below his chin, and tucked in his well-worn coveralls. Buck's stout and small frame made him an ideal mechanic. He could get into tighter spots than most of his elfin counterparts, and he had the strength to lift, push, pull, and tug anything into place or rip them apart.

With an extremely exceeding hairline, he wore what was left of his rust-colored graying hair tucked up in an old blue ball cap with a big *KC* in dingy white letters on the front. When not wrenching on vintage planes, he enjoyed listening to baseball on the radio. The stocky little man rooted for the boys in blue who hailed from Kansas City whenever he could. The first time he brushed against the sport was in 1985, when the Kansas City Royals had a fantastic season that led them to take the World Series. In all his years he had never seen a more noble sport.

Like everyone else behind, Buck was also born with another name. Human names made it much easier to deal with the public when it was necessary. This was a convenience from time to time, to acquire parts that were needed for maintenance and various projects. To the average human, Buck appeared to be just the short biker type. Other than his size, he blended in quite well.

Buck was born Beladar and son of Belvor. Belvor was a very skilled blacksmith who made blades and tools that had never been seen since the age of magic. This skill was passed down from generation to generation. With mankind's advances in metallurgy and manufacturing techniques, Buck had taken it one step further. With these advances, his young apprentice, Nedloh would have a lot to learn, and much more to contribute in the future.

Most dwarves were content to labor below ground, working with the stone, and from time to time, quarrying gold and jewels—deep within the Wyoming Mountains were no exception. The ore and the precious stone fueled the growth of the fortune, enabling the small fleet of aircraft to be bought, restored and maintained. There were still a few of the stout race that preferred to spend most of their days above the ground. Some, like Buck's nephew, even looked towards the clouds for adventure.

Nedloh had been as mischievous as any 95-year-old dwarf, but also very ingenious and a quick study. His first attempt at building an aircraft almost got them discovered by the United States military. Its revolutionary flight controls and construction were unlike anything of the time. The craft was controlled remotely by the thought patterns of the pilot. It was constructed of a new composite honeycomb material that had never before been used. No man had ever seen a similar material. To the aircraft's misfortune, it was extremely fast but the range of control was very limited. It finally crashed somewhere outside Roswell, New Mexico in the 1950s. The discovery of the craft created quite a commotion. Since then, Nedloh had been forbidden to work on any more secret projects on his own. The advances that he had brought forth were still being tested one by one, and they were slowly integrated into the existing aircraft.

"Well?" Nedloh was more than excited to hear how his fly-by-wire system worked.

"Don't worry, me lad. You did just fine." Buck gave him a firm pat on the shoulder. "Now help me get her towed to her bay. We'll give her the post flight and run her maintenance checks. Jump in there and ride the brakes."

Buck was already hooking up the tow bar and a small, stout aircraft tractor was pulling up to the other end of the tow bar. Like the morning of *Ithenor's Feast*, a major dwarf holiday, the young dwarf grinned. Nedloh always jumped at the chance to sit in any aircraft. One day he hoped to fly. He practiced any time he was not wrenching with his uncle on computer simulators that he and Conner designed. Each aircraft had its own simulator. The simulators were linked to each other through a network. One could not get more real without leaving the ground.

"Hey Buck," Connor called as he watched his ground crew hook up the *Dragon's Heart* and wheel her into the modern layer. "I am going to visit the library. I need to check something."

"Gotcha, ladle! If I need anything, I'll know where to find ya." Buck grinned and went immediately back to the task at hand. Connor always wondered where his head mechanic had gotten his Celtic accent. He had known Buck all of his life and he had never known him to have been anywhere near the Emerald Isle.

Chapter 2

Isabelle Thompson had no idea how or why she ended up in the middle of nowhere. Wyoming was a far cry from the excitement and activities of Kansas City. The tall, thirty-something woman did know one thing: the Cadillac V8 in her old Chevy was thirsty, she was broke and without work. Feeling a little nervous, she started watching road signs and praying for something to pop up.

As the daughter of an automotive technician, she started turning wrenches with her father at an early age. As a little girl, she liked playing with Hot Wheels and model-car kits more than dolls and dresses. Cars and all things mechanical had always been her passion. For as long as she could remember, she always had her hotrod. The 1948 Chevy sedan was the first and only car she'd ever own. Her dad had bought it for her for her as a *Sweet 16* present. Although it was far from sweet when she first laid eyes on it, she and her dad labored to give it a ground-up overhaul. A 500-cubic-inch monster from a 1971 Cadillac replaced the original 216 cubic inch Chevrolet engine. The manual, vacuum shift transmission was also replaced with a more modern automatic. Sporting a fresh charcoal-gray interior, performance stereo, and deep purple paint, it was finished before her senior year of high school. She had driven her date to the prom in it.

All the boys were envious. Many lost to her in street races or at the high school drags that were held twice a year at the local drag strip. The downside to her intense passion for all things mechanical was the extreme loneliness. Since she was an attractive young woman, the guys did not take her seriously and she could not talk cars with the other girls. She did have a few girlfriends with whom she could share her interests. Isabelle was not all tomboy, and she did have a soft side. Although she rarely showed it, it was there. Not many girls can rebuild a carburetor without breaking a nail.

Isabelle was taller than most women were. She stood at six feet with a very feminine build. This also made her more intimidating to most men. Her perfect complexion made her look as if she were in her mid-twenties instead of her early thirties. She was thin and well-proportioned for her height. Her stature gave her strength that matched most men as well as the grace the made any woman envious. Isabelle kept her long brunette hair in a ponytail. While working on anything mechanical, she kept it in a tight bun. Her brown eyes had shown a deep trust that could be rarely seen in a human. She also had a wisdom and street smarts that rivaled any midtown street hood.

After a stint in the military working on helicopter gunships, she was discharged. She got her FAA mechanic's certifications before leaving the service. She had quickly gained a love for aircraft, especially for World War II fighter planes, but never lost her love of cars. Pratt and Whitney radial engines, as well as liquid-cooled V12s, were her favorite power plants.

The economy was terrible in KC. No one there would take a female aircraft mechanic seriously. After a few poor choices and a run of bad luck, she packed up everything she could into her old Chevy and started driving. With only $500 in cash and all that could fit in her car, she headed northwest. Without a map or any particular direction, she drove.

It felt odd to her, but no matter where she went, she had a feeling that it was the direction in which she should be going. The roads looked strangely familiar, and she never felt lost. It was an extreme case of déjà vu. At night, she would dream that once again she was driving. The next morning the scenery would be similar to from the dream the previous night. She had a couple of mild psychic encounters when she was younger, and it seemed that, as of late, they were getting much stronger.

As she looked down at the gauge-cluster of the old Chevy, worry crept into the back of her mind. She was miles from any town and her gas gauge told her that she was about to get some exercise if she could not find a filling station soon. The monster of a power plant in the street rod gave her a smooth and dependable ride. It was also very taxing on the pocketbook. Fuel economy was not what she had in mind when she dropped the old Caddy motor in. Realizing she had no money left and no job, worry gradually became panic.

Passing a green road sign with a familiar airplane on it, she felt a sense of calm wash over her. Thinking to herself that she may be able to get some gas and maybe some work, she began to let off the gas pedal. Flipping the turn signal on, she made a turn onto a well-kept gravel road. She did not even see the sign that was posted, "Private Drive."

Connor made his way to the elevators that went up into the tower. As the door closed behind him, he did not press the button to go up. A down arrow illuminated immediately after pressing the panel. The elevator doors opened to the small and magnificent city carved from solid rock miles below the hangar.

Elves preferred more open spaces to the smothering stone city that lay beneath the thousands of acres that were held as their private sanctuary. The City of Estal was cut from the stone of the earth to house the stay-behind dwarves, the elves, and their families. The size would have boggled the human mind but was only a flicker compared to the grandeur of the great dwarf city of Shangri-La.

It had taken generations for the dwarves and elves to carve their humble dwelling. The dwarves did all they could to make their elfin brothers feel at home. There were open courts and many statues of trees carved from the stone pillars that held up the ceilings of their city. Electricity had been piped in from the outside, which was generated by a multitude of air turbines located on the vast property. The lighting was cycled up and down to simulate the occurrence of day and night. What was done in the times of old by magic, now had to be accomplished by human technology.

Connor stepped out into the subterranean courtyard. The residences of Estal were going about their daily business. All who Connor passed would wave or give a brief hello. Connor was essential to this small community. He made it possible for all who worked and toiled underground to have some contact with the world above. The radios he had brought to them sixty years ago eventually gave way to television, cable and satellite television.

The library was tended to by the elders and keepers of *The Knowledge of the Past*. This was a chamber that housed many books and scrolls on magic and knowledge that had all but gone from this world. There were books on practical magic, such as the *Book of Dwarf Smithing* as well as the *Historical Books of Merlin.*

Magic had been locked away for the safety of the once very young humankind. Its knowledge and practical uses had been stored here for the times that it would be needed. The Council of Elves and Dwarves had done this before they set off to explore the stars. It was also predicted by a very ancient elf woman in one of these many books that the magic would one day be set free by the greed of mankind. It was because of this prophecy that the small group would remain behind to protect mankind, and call the races to return home once again.

Connor passed through the ancient wooden doors with his leather flight jacket still in hand. Quickly glancing at the occupants of the chamber, he proceeded into a single, smaller chamber set off from the main room. He stepped through a narrow doorway that separated the smaller stone room from the larger. Draperies blocked out most of the light from the adjoining larger room. It took Connor only a second for his elfin eyes to adjust to the considerable differences in light. It did not take him long to find the object of his interest.

For eons, the safety of the locked away energy, once known as magic, had to be monitored and safeguarded. It was buried deep within the earth in the form of a crystalline formation so that it was out of the hands of all mankind. The only way that this could be monitored was through a smaller formation that was embedded into the wall of this very room. It was a small hollow stone in which a formation of crystals on the interior had been linked to the larger stone. This smaller stone kept the great power safe. The prophecy had foretold that when the Negastone, the keeper of all the mystical energies, was close to being discovered, the smaller Skystone would awaken. If and when this time ever came, the races would be called back home to protect all who lived.

Connor's feelings and the waking dream in the cockpit put him on edge. Although he did enjoy his visit to his distant past, he could not help but wonder what was in the immediate future. The Skystone was calm at least for now. That still did not set his mind at ease. There was no need to save mankind at this very second, but Connor knew that could change in half of a breath.

"I'm sure there is plenty in the hangar to keep me busy," he said to absolutely no one as he made his way back to the elevator.

Isabelle drove for what seemed like miles, through a forest of huge electricity-producing windmills that covered the rolling Wyoming hills. Their three blades gracefully turned in the spring breeze. The acres of wind turbines soon gave way to a small farmhouse. Behind the house, there stood an extremely large hangar and an active runway. It had the standard orange sock that had been opened to form the nylon cone by the air currents. By the looks of the building in back, she figured it could hold a couple of jumbo airliners. She marveled at its size as her eyes were caught by a sign that read, "Deliveries in the Rear" with a white arrow pointing to the side of the building opposite of the flight line.

There was an aircraft control tower that was part of the hangar. The scale of what had to be a small-time farm airport was astounding. Shortly, she was even more impressed when she spotted a World War II Messerschmitt BF109 that had once been the pride of the German Luftwaffe, sitting next to other vintage planes.

As she pulled up to the small glass door that was marked, "Administration and Deliveries," her car sputtered and died. She noticed that needle on her fuel gauge was stuck on the *E*. It was only a minor miracle that she had gotten this far. Most people would say it was luck, some would say it was fate, but she liked to think that a higher power had something to do with it.

Isabelle remained behind the wheel for a moment after she put her car in park to collect her thoughts. There was no going back now. She was out of money, now out of gas, and low on options. Only one choice was in front of her—surely an operation of this size had something she could do! She would love to get her hands inside the

Messerschmitt or whatever other treasures that may lie inside, but at this point, beggars could not be choosers. She would be happy to make coffee or clean toilets. Stepping out of her car, she made her way to the entrance to the building. She paused, took a quick look to see if anyone was watching, then slipped around the side to the monstrous hangar doors that were wide open.

Chapter 3

Darkness, cold, and hunger...these were the only things that could be felt. Of these, the entities were aware, but all other senses had failed. Why? Where were they? How long had it been since they were imprisoned? Days? Months? Millennia? They did not know. Their hunger was growing. They needed to feed, to consume. They needed freedom. They were not alone. There was a goodness with them... such an *awful* goodness... they needed to escape and scatter.

Just off Highway 180 near Flagstaff, Arizona, the students from Kansas University were busily investigating a gravitational anomaly deep within the earth's crust. The mesas in the Arizona desert surrounded them. The latest satellite-measuring equipment discovered a meteor-impact crater that created a substantial increase in the earth's density, more so than in the areas surrounding it.

The Board of New Studies decided that portion of the geology department's yearly budget could be used to fund this survey. It took a little politics and a lot of red tapes, but the study was approved by the state and federal governments.

The field camp had only been set up for a couple of weeks. The head of the geology department and leading scientist in the field, Dr. Emmitt Strouse, was leading the study and excavation. It was quite an undertaking. Scientific equipment and computers, as well as plenty of wheelbarrows and shovels, were kept in mobile laboratories. Surrounding the site was a small tent city. Miniature domes of rainbow-colored nylon dotted the surrounding area to make up the students' temporary dormitories.

The students labored as an ant colony, each one busy with their assigned task in their fields of study. Much of the earth was moved by hand. Routinely, the layers of soil would be tested for mineral content, settlement, and dated as they went down several hundred feet. Every sample had to be cataloged and stored in another trailer or carefully sent back to the University.

Dr. Strouse had been with the university for 10 years. He had liked the city of Lawrence, Kansas. It had all the charm of a small town with all the conveniences of a big city. Being a big outdoorsman, the area also was well suited for his hobbies with a state park right outside of town. When he was not teaching, he would spend his time camping, fishing and enjoying what Mother Nature had to offer.

Even though he was tall, handsome and charming, the college professor had never married. The bachelor life had suited him well. Outside of his work, his black Labrador had followed him everywhere and had been his best camping buddy. He felt no other need for companionship. Fanny had been his four-legged best friend for the past fifteen years. She had been put to sleep four months earlier due to failing health and old age. Since then, he had thrown himself into his work, being the only way he knew to fill his time.

Emmitt was the top geologist in his field. Kansas University was very fortunate to have a professor of his caliber. He could have made considerably more money working for any megacorporation doing geological surveys, but teaching was his life. Shaping young minds and sharing the secrets of what Mother Earth had to give was like no other joy. His slightly receding, salt-and-pepper hair gave him a heroic appearance. Many of his students called him John Wayne. He did not mind. Actually, he thought of it as a great term of endearment. All loved him.

The department had been studying an impact crater in the Painted Desert outside of Flagstaff, Arizona through satellite imaging for some time. The gravitational anomaly itself was the target of this particular study. The center of the crater had a significantly higher density than that of the area around it, causing a difference in the earth's gravity.

Dr. Strouse had theorized that the meteor itself, hidden under layers of earth, caused this anomaly. This could possibly be a new element to add to the Periodic Table. Regardless, new secrets of the universe were about to be unlocked. He had no idea of what it was comprised, but he was hoping that it was something of extreme significance to the scientific world.

It took several weeks of digging, dating and cataloging to even come close to the source of their study. Core samples of soil were constantly being removed and taken to the laboratories for analysis and dating. Each meter they dug spanned hundreds of years into the past.

"Dr. Strouse, come and check this out!" a young short blonde haired student shouted. Dr. Strouse looked up from a stack of printouts from the latest soil sample tests. Hearing the urgency in her voice, laced with the thrill of discovery, he jogged to the edge of the dig and quickly scampered down the ladder.

"According to the sonograms, we are getting close." The noble professor picked up printouts of the latest sonograms and studied them quickly. "Did you find anything, Miss Jones?"

Penny Jones was an attractive young woman even when covered in dirt. She was a hard worker and a good student. It was refreshing to finally have someone young and as passionate about the earth and its secrets, as he was. Having no children of his own, he treated all of his students as if they were his kids. It was a frame of mind in which he put himself every year, to keep himself out of the Dean's office and out of trouble. He had seen several of his colleagues up on sexual harassment charges. Many of his associates had fallen to the temptation and appeal of their young attractive students.

"Well, Professor, we have found something interesting!" William Stewart chimed in. Stewart, a student from Michigan, was one of Dr. Strouse's top studies. With a supporting major in paleontology, William was an interesting asset to the team. "We are maybe ten feet from the meteor and we discovered the remains of a large animal."

"What kind of animal, Will?" Dr. Strouse took off his straw hat and scratched his receding hairline.

"Well, professor, I am not sure. At first, we thought it may have been an undiscovered dinosaur, but the bones haven't yet fossilized. I have a sample here, ready for analysis and dating."

"Hmm…" Dr. Strouse pondered this discovery. "Okay, fine. Get the sample up to be dated and then get this thing excavated to see what we have. We just may have two discoveries!" Emmitt was proud of his pupils. They had done well, and it was not every day that one could be part of a major breakthrough.

William was nudged by his co-ed companion. "Tell him the rest!"

"Oh yeah, I almost forgot! Based on the sonograms, the skeleton is intact, but it appears to be curled around the anomaly. It is if it were actually holding or protecting it."

Looking at the images shown on the laptop's screen, Dr. Strouse could see the beast curled around the meteor in a fetal position. The head and long neck were tucked under as if it had hit the ground head first. By the imaging, one could see horns and what appeared to be wings and a tail. He raised his brow in curiosity. Dr. Strouse lifted an eyebrow to this bit of intriguing information.

Curious, indeed...

"Let's get busy and see what we have! Don't forget to document everything." With that in mind, the two students turned around and jumped back into the activities. This had gone from a geological study to an archeological find.

The students then worked around the clock to uncover their new discovery. Pictures were drawn and computer models were made. In the middle of the ancient animal bones was a large stone. It was carefully brought to the surface, measured, weighed and marked. The outside was rough, but it was a perfect sphere that measured ten feet in diameter.

The stone had been the source of the gravitational anomaly. It had taken additional lifting equipment to hoist it to the surface. Three large construction cranes were used to their capacities. The stone had weighed in at 90 tons.

The most curious thing about the stone was that it was comprised of the stone from the surrounding area. It was as if a boulder from the area had been implanted into the rock beneath them.

William was totally baffled and excited by the animal's osseous matter as well. Pictures were taken and drawn of the complete skeletal system. Maps of bone locations were marked and documented. A piece of green-knobby flesh had been found with the bones. Initially, the student paleontologist had mistaken it for an odd emerald-like pebble. After closer examination, he had concluded that it was indeed a part of a much larger reptilian scale. His theory of it being a lost dinosaur would have been correct, except for the fact it was buried relatively recently, compared to the prehistoric dinosaurs. The creature also had wings. Not since the Pterosaurs, had there ever been a flying reptile such as this. The carbon dating had placed the remains as early as three thousand, five hundred years ago. This was millions of years after the extinction of the last known dinosaur. As answers were found, more questions arose.

William had been seated at his computer all afternoon. His mind was totally aghast at what he had before him on his screen. Pictures and measurements had been taken of all the bones that had been recovered from the site. He fed the information into his laptop to create a model of what the beast may have looked like.

"A dragon?" Dr. Strouse could not believe that had come from his own mouth. Dragons were not real, and they have never been. They were beasts of myth and legend. To his confusion, the model created by the undergraduate paleontologist looked remarkably like that of the mythological creature. To top it off, it was surrounding or protecting its meteor. "Are you sure you're not pulling my leg?"

"No, this is no joke. Yes, Professor, it appears to be a dragon. I can't believe it myself, but there it is. The facts don't lie." He motioned to the computer screen.

They found the source of the anomaly. The fact remained that the newly discovered creature's remains were surrounding it. Dr. Strouse was purely a geologist, so he was thankful to have William on his team. The young man had come in handy. Emmitt would not be surprised that the only reason that he wanted to be on this survey was because of pretty Miss Jones. He suspected that the two college students had a romance going on for some time. So be it. As long as it did not interfere with their studies, and as far as the doctor was concerned they were all adults.

Dr. Strouse left the computer lab trailer in total awe. On his way back to his tent he was brought back to reality by sudden gale-force winds. Quickly putting his hand on his straw hat to keep it in place, he feared for the integrity of the site. He was aware that storms materialized rapidly in the heat of the southwestern desert.

"Get the site secured! I need a tarp on the stone and on the site of the remains!"

He quickly started back to the computer trailer to fetch Will. Will was already out the door and sprinting toward his discovery. The team was frantically scurrying about to cover up the site. Too much work had been done to lose everything to a freak windstorm. The young man began staking down tarps across the dig.

The wind continued to blow. Tents had been battered like large wounded butterflies and several had been uprooted. Most of the students had taken refuge in the trailers as soon as the site had been secured. The trailers still rocked like ships on the ocean but there was much more protection from blowing sand and debris than there had been outside.

As the wind blew, clouds formed from nowhere. The clouds were dark and ominous, as lightning flashed in the Arizona sky. With his curiosity getting the best of him, Dr. Strouse left the safety of the trailer that had been his office. He went outside just as the lightning broke through the darkening skies. The sand tore at his skin, but he seemed to pay little attention. Instead, he was drawn to the stone that had been covered by the large construction tarp. The lightning strikes were close as they had begun pelting the ground. Each bolt grew closer to the stone.

Warmth? Something was different. Something had changed. They no longer felt cold. Darkness was there, as well as the hunger and the desire to be free. *Awful* goodness still was among them. They could feel the outside, but they could not have it. They were not free, but they could call it. They could call the wind and the sand. They could call the power from the sky... closer. Freedom was at hand. It was just moments away. They felt the electricity in the air growing stronger, closer. They could touch it and pull it to them.

Dr. Strouse was entranced by the electrical storm. Closer and closer the lightning danced across the sky and the desert floor. It came closer to the site. Horrified, he tried with every molecule of his being to run to the shelter of the trailers, but he could only step slowly towards the huge stone. It had seemed to be drawing the atmospheric electricity along with him, perhaps toward it. Fear and curiosity coursed through his soul. It was like being in a bad movie in which he had no control. The latter overcame the first. He was but a puppet of some unseen force. He watched his own hand in horror. Pulling a small knife from his pocket, he freed the stone from the tarp.

Lightning flashed and a bolt of bright blue energy hit the stone. The concussion of the strike sent the doctor flying through the air until gravity grabbed his flailing body, and slammed him back to the ground, rendering him unconscious. As abruptly the storm started, it ended almost immediately after the doctor's crash landing. The students watched the surreal happening from the trailers. Rushing out from the safety of their shelters, several ran to his aid, while others hung back, either leery of the stone or staring in awe at the sky.

Those who had their focus on the stone noticed that it was now in two complete halves. It was hollow and had a rainbow of colored crystals surrounding it. The multiple colors gave an eerie glow. It was like someone had bottled the *Aurora borealis*. What they could not see was the vaporous light that wafted up from the bisected stone. The colors soon vanished as the sun returned and reflected off the millions of facets in the stone. All the light camouflaged the dissipating shadows that were trapped within. The darkness escaped unnoticed.

The dark prisoners held within for eons scattered as soon as they were freed. The *awful* goodness was too much to bear, although one did not wander far. It felt drawn to the power and intellect of a single corporeal being. It had been drawn in by the warm comfort of innocence and wisdom, knowledge and power. This being that was a magnet to the dark magic would be used to rule and conquer. There was so much that could be taught to the crude beings in exchange for nothing less than perfect obedience.

The dark mystic energy found its way into the professor's soul. From there, it reached for his mind and began slowly to envelop his thoughts: controlling them, corrupting them, and then becoming one with them. Both would share knowledge. The professor had no choice in the matter. He was but a victim of a greater being which possessed no body. It was a being that had been born ages before in darkness. The human was weak and injured, but the body and bones would be healed and in time and made invincible. The man's hazel eyes, full of knowledge, seemed to burn. As the darkness absorbed the man's mind, body, and soul, the windows to that soul darkened and became as black as the evil itself.

Darkness was aware of the new world in which it had entered. Its new vessel had much knowledge that it needed. It would freely give the knowledge that it had kept for so many eons. It would share its knowledge that could grant one's deepest desires or one's wildest fantasies.

Learning all the knowledge that the doctor worked so hard all his life to acquire took less than an instant. It began to twist the knowledge into something that could be used to gain control. The first thing was to change the name of the insignificant human. From now on, they would be known as Esuorts, Dark Lord.

Chapter 4

Amanda had been on the bus for two days. Her appearance had shown it. Her auburn hair was stringy and unwashed. Her jeans were dirty and torn. Her white blouse had a mustard stain in the middle that had been a souvenir from the last roadside diner, a sign of her unsettled and nomadic life. Everything she owned was in the backpack next to her, accompanying the five dollars and seventeen cents in her pocket. She stared out the window and paid no attention to the weathered fence posts holding up the strands of barbed wire that blurred by. She was somewhere else. Her body may have been physically on a bus somewhere in Wyoming, but her mind was already at her destination.

She could see the huge building with many planes. They were neither shiny nor new jets, but airplanes right out of an old black and white war movie. People, short and tall, busied themselves about the outdated aircraft. They were moving, painting, washing and fixing them, as their forefathers had eons ago. She knew they were elves. She had often encountered them in the books she had read, and in the movies that allowed her to get away from the chaos of the life that had surrounded her. That was before it had become too much for her to bear. She dreamt of the elves. Her dreams taught her to be strong and brave, but only in those dreams did she have the qualities.

She knew she would be safe here with the elves. Amanda had dreamt of the place often. She knew it was real, and she would find it. At this place, she would be needed and loved. She knew she would find a home here. The young woman knew that the elves and dwarves would take good care of her. No one told her these things, she just knew them. She was a long way from the suburban city of Bonner Springs, but the girl knew where she was going, and she knew where she belonged.

Being only fifteen, Amanda had been through twelve foster homes since her parents were killed in a plane crash seven years prior. In the same crash, she was miraculously thrown from the cockpit unscathed, but not unscarred. The memory of that day played through her mind like a low-budget horror movie. Her body was in perfect health, but her soul was slowly withering. The elves and dwarves would help.

She had been repeatedly beaten and abused by her foster father for uncountable reasons, but the final time was while her foster mother watched. She helped herself to two-hundred dollars from his wallet and hitched into town to buy a bus ticket.

Her destination was Lancaster, Wyoming. She did not know where she was going but instead sensed it. Of all places she felt she had to go, Wyoming called to her. It called to her so intently, that she had dreamt of this very stretch of road.

She was jolted out of her daydream by the deceleration of the bus. She quickly looked around to get her bearings. This was where she would get off. She was not quite to Lancaster, but she was at the last diner before she would arrive at her ticketed destination. This is where she would leave the bus and take up the road on her own. She grabbed her pack and filed off the bus with the other handful of passengers.

Inside she found a corner booth near the ladies' washroom. It did not take long for a middle-aged woman wearing too much bright-red lipstick to come to take her order.

"I'll have a bowl of soup and a glass of water, please." She said trying to conserve her last few pennies.

"Sure hon, I'll get it right out to ya." The waitress smiled at her and hurried away.

She quickly returned with Amanda's order, along with a big slice of apple pie and a heaping scoop of vanilla ice cream on the side.

"I didn't order this," she said in horror. She feared that she would not have enough to pay for it.

"It's in the house, sweetie. You will need your strength if you are going to make it to the hangar tonight. It's a bit of a walk, but you'll be okay. Look for the winged tiger when you get there," she instructed. "I would advise you to eat the dessert first before it melts all over." Then she turned with a smile and walked away.

Amanda watched her curiously. She did not watch for too long as her hunger reminded her of its presence. She greedily went to work on the pie and ice cream. The soup was very good. She did not know if was because it had been a while since she had a decent meal, or if she were getting used to diner menus. As soon as the soup bowl was drained, she decided to pay her bill and slip into the bathroom. She looked around for her waitress, but she was nowhere to be found.

She waited for several minutes until she found another, although much younger waitress passes by.

"Excuse me, do you know where my waitress is? I need to pay my bill," Amanda asked nervously. "She was the older lady with the bright lipstick."

"There isn't anyone like that here. Everyone else called in sick and I have been here alone all day." She smiled politely and said; "Your father already took care of your bill, hon." The woman went about busily busing another table.

"But I am alone, and on my way to my aunt's house." Amanda had lied, although the point was moot. The woman was already busy with other customers. She got up to go hide in the bathroom, but she noticed that the bus had already left. She was supposed to walk. She felt the calling. With her backpack slung over both shoulders, she slipped through the door and out into the parking lot unnoticed. She stopped, turned to her right, and began heading up the road. She did not know how long it would take, but she did know where she would be once she got there.

To anyone other than Isabelle, the huge hangar would be intimidating. Isabelle felt like she had died and gone to heaven. Her heart skipped a beat when she scanned the variety of aircraft that was sprawled about the massive structure. Her eye was caught by one aircraft in particular. She immediately recognized the Curtis P-40B.

She momentarily forgot why she was there, and wandered over for a closer inspection. Except for the strange propeller design, she was very impressed with every detail in its restoration, from the teeth on the nose to the winged tiger on the tail. She walked around the aircraft with her left hand on its metal skin. Caressing the skin and feeling the rivets that joined the panels, Isabelle was enamored by the fighter plane. The woman had enjoyed and read about historic aircraft. This had been one of the most predominant fighters of the allies. Others like it had served in every theater of the Second World War. She wondered what it would be like to fly into battle in such a sturdy craft. As if in a dogfight, she imagined herself rolling and juking, while trying to line up her sights on the unfortunate Mitsubishi Zero that happened to be in her path. With all six machine guns blazing, she saw the Zero begin to smoke just before it burst into flames and plummeted into the Burmese jungle.

"I can't see a blessed thing in here!" A gruff voice from the cockpit shocked Isabelle back into the present. "Ned, be a good lad and bring me a torch." Isabelle quickly looked around. Her eyes easily found the toolbox resting near the right tire. Opportunity! She easily rifled through the box and found a small yellow flashlight. She bounded up the service ladder in only a few steps. She levered the flat black switch on the side and ignited the beam.

"Thanks, lad, shine it right over here. I can finally see what I be a doin'" She watched a stout little man in dirty coveralls fight with a twisted wire on a bolt. His growing frustration was obvious to her. After a few more colorful metaphors from beneath the little man's beard, she took action.

"Here, allow me." Isabelle shoved the little man in greasy coveralls out of the way. She took the wire and the cutters from his hands and began to go to work securing the bolt. He was surprised at seeing the young human woman instead of his nephew. He could do nothing but stare, bewildered.

Her hands danced in front of his eyes as she deftly twisted the two strands of wire into, then over and under the braid, wrapping them around the head of the bolts. This prevented the fasteners from becoming loose and removing themselves during flight.

Buck covered his astonishment with mock anger. "What do ye think ye be doin' in here, lass? This be private property or didn't ye read the signs?"

"It looks like I just did a safety on that actuator bolt." She quickly realized she was a stranger and began to feel ashamed of herself for barging in.

"I'm sorry. I was running low on gas and funds, and I saw this small airport. I wondered if you could use a mechanic, secretary, or a janitor. I am not picky. I just need work. I am Isabelle... Isabelle Thompson, by the way." She offered her hand to the little, bearded man.

"Buck is who I be." He took her hand with fading gruffness.

One gaze into her big brown eyes, and it was all over. His frustration and shock vanished quicker than it had appeared. "Where did ye learn to do a safety wire like that?"

"I was in the Army for a while, working on the Apache gunship." She tried to be as strong and confident as she could without losing her feminine charm. It appeared to be working.

"Well, if you have your certification, I can't say no to a job like that. Safety wiring will be me death. Let's go have a wee spot of tea, and I'll see what can be done."

Together they climbed off the plane. Buck lead her into a small lounge, then busied himself with a kettle of water on a small stove. "You make yourself comfortable while I go find the higher-ups and see what can be done." He was off and back into the hangar, but not without pausing in the doorway. "Now ya stay put, and donnet ye go wanderin' off. There be liability issues, ye know!" He quickly added, almost as an afterthought.

When he was off, she laughed inwardly. The little man reminded her of Grumpy from Snow White and the Seven Dwarfs. She sensed what Alice must have felt when she fell down the rabbit hole. What a day this had become.

Connor made his way across the hangar towards the *Dragon's Heart*. He knew how much Buck hated to do safety wire, and the flight controls had a lot of them. As he walked past the mammoth doors, a reflection caught his eye. He looked out to get a second look. He was right the first time. There was an old Chevrolet parked outside. As he turned to investigate the out-of-place auto, he heard Buck's booming voice echo from behind him.

"Connor, m'lad! I think there is someone who ye need to meet in the office." Frustrated by this distraction, Connor changed directions once again.

More than a little nervous, Isabelle waited patiently for whatever was to happen next. She had helped herself to a Styrofoam cup and a tea bag; she poured it full of steaming hot water, hoping it would calm her nerves. Through the door stepped a tall and handsome man. Isabelle quickly corrected herself. He was a tall and *beautiful* man. His emerald eyes quickly searched her soul, and they set her at ease. Not knowing what had just happened, she felt her body instantly relax the moment their eyes met.

Was it the tea?

"Bob Connor," he said with a warm smile and extended out an almost dainty hand. "What can I do for you, young lady?"

Isabelle was smitten by his masculine beauty. His features caught her, and her eyes could go nowhere else. She looked into his deep green eyes and could see life ceaselessly. To her, his eyes appeared to have flecks of emeralds that made them sparkle. She took his hand and was shocked at the firm, but gentle grip. She smiled inwardly at the obvious flattery. He had to be almost ten-years-younger than her. This could not be the one in charge. The whole moments around her presently seemed to be from another place. They seemed to belong to someone else. She could not remember moving her lips or uttering words. "Well, I was wondering if you had a position available."

She had finally come back to Earth. She had remembered that she was out of gas and had barely a dollar to her name. She was hoping against all hope that she could find something here. She did not know what she would do. The tidal wave of reality crashed down on her and swept every ounce of courage and fortitude out to an emotional sea. Her eyes blurred with tears and a lump burned her throat. "I drove up from Kansas City looking for a new start. I got this far and I am now out of gas and money."

Before Isabelle knew it, her heart was open and spilling out onto the floor in front of complete strangers. Connor comforted her to the best of his ability. The elf had that effect on human women many times. They easily opened up to him. He had to make sure that this human woman could be trusted. The wave of sudden emotion told him she had no desire to deceive. He held her hands in his and sent her calming thoughts. Buck handed her a tissue. She immediately responded, and with a thanking smile took it from him to dry her eyes.

Isabelle felt a calm wash over her. She gathered herself together.

"I am so sorry. I don't know what came over me. I never break down like that. I am so embarrassed."

"Don't be. It sounds like you have been through a lot. Buck here says you told him you that you have FAA certifications. If that is true, we can see what we can do to help." Connor could not leave anyone in distress. The Rider in him had always shown through. Isabelle, being such a beautiful woman, did not hurt either.

She reached across a table for a pen and a scrap of paper and began to scribble down a series of digits. With tears in her eyes left over from her emotional crash, she handed the scrap to Connor.

"Buck tells me you can tackle a mean safety wire. That's saying a lot. He's the best I have ever seen. He just hates doing it." Connor picked up a cordless receiver and made a call.

"Maggie, call the FAA in Oklahoma City and see if these numbers belong to an Isabelle Thompson. Give me a callback. If they do, start employment paperwork as a level-three mechanic. Uh huh." he said to the woman on the other end, "Let's just say she comes highly recommended." With that, Connor smiled and hung up.

"Now all we have to do is wait a few minutes until Maggie calls me back." Connor wanted to keep her out of the hangar for a while longer. It is going to be hard enough breaking the news to her. He knew she could be trusted with their secret, but it was not going to be easy on her. "In the meantime, that has to be your '47 Chevy out there. I would love to have a look if you would be so kind as to give me a tour?"

"Actually, it's a '48." she countered. She loved every chance she could get to brag on her baby. "I would love to, but only if you promise to give me a tour of your flying museum."

"I think we can arrange that," Connor smiled and the deal was done.

Amanda didn't know how long she had been walking. The sun had been getting low in the sky. She knew it would be dark in a couple of hours. With every step she took, she let her mind wander...

It was a sunny Saturday afternoon. Eight-year-old Amanda loved to fly with her father. Today was special—Amanda was having a picnic with her parents before going up. The three of them enjoyed sandwiches, cole slaw, and potato chips along with freshly brewed iced tea. Afterward, Amanda's father Jim pre-flighted the small four-seated Piper Cub and got it ready for their adventure.

Amanda had been looking forward to it all week. She told her teacher and the other kids at school all about it several times. Flying fascinated her. She often took photos of their trips for show and tell. She studied in her off time about big things like theories of flight. She had done many reports on the subject for school. Her dad even allowed and encouraged her take lessons.

Today her dad wanted to fly and she would let him. It did not take long before the quick inspection was over and they were on their way. She sat up front and her dad let her take off. She loved the thrill of leaving the ground. She would watch the runway as if she were driving and eventually when she pulled back on the yoke, her car slowly and steadily left the ground.

Today her dad was the pilot. Jim Raymond was an excellent pilot. He always paid attention to every little detail. From the preflight and in-flight gauges to the post-flight inspection, Jim checked and double-checked everything. Today was no exception. After looking long, nose to tail, checking the logbook twice, he was confident that the Cub was more than competent to carry his greatest treasures.

Smiles were all around during the textbook takeoff. It was not long at all before they were high over Clinton Lake surveying all the beautiful sailboats. The little plane banked and dove to provide a better angle of the summertime activities going on the smooth water below. Amanda was amazed by the colors of the different sails.

The flight was uneventful. It took them over the lake as well as a patchwork of fields. Amanda was amazed when she saw that one farmer had planted his crops so that you could see three sunflowers in a vase. When she got to her crayons, she would draw that same picture. Heading back to the small Lawrence airport, she knew that there was nothing left to see on this trip. She snuggled in for a small nap.

No sooner had she dozed off when her father's voice woke her up. "May Day!" There was a stressed tone in his voice. "Lawrence Tower, this is

November Six Three Niner-Lima-Fife. We are approximately two miles from the runway with no fuel pressure. Please be advised that we have lost our engine and are going down."

Panic flashed in her mother's eyes as she reached forward to check Amanda's seatbelt. "I don't understand," Jim said." I checked everything myself."

Jim fought with the controls to keep the plane's nose up to try to glide the craft as much as possible. Amanda knew that this was going to be bad, and there was nothing she could do. She cried.

Amanda woke on her back in the tall Kansas grass. She heard people shouting her name. She thought that maybe her mommy and daddy were looking for her. With a little effort, she rolled over and pushed herself onto her feet. She quickly judged the direction of the sound by the yelling and the sirens and ran off screaming.

"Here I am Mommy! Daddy, where are you?"

She quickly saw what looked like the plane in which they had flown earlier, only it looked like somebody had crumpled it all up. There was an ambulance with the wheeled tables she had seen on TV with sheets on them. She remembered what that meant on the shows.

She started crying all over again. "Mommy! Daddy!" She managed to get out between her sobbing breaths. She was alone.

Amanda brushed away the tears as she neared the dark hangar doors. She reached for the knob on a side entrance just below the tower. "Please don't be locked," she whispered. As she grasped the knob there was a click. She turned it and stepped in.

She found her way into the big hangar. Most of the lights were out except for a few over one lonely plane. It was green and tan. She tiptoed over to it. She smiled when she looked down the side. There on the side with blue wings was an orange tiger that was painted to look like it was flying through the air. With exhaustion overtaking her, she climbed up into the cockpit, out of sight, and quickly fell asleep.

Chapter 5

Conner slid the cordless receiver into his back pocket and escorted Isabelle out through the hangar and past the behemoth doors. Around the side of the hangar sat the old Chevy. The sunlight reflected off the minimal chrome trim. The wisps of clouds mirrored in the deep purple enamel. With one look at the Detroit masterpiece, the elf knew it was not stock.

Isabelle beamed with pride. "I replaced the original Babbitt bearing six cylinders with a bored and stroked 500 Caddy. A 400 turbo hydromatic now transfers the torque instead of the original vacuum shift manual transmission, and a Dana rear puts the power to the ground." The woman loved talking in the dialog of street rodders. She lifted the hood so that Conner could see her best work. The engine compartment was completely filled and neatly organized. Chrome and polished aluminum adorned the monster V8.

"I am impressed. It's pretty too. I see you have a performance Quadra-Jet. What, you don't like fuel injection?" Conner tested just to see how much she knew. So far, he was very enamored with her mechanical abilities. This masterpiece of a car was proof she could handle a wrench and was not afraid to get dirty.

"Computers are fussy. I can work with them, but mechanicals is more reliable. Besides, I prefer to feel my work than let some machine tell me if it's right or wrong," she shot back. As she guided the tour, Conner attacked her knowledge. He asked questions about mounting the monster to the frame rails and what kinds of modifications made it fit. Each time he quizzed her, she parried accordingly. When it came to the automobile, she was a whiz. It was time to put her to the true test.

"The transmission bolted right up, but I did have to fabricate my own engine mounts. I replaced the leaf springs with air bags for a better ride, and the front suspension is out of a 1974 Ford Pinto. That way I have rack and pinion with independent front suspension. She handles like a sports car." Isabelle smiled. She knew that she had passed Conner's car quiz.

"That is some work you have there!" The phone rang in his back pocket. "Conner here, whatcha got, Maggie? Really? Okay. Make it happen." He hung up and smiled.

Conner decided to shift the testing to more practical applications. He wanted to let her wait a bit before actually making the offer, but as he was speaking with Isabelle, Maggie was already working on the standard hiring package. "Let me show you some real artwork." He motioned her back into the hangar.

The tall woman's face lit up like the Fourth of July. "Pick one," he said. She thought he would never ask. Immediately she started for the P40. "Except that one, at least not yet."

Her disappointment was short lived. She quickly spotted an old F4U Corsair with the engine out, and on the floor next to it. It appeared to be in mid-restoration. She changed directions and headed for it. Men similar in stature to Buck were busy with the little plane. Isabelle could still see the name "Amy" hand-painted on the original paint.

"We bought her from a farmer in Burma." Buck came up behind them. "She cost us twelve goats and a year's supply of soda." Buck was proud of the price that he paid for the Navy fighter.

"Rumor has it that this plane was an actual member of the Black Sheep Squadron." Conner boasted.

"I see you have modified the original Pratt and Whitney 2800." Isabelle once again impressed Buck and Conner. All they could do is look at each other in amazement. Was there anything that this young woman did not know?

Isabelle climbed into the cockpit to look around. Most of the original gauges were still intact. Many were in desperate need of repair or replacing. Faces were faded and the lenses cracked. "She could use an updated cockpit, though," Isabelle informed her new friends.

"I didn't think you liked computers," Conner said with a mischievous smile.

"Fresh avionics will lighten her considerably, as well as make her much easier to fly, and less stress on her pilot," she continued without missing a beat. Isabelle was right at home talking about aircraft or cars. She was not shy in the least bit.

"Do you fly, Miss Thompson?" Conner queried.

"No, but I always wanted to learn. By the way, you don't have to call me *Miss*. I am not that much older than you. *Isabelle* will be fine, or all my friends call me *Izzy*."

Conner smiled inwardly as she compared their ages.

If she only knew...

"I am a licensed instructor, maybe we can work something out," Conner continued his offer. "Okay, I have heard enough. How would you like to head this project?" he offered.

Isabelle's heart leaped. She tried hard not to show her enthusiasm, but it was hard to contain. She wiped her sweaty palms on the back of her jeans. Sweeping her hair out of her eyes with her left hand, she offered the other to Conner. He took it immediately, sealing the deal. "I can start as soon as you would like me to."

As they were speaking, Conner felt an extreme surge of energy hit him. Like a bolt of electricity, each cell in his body was instantly awake and alive. He had not felt energy like that since his days as a Rider. Even then, it was not as strong. His body was numb for months after the magic was hidden. He could still wield some for healing, but only in the stone city underneath. Since he had been chosen by Emorthra as a Rider, his ability to wield magic was as strong as most wizards of that time, if not greater. It was quickly evident what just happened, but before he could share his body shut down. Darkness encompassed his vision, and his legs could not support him. He fell to the floor.

Isabelle was stunned as she watched him drop to the ground. All around her and Buck, everyone except the shorter mechanics looked temporarily disoriented or held their heads for a moment. Conner was still unconscious. She had no idea what was happening. The events of the day should have made her nervous. No matter what had just happened she still felt at ease with her surroundings, although a little apprehensive.

"Help me with him, Lass. There is something you need to know." Buck began to pick up the elf. He could have easily done it himself, but Buck thought it would be better to let the human woman think she was helping. He knew she was going to find out their secret eventually. He had just hoped that Conner would have been the one to tell her. The elf was much better at influencing humans than he was. "Come with me." He instructed as they picked Conner up off the floor.

They carried Conner to the elevators. On the ground floor, Isabelle was curious to why the short man pushed the down arrow. She was amazed when the elevator actually started going down. Buck always had an upfront approach. To him, there was no delicate way to make this statement. Conner could always find one, but not Buck.

"Lass, you were going to find out eventually, but I was just hoping to break it to ye easily..."

"What do you mean?" She started to get nervous.

"Oh, dannot worry ye pretty little head, Lass. You are safe." Buck continued. "As a matter of fact, ye be safer than any of your kind has been in thousands of years."

"What do you mean *my kind?*" she asked.

As an answer, her questions the doors opened into the underground city. "Welcome to Estal, m'lass." Buck extended his arm out.

Isabelle stepped out of the elevator, but could not make her legs move any further. She was stunned by the sheer size and detail of the complete city carved from limestone beneath the hangar.

"You see m'lass, all is not as what it seems." Buck started with a smile. He had always been proud of the city he had helped build.

"Where did all this come from?" Isabelle was paying little attention to Buck at this moment. "Who carved all of this?" She asked.

"It took us a few thousand years, but we did." Buck tried to help the young woman to the best of his ability. "It is still under construction in some places."

She turned and looked down to him. "Who is WE?"

"Those of us who stayed behind... We dwarves did most of it." Buck began to explain without a moment's hesitation. "Mining and working stone are what we do best. I am one of the few who actually spends most of my time up top. The boy would be lost without me." Buck looked down at Conner's limp body.

"Dwarves?" Isabelle asked. "So you are a dwarf?"

"That I be," Buck assured her proudly. "Beladar, son of Belvor, at your service."

"As in *Snow White and the Seven*?" she questioned.

"Well, that story is not such a fairy tale, but it didn't quite happen as the books and movies explain it. There were ten of us and no poison apple. But anyway..." Buck stopped himself, "that is a story for later."

"So I suppose that Conner is an elf." She said with all the sarcasm she could muster.

"You are quick, Lass." Ignoring her sarcasm, Buck brushed back the unconscious elf's hair, revealing his ears.

It was too much for her human mind to take. Shadows crept into her vision and everything before her eyes swam and went dark. She fainted.

Buck was surprised the woman took as much as she did before she went out. He quickly got the attention of a few of the dwarf women that were busying themselves about the city to help. "Take her. Make sure she has a comfortable room and clean clothes. See to her every need when she wakes up. Get Maggie to help. She would feel more comfortable with Maggie. That will be easier on her." Buck took charge quickly in Conner's lack of consciousness. He turned to two elves that had been standing watch over the library. "You! Post outside her door. Make sure she does not wander around by herself." He instructed the first. "And you, get relief from your captain and join him." Buck pointed to the first. "Let him know of my authorization." Neither said a word but complied quickly.

Nedloh came through the elevator door and up to his uncle. "What's going on Buck?" Nervousness was heard in his question.

"I don't know, lad, but I'm gonna find out in a moment." Buck started toward the library. He stopped and turned to his nephew. "Make sure Conner is well. If he comes around before I am done, have him find me. Tell them up top to shut down for the night and make sure everything is locked down." Buck gave the final instructions. The younger dwarf complied smartly. The older dwarf returned to his original heading.

Chapter 6

Darkness came quickly upon the entire world. Today it had nothing to do with the sun. Across the globe, it spread. Like a plague upon humanity, the magic within the stone covered the earth. It filled every canyon and valley. Up every mountaintop, it climbed. It was invisible to humankind and would soon be man's end.

Deep within the caves across the planet, beady eyes opened. Blinking the eons of sleep away, goblins once again awoke. On that day thousands of years ago, with the magic locked away, the goblins' long sleep began. With no dark magic to sustain them, they had turned to stone. They looked like hideous statues carved into some grotesque combination of a man and a wild pig.

Barock yawned. The vilest creature that ever walked above or below ground was once again stirring. Goblins were again awake and hungry. After such a long sleep, only one thing would satisfy their appetites: the flesh of man.

With empty bellies, they crawled out of their dark holes to begin to hunt for their masses. This night would not bode well for the human race. The goblin king grunted and squealed for a scouting party to go above ground to assess the food supply. He called a dozen of his best trackers and scouts. In their very rudimentary dialect, he gave them instructions to see how much man flesh was available in the meager villages in which he remembered. He also commanded them to bring to his samples. If it were worthy of consumption, then raiding parties would be formed to feed all. The twelve gave their acknowledgment, turned and left to prepare.

Deep in the bowels of the Earth, the scouting party donned their armor and picked up their arms for the journey. They too hungered. They would nourish themselves with whatever they could find when they left their caves and holes or perish. On the hunt, they split into three parties. They all agreed to their language of snorts, clicks, and squeals to return by dawn to report and feed their king. They all feared failure.

The sun had just set. Anne had been working late all week. Leaving the busy city for the last time this week, she knew she needed a long weekend. As her Toyota left the bright lights of the crowded city, she breathed a sigh of relief. The buildings faded into fields and forests. She felt her muscles loosen and the stress melts away as she drove. The winding Arkansas road out of Little Rock always calmed her.

The thought of her husband waiting with a hot meal and cold drink put a sense of urgency in her driving. Her eyes never strayed from the winding road.

They sniffed the air as the first set of goblin trackers discovered something new. As they came out of the trees, they were intrigued to see a winding river of flat dark rock. It was black as pitch and smelled of tar. The stone seemed to be made of tiny stones, covered with an oily tar of which it smelled. Quickly, one was chosen to investigate the recent find. Three stayed back in the trees under the cover of darkness, the youngest sent forward. He stopped to feel the river's cool rough texture, sniffing, touching and tasting. The one goblin could taste the tar, oil, and other unfamiliar substances. The middle of the flat, motionless river had a thin strip that was the color of the nasty sun. He crept further out to see.

The scout was completely engrossed with his investigation. He was in the middle of a strange stone river. He was feeling the smoothness of the yellow line. From up the river came a strange sound. Redirecting his attention, he stood and looked up. His pointed ears perked up as he cocked his head in the direction of the sound. What beast could be making such a sound? He wondered if it could be the great cats that make tasty morsels. He stood facing the direction of the noise with his goblin ax at the ready. Before he could see the beast, two miniature suns blinded him. What magic was this? He was motionless and unable to move in the middle of the stone river.

Anne rounded the curve as she did countless times before. She was always cautious of deer crossing the road in the early nighttime hours, just after the sun had set. In a split second, she saw it. There was a hulking grotesque man dressed in rags and metal plates standing in the middle of the road. He was holding a very crude ax. With a pig-like face, the massive form stood motionless in her headlights. She was stunned. She quickly tried to figure out what was standing in her way. Whatever "it" was, it was not moving. It acted as if it had never seen a car.

She swerved to avoid hitting the strange creature but failed. At her current speed, the impact was unavoidable. She clipped the monstrosity with her driver's side front fender. The massive beast rolled off the hood and bounced twice on the pavement. With tires squealing, she struggled to regain control of the little Camry. The ditch and trees came too quickly for her to correct her course. Glass and sheet metal impacted a large oak with a terrible crash. She lay slumped over the steering wheel surrounded by deflated airbags.

They saw the younger goblin roll across the front haunch of the strange creature that had attacked.

He had stopped just a few feet from where they were hiding at the forest's edge. Stunned and disoriented, it got up. The huge beast lay against the trees. The beast, wounded and motionless, still growled. It had lost one of its bright shiny eyes in the attack as the other, buried, had shown off into the trees. The party was also cautious of the angry red eyes glowing behind it.

The group quickly ascertained that the beast had two heads and discussed how to keep from an attack from the second. It was a very strange creature indeed. They drew their weapons and the leader decided on a broadside attack. This would still leave plenty of shiny smooth flesh for them. Bringing down their axes and swords on this monster, they were bewildered. Smashing the skin made no cuts nor drew any blood.

One looked into the clear crystal membrane. He noticed a human slumped over and bleeding. The beast had appeared to have just fed and not yet digested its prey. This was a good thing. The leader cleaved the cool, smooth surface and it shattered. Grunting at his discovery, he pulled out the tender human female. The other three looked at the limp woman who dangled in the goblin hands. They howled in victory.

A second scouting party came out of the woods in a Little Rock suburb. The village they saw before they had been a lot different from how it that had been before their sleep. The houses were no longer made of thatch and sod. They appeared to be made of bone or skin and scales of a creature that never been seen by goblin eyes. One thing stayed the same, the window. Through which, the second party spied an ancient woman in a room that appeared to have the purpose of food preparation. There with the old woman was an orange tabby waiting for its evening meal.

The striped cat purred and paced back and forth. It rubbed its back and tail on its owner's arm as the old woman held down the lever of the can opener. He knew the sound of the whining motor well. Patently, he watched the can turn around. The smell of tuna enticed his nose. There was something else in the air. It smelled of stale, rotting meat, a smell of evil. The odor that wafted past his nose was faint. It still floated on the wisps of the conditioned air. The stench, disguised by the delicious smell of tuna and the cinnamon and apple, eased in from the wall by the floor. The old orange cat scanned the room to see from where the vile odor was coming. The cat wandered about the room, and his eyes forced to stop by the window.

From the time before time, all cats knew about these vile creatures. There were legends told to young kittens to keep them in line and out of trouble. They fed on human flesh, and cats were always guardians and protectors of humankind. It had been thousands of years since the creatures roamed the Earth's surface. The old tabby had seen them plain as the stripes on his tail. Through the window, they were watching. Goblins!

The old woman opened the can of tuna flavored processed meat. Her orange cat hissed. He arched his back high and stared out the window. "What is it, Alfred?" she asked as if he were to answer back.

She followed his gaze out the window. She quickly discovered what had his attention. She was temporarily transfixed by the ghastly site. As she looked out, she saw two of her kitchen windows full of hideous faces. Glowing eyes accented warthog-like features. The clanging of metal off her linoleum floor as she dropped the can brought her back to her senses. She reached for an olive green telephone hanging on the wall. Instinctively she dialed the emergency line.

At the Little Rock emergency call center, Sally was busy at her station. The young blonde woman sat at her computer terminal with her headset and her Diet Coke. As she did every night, she took every call with the standard "Nine-one-one, what is your emergency?" Tonight was no exception. Now she was on a call with a frantic elderly woman who lived alone.

"Yes, ma'am. I understand that you live alone. You have to calm down for me." Sally's voice was soothing. She learned quickly how to calm a caller without getting excited herself. Her level head helped her keep her wits about her on a nightly basis. In a major city such as this, she had probably every type of call one in her profession could hear. Tonight was just another night in Little Rock.

"Okay," She paused as she tried to get a word in with the frantic woman. "Are they in the house, ma'am? Sally talked her down as she sent the information through her terminal to police dispatch. Within seconds, confirmation came back stating that a patrol car was in the area and that an officer would be at the woman's door within seconds. Until the officer was there, Sally's job was to keep the woman calm and on the line until help arrived. The health and safety were her main priority.

"The officer is at your door right now, ma'am," Sally assured her. "I am going to let you go now so you can talk to him." After the enthusiastic thanks from the woman, she ended the call.

After advising dispatch that he had left his vehicle, Officer Bill Franklin proceeded up the steps and to the front door. The information that he received through dispatch was that an elderly woman, by the name of Betty Havisham, reported prowlers. According to headquarters, four large men who were allegedly wearing Halloween masks had been looking through her kitchen windows. They may still be on the property. He went to the door to let her know he was there to help and to look around.

Bill Franklin was by no means a small man. He had to have his uniform custom tailored to fit his six-foot-four-inch frame. All three hundred and twenty pounds of him were lean muscle. Betty was extremely relieved to see such a man filling her doorway. His arms were barely contained in the short sleeves of his uniform shirt.

"Mrs. Havasham?" He wanted to make sure he had the correct address.

"Oh yes! Thank the All Mighty you are here. Please come in." She was delighted and relieved to see her uniformed savior.

"That's okay, ma'am. I am just going to check around the property first, just to make sure you are safe. I want to make sure they are gone," he assured her. "Then I will take a look inside. You are alone here, is that right ma'am?"

"Yes, I am... well, except for Alfred."

"And Alfred is your husband, Mrs. Havasham?" he asked as he was writing in a small notebook he pulled from his left breast pocket.

"Heavens no, officer," she smiled. "Alfred is my old, orange tabby cat."

The words "I see" were the only things that would come to mind as a response. With that, Bill closed his notebook and put it away in his pocket. Stepping off the wooden porch, he pulled his large flashlight from its ring on his holster belt. The bright white beam illuminated instantly with a push of the rubber-covered switch.

The beam swept the lawn of Betty Havisham. His trained eyes followed. He also looked at the windows on the house as he walked around it. He examined intently for any signs of an attempted forced entry. He also looked around trees and small garden shed. His senses were alive and ready to notice anything out of the ordinary. He heard every breath he made. To his ears, his breath was as loud as a jet engine overhead. Now that was the only sound that came to his ears. He quickly realized there were no other sounds. There were no dogs, cats or even crickets chirping. That ended abruptly with a rustling in the shrubs in the far corner of the yard.

His heart pounded in his chest. He quickly aimed the beam of his halogen flashlight on the bushes. He immediately caught the reflection of a pair of eyes. The next thing that came to his ears was an awful squeal. It was similar to that of the wild razorbacks he had seen and hunted often times as a boy growing up in the backwoods of Arkansas.

He drew his 9mm from its holster and thumbed the safety lever to the firing position. From his own personal experience, razorbacks were not pigs with which to trifle. He called the boar as he had done so many times in the past. It was very rare to see one this far in the city, but because humanity continued invading their habitat they pushed deeper and deeper to broaden their areas. Bill supposed that from time to time, one was bound to move those divisions farther.

Instead of the wild pig he had expected, a large creature stood up from behind the shrubbery. The only things that even resembled a feral pig were the face and head. From under its snout grew two large and jagged tusks. It was uglier than any wild hog he had ever seen. It must have been almost seven feet tall. By looking at it, Bill would have guessed that it had to have weighed over five-hundred pounds. Staring at it, he could see an evil cleverness in its eyes. It started toward him.

"Stop!" Officer Franklin ordered the massive creature. It only paused and cocked its head slightly in bewilderment before it continued. This time, it came at him at a faster pace.

Bill fired his first into the creature's chest. It ricocheted only leaving a dent in its crude armor fashioned from iron and leather. Without so much as a pause, it continued. This time charging from across the yard, it let out an ear-splitting howl. Four more rounds were fired from the 9mm. This time, the rounds buried themselves directly into the monster's forehead. In mid-step, it fell just inches from his feet.

"Dispatch, this is two-nine-five," Bill said into his handset, attached to his shoulder.

"Go ahead two-nine-five." The handset answered him.

"Request backup on Elm. We have a suspect down and three more possible. You may want to call in the sheriff also for assistance." He paused to choose his words carefully. No one would believe this without having seen it. "I also need a coroner and someone from wildlife control out here as well."

"Roger that, two-nine-five."

"Two-nine-five, out." Bill ended the transmission.

He squatted down to investigate the carcass that lay at his feet. It took quite an effort even for him to roll the thing over on its back. The first thing he noticed was the horrible smell. He thought it reminded him of rancid meat and a nasty case of body odor combined. Once he had the beast on its back, he went in for a closer look at the monster he just put down. By no means was Bill prepared for what he saw.

"What the...?" was all that he could manage to mutter. He pulled out his pocket notebook once again. He wanted to make sure that he got every detail so that there were no mistakes on his report. It was going to be hard enough for his chain of command to believe him, even with pictures. Bill felt a vacation in the very near future would be required.

As he was jotting down the details of what had just transpired, the sounds of more grunts and squeals came to his ears. He knew immediately that they did not come from a pig. Bill stood up with his side arm and flashlight at the ready. Scanning diligently with the bright white beam, he found nothing.

Howling started once again. His heart sank. From the sound and direction, he knew they surrounded him. He heard no movement. Shining the beam at the tree line, he scanned. His eyes desperately searched for movement in the darkness of the Arkansas night.

His heart skipped a beat, and he froze in his position. He suddenly felt hot, rancid air blowing down his neck. He slowly turned his body to see what was behind him, but he already knew. This one was almost as big as the first and just as ugly. Bill had to tilt his head back to meet its gaze.

For what seemed to be hours, Bill Franklin stared at his opponent in terror. Without losing eye contact, he noticed that they enclosed him. He could see the other two beasts in his peripheral vision. Things from his childhood rushed back to him. He remembered the stories that Granny used to tell him. There were monsters long ago that would take children and sometimes adults away to their caves and tunnels, and then devour them. He tried to remember what Granny called them.

The monster he had been facing drew a huge sword from a sheath on its back. Bill, at that moment, realized that he had his 9mm still drawn and pointed at the creature's chest. He squeezed the trigger repeatedly. Within a few seconds, the bangs from each launched round were replaced by clicks of an empty magazine.

The creature holding the sword staggered back only half a step as his armor deflected the force of the human's weapon. He did not fall. Instead, it brought the blade down on the shoulder of the large human. The other two beasts watched as the right arm of the human fell to the ground with the weapon, and still pulling the trigger.

Bill looked down as his precious life fluid poured out onto the ground. The brachial artery had been severed from his arm. Darkness quickly overtook him. Soon he could hear nothing and saw the same. The last thing that escaped his mouth has what he finally remembered that Granny told him, "Goblins!"

Curious onlookers dressed in their pajamas hovered just outside the yellow police tape. Most had been brought from their nightly repose by the sounds of the strange howling and gunfire. The flashing lights of emergency vehicles illuminated the entire neighborhood with pulses of red, white, and blue.

Inspector Reynolds from the Little Rock Police Department was looking for the massive creature that lies in the backyard of Mrs. Betty Havasham. The team that had come from Arkansas Fish and Game had never before seen anything like it. A team of scientists from Washington was supposed to take the carcass later this morning. The inspector figured the government would probably take the corpse, study it and then hide it like the aliens in Area 51. He took over a dozen photos with his cellphone camera, just so he could make a few bucks with the tabloids after this had all blown over.

A white chalk outline marked where Officer Franklin's arm fell. The rest of his body, along with his weapon, were nowhere in the immediate area. They would have better luck in the daylight with the search. He had theorized that after the beast severed the officer's arm, an officer would have shot it at point blank range, killing it. Judging by the footprints, Officer Franklin must have followed two or more into the woods where he bled to death. They would find him in the woods, after sunrise. Until then, all that Inspector Reynolds could do was gather as much information from the scene as he could.

The last scouting party went on a much longer and more important quest. They traveled the deep caves and tunnels for several weeks. Their task was to find the source of the magic that had awakened them. The leader of the party had a small crystal that hung from twine made from the hair of a black unicorn. This would point the direction of the strongest magic source within two-thousand leagues.

As they moved along, they mapped the tunnels from their home grotto to their final destination. The crystal would glow shortly before a change of direction was indicated. At the cross tunnel, it would then turn and point down the corridor that they needed to take. Each tunnel, corridor, and the passage was meticulously marked, both on the parchment as well as on stone walls.

Winding through the catacombs, they eventually felt themselves climbing toward the surface. The party of four knew that they were about to reach the origin of what had awakened the race of goblins. The bright daylight streamed into their exit, blinding and burning their eyes. Goblins despise the sun. When they did venture out above ground, they only did it in the cover of darkness. Goblins' eyesight allowed them to see even in the total absence of light. The four would wait until nightfall to continue their quest.

Among the mountains and mesas of the Arizona desert, in what had been a small geological survey camp, the world had changed. A new being with great magical powers shaped this new world. Using his newly released magical abilities, he had altered the inhabitants of the camp to suit easily his needs. Almost a hundred students now became his minions. They did so against their wills, and their minds had been drained of useful knowledge. The rest of the minions were wiped clean and made simple. All were made obedient.

The self-proclaimed Lord Esuorts wielded his new dark power with ease. Stone provided him with a virtually impenetrable fortress and a seat of rule to begin his conquest. It blended in with the surrounding terrain. Great walls formed around the stronghold for protection. In the middle, he thrust up a great tower for his court. Inside this twisted palace, he set up his study and war rooms.

His forced subjects were warped and twisted. He created new races of men. Some, he had made small and thin. These *Ratticans*, as he called them, he designed to fit into small spaces. They ran the plumbing and heating ducts as well as the new power called *electricity* throughout the palace. They scurried about with pipes, and rolls of wiring and ducting.

The new sorcerer shaped other men and women into hulking beasts. They did much of the heavy lifting and building. Many also acted as Lord Esuorts security force. They watched for prying eyes that may attempt to stop his conquest. They were outside the gates and on a few ridges around the fortress. He simply called these brutes *heavies*. At over eight feet tall, and close to a thousand pounds of pure muscle, they would soon be a formidable army. He made certain that each *heavy* female would give birth to twins, and that the offspring would mature rapidly. He had an army ready for his conquest of the planet.

Lord Esuorts twisted the last and fewest of the survey students to interface with technology. The new magic was created as he had slept for all those eons. Each new creature had part of its brain warped to process billions of gigabytes of information in a fraction of a second. These new technicians could process more than a hundred of the world's fastest supercomputers at once. They also routed information to terminals throughout the fortress. Humankind had become dependent on computers. This technology had made the race complacent. They had become user-friendly and plugged in. This would be the weapon that Esuorts would use to bring about their downfall.

Sunlight failed. As it went to bed below the horizon, the darkness once again ruled the world. The remaining scouts slithered from the safety of the tunnels in which they had remained hidden. Not far from their exit was a massive stone fortress. It appeared to have been belched from the earth itself. The crystal indicated that the source of the magic lay inside. They agreed that getting in would be challenging.

Goblins were not adept at covert operations. They preferred a direct approach. Three hid in the rocks just outside the gate. They waited in ambush. The fourth goblin went straight up to the main gate.

Guarded by one of the dim-witted heavies, the gate appeared to be the only way in or out of the stone fortress. The night was quiet. Nothing stirred. An extremely large human stood to watch over the gate. Steel doors had been framed and set into massive stones. The rock seemed to have flowed around the massive hinged gates.

The heavy guard stared into the night. With nothing to keep him occupied, his brain seemed to drift away to a life he once had. He awoke from his dream-like state with the arrival of a large intruder. From out of the darkness, it came. The stranger stood just a few inches shorter than did the heavy guard. The new arrival had his sword drawn in preparation for an attack.

With a crude blade his hand, the goblin scout marched straight up to the guard. It had never seen a man so large. That did not matter. The human was going to fall this night, by his sword. The human waited, armed with only a crude steel pipe that was eight and a half feet long. As it saw the goblin approach, the man stepped into the stranger's path.

"Stop!" the monster of a former man bellowed. Its voice was deep and gruff.

The goblin charged the massive human with its sword held high overhead. It brought the blade down in an attempt to cleave the man in half. The blow was easily blocked. Sparks flew from where steel met. The human was quick to defend but unschooled in the art of combat. The scout quickly regrouped. Stepping sideways, he sliced horizontally at the human. The brute of a man was not fast enough this time. His body slid into two halves with the follow through of the goblin's blade. The heavy howled in pain.

The remaining three scouts joined their leader at the body of the fallen human. As they stood discussing their next move, a decision was made for them. The gates opened. Almost a dozen heavy males quickly engaged the four intruders. The goblins responded with their swords. Steel clashed and sparked. Several of the massive men fell, but sheer numbers quickly overtook the four. Battered, beaten, and unconscious, the limp bodies of the intruders were drug into the fortress.

Chapter 7

Conner's eyes snapped open. He knew exactly what had transpired. "You were definitely not what I expected to see first thing." Buck had been sitting with the elf since he dropped to the floor twelve hours ago.

"It's nice to see you too, Lad." the dwarf smiled. "Do ye have any idea of what happened?"

"Yeah." Conner sat up rubbing the back of his head. He was still dressed in his flight suit. "I don't think we are going to like it much my friend."

The elf got up and showered. Refreshed and in a clean flight suit, Conner had many questions to answer, but first he needed to check on his guest. He knew that Isabelle would be confused. He was hopeful that Maggie would soften the blow a bit.

Isabelle woke in a room that was strange to her. The décor flowed together very organically. Earth tones of brown and green blended with hues of blue on the ceiling. The room was small, but it had a wide-open feel to it. She was dressed in a fine silk sleeping gown, between silk sheets that were both light and warm. The bed itself seemed to cradle her. She felt rested and at peace.

She was alone in the room except for a woman she had once seen. Clearing the sleep from her mind, events came back to her. Maggie. The woman beside her bed was Maggie, the receptionist. She smiled at Maggie. "Good morning." The young woman said in almost a whisper.

"Did you sleep well?"

"Yes. I did, thank you. I had the weirdest dream, though." Isabelle sat up. She felt extremely comfortable talking to Maggie. It was almost as if they had been lifelong friends. Without waiting for a reply she went on to tell of what she thought were nightly visions. "I dreamt that Buck was a dwarf, as in Snow White, and Connor was an elf." Maggie just listened contently. "There was a huge city under the hangar where they lived. It was carved out of stone by the dwarves."

"They do enjoy their work," Maggie stated. "The dwarves are a very proud people."

"Come on! You have to be kidding, right?" Isabelle began to worry.

"Isabelle, it's no joke." She brushed her long red hair behind her right ear revealing its elfin point. "Listen, something big is happening. It is something that will change the world. Girlfriend, you are in the safest place you can be right now." Maggie began to reassure her. "Conner will find out what is going on. Be ready to make some life changes."

Isabelle was speechless. She should have been horrified, but something about Maggie calmed her fears. Somehow, she knew she was where she was supposed to be.

"I will go and see if I can find Conner," Maggie told her. "In the meantime, there is a shower in there with all the necessary toiletries. You will find anything you could need. There is a clean flight suit in the dresser. I think you will also find the necessary underclothes as well. You will find this job is like a family. We take care of our own." With that, Maggie left.

Conner decided not to visit his new friend empty handed. He stopped and picked up some elfin cakes and pastries. He knew that Isabelle would be hungry. He, himself, was famished. A bit of breakfast and tea would go a long way in easing Isabelle into her new environment. Minds think more clearly on a full stomach. His was no exception.

The elf wheeled a small cart loaded with a variety of honey cakes, as well as sweet cookies and tea to Isabelle's room. A bowl of fresh fruit not only served as a beautiful centerpiece but also was a very enticing addition to the morning meal.

"Oh. I see elves do like to bake cookies in their trees." Isabelle stepped out of the bathroom in a clean flight suit while towel drying her hair. She did not know what to think about the prior day's events. She handled it the only way she could, with her dry wit and humor. She had many questions for her new boss but did not know where to start.

"I thought you might like a bit of breakfast before I try to explain. I am ready for you to drill me with questions, afterward." Conner wheeled the cart over to a simple but elegant table in the corner. He crossed his arms and leaned against the wall waiting for Isabelle to get started on her meal.

"What, no eggs and bacon?" she jokingly asked.

"Well we are not quite the type that you see making cookies in TV commercials, but we are tree folk. At least we used to be..." Connor pulled up a second chair around the table and sat down.

Helping himself to a honey cake, he began his narrative.

"Elves and dwarves have been around for longer than the earth itself," he began. "We actually arrived here as what human scientists call the Mesozoic period. We lived in peace with your friendly dinosaurs for millions of years. We even had some of our own."

Once again, Isabelle's head began to spin. This time, she kept it under better control. "You mean to tell me that you have been here since the dinosaurs?" She could hardly believe what she was hearing.

"Exactly! Some of them developed intelligence and a magic of their own. Since they were of this world, their magic was far more powerful than ours, but I will get to that later." He nibbled at his breakfast as he explained.

"We came here from the stars. All of those who are old enough to remember decided to make the journey to the other life awaiting us on this side."

"So now you are telling me that you believe in a heaven?" Isabelle could not believe what was coming to her ears.

"Yes. We always have known there was a great creator of the universe. We are here in this life not by accident. Your arrival in Estal is also not an accident. This is the same for the return of the magic. All that happens in our lives is either allowed to happen or is caused to happen. Either we learn from each lesson or we do not. It is our choice. We elves have learned to pay closer attention to our lessons.

"Back to the original topic," Conner made a course correction for his conversation. "As humans are starting to realize, most dinosaurs came to an abrupt end, but not all. Some of them evolved and became quite intelligent. They also became more powerful with the magic of this world. They became our friends, the race of dragons.

There was a big war of magic. Goblins had discovered it and twisted it to evil, to suit their greed. To try to put an end to us, they brought down a great rock from the sky.

The dragons told us about this upcoming and potentially cataclysmic event. They came to us for help. We had discovered that the great meteor coming toward this planet was from the Mars asteroid belt. We had plenty of time to prepare."

"Couldn't you stop it with your magic?" Isabelle asked. She stared into his eyes as a child. Engrossed by the new accountings of history, she could scarcely take her eyes off the elf.

"That option was discussed, but it was not what was to happen. We knew that we had to form an alliance. We went to the dwarves for help. The dwarves were thoroughly impressed with the dragons. After much deliberation, they agreed to help. They would keep us safe underground in exchange for one thing—they wished to have protection from the goblin hordes themselves. Their numbers were too few for an effective army against the number of magic-wielding goblins. Magic was the only thing that had helped us survive until this point."

"Goblins?" Isabelle felt as if she were getting a history lesson from J.R.R. Tolkien.

"The three races joined into a lasting friendship. The dwarves quickly quarried homes for the dragons and us." The elf shook off the interruption without missing a beat. "The friendship between dragon and elf had been strengthened only by time spent together. Since the elves and dragons had a longer friendship than with dwarves, it was stronger. Our bond became extremely strong. It went so deep, as to bond the very soul of some dragons to elves, and even some dwarves. Dwarves realized this but were still jealous. It was hard work maintaining our friendship with the dwarves, but it worked out in the end.

The rock did strike the earth. The dinosaurs did all die. What the goblins did not realize was that the event also caused new animals to evolve, and others to adapt. When we left our shelter toward the end of the ice age, we were on what seemed to be an entirely new planet. The land had changed as well as its inhabitants. The world was alien to us. The elves returned to the surface extremely thankful to our new friends, the dwarves. We immediately rebuilt our greatest city, Atlantis."

Conner did not think that his audience of one could get more interested. Her eyes just grew wider.

"We decided to take advantage of our bond with our friends, the race of dragons. We formed a group of protectors. It was kind of like the knights of your medieval times. Dragon and rider bonded for life. We became *Skymate*. We protected dwarves and ourselves from the goblins. We also discovered that we were no longer the only intelligent beings on the planet.

We discovered the rise of humankind. We helped the new race. We shared our knowledge of magic and technology. They showed us other intelligent and noble beasts. We met the race of winged horses and the great griffins. Many humans joined our ranks as Skymate. When they bonded with their Skymates, it increased their life forces greatly. There were many brave and noble men and women worthy of being called *brother* or *sister* by elf and dwarf.

Overall, humankind had become warped and perverted by magic. Many have lusted for world conquest and power. A council of dwarves, elves, man and dragons decided that the magic should be locked away and hidden. There would be a time for man to take his place as the dominant race of Mother Earth. Dwarves, dragons, and elves began to prepare for their return to the stars.

A great emerald dragon volunteered to bury the magic deep within the earth. He was my Skymate." A tear welled in Conner's eyes at the thought of his brother in arms. "Afterward, he has never seen again."

Few of us were to stay back and watch over humanity. No dragons remained. They had made their sacrifice. I was one who remained. Buck's clan had also stayed. A few of my elfin friends joined me."

The meal had long been over. Conner quickly realized that this revised history lesson went on entirely too long.

"Please excuse my ramblings." Conner apologized, "but you have work to do. I have a strange feeling we will need all the aircraft up and airworthy as soon as we can."

Conner got up as soon as Isabelle began to stand. He guided her to the door and opened it for her. "We can talk more on the way up."

Isabelle was totally lost in thought. Absorbing all she had heard was not as easy as one would have hoped.

Amanda awoke in the cramped cockpit to voices busy about the hangar. She quickly reviewed the events of the prior day. She remembered the long walk and what the waitress at the diner had told her. Part of her knew that she was not supposed to be in this plane. Another part of her knew she was exactly where she was supposed to be. Her back was stiff from sleeping in the cramped cockpit. She needed to slide out and find the elves as soon as she could.

Conner escorted Isabelle throughout Estal, giving her a quick tour of all the small shops and places of business. "I first brought the radio here before I left for China and the Burmese jungle in the early 1940s. TV came along afterward in the 50s, and in the 80s came cable. About 20 years ago, we got our own satellite."

"So you are telling me that you are over 100 years old?" Isabelle was still trying to figure everything out.

"No, I am not. Isabelle, elves do not have a natural aging process. We do not grow old. The only time we can die is if we are killed in battle or if we decide that we are tired of living."

Conner continued to explain. He stopped and looked directly into her eyes. "Isabelle, I am over four thousand years old." She felt something touch her mind. She no longer had doubts about what he had been telling her. It was as if a picture suddenly came into focus or pieces of a puzzle put into their proper places instantly. The look of confusion melted from her face, as questions popped in. "So, where does your money come from?"

"Well, since we have been around for quite a long time, we have been able to amass quite a bit of money to keep us afloat, as well as provide a few comforts. The dwarves have a tendency to strike a line of precious metals from time to time, and they are always finding rare and precious gemstones." He was happy to tell her how they funded the small elfin-dwarven nation.

"Most of our electricity comes from the wind turbines you saw on your drive in, as well as from hydro-electric generators and geothermal means." They stopped at the library and paused at the door. "I am going to have to ask you to wait here. No human has ever set foot in this place. Knowledge is very sacred to us. Some of what is behind these doors are not for humanity at all. Some you may learn in time." He gave her an apologetic look. "I must check on something. The answer to what happened yesterday is inside. I will only be gone a short time." With that, he turned and went through the intricately carved wooden doors. She stood outside. She was alone and hurt.

Conner quickly navigated the shelves of books and scrolls of ancient magic. Something was different about them. Some seemed to glow while others seemed to sing. It gave him more concern for alarm. He made his way to the small stone chamber in the back. As he entered, his suspicions were verified. He pulled back the tapestry that blocked all light from entering the room and was blinded by the brilliance that shown from within. The Skystone lit the room with a peculiar luminescence—magic released itself from the stone that had bound it all these eons. Conner urgently needed to find Buck.

When he returned, the expression on her new boss's face was quite different. Isabelle noticed that Bob Conner looked deep in thought. Although it had been only the second day, she felt as if she had known him all her life. She felt very comfortable here, no matter how much like a fairytale her life had become overnight. This was different. The expression on his face made him look alien to her.

"Is everything all right?" she asked. Knowing she had no right to offer assistance, she did it anyway. "Is there anything I can do?"

"Well to answer both those questions, I don't know." He stopped for a minute and looked seriously into her eyes. "Life as we know it has drastically changed." He gently grabbed her arm and pulled her back toward the elevators.

"I need to find Buck." They stepped out of the elevator into the hangar. Conner spotted Nedloh first.

"Ned! Come here for a second." He motioned to the young dwarf to him.

"Have you seen your uncle?"

"He is working the *Griffin Claw* refit. Why?" Nedloh sensed the urgency in the elf's voice.

"Thanks, I will explain to everyone later." Conner started toward the B17 at a brisk pace. Abruptly, he stopped and turned to his young dwarf friend. "Can you modify an inboard GPS to detect a high concentration of magic?"

Instantly the questions that had arisen in Nedloh's mind were answered. Curiosity was replaced a nagging fear. "Sure I can. It will take me a couple of hours, but no problem."

"Good. Have it installed in an hour. I am taking off." Conner started toward the bomber again and once more stopped.

"Miss Thompson, the Corsair is all yours. Get it up and in the air and you will get your wings. I am going to need you. Whatever you want or need for it, get it. Money is not an object. I trust your judgment. Just get it ready to fly. I need to be able to depend on it!" The elf walked away. This time, he did not stop.

"When he gets like that, just do as you are asked, and stay out of his way." The young dwarf advised the new recruit. "And, Miss Thompson is it?" Isabelle nodded. "He trusts you. That does not happen easily with your race. He knows something about you that you do not. Listen to what he has to say and you will be a credit to your kind."

Isabelle let what the small man told her sink in as she went to work on her Corsair. It took several minutes to realize that she had an F4U Corsair. She looked at it from a distance and saw what it could be. She was going to make it hers.

Conner reached the *Griffin Claw* and shouted up the entrance hatch. "Beladar! I need you down here A.S.A.P!" Conner waited anxiously.

Inside, Buck heard his given name called. Something must be serious. He quickly gave instructions to a fellow dwarf and an elf that was assisting in finishing the task at hand. Now that he was free, he quickly made his way through the bomber and down the steps. He was wiping his broad hands on a shop towel as his feet hit the hangar floor.

"Now, what is all the excitement 'bout, Lad?" Buck stuffed the dirty rag into his back pocket and folded his thick arms across his chest.

"The time has come." Conner was calm and concise with his words. "Magic is once again loose in the world of man. We need to find it and put it back." Buck had never seen Conner like this.

"Ned is modifying a GPS to help me find it. We can discuss what to do about it better when I get back. Have the refuel points ready." Conner put his hand on his friend's shoulder. "This is exactly why we are here. We were responsible for teaching it to humanity in the first place. Let's not make the same mistakes again." He turned to start back toward the *Dragon's Heart*. "Walk with me." Buck fell into step next to the elf. Although he took two steps to Conner's one, he kept up with ease.

"Aye, Lad. I will have all our friendly refuel points on standby." Buck mentally ran down the list in his head. Maggie would have all the numbers. "Anthriel," He stopped and turned to the elf. "If the magic has been released, by no means was it an accident." Conner looked puzzled. "What I mean to say, Lad, is something most unpleasant is afoot. We should prepare for the worst."

"Good thinking." Conner agreed. "Make sure every warplane in this hangar is armed and ready to fly in a week. I will get on the uplink and send the signal as soon as I get back. It is time for our kin to come home." The two friends continued to walk toward the P40 as they discussed strategy and details. Buck knew there was something that Conner did not tell him. With the return of magic, it could have been anything. He learned years ago that Riders could know things without ever learning or hearing. Sometimes it was like a premonition, other times, like instinct.

Amanda was startled as she heard voices outside the cockpit. She slowly peered over the edge. She looked past the blue star painted in a white circle on the camouflaged wing. An extremely short man was talking to a taller man. The tall man was looking directly at her. They were not men at all. The tall one was very pretty. He was an elf. The shorter was a dwarf.

"Um, I am sorry. I didn't break anything, I promise." She was very scared as she stepped out onto the left wing. The tall one just smiled and motioned her to him. Looking into his eyes, even from that distance, her fear melted. She took a few steps out onto the wing and sat down just before the machine gun barrel. The elf reached up, put his hands on her waist to help her down.

"Welcome, little one. I am Anthriel. Everyone calls me Conner. It's much easier." Conner gently sat her down on the epoxy floor. Buck could not believe his eyes and ears.

"How did you get in there?" Buck asked. Conner once again placed his hand on Buck's shoulder. He was quiet.

"You wished the door to be not locked last night didn't you?" Conner asked the young woman. Looking down at the floor, all she could do was nod her head. "I saw you in my dreams last night. I didn't remember that you were here until just now, I am sorry."

Amanda was relieved. Once again, remembering the diner, she felt more at ease. She knew that she was right where she was supposed to be. She smiled at Conner and handed him the leather flight jacket that she had used to keep warm the previous night.

Maggie had come out of her office to collect a stack of parts order forms from her box. She looked up and saw Conner standing by his plane with an extremely young woman. *What stray has he picked up this time?* She smiled as the thought went through her head. She did not wait for Conner to address before she went to him.

Just as Conner looked up toward the administrative office, he saw Maggie already walking toward the three of them. Maggie would take care of this special one until he got back. She was always great at entertaining special guests or new members of the family.

"You must be Amanda," Conner told her. The look on her face was sheer amazement.

"How did you know?" Amanda was bewildered.

"Just as you have dreamed of us in the past, I dreamed of you last night. You are safe. I know who you are, more than even you do. I will personally make sure that nothing bad will happen to you again." Conner was not one to go lightly on promises. Buck realized that there was something special about this girl. Conner was not just talking.

"Maggie, are you caught up for today?" the elf asked his office manager.

"Just these parts requisitions and..." She started to say his elfin name, then remembered the girl.

"It's okay, Magnethella. We are among friends." Conner smiled at the look on Maggie's face. "Have your assistant to take care of it, as per my request. You have had a change of priorities." Maggie nodded acknowledgment. "Take her down and get her a room. Make sure she gets something to eat and clean clothes. I think a pink flight suit would be fine. Let her know all about us. I will see her when I get back." Maggie took Amanda into the office as she gave her assistant new instructions.

"What was that all about, Lad? You are just taking in stray humans left and right." Buck was more than worried.

"That little girl there is going to save her own kind from total extinction and she does not even know it. As for our Miss Thompson, she is more valuable to us than just a crackpot mechanic is. Look at her." Both of them looked across the hangar at Isabelle. She was working hard as well as guiding her crew. "She is a natural leader. I need Isabelle as a wingman."

"Lad, you act as if we are going to war." Buck was thinking that if an elf could lose his marbles, this would be exactly how he would act.

"We just very well may be." With that, Conner began to preflight the *Dragon's Heart.*

Within minutes of beginning the preflight, Nedloh came running with a metal briefcase. He was once again beaming with pride. He quickly climbed up the fighter and into the cockpit.

"What do you have, Ned?" Conner quickly joined him at the cockpit. Ned pulled a screwdriver from his back pocket and went to work.

"Well, I started with the same model GPS tracking system you have now. I didn't want to re-compute weight and balance or modify your gauge cluster. I then added the typical magical location system from days of old. The hardest part was finding a unicorn hair and crystal with the right resonance. Harmonics are very important in a situation like this. Then I had to modify the software. Mankind never thought about looking for anything magical. So I had to make sure the computer not only knew where you were but where you wanted to go."

"Keep it up and you will put your uncle into retirement." Conner was amazed absolutely with the young dwarf's genius.

"I could never do that, someone has to complain," Nedloh smiled as he put the last screw back into the P40's gauge cluster. Conner gave a slight chuckle at the joke that he made at his friend's expense. He finished his preflight.

Chapter 8

Outside the hangar, Conner fired up the modified Allison V12. The *Dragon's Heart* roared to life without a puff of smoke. He quickly gave his flight controls a test for dragging and binding. All was smooth. He slid the cockpit shut to dampen the noise from the props. It was always too hard for the person on the other end of the radio waves to hear over the noise created by the spinning blades.

"Estal Tower, this is Delta- Hotel-Zero-One-Niner-Alpha, ready for immediate departure," Conner said into his headset. He zipped his leather flight jacket as he waited for a response. He could feel the young girl's energy very strongly through the jacket. Closing his eyes, he could see her life flash before his mind's eye. He saw her happy childhood that included her flight school. He also saw it ripped away from her by tragedy. It was replaced by abuse and neglect. This young woman was special. The events of her life had made her that way. He knew that she could use magic.

There is yet another. A familiar voice of long ago told him. His eyes snapped open.

"Delta- Hotel-Zero-One-Niner-Alpha." This voice came into his head through the headset. "You are cleared of all traffic. Good flying, Conner. See you when you get back."

"Roger that, Tower." With that, Conner turned on the global positioning system and pushed the power lever forward. He taxied to the runway. With his speed increasing, he remembered Bernoulli's principles of fluid dynamics. He pictured, in his mind's eye, the air moving across the wing, and creating the area of low pressure on the top of the wing, thus causing lift.

Quickly the earth dropped away and he was once again airborne. The skies were his domain. This time, it was not for fun. As in the days of old, he had a mission. The GPS ran quickly through diagnostics. Conner prayed that Nedloh had not gotten a variable wrong in the programming or a wire crossed. After a couple of seconds, the instrument showed to be working properly. It let Conner know via a liquid crystal display readout, that all was functioning and that the module was reading four satellites. He knew right away that this must have been part of the new programming. This model originally triangulated the aircraft's position with the use of only three satellites. The fourth must have belonged to the elf and dwarf delegation.

A standard arrow pointed the direction of north as well as a smaller blue arrow that indicated the direction of his heading. To his surprise and amazement, a ghost arrow pointed the direction in which he needed it to go. This one was pointing to the southwest. He banked the Warhawk and adjusted the nose of his warbird so that the heading and ghost arrows agreed.

He flew for the eight hours that the FAA allowed in one day. He landed at the Kansas City Downtown Airport. He had flown southeast to disguise his approach in the case that someone would track the direction in which he came. The landing was once again flawless at the small airport.

"What brings you into town, Conner?" A familiar voice came to the elf's ears as Fred Myers stepped out of the fuel truck.

"Hey, Fred," Conner shot the fuel man a charming grin. "I'm just passing through. Is that hotel down the way still open?"

"You betcha!" Fred pulled the hose and nozzle from the truck and walked over to the fighter. "Sorry, you're not staying. It's been a while, and I still owe you a beer." With a remote in his hand, he began to fuel the plane.

"I'm afraid I'll have to collect next time, buddy. I have to get going early tomorrow," Conner explained. He could see the disappointment on his friend's face.

"No problem, Conner." Fred quickly smiled. "Is this bill still going to the same place?"

"Yeah." Conner pulled the bags out of the storage compartment in the belly of the plane. Putting them down on the warm concrete, he walked over to sign the bill. Within a few minutes, Fred finished. Loading back up into the truck, the middle-aged Kansas City man drove back to the hangars. Gathering his bags, Conner waved as his friend drove away.

Conner secured the *Dragon's Heart* for the night and called for a cab. Conner stayed the night in a nice, but inexpensive downtown hotel. As he checked in, he requested a 5 A.M. wake-up call. Elves never slept much.

Isabelle quickly made a parts list from her thorough inspections of the Vought-manufactured Corsair. She was so lucky to have a usable copy of the original manuals. She also had a quick and accurate crew of both elves and dwarves to assist her. She took pictures of the original nose art, which consisted of the name *Amy*, and a buxom brunette in a bikini. What men did to entertain themselves never ceased to amaze her. She also noted a number of kills under the fogged and cracked canopy. New panels had been ordered to replace the original glass. Lexan would lighten the fighter quite a bit. This was only one of the many modifications she planned to make.

She climbed into the cockpit to reassess the gauges. She made a list of what had to go and what had to be updated. There was not much room to get to the fight controls under the floor. As she removed the seat, an envelope yellowed by time, fell to the floor. Picking it up, she noticed the faded red lipstick in the shape of woman's delicate lips over the flap.

Sealed with a kiss...

She sighed as she thought of the romance of two lovers separated by war. She gently opened the yellow flap. She slid the paper within out into the world. Opening the folded paper, she began to read...

My Dearest Love,

I hope this letter finds you well. We are all praying for your safe return. President Truman comes into the living room every evening to keep us updated. I always hope I may catch a glimpse of you on the newsreels during the matinee on Saturday.

The victory garden is doing well. Tomatoes are just starting to turn. I know they are your favorite. Oh, Baby, how the vines are loaded. I should start canning next week. I am going to trade with Martha Havisham for some raspberry preserves. Her garden seems to be growing as if touched by magic. You know that her husband could not go because of his knee. He so wanted to. He does what he can to help with the copper and rubber drives.

I hope Pappy and the rest of the boys are behaving themselves. I am sorry I must keep it

short this time. As you know, loose lips sink ships.
Know that you are in my thoughts and prayers.
Come home to me soon.

With all my love,
Amy

As Isabelle finished, she folded the paper and returned it to the envelope. She sat in silence thinking about what she had just learned. She now knew where the gull-winged fighter got its name. She also knew in fact that this plane was a part of the famous Black Sheep Squadron. It now belonged to her.

"Since you are already giving her a refit, why don't you upgrade the flight controls?" Nedloh snapped her out of the haze of romance and nostalgia brought to her by the little-yellowed letter.

"What do you have in mind, Ned, is it?" She slid the envelope into the left breast pocket of her flight suit and pulled the zipper shut.

"Yes, it is, Miss Thompson. I think you will like what I've got." Nedloh assured her.

"Please call me Isabelle" She always felt so uncomfortable with any kind of title. It drove her nuts when others called her by rank and last name in the army.

"Okay, Izzy." Nedloh gave her a smile that could melt icebergs. It made Isabelle feel fifteen again. "I came up with a fly-by-wire system for Conner's P40. It runs totally by computer inputs from the flight stick and pedals. I even incorporated a forced feedback to give the controls a realistic feel. It can be adjusted to the comfort of the pilot."

Isabelle was impressed. "How soon can you get me the controls?"

"I can have the servos and programmed boxes to you the day after tomorrow. Maybe later, if..." Nedloh stopped short.

"Is there something you are not telling me?" Isabelle had a feeling that there was about to be more added to this deal.

"Well, I have been working on a few other things." Nedloh started. I have a program that would read your brain waves and adjust the controls as you desired."

"You mean read control by remote thoughts?" He definitely had Isabelle's attention.

"Well, yeah, to start." He continued.

"What do you mean, 'To start'?" A red flag just popped up for Isabelle.

"I have been working on this for years. You may have heard of one of my remote-controlled craft crashing in Roswell in the late 40s."

Isabelle started laughing hysterically. "You mean to tell me that Roswell is real and not just something made up by the tabloids?" Her face had turned bright red in her hysterics. "And to top it all off, it's not even an alien, but a dwarf playing with toy airplanes?"

Nedloh pretended to be insulted. "I worked hard on that plane. It has taken the rest of the world almost fifty years to even come close to my ideas."

"I'm sorry," Isabelle was trying to catch her breath. "I just found it ironic that instead of little green men from another planet, it turned out to be little, bearded men from fairytales. I'm sorry. Please, go on." Isabelle tried to keep a straight face.

"Well, I wanted to take it one step further by incorporating my artificial-intelligence program, so that your aircraft will be able to respond to you." Nedloh thought that if he got into the details right now he would lose her.

"That sounds interesting. So you are saying that this aircraft could have a mind of its own?" Isabelle asked.

"You got it. And it would only respond to you and whomever you wanted it to." He assured her.

"When can you have it ready?" Isabelle was on a timeline and did not want to disappoint her new boss.

"When do you want it? You're the boss." Nedloh was feeling more than a little sure of himself.

"She goes to paint in four days. I need it ready to install by the end of the week."

"No problem Izzy. We will have to pull a few all-nighters to get the AI like you want, but it will be ready. What do you think?"

Isabelle held out her hand. "I just think you sold your first AI, Ned." He shook her hand to seal the deal. They had the start of a great friendship.

Chapter 9

After a few hours rest, the elf headed back to the airport. The skies were already light in the early summer morning. Stepping out of the taxi, Conner paid the cab driver and left him a nice tip. As he walked through the security gates to the P40, he felt something strangely familiar. As the sun peeked over the horizon, he felt life. Conner could feel the heartbeat of the birds. He could even feel the beetles scurrying across the warming concrete. This was a feeling he had not had in so long. He remembered that this life was the source of all elfin magic. It came from the earth and everything living on it.

The elf decided to try a small spell. Holding a set of keys as if he had a remote door lock, he pointed his hand toward the P40.

Ellá mone Benatté...

These words came to his mind easily. He remembered the elfin meaning, "Allow me entry". With this, he heard the security latch release of the cockpit and the canopy slide open.

His entire race had the ability to use magic to varying degrees. Some were inclined more for healing while others were to grow things. Some even had the ability to temper steel to make the finest weapons and armor. Elves had never forgotten this unique ability, though they have lived without it for so long. They had gotten through the last few thousand years as humans have.

While doing his preflight inspections, Conner had his attention divided. Looking over his mechanical-winged steed, he thought about the significance of the past week's events. His mind was abuzz with possible scenarios of the *hows* and *whys*. The only conclusion that came to his mind pointed to the need for more information. He should reach his destination today.

Preflight completed, he once again woke the V12 and taxied. He got clearance and instructions for takeoff. He was on his way.

As he flew from the busy city, he invoked one more small mental incantation, *"Seirenthé velethulé!"* [Shape my time.]

The world below him came almost to a complete standstill. Birds seemed to hang in midair. Clouds did not move. Human life below moved so slowly, it could not be discerned. He should have thought of this yesterday.

As the world around his P40 stood virtually motionless, he continued normally through his own time. His navigation worked without hindrance.

The crystal and the hair of unicorn were unaffected by his elfin craft. As what had been hours to him, only seconds passed for the rest of the world. He grew close to his destination in mere moments.

On the floor of the Arizona desert, his keen elfin eyes spied where the source of the magic originated. Great rock formations forced from the earth were in the form of a large dark fortress. At first, it blended in with neighboring mesas and rock formations. A twisted stone tower marked the middle. Perverted human forms stood motionless. They were frozen in their daily routines by Conner's spell. He banked the *Dragon's Heart* to the left for a closer look. He was horrorstruck as he saw the twisted forms of man that were spawned. He was not prepared to find such atrocities, nor was he ready for what else his eyes discovered. In what appeared to be a courtyard, four massive humans have frozen escorts to four skilled captives. Goblins never gave anyone a warm fuzzy feeling.

Investigating the tower more closely, Conner noticed satellite dishes and receiving equipment. With a small onboard camera, he began taking several pictures of the stone fortress and its surrounding terrain. With the photographs and his own eyes, he had enough intelligence for one day. It was time to start back and get in touch with Buck.

Illith dué mellinathia! [Share my time.]

As Conner headed back for Wyoming, time around him sped back up to merge with his own.

The money they had acquired over the years had afforded the elves and dwarves a few extra goodies. One was a private satellite as well as some high-tech jamming and encryption equipment. Nedloh designed most of the gear. Conner smiled at the thought of the dwarf's rabid genius. The main codes used elfin numeric symbols and algorithms. Tolkien was the only human who ever published anything with the elfin language and most of what he knew, the literary genius took with him to the grave. Conner remembered what a good friend he was.

Conner set his radio to broadcast in the red. He would bounce his signal up into orbit and back to Estal. The LED on the radio blinked three times, and then glowed red.

"Rider to Estal," he repeated three times.

He waited only a few seconds for a reply between each.

"Go ahead, Rider. This is Estal. We have you secured and in the red." Buck's voice came back at him.

"Estal, I have hard intel on what we were looking for. It's not pretty."

Conner tried to keep emotion from his voice. "It looks like nothing good is coming of this. Continue with your preparations and I will see you when I get back."

"Estal acknowledges. I will make it happen." Buck replied.

"Roger that, Estal. Rider out." Conner finished his transmission.

"Estal out." Buck ended the transmission. The LED blinked and glowed green once again.

Chapter 10

Lord Esuorts sat in his throne room. A large cluster of monitors and computer screens suspended from the ceiling. They tied in with each country's spy satellites and camera networks. It was a perfect blending of magic and technology. He watched, calculated, and planned his conquest with the information he procured. He could see any city's traffic, bank or ATM cameras worldwide. He could tell who would be easy to shape, and who would perish. He stored the collected information with the technicians. Because of this, he made certain that this room was the most heavily guarded. His technicians could not be lost.

Momentarily, he had a strange feeling. The sorcerer inwardly queried. He knew the screens before him would reveal the answer. He watched continually. His eyes saw nothing out of the ordinary. With a thought and a wave of his hand, a technician approached the station and plugged in. Instantly the picture was enhanced and slowed. Several times the image changed as it became clearer until a recognizable shape came to view.

"There," he pointed, "That is what I am looking for." Esuorts stared at the tiny dot that blinked onto the screen for just a split second. "Again," he commanded. This time, the picture froze on the tiny dot and enlarged several times. The sorcerer rested his chin in his hand with his index finger over his upper lip. He watched as the shape of a WWII fighter formed on the screen.

"Aircraft of that time are not stealth. The only way it could be undetected is the one way I detected it—magic." He was the only one who had the power. Feeble human minds could not discover nor learn to wield the *awful goodness* locked away with him. This had to be something else. It was something that could impede his conquest. Esuorts hated annoyances. This was his first. He would find out more.

He decided to act now and ponder these implications after he had crippled the world.

"Upload the virus and await my signal for its release." He smiled. He was proud of his new pet. Not only would it infect every computer, but every human in contact with them as well. After its release and activation, he would be able to reshape his subjects as he saw fit. The world would be on its knees soon enough. He would strike while he still had the element of surprise on his side. This insignificant plane troubled him still.

Where were his manners? He had guests in which to tend. How could have he had forgotten the four large friends who came to visit in the night? How much more would want the power he had.

"Bring me, my guards. I require an escort to the detention levels."

Within seconds, four heavy guards appeared in his chamber. With having guests drop in unannounced twice now, Esuorts had become more distrustful. His mind would be more at ease when he controlled the world. For now, he would surround himself with his guards.

He needed to find out more about his first four guests. He was impressed with their size and tactics. Lord Esuorts was almost certain there were more. He just had to find them. A benevolent smile formed as he contemplated meeting his new allies. Through the corridors, he contemplated all he had accomplished as well.

He was pleased with what he created thus far. He had increased security as well as updated the arsenals of his infant armies. After his Ratticans had finished with his tower, Esuorts ordered them to develop new weapons that were far greater than anything seen by today's modern armies. Superior firepower and numbers would bring this world to him. Without the world's computers to guide them, the nations' armies would be helpless; crushed as quickly as a cockroach underfoot.

Lord Esuorts' musings ended as the guards led him to the detention cells. These cells were no more than pits twenty feet into the floor. The walls were completely smooth. Escape was impossible. With just a wave of his hand, one of the goblin scouts floated up to the evil lord. It floated within six feet of the smooth stone floor. Esuorts purposely dropped him to the stone.

Fear shone in the mighty goblin's eyes. It bowed before the sorcerer, hoping to be spared.

"What are you and where do you come from?" he asked the scout.

Squeals and grunts were all that came back as a reply. Disgusted with the language barrier, the new dark lord nodded his head. "Now, let me ask you again, what are you and where do you come from?"

"We are of the Goblin people." The scout's hands went to his throat in sheer terror. "What have you done to me?"

"I am asking the questions. The slight change in languages will be nothing compared to what will happen if you do not answer my queries." Lord Esuorts was making no idle threats.

"Many apologies, my lord. We are but humble goblins on a quest for our king." The goblin was still in shock from the human language coming from his mouth.

"What is this quest you speak of?" The corrupt mage was genuinely curious.

"We are one of three scouting parties." the goblin began to explain. "The first two were sent in search of food for our people. His majesty sent us to discover the source of the magic that woke us. We had to return with it, if we could."

"So you shall. So you shall." Lord Escorts' mind was like a trap. He knew from where his new army would come. This race of goblins would augment his forces well.

The monster slept—massive, yet small enough to avoid detection by the human eye. It consisted of ones and zeros lurking in an immense computer system. It waited to be unleashed onto the world. It too was a blend of technology and magic. Made of electricity and binary code, it would strike out everywhere computers were used. It spread like a plague to everything that could process information. Its sole purpose was to feed on the human brain.

As one sat at a computer terminal, it would feed on, and spread to the greatest computers ever created. It went past chips and circuit boards. Traveling on the World Wide Web, it would find its way to humans across the planet devouring all human knowledge.

Inside the world of cyberspace, a living creature not only preyed on living minds but on circuits and hard drives. Like a beast of our nightmares, it watches and waits. Without discrimination, it pounces. Instead of talons and teeth, light flashes and audio soak into the victim's brain. They sit at their laptops and desktops unable to look away.

Flashing colors hypnotize and trap the poor souls. With the brain paralyzed, DNA is recorded and rewritten, creating monsters for the Dark Lord to rule.

Not stopping there, the beast travels farther along the web. It finds bank and government computers. Absorbing the information, it amasses all known knowledge. Once all knowledge is acquired, systems shut down, and nations are crippled. If anyone survives the beast's attack through the boxes, their world is no longer accessible. Money becomes worthless. Utilities such as water and electricity stop instantly. Even traffic lights take on a mind of their own, resulting in thousands of deaths worldwide.

As humankind relies on chips and circuits, computers that humans created, their very inceptions turn on and become the plagues that they have fought so hard to exterminate.

Chapter 11

Conner no longer had time to play FAA games. He needed to be back at Estal hangar as soon as possible. Magic had been used to twist life. *Magic* had to be used to stop the atrocity as soon as he could. The elf knew that only magic could be used to defeat this evil that had been born of the same. Everything in the universe needs balance, and magic was no exception.

Illith dué Mellinathia.

Once again, time surrounding the P40 came to a near standstill. To him, time remained the same. He set an alarm on his watch and let his thoughts wander.

He felt it coursing through every cell of his being. It took him back the days of old. He remembered his life as a Rider on his friend's back. He had watched Emorthra hatch when he was but a youngling. His first responsibility as a Rider in training was the care and feeding of his dragon hatchling. The young elf cleaned Emorthra's dragon keep, as well as bathed and fed this Skymate. The two quickly became more than friends.

Anthriel had other responsibilities, as did Emorthra. The elf, schooled in magic, learned how to heal and levitate objects. He even learned to bring necessities of his survival from Earth itself. He learned how to make his very existence depend on magic. He relied on himself and his Skymate first and foremost. His elders taught to him that for every action, there was an equal and opposite reaction.

"There is only so much water in the world," he remembered his instructor telling him, so many years ago. "If you bring forth a spring in which to drink, but do not send it back when your thirst has been sated, a well or river somewhere else in the world may go dry. This may cause others to suffer for lack of water." Ehteneite was very wise. He was very much like a father to young Anthriel. He even schooled the young elf in hand-to-hand combat as well as the use of the sword.

Anthriel was not the only one to have been educated. Dragons were born with basic knowledge. This was augmented by elfin knowledge and understanding. Emorthra also learned air-to-air combat tactics from wiser dragons. He had to learn to fly and maneuver through the air with great plates of armor covering his scales.

Of all the things the young elf learned, nothing pleased him more than the day he had learned to make a saddle. It was the day that he learned to fly on his friend's back. From this day forward, whenever his lessons seem to weigh him down, he would mount his mighty emerald friend and dance with the clouds. Nothing thrilled him more than looping and rolling through the blue of the sky. He loved to feel the mist of the stratus clouds on his bare skin. Nothing was more refreshing than time in the air with his dragon friend.

The beeping of his watch brought him back. He once again whispered the words that merged his time with the rest of the world. "Estal Tower, this is Delta-Hotel-Zero-One-Niner-Alpha, requesting permission to land."

"This is Estal Tower. You are cleared for approach and welcome home, Conner." The elf in the tower radioed back.

"I wish I had something to celebrate, but I am afraid I do not bear glad news. Please have Buck meet me in the hangar."

"Roger that, Delta-Hotel. Tower, out."

Conner taxied into the massive hangar and parked the P40 into its bay. Papers and shop towels blew everywhere. The gusts came to an abrupt halt as the propeller and engine died. Buck was already moving toward the plane as fast as his short legs could carry him. Conner loosed himself from his harness and parachute and climbed out as the dwarf reached him.

Conner whistled to one of the elfin ground crew. The crewmember ran from across the hangar floor, reaching the P40 the same time as Buck.

"Ye elves like to show off any time ye get." Buck snarled.

Conner tossed down the rolls of exposed film. "Get these developed and bring them to the war room. I need you to make *One Hour Photo* look like it takes a week."

The elf was gone so fast to the elevator Buck barely saw him move. "We have a lot of work to do, my dwarf friend," Conner said earnestly.

"I was afraid of that, lad." Buck let Conner know that he had his back. "I have made some calls, and we shall be getting some new equipment in the next day or two."

"Great! I hope we are thinking along the same lines." Conner half asked and half stated.

"I think we be, lad," Buck assured him.

Conner walked toward the Corsair. He saw right away, Nedloh working with Isabelle. "Well, where are we standing?"

Isabelle, startled by Conner's question, recovered quickly. Wiping her hands on an already dirty shop towel, she climbed down from the old navy fighter.

"Well, the landing gear has been gone through. We put in new seals, hydraulic fluid, and have the air pressure right where it needs to be. We have new tires and brakes. She explained. "The Lexan canopy came this morning, and that is next. It will be ready for paint tomorrow and Ned's new flight-control system as soon as it's dry."

Nedloh popped his head out and smiled in mock innocence. "What new system?" Buck asked.

"Something he has been working since Roswell, I think," Isabelle explained. Buck just gave his nephew a warning stare. Nedloh answered him with a mischievous grin.

"It's your funeral, lass," Buck said in reply, as walked off with Conner.

"By the way, Miss Thompson, your flight lessons start next week," Conner stopped and turned to tell her. "Don't worry; the company will pick up the tab. We are going to need all the pilots we can get as well as planes." Isabelle did not know what to say. She was happy to be getting flight lessons, but something in her boss's voice that told her Conner was not giving her the whole story.

Chapter 12

Amanda rested comfortably in her room. Estal was more than she had ever hoped for. The elves had been so nice to her. For the first time since the crash, she felt safe. After a small knock, Maggie opened the door to find the young the woman staring around the room in awe. The pink flight suit felt different, but comfortable, on the young woman.

"How are you doing, dear?" Maggie asked.

"I'm feeling much better now, thank you." The young woman replied. "The suit feels a little weird. It feels so light... almost like I am wearing nothing at all."

"That is the elfin cloth that it is made from. It's lightweight, cool and warm. Above all the suit is more flame resistant than any Nomex weaves. We could find something more suited if you would like."

"No, that's okay. It's quite comfortable." Amanda knew the elves had taken her in. That meant a lot to her. She did not feel like intruding upon their hospitality more than she had to.

"Fine," Maggie said with a smile. She had a feeling that the young girl was trying not to be a bother. "How about we go find something to eat and take a look around."

Amanda's eyes lit up. "I would love to!" She could barely contain her excitement. The young woman had been eager to explore ever since she went down a few hours ago. The shapes and stone carvings drew her attention immediately. Now she will get a closer look.

"You are a guest here, Amanda. Once you are a friend of the elves, you will remain so until you pass into the next life. You are free to come and go, but you should never tell our secret to anyone else. This is a grave responsibility. Do you understand?" Maggie asked her.

"Yes, I do. I knew I was supposed to be here. You took me in when I had no place else to go. I promise never to jeopardize that." Amanda swore her oath and pledged her friendship to the elves.

"Now that the serious stuff is over, let's go get something to eat and explore." Maggie was more upbeat. Her smile was contagious. Amanda could not help but return it.

They left the guest area and traveled down the corridor to the main hall. Amanda was enamored by the stonework. The stone trees that supported the huge ceiling amazed her. As they walked, Maggie explained to her how the dwarves carved them and told her the story of how the elves became friends with dragons and dwarfs. She told the young woman of the Riders and Conner's part in all of this. Over breakfast, Amanda learned much about her new friends. She loved the stories. She liked the stories of the Riders most. She listened to Maggie intently.

Amanda passed the day with her. Before she had known it, it was time for evening meal. They dined on salad and fruit. Isabelle joined them briefly. The other human woman was covered in grease. She knew there was something special about Isabelle. Amanda remembered seeing her and the elves in her dreams.

"How is *Amy* coming?" Amanda tried to get a conversation started. Any other time, the younger woman would have been shy. She felt comfortable here. She had nothing to hide, nor need to feel shame.

"Excuse me?" asked Isabelle, startled by the younger woman's question. "Oh, I'm sorry, *Amy*, the Corsair! She is coming along greatly. She should be back from paint the day after tomorrow. I just need to pick a color."

"Amethyst!" Amanda exclaimed without batting an eye.

"What was that?" Isabelle inquired, temporarily confused.

"It is a pink color with a touch of purple," the girl countered.

"That would be great—a far cry from original navy blue, but neither is the rest of the old bird." Isabelle really liked the idea. "Amethyst it is. Thanks for the help." She smiled at the young woman.

Isabelle got ready to return to work. She had a lot to do still. She stopped in her tracks and turned to Amanda. "If you would like to come up and help, or just sit back and watch, you are more than welcome."

Amanda looked at Maggie for approval. "Just stay out of trouble. There is nothing for me to show you until Conner is ready for you," she said with a smile.

"I would love to." Amanda smiled as she hurried to finish. She quickly fell in step beside Isabelle as they headed toward the elevator. Right away, she admired the older woman. Amanda felt as if she had a big sister.

Buck sat with Conner in the elf's office. A multitude of aerial photos taken from the P40 was scattered across the desk. "I do not like it a wee bit, lad. This is far from natural. This is blasphemous."

"I concur, my friend. I am afraid that whoever is using the magic also has access to satellites. The elders and I have put multiple shielding spells on our network and orbiting relay. Our system has downloaded and archived every piece of information that our data banks can hold."

"I can link through the US satellite system and relay everything on a separate terminal that Ned can put through together," Buck proposed.

"Good idea. If that goes down we know that our new friends in magic are involved." Conner agreed. "By the looks of the fortress, whoever has control of the darkness is not just in it for the money. They are playing for keeps"

Amanda watched Isabelle for hours. She helped when she could. The older woman was amazed at the knowledge of the younger. "I used to fly with my dad," she smiled

"Really? I can tell you know your way around a plane." Isabelle loved to talk with the girl. "Where are you from?" she asked.

"I came from a small town outside of Kansas City. We used to fly out of the Lawrence air terminal." For some reason, talking to Isabelle was not difficult. There was something about the woman that opened her up.

"You have to be kidding! I am from Kansas City. I know where Lawrence is!" Isabelle was flabbergasted. She was so far from home with a young girl who practically came from her hometown.

"So, what happened to your parents, if you don't mind me asking?" The smile suddenly melted from the younger woman's face. She immediately felt bad. She knew she struck a nerve. "Hey, I am sorry. It's none of my business."

"No, that's okay. I really feel comfortable talking to you. I was eight when my parents were killed in a plane crash." Amanda began her story.

"I know it must have been a blessing and a curse not to have been on that plane." Isabelle tried to understand.

"You don't get it, do you? I was on that plane. I was thrown from the cockpit and miraculously landed without a scratch."

Isabelle did not know what to say.

"I had been in a dozen foster homes. Nobody wanted to adopt a girl as old as I was. Weird things always happened and no one would keep me. Finally, my last foster father beat me while my foster mother watched. My caseworker got tired of moving me so she just left me there. Finally, I emptied the cash in his wallet right after payday and hopped a bus. Now, here I am."

Isabelle let the socket wrench she was using slip from her grasp. Before Amanda could react, the older woman's arms were wrapped around her. Amanda could hold it back no longer. She wept in Isabelle's arms.

Time passed quickly. She knew that Amanda had a rough day. It could not have been easy baring her soul like that to a total stranger. The girl had fallen into a strange environment, as had she. Isabelle felt that they could help each other deal with the nuances that their lives had brought them. Only time could tell what adventures lie before them.

By the end of the day, the women had bonded. They both knew that they were exactly where they were supposed to be. They discussed their journeys to Wyoming and the dreams of the roads that brought them there. Isabelle was very intrigued with Amanda's narrative about her last stop at a diner. Isabelle also found the mysterious waitress to be peculiar.

Conner looked hard at the military forces he had, which were sparse. As long as magic was involved, he knew that he could not count on human governments for help. The elf actually preferred it that way. The knowledge and power that magic represented were too great for any human nation to wield. It was more powerful than nuclear technology. He could not risk it. At one time, he could have counted on the Native American Nations to help, but most had become bitter and would use it to seek revenge on the white man.

They had a small contingency of elves and dwarves—hardly enough to stop a sorcerer bent on world domination. He would definitely have to call the Races home to assist. Humankind had come too far to give up on them now. Technology replaced the magic of old. In a way, it had become a new magic altogether. Wielded by mages of the World Wide Web, the spells were written in binary code instead of runes of ancient languages. These new mages could create entire worlds on laptop screens from which to adventure in or learn. The combination of these two forms of magic could be deadly.

Picking up the receiver on his desk, Conner dialed an internal number. "I want every channel on radio or television turned to a news network. I need these monitored around the clock. Make sure they are spell shielded." He gave his orders to the dwarf in charge of security who was on the other end. Coranth listened intently. "I also need to have our computer systems separated as soon as the downloading is complete." The elf added.

"No problem, we are finishing downloading every human archive as we speak. I already have four of my team monitoring all the major networks. We are recording on the new crystal storage system. The CSS will hold every bit of information that the world has to offer five hundred times over. So, we can record from now until doomsday on one cube," the security dwarf assured.

"Good work. Let me know of any changes." Conner did not want to alarm anyone yet. He did not want to let it slip that doomsday may be closer than expected. He turned on the set in his office and leaned back in his chair in thought. It was hard to plan contingencies if he had no idea who the enemy was, or what their plans were.

Chapter 13

The four goblin scouts escorted Lord Esuorts and twelve of his personal heavy guards. The sorcerer's plan was to meet with the goblin king and demand his allegiance. He would make it beneficial for either party, but one way or another the sorcerer was going to get his army.

As they traversed the catacombs and tunnels that initially led the scouts to Esuorts, the sorcerer had plenty of time to further his plans. The small plane weighed most heavily on his mind. His own personal air force would be needed to defend his holdings from any attacks that came from the sky. It was a small matter. The thought of the dragon skeleton came to mind. He would create his own flying beasts to devastate the world from the sky. Once he had rendered every computer helpless, modern air warfare would be all but impossible. A smile formed on his face as designs for his new, magnificent, flying beast formed in his mind.

Barock studied the carcasses that the first two parties had returned. Human flesh had become soft and delicate. It was much more tender than he had remembered. The young female that had been brought to him had been a most exquisite morsel. It had been prepared rare with cave mushroom gravy. The other was tough but lean.

The king's dining chamber was lit with ornate iron torches placed on the walls of the large cave. A large fire roared in the center of a big stone hearth placed in the middle of the great hall. Goblins were not much for quarrying or working with stone, as were the dwarves. They preferred to find a cave that suited their needs and move in. Improvements would be made as they saw fit.

The dinnerware, golden goblets, and knives had been stolen from men, dwarves and others that fell prey to goblin pillaging. Barock knew that the time for ravaging man had come to an end. It was going to be the new age of goblins. Goblins would herd men, as men do cattle. They would have plenty to eat. The flesh of man would be made to serve the goblins' desires.

As the goblin king feasted with the successful parties, he discussed with them the availability of food. Soon raiding parties would be formed to gather for his hungry peoples. The youngest and most tender would be saved for him. In the language of squeals and grunts, the scouts had told their king of large villages throughout the top world. They also told them of the beasts that were made of steel and carried men in their bellies. These were a challenge, but they could be overcome with enough force. Nothing could keep a goblin from its meal.

As the feast continued, the lord of the underworld inquired if the third party had reported yet. His adviser grunted a negative. This worried the goblin king. As the mighty goblin gnawed the tender bits of meat off the bone, his herald entered the dining chamber.

The younger, smaller goblin told him of the return of the third party. He also informed him that they had returned to the realm of goblins with a human. In the language of the hulking beasts, the small one informed his king that this human requested an audience with his majesty.

"What business does this human flesh want with me? Let it be quick or let it be my next meal." The king of goblins was infuriated with them bringing a human back.

"It claims to have brought the magic in which you seek." The smaller goblin cowered away in fear of his king's anger. The small goblin herald shortly reappeared with a tall elderly human with eyes as black as night. "Lord Esuorts, your majesty." The goblin announced his presence.

"What do you want with me, my supper?" Barock grunted and squealed.

"I am sorry, I do not speak swine." Lord Esuorts waved his hand and the goblin king made a slight gurgle in his throat as his vocal cords changed.

"How dare you insult the honorable language of the goblins!" The king of the underground was taken aback by the human speech that came from his mouth. His threatening tone quickly melted away with the horror of what came from his mouth.

"Now that we can communicate better and that I have demonstrated a small measure of my abilities, I would like to discuss your allegiance to me," the human lord of dark magic smiled with confidence.

"What is the meaning of this?" The confusion caused by the change in speech quickly faded. Anger had once again returned, joined by contempt for this intruder.

"I owe you no explanation. Since I hope for a peaceful cooperation from you and your goblin army, I shall grant you one." The dark sorcerer began his own version of diplomacy.

"My intent is to rule this entire planet. You can either assist me, of which you would be rewarded with plenty of the sustenance you require, or you can perish like the rest of those who choose to oppose me." Lord Esuorts made his point quickly. Since the plane was spotted spying on his plans, he had no time for pleasantries.

"We goblins are strong and our armies can defend us from anything you bring," the king boasted.

"Are you so sure?" The dark lord waved his hand and the goblins at the table began to scream and melt in front of the king. A smile grew like a fungus on Lord Esuorts' face. Barock stared in whatever expression of horror a goblin can make. "Let me ask you again, will you assist me in my conquest."

"Okay, you have my attention, human." Barock paused as he watched his best trackers melt into puddles. "You are very convincing. I think we may work well together."

"Good! Now that I do have your attention, I need you to swear your allegiance to me," Esuorts demanded.

"I may assist you, but goblins do not swear allegiance to their food," Barock added with smugness.

"Then I'll tell you that I don't want to have to watch my back with you. Since you cannot make up your mind, you can be food," Lord Esuorts smiled as he held out his hand. A glowing sphere of blue light started in his palm. It shot out toward the swine-like goblin king. Before the court's eyes, the wart-ridden and wrinkled skin of the massive goblin changed into that of a pale, smooth human. His shape transformed itself into a young woman.

"What have you done to me?" the newly transformed young woman shrieked in horror.

"Now, now," Esuorts scolded. "That is no way to make a scene in front of very hungry goblins." As he said that, a guard came, grabbed her and took her off to the kitchen. They had no idea that this woman was their former king. "Now," Esuorts bellowed in the hall at the top of his lungs, "I claim the throne of the goblins! You will serve me! You will obey me or you all will perish!"

The herald kneeled at the sorcerer's feet. "What is your bidding, my master?" The small goblin groveled at the human's feet.

"For you, I have a special task. You will rule until I send for you. You will be my General of Goblins, as well as my liaison to the goblin people. No commands will be followed unless they come from me." The small bowing goblin grew before Esuorts. He grew to be the greatest of goblins—his allegiance given only to the sorcerer.

"I will not fail, my lord," he answered in a booming voice.

"I trust you will not. I will go and make ready. Our days of ruling this planet are nearby. Prepare your armies. Take all necessary steps to arm and feed your ranks. Chaos is now! A new age is at hand!" Esuorts was almost mad with the joy of his plan was slowly coming to together, just the way he wanted it. He turned and left the goblins with as much confidence as he had come.

Chapter 14

What had usually taken most men months to overhaul of the Corsair, had taken Isabelle and her team of elves and dwarves only a matter of weeks. Conner was impressed with the efficiency of the human woman, as well as her attention to detail. This would be an asset to whatever trials would come before them in the coming months.

The human woman was strong and quite intelligent. Conner also believed that she might possess the ability to use magic. If dragons were still on the planet, she would have been a candidate for bonding. She had the makings of a great Rider. This, Conner felt, made the woman very intriguing. He needed to see if she had the instincts to match her skills.

Conner crossed the hangar to the Corsair. He smiled as he looked at the amethyst hue, instead of the original navy blue. The belly remained gray. It was very bland in contrast to the bright pinkish-purple of the top portion of the fighter. He found it fitting that the original name of the plane had been retained. On the nose, the name *Amy* was

airbrushed in the same silver and script of the
original hand-painted nose art. It was definitely a
girl's plane.

"That thing has come a long way in a few short
weeks." Conner started in just to get the woman's
attention. "It looks good, but will it fly?"

"I don't know. Everything works as it's supposed
to, and the engine purrs like a kitten." Isabelle
reported. "We just need someone brave enough to
take her up and see how she handles. Let me know
when you find someone," she jabbed.

"Would you feel safe in her?" Conner's query was
more to check her work without getting too picky.

"I would in a heartbeat," Isabelle replied without
hesitation.

"Good. I will give it its first test flight, and then
you will have a crash course in the principles of
flight tomorrow. First, let's have some dinner. I will
buy if you drive. I have wanted a ride in that hot rod
of yours ever since I saw it." Conner was looking
forward to some time with the woman for a while.
He also thought that it was time that she knew a
little more of what was going on.

"That would be great. I could use a burger and
fries. Let me get cleaned up." She climbed down
from the cockpit and went to go change. "Give me
half an hour and meet me out by my car," she yelled
back at Conner as she walked backward toward the
elevator.

Conner had been standing by the old Chevy for almost ten minutes when Isabelle finally got there. He was more than stunned. He was amazed how she looked out of her flight suit. Her jeans fit her body perfectly. A short-sleeved black Holley Performance bowling shirt covered her shoulders where her pink camisole did not. Her long dark hair was pulled back in a ponytail. She wore just enough makeup to bring out her features. She really did look amazing.

"Wow," was all he could manage to say after he picked his jaw up.

Isabelle smiled, as she knew that she had accomplished her mission of grabbing his attention. "Oh, this? I just threw it on." She quickly changed the subject. She did not want him to know that she picked it out purposely. "So where are we going to eat?"

"There is a great little diner just down the road a couple of miles. They have the best apple pie." Conner tried to tempt her. Isabelle did not care what they ate or where they went, she was just thrilled to be out with Conner. She did not know anything about elfin courting rituals, but in the human world, this would be considered a first date. She was sure he had been around long enough to know better.

She pulled her key chain out of her purse and hit two buttons on the automatic door release. Both doors popped open. "I was wondering how that worked since you seemed to have removed the door handles." Conner was no less than amazed.

"I like the clean, shaved look. That is why I kept chrome trim to a minimum." There was nothing in the world she liked more than talking about her baby. Now she really had a chance to impress him. "Are you ready to go?" she asked.

"Sure," Conner said as he climbed into the car and buckled up. Isabelle slid into the driver's side, put the key into the ignition, and fired up the 500-cubic-inch Caddy motor. He knew she must have felt the same way about this car as he did for the Warhawk. It must have given her a great sense of pride and accomplishment. Conner watched the woman put the car into gear, and off they went.

Conner and Isabelle walked into the diner that had been usually full of tourists and bus travelers. This evening had been much quieter than normal. They picked out a nice quiet booth in the corner. The red vinyl cushions were plain and what was expected in every typical American eatery.

As they perused the menu, a middle-aged waitress with bright red lipstick came to take their order.

"I'll have a double cheeseburger, order of fries and a diet cola," Isabelle ordered first and handed her menu back to the waitress. The waitress turned to Conner who had his nose buried.

"Hey there, hon. Long time, no see," the waitress said as she recognized the elf. "How is the little one doing?"

"She made it to us safely and is adjusting quite well. By the way, can you give me a clue to what is going on?" he asked the waitress.

"I could, but then I would be doing your job for you, now wouldn't I, Sweetie? I can tell you that you have a rough time ahead and the world is changing before you, as we speak. Among you, there will be a light that will shine through the darkness and will fall on this world. Now what can I get you?" she asked him again impatiently.

"Okay, I'll have the whole-wheat pancakes with extra syrup, not that imitation stuff, and a glass of unsweetened iced tea." Conner closed his menu and handed it back to her, and she went off to put their order in.

"Oracles are so hard to get information out of, sometimes. They always get a kick out of being all mystical or talking in riddles. Don't you hate that?" Conner asked. He tried to be upbeat, as he pondered the oracle's words.

"Actually I have no idea of what an oracle is, nor what you're talking about. I have never met one." Isabelle looked quite confused.

"Oh, I forgot," Conner said apologetically. "An oracle is a mystical being that pops in our world from time to time to give us wisdom and guidance. The problem is they always speak in riddles or never give us all of the information. We have to figure out a lot for ourselves. It keeps us thinking and on our toes," Conner explained the best of his ability.

"I think I get it. How does she know Amanda?" she asked.

"The girl probably stopped in here on her way to the hangar the day before I found her in my cockpit," Conner explained. "She doesn't just appear to elves. They have been known to appear to humans as well. Besides, I would not be surprised if she has something to say to you before we leave."

The whole conversation confused Isabelle. She did not want to admit it, but it was very odd for her. "So, do you think that you can take *Amy* up tomorrow?" She quickly changed the subject to something she could handle.

"Sure. I can't see why not. Just run with me through the logbooks and walk her with me for a thorough preflight." Conner understood the change of conversation. He knew that it takes most humans a bit of getting used to when it comes to magic and the mystical.

"I can do that. I can show you all her new goodies. I think you may be impressed." She glowed with pride.

"We'll see," the elf said simply as their food arrived. "It looks great as always!"

They ate quietly. Isabelle was hoping for a little more than shop talk at the table. She kept looking up at her new friend who was enjoying his pancakes. She looked around to see how busy the place was. She had a few questions and was hoping to get him to open up.

"Oh, don't worry, the only person that can hear our conversation is the oracle. She knows a lot more than I do," Conner assured his companion. "To anyone else in the diner, our conversation blends in and no one can make out a word we say."

"Um, okay. So how long have you been here in Wyoming?" She asked.

"Well, since our races left, about four-thousand years, give or take," Conner said without hesitation.

"That is amazing. You have lived that long." She did not know what to think her romantic interest had been on the Earth longer than Christ had. That raised another question. "All our religious beliefs are null and void?"

"Depends on which faith you follow," Conner said calmly.

"I was raised Catholic," she countered.

"Oh," he said not to any ease of her mind. He put his fork down and folded his hands together as he solemnly gazed into her eyes. "Basic Christianity is valid. Christ was sent down to save the race of men. He is actually quite an interesting fellow. His miracles were beyond any magic done by elf or rider. The power of The Creator is equal to none. More people should follow his teachings. If they would, the world would not be in the state it is,"

Conner had told her with conviction. "As for organized religion, there are too many people in charge of too many people." Isabelle was confused again.

"You see, with all the religions and different versions of Christianity, too many people take charge and push their own beliefs onto others who cannot think for themselves. I feel that organized religion should give a person basic information, and if they truly follow The Creator, then He will guide them to Him."

Isabelle was amazed at his answer if not shocked. "So do you believe?"

"Faith in The Creator, I do have. He led our races here and lets us stay," Conner told her. "We talk daily and I seek guidance quite often from him. Therefore, yes we elves do. We just have a bit different relationship."

During the conversation, many things became clearer to Isabelle. She knew she had a big role in whatever was to come in the immediate future. She was honored to be a part of it but also frightened. Feelings returned to her that she had not had since she was in the military. She had high regards to serving her country, but when she was fixing helicopters in a country riddled by war, she was extremely uncomfortable.

Thinking about the immediate future, she changed the subject again. "Can humans use magic, or is it just for the elves?"

"Actually, since it has been released into the world, we should start to see it pop up more often. We need to keep our eyes and ears open to the news. Just because the magic was locked away, does not mean that humans were not born with the ability to use it. That ability usually manifests itself in what your scientific world calls extra-sensory perception. It was similar to déjà vu or anything unexplainable that could happen. You know *X-Files* kind of stuff?" Isabelle thought of the dreams she had that brought her to the elves.

"Yes, in time you can learn to use it as well," Conner said, almost reading her mind. It had been enough for Isabelle. They finished their meals in peace.

As soon as they had finished and the last fry was gone, their waitress reappeared with two slices of apple pie with vanilla ice cream on the side. She smiled and set them down in front of the two. She looked at Isabelle. "Listen to his wisdom. You are going to be needed by your people." She paused. "Oh, and your plane is not the only *Amy* in your life that will fly. Amethyst is a noble color. Enjoy. It was good seeing you again Conner!" She walked away. Isabelle was confused again.

"I told you," Conner smiled at Isabelle. She was instantly calmed. "Try not to think too hard on it. Keep it in the back of your mind and let it unfold itself. You will understand it one day." He reassured her as they finished their dessert.

On the way back to the hangar, they drove is silence. Isabelle was trying to digest more than the cheeseburger and fries.

Conner was the first to speak. "I am sorry this was not quite what you were expecting," he started. "You have to understand, that there is more than a massive age difference between us." He began to recognize that he had feelings for her and did not want her hurt.

A simple "I know." was all she could manage to say as she fought to orient herself in her new spinning world.

"Riders were the only humans who lived anywhere as long as an elf. There had not been dragons or any other mystical beasts in over four thousand years." Conner tried to explain. "The world is changing. We don't know what is around the corner." Conner gave her a solemn look. "Sorry, but I do want you to know that I really enjoy your company." He left it at that.

Chapter 15

The next day, Isabelle tried to keep focused. She went over the Corsair from nose to tail with Conner. She felt shot down the night before in her own romantic dogfight, but her professionalism did not show it in the least. She set her emotions aside and concentrated on the preflight. Someone else was going up in her aircraft. She had been in charge of the overhaul; she would be responsible for any lives lost. She had to be sure everything was checked and double-checked.

She could tell that the elf was distracted. Was it because of last night, or was he nervous about the test flight? If it was the flight, all she could do was to assure him that there were absolutely no discrepancies with the old war bird. She knew that the plane was better than when it came off the assembly line almost seventy years ago. If the cause for his distraction had been last night, then she could take pride in catching his attention. Isabelle had to remind herself that this was no everyday guy. Although he was male, he was not human. She would definitely have to make sure she paid as much attention to the details with him as she did with her aircraft.

Conner, on the other hand, had total faith in Isabelle, but his mind was not in the preflight. The books looked great, but last night bothered him. Isabelle bothered him. She had only been there for a couple of weeks. She had adapted so well, he could not imagine the hangar without her. He still could not get the picture of her in jeans out of his head.

He knew that he was falling for this woman. He also knew the pain of watching her grow old and eventually dying. He had been through that pain too many times. Conner felt pulled in two different directions by his heart and his logic. He resolved to be with her whenever he could and enjoy her company just as often.

Amy had been towed out to the flight line for the initial test runs. Isabelle sat outside the small plane. She could communicate with Conner through a fifty-foot communications cord that plugged into her headset and connected to the wing. She had installed the internal communications system's cord while she had overhauled the Corsair. Conner liked the idea so well that he had Ned install them in all the aircraft that did not already have them.

Conner went through the flight controls. They were smooth and efficient, very much like his P40. After testing the rudder, ailerons, and power controls for operation, it was time. Conner cleared the props and Isabelle unplugged. If anything happened, she did not wish to be dragged alongside the aircraft. She backed away and gave Conner the thumbs up.

Conner acknowledged and toggled the power switch to the *on* position. The gauges jumped to life, showing everything in the green. Double-checking his gauges, he reached down, flipped and held the momentary start toggle in the *up* position. The 2800 Pratt and Whitney chugged, sputtered and then roared to life. A smile appeared on Conner's face, as if by an invisible pencil.

Isabelle's heart almost leaped out of her chest. No matter how many overhauls she had under her belt from the military, she never got used to the feeling of accomplishment. This was a little different. This was a 70-year-old warplane. She had put it together from almost nothing. Elves and dwarves fabricated many of the replacement parts by hand. Isabelle, amazed by the artisanship, felt no human could ever build anything as good or as fast.

The amethyst Corsair roared on the flight line. Isabelle could hear the change in pitch as Conner took it to full power for several minutes and then back. She watched him intently. After the engine came down to idle, Conner once again gave her the thumbs up. He released the brakes and the plane began to roll forward. She smiled as the elf taxied the old navy plane toward the runway. He lined the nose up and increased power. The warplane rolled forward, quickly picking up speed. Three-quarters of the way down the runway, the wheels came off the ground and she was airborne.

Gaining altitude, he retracted the landing gear. As soon as they were stowed, he poured on the speed. Isabelle watched with excitement as Conner banked the Corsair hard right. He leveled it out and banked it again hard left. As the plane leveled out, he began to climb. Conner was impressed with the responsiveness of the controls. The gull-shaped wings of the *Dragon's Heart* would in no way be able to outmaneuver this plane. It brought a smile to his face as the G-forces tossed around his stomach. It was time to push it to the limits.

He spared no horsepower, nor was he easy on the controls. If he did not tear the engine off the struts nor rip every rivet from the fuselage, he would be happy. He was trying everything in his power to do so. What impressed him more than the handling was the speed. The old bird was fast. The airspeed indicator read of 475 miles per hour. It was much faster than the Warhawk as well.

Without Isabelle knowing, Conner had Ned make sure the guns were cleaned, oiled and operational. Also without her knowledge, the ammunition magazine in the belly had been loaded and ready to be tested as well. Conner wanted to make sure he had whatever resources he needed, come what may.

The elf brought the warbird to the deck. Fifty feet from the ground, he brought his air speed down for a strafing run. Isabelle watched in wonder as he flew her bird only feet from the Earth. Wooden targets popped up. She could distinguish the silhouettes of tanks, jeeps, and various vehicles. She also saw representations of what appeared to be men on horses and some shapes she could not identify.

Thundering low to the ground, Conner pulled the trigger on his flight stick. He released a hail of bullets that shredded every target in his way. He spared nothing. Isabelle was amazed that the weapons were operational. She did not remember overhauling them. Part of her was amazed at the sheer destruction of the Corsair's machine guns, yet part of her was appalled at the devastation.

After the run, Conner pulled up on the nose and banked the bird right, bringing it back into the flight pattern. He was on approach to bring the refurbished Corsair back in. Isabelle snapped out of her amazement. Anger quickly overcame her.

"What was that?" Isabelle did not even allow his elfin feet to hit the ground.

"I wanted to make sure she was completely ready for whatever is in our future." The elf tried to calm her excitement.

"What is that supposed to mean? What are you getting ready for, World War Three?" Isabelle was so angry she could barely breathe. The putrid emotion seethed from her like an uncontrolled wildfire.

"Unfortunately, World War Three will be like a friendly game of chess compared to what we could be in for." Conner looked deep into her eyes and instantly calmed her, but only for a few seconds.

"Don't you dare give me that elfin-charming-thing that you do! I am not falling for it this time." Isabelle had broken the elfin charm spell on her own accord. She was very unaware. Conner, on the other hand, was completely astonished. Only extremely gifted magic users could have broken through.

"Okay. We need to talk. Let's go inside. You really need to see something." With that, they started inside. Conner and Isabelle passed through the massive hangar doors. "Hey Ned, can you make sure *Amy* gets refueled, rearmed and put away?"

"Sure thing! I will make sure she is ready to go when you are." Nedloh assured the elf.

"Thanks. Have Buck join us in my office." With a nod, the younger dwarf followed the instructions.

"It seems like everyone knows what's going on around here but me." Isabelle broke her silence.

"Need I remind you, Miss Thompson, that you are an employee here? The fact that you may be needed to help save humankind is beside the point. The only thing you need to know is what I feel you need to know. Consider what you are about to learn a bonus."

Isabelle was instantly humbled. The anger subsided a bit. The shock from Conner's outburst not only astounded her but made her feel like she was a child again, being scolded.

The elf read that in her face instantly. "Hey. Um, look. I am sorry. There is just so much to lose here. It has already started, but I don't know the extent of the damage. What we are up against is also quite a mystery." Conner tried to explain the best he could the intensity of the situation before he actually showed her what he knew.

Buck was standing by the desk when the two entered. A grim face hid behind his rusty beard. "It don't look good, m'lad." Buck slid a disc into the player that had been set up with a television on a table in Conner's office. "This was what we got from the world satellite news channel before we lost it."

The picture came on as soon as the disc settled in. "The amount of devastation is still unknown." The middle-aged blonde woman stated from behind her news desk. She had her hands neatly folded in front of her on a small stack of notes and papers. Isabelle could tell she was incredibly shaken. Although her maroon business suit was neatly presented, Isabelle looked past the perfect makeup and into her eyes. She could tell that the news anchor had been crying.

"Reports have been coming in from all over the globe of creatures destroying cities and taking prisoners." The camera cut to a scene of several slimy-winged creatures with pig-like riders on their backs destroying buses, picking up frantic people from the streets and carrying them off to some assumed lair.

Isabelle just stared in disbelief. "That's not all, my friend." Buck grimly attested.

"Nations of the world are crippled, due to a computer virus that has infected every major database worldwide. We are asking you to stay in your homes. Basic services are out across all nations and superpowers. The president has placed the United States under martial law until further notice. Forces are slow to mobilize due to communications failures. The president..."

The screen went blue. The words "No signal" instantly appeared in the right-hand corner of the screen in white block letters.

"I knew it would not be pretty. I have no idea what the goblins are riding, but they are definitely on something nasty." Conner was still staring at the screen. Isabelle could do nothing but hold her hands over her mouth in horror.

"They looked like some perverted form of a dragon." Buck was still noticing the hideous monsters that had become the goblins steeds.

Conner turned to Isabelle to find her in shock. "Look, Izzy..."

She slowly blinked through tears and became aware of her surroundings. "This is where I need you. I don't know how much flight experience you have, but I need you on my wing. We have a lot to do before this is over." Conner gently put his hand on her shoulder.

"There is something about you. You have a quality that not one of my other pilots has. You need to be up there fighting for your people. Now, you need to go get some rest. It has been a very big day. We will start at zero-five-thirty tomorrow. Be ready for anything."

Isabelle left Conner and Buck to do their planning. She rode the elevator down to Estal. When the doors opened, she saw that the whole city was in preparation. Every dwarf and elf bustled about the underground city with a mission. There was no panic or fear in their eyes, only the tasks at hand. This was why the elves and dwarves remained here. They had been here to protect humankind. She, along with Amanda could not be in a safer place.

Amanda! Isabelle had to check on the girl. She had no one else. She knew she would be safe, but she had no idea in what kind of state she would find the girl. She almost ran to Amanda's room.

She opened the door to find the girl sitting on the bed, staring off into nothingness. "Goblins... the bad man has sent goblins." Amanda slowly turned to Isabelle, still in a daze.

"The elves will help. They always help. You will too." The girl seemed to stare directly through

Isabelle. "The bad man has bad magic. It is very strong. The dragon riders have stronger magic. The elves will have a hard time stopping him. Nothing will be the same ever again." Amanda snapped out of her waking coma with blinking eyes. Tears began to flow. The teenaged girl ran and threw her arms around the tall woman for comfort. Isabelle easily lifted her off the ground and took her back to her bed.

"Don't worry kiddo. You are in the safest place you can be. Let's get you to bed. Tomorrow is a new day. It can only get better."

"We will make it better," Amanda told her as she slid under the covers.

"You bet we will. I promise you, we will stop the bad man." Isabelle tucked the girl in and kissed her on the forehead. Instantly the girl was asleep. Isabelle quietly closed the door as she left and headed just down the hall to her own room. Bed began to sound better with every step to her room she took.

After a warm shower, the stress of the day melted off. Tomorrow would come extremely early for her. She slid beneath her own silken blankets and she was quick to dream.

Chapter 16

The fleshy, mottled gray and brown bag had a rough ovate shape to it. Within it rested a perverted semblance of life, a slimy body wrapped in transparent wings of the membrane.

The dark conjurer had started an air force all his own. With the goblins as riders, he would dominate the skies of his new world with massive, toxic beasts that would strike fear at his new subjects.

The goblins were quick to learn the breeding and care of his new abominations—his new creatures. Although a few goblins actually had become nourishment for his new pets, Lord Esuorts was sure they would learn quickly to conquer and tame these beasts. If they could not, they deserved to become the first meals of the Necrogulls.

He stood in the pit as the stronger hatchlings quickly devoured the weak. Deep underground, great grottos had been found to breed and tame these new amphibious beasts. They had skin like wet suede with a layer of bone plating for armored protection. The pit was filled with rancid water. Just out of the egg sacs, the larvae swam in swarms of iridescent eating machines. Small wings on their bodies acted as fins as they floated through the birthing brine like rabid underwater birds.

Trandok had seen three generations mature in almost as many weeks. Lord Esuorts created these vile beasts to breed and mature quickly for his great army of the sky. The goblin general was dubbed the first rider of these perversions of the great dragons of old. It had cost him his left hand in doing so. He now proudly bore a harpoon-tipped hook that replaced his left forearm and hand. A blade was interchangeable on the base and attached at the elbow. He would have been fed to the attacking monster if he had not killed the beast that took his left hand, with his right. This gained him great favor with the sorcerer.

Immediately after each monster was born, goblins separated the larvae into their own maturation ponds. Technicians then implanted each larva with bioorganic technology in the form of computer chips. The magic was implanted in the brains of the winged beasts to control their temperaments and ravenous appetites. This also allowed for communication between the rider and beast as well as between beast and Esuorts. The battles to come could be orchestrated more efficiently with this new computer magic. Trandok was quickly learning this magic.

This new generation would be the strongest yet. This brood counted over fifty healthy winged steeds. After consuming the weakest of the brood, the hatchlings were quickly separated for the technician's implants. Trandok was sure to ride soon. He was the strongest and most cunning of the Necrogull handlers.

Just after a week, the winged eating machines developed their hind legs and began breathing air. They no longer needed the putrid ponds to survive. Old and sickly humans were used as sustenance for the growing abominations. With keen eyesight and sense of smell, hunting was easy for the beasts.

At maturity, the monsters were as long as a tractor-trailer. Their bones were hollow but strong. Tight, compact muscles also added to the strength. The wingspan was equally impressive. The heads of the beasts were considered small and diamond shaped except for their massive lower jaws. The mandibles did not join to form a chin. Instead, the lower jawbones on both sides ended with teeth larger than a broadsword of old and twice as sharp. These massive lower fangs were serrated and could sever an elephant in half with one pass. The lower fangs also had a unique muscle structure. The sword-like teeth could pivot forward to expose glands that could project a stream of acid. This stream could shoot several hundred feet. Even out of range of the toxic blast, a cloud of acid vapor could kill any living thing within a quarter mile.

Trandok was trained and ready. His Necrogull was obedient only to him. It was fully mature, strong and healthy. There were only eleven other riders and Necrogulls ready for the first hunt. He would lead his party and bring back food for his people and carve a new world for his dark master. Tonight they would fly.

Esuorts was impressed with his new pets. They were strong and powerful. Without the world's air forces, they would make short work of whatever defenses the nations had to offer. World powers could no longer communicate with each other. Thanks to his virus, computers were useless. Chaos and anarchy would soon ensue. Thanks to him, world devastation was at hand. From the ashes, he would rise as a world leader to mold the Earth as he saw fit. He would be worshiped and praised. Any that did not die.

He sipped soothing tea as he watched the breeding grottos. Goblins were not quite as dumb as they seemed. They were serving him well. He would have to find a way to reward them, but for now, he had plans. He had let loose a few weaker Necrogulls to the wild. It was a test to see if they could breed on their own. The monsters had already torn apart a couple of major cities. They fed on everything in sight. With goblin raiding parties on the ground and his special forces of heavy troops, civilization was falling quickly. It was time for the next step. He would send forth a small party to test the defenses of the greatest nation on the planet. It was time for rider and beast to join.

Dragon Squadron

Tonight he would send his children to the White House.

Chapter 17

Four o'clock came excessively early for Isabelle. A shower to wake her up, and some breakfast would do her well. The water was cool and made her skin feel alive. She always enjoyed a brisk shower in the morning. Her breath was taken away as she stepped in. The water seemed to wash the sleep right out of her body. The elves really knew how to do things. She felt as if she were bathing under a forest waterfall. The only difference was the fact she could adjust the temperature of the water to suit her needs.

She laced up her black boots. They looked like something from a military surplus store but were much more comfortable. She had never worn tennis shoes as comfortably. They were lightweight and breathable. They were of a synthetic material that had the look and durability of leather. Along with a pair of gloves and her flight suit, she was fire resistant from the neck down. The military was a long way from materials like these. She was cool where she needed to be and warm where she needed. The elfin materials were amazing.

She showered, dressed, and was ready in a quick thirty minutes; she still had plenty of time for breakfast. Finding her morning meal was next on her agenda. She opened the door and stepped out into the stone corridor, then immediately ran into Conner.

"I see you are up and ready." Conner started first.

"Um, yeah. Good morning." Isabelle was already off her guard. Conner's face was not what she expected to see first thing. "I thought I would get me something to eat before we started."

"What a coincidence, I was just coming to see if you would join me," Conner smiled. His gaze once again melted her heart as he charmed her.

"You are doing it again!" She caught him. This time, she picked up on it much more quickly.

Conner just looked sheepishly at her. The spell he had used had gotten him married several times in the past. He was still amazed that Isabelle broke it so quickly. "You know, Izzy, you're right about the charm I used." Conner began as they walked toward the dining hall. "I tried it last night to calm you down, and only that. I was extremely surprised when you broke the spell. I thought it was a fluke until just now.

"So I guess elfin magic is not as strong as you remembered, now is it?" Isabelle started to feel a little sure of herself.

"Actually, it's quite the contrary. Your magic is stronger than I have ever seen in a human. I have seen a lot of your kind as sorcerers and mages, witches and wizards, but they have never broken an elfin charming spell that quickly." Conner started to explain to Isabelle as the color drained from her face. "This can be a bad thing if you are not properly trained in the use of it. We will have to make sure you get that proper training." Conner firmly grasped each of her shoulders and looked deeply into her eyes. "You have a lot on your plate right now. We are never given more than we can handle ourselves, but we are given friends to help us with our burdens. You are not alone."

Isabelle let out a deep sigh and cleared her head. Conner's words quickly sank in and hit their mark. "Okay, one thing at a time then," Isabelle told him.

They ate their meals which consisted of blueberry muffins and coffee quietly. Isabelle had much on her shoulders in a very short time span. Conner knew this and felt very sorry for his new friend. On occasion, he would look up from his breakfast at the woman, wondering how she would pull through. He was sure with her strong spirit, good heart, and his help, she would be just fine.

Isabelle was digesting a bit more than a muffin. Her head was absorbing all the information that had been given to her. It still felt like a dream. It felt like a dream moving into a nightmare, more every day. Somehow, she knew that she was going to be okay. She trusted Conner, as well as the rest of the elves and dwarves. She had made friends quickly. She felt that the bonds that had taken place were almost like family. Conner would not let anything happen to her or Amanda. She quickly smiled. She was in for quite a ride.

"Now let's see if we can get you into the air," Conner said as they had finished their coffee. Isabelle smiled. She had always wanted to fly. She had been in many simulators, fixed-wing as well as rotary-wing. The military had the best.

"I know the basics," she informed Conner. "I have lots of stick time in simulators. Just help me get her started and we can go from there."

As they walked through the hangar, Isabelle felt her stomach starting to protest. Her lifelong dream of flying was about to be fulfilled. A crew of elves and dwarves were busily readying the two aircraft. The *Dragon's Heart* was parked on the tarmac next to *Amy*. The bright amethyst paint greatly contrasted to the flat earth tones of the P40.

"Well, if you can't shoot them down, maybe you can blind them." Conner joked.

"That's very funny, pointy ears," Isabelle reported. "You didn't seem to mind her yesterday."

"Hey, I was just joking, lady. There is no need to get racist." Conner had a mock look of hurt flash across his face. "Anyway, let's see if you can fly as well as you can turn a wrench. Climb in."

Isabelle climbed into the cockpit with Conner standing on the wing outside.

"Now, are you familiar with the flight controls?" Isabelle nodded an affirmative as she stared at all the controls. She recognized most of them. "That is the air-speed indicator, altimeter, fuel, and artificial horizon." She pointed out the ones she knew.

"Not too bad for a wrench jockey with only video games for stick time." Conner was pleased with her knowledge. "This screen is an updated global positioning system. They work on our satellites alone. That," he pointed, "is your rounds counter, your engine RPM, oil pressure gauge, and this little baby is something a bit new. This is what you had Ned put in. This is the artificial intelligence module. She can fly herself if needed. She is also equipped with a target acquisition system." The elf pointed to the main screen in the middle of the gauge cluster. "It identifies targets in red and friendlies in green. *Amy* has been loaded with a pilot training program to help get you started."

Conner and Isabelle spent over an hour going over instruments and procedures. They covered everything from *Amy's* functions to radio procedures. Isabelle was bombarded with knowledge. She was fascinated and absorbed it all quickly. They went through all the flight controls, one by one. Many times Conner demonstrated with his hands the actions of the plane as certain controls were used. Memories of simulator time came flooding back to Isabelle. She quickly became anxious to get in the air.

"Ok, Rookie, let's see what you know." Conner jumped down and jogged over to the *Dragon's Heart*. Isabelle stared blankly at the console for a moment. She strapped on her kneeboard and began to write down power up procedures as she went through them.

She flipped the electrical power switch to the on position and then flipped on the AI. "Good morning Isabelle." *Amy* cheerfully greeted her pilot. The AI had a pleasant voice. It had authority, but she knew that her pilot was in command.

"Um, good morning *Amy*." she stammered. She was shocked that her airplane was talking to her. *Amy* began guiding Isabelle through the startup procedures. Piece by piece, the human pilot absorbed the information.

"In the case of an emergency, I can perform most of the startup procedures for you. The only thing that you have to do is flip that red momentary switch to your far left. It is marked *ignition*. Go ahead, give it a try." There was almost a hint of mischief in the synthetic female voice. Isabelle flipped the switch up and held it. A small whine came from aft of her seat. Isabelle recognized the fuel pumps. There was the sound of the starter motor spinning, followed by the Pratt and Whitney radial quickly roaring to life.

Isabelle's stomach still flipped. Excitement replaced nervousness. She looked over at the P40 with a large grin. Conner was motioning to his headset and microphone. Isabelle had almost forgotten the radios. She quickly programmed the frequencies. "Radio check, do you read me, Izzy?" Conner's voice immediately came to her through her headset.

"I read you, Lima-Charley, Conner," Isabelle replied, remembering her communications procedures from the military.

"I have you the same," Conner confirmed. "Okay, for this flight my call sign, I will be Dragon Leader. You will be Rookie One."

"Roger that Dragon Leader." Isabelle winced slightly at the thought of being referred to as a rookie.

"Hey, you are pretty good at this radio stuff." Conner sent his compliment with earnest.

"You forget my background, Conner," Isabelle reminded.

"Sorry!" Conner fired up his P40 and began to taxi her to the runway.

"Follow *Amy's* instructions and line up behind me."

"Okay, *Amy*. Let me see if I can do this one myself," Isabelle ordered her electronic copilot.

"As you wish, Isabelle, I am here if you need me. I will remain on so I can learn maneuvers and get to know you better. I am designed to be your best friend while you are in the air."

"Well if you are designed to cover my back, please call me Izzy. All my friends do." Isabelle smiled in amazement at the little friend she had in her plane. Her new friend *was* her plane.

"Thank you, Izzy. I am honored." *Amy* replied. "Now take us up."

Isabelle released the brakes and pushed the throttle lever forward. *Amy* was in motion. She taxied the small navy plane behind the P40.

"Tower, this is training flight Alfa-One-Niner, requesting take off." Conner cleared with the tower.

"Training flight, this is Tower. Traffic is clear you are ready to go for takeoff." Isabelle immediately recognized Ned's voice. "I have a lot of work in that bright bird of yours, Izzy. Try to keep it in the air."

"Don't worry; I am highly allergic to crashing." Isabelle retorted with her usual dry humor.

"Quit flirting with the tower, Rookie. Let's get going." Conner chimed in.

Pushing his throttle forward, he taxied down the runway and was in the air three-quarters of the way down. This was it for Isabelle. Taking a deep breath, she followed suit. Throttle forward and brakes off. *Amy* quickly picked up speed. Shortly before the end of the pavement, her wheels left the ground. Isabelle was airborne in her own Corsair.

She gently gained altitude. The little plane's wings wobbled a bit as she searched for the landing-gear switch. Quickly found, the gear stowed.

"Very nice!" *Amy* complimented.

"Why thank you."

"Rookie-One: nice job. Next time, do it without *Amy's* coaching," Conner chuckled.

"Dragon- Leader, this is Rookie One. AI," *Amy* quickly shot back. "That *was* all Izzy. AI Out!"

"Thanks, girlfriend," Isabelle smiled.

"My pleasure, girlfriend," *Amy* answered with something that almost sounded like a giggle.

Isabelle loved the feeling of being in the air. The Corsair quickly became an extension of herself. Her hand felt like it became part of the flight stick. The pedals felt like they blended in with her feet.

"Okay, Rookie, form up on me and let's see how you can fly in formation," Conner instructed. Isabelle quickly matched his speed, slid up on his right wing, and fell back a few yards to offset the formation.

"Not bad!" Conner was extremely impressed. "I guess you have spent a lot of time in simulators."

"Well, I will admit it is a bit different, but I am a fast learner," Isabelle answered.

"Okay. So far, so good. Want to try a game of Follow the Leader?" Conner asked. Isabelle could see the grin on his face.

"Sure, why not." Isabelle was confident, yet still apprehensive. She knew she could use all the skill she could get. This is one way to do it.

"Okay, go!" Conner poured on the speed. Pulling back and to the left, he banked the P40 in an upward climb. Isabelle did her best to follow. She was not quite a precise in her maneuvers, but she managed to keep up. Conner rolled, dove, and juked the Warhawk. With each passing maneuver, Isabelle began to match her *Amy* to anything that Conner threw at her. With the few hours of flight, she learned to roll, bank, dive, and spiral. Conner taught her simple dogfight tactics. Every mock engagement Conner lined his crosshairs up and called his shot. He was amazed by how quickly she learned, though it would still take a while before she would be ready for combat.

"All right, Rookie, I am impressed. I have not seen someone take to flying like that in a long time." Conner knew his compliment fell drastically short of how he truly felt. He was right about putting her on his wing.

"Thanks, Leader." Isabelle glowed inwardly with accomplishment.

"Did you hear that *Amy*?"

"Yes, I did, Izzy. Your talents are quite impressive." A pleasant voice sounded from *Amy*. "I think we will do much better next time."

"That is a promise, girlfriend," Isabelle smiled as a thought popped into her head. "Dragon Leader, Rookie One..."

"Go ahead, Rookie."

"Last to the tower buys dinner at the diner." Isabelle challenged.

"Roger that! First one back drives!" Conner smiled and pushed the throttle lever full forward. The P40 eased away from the pink Corsair.

Isabelle slowly pushed hers forward as she began to catch the Warhawk. Even with Conner, she waved at him as he sat in his cockpit. She flew by.

Nedloh watched through his binoculars as the two planes came in the flight pattern. He could tell that they were moving at top speed. Only one-hundred feet from the ground, the Corsair was in front. Isabelle seemed to be pulling away from Conner. He motioned to his uncle who raised his binoculars.

"For the love of..." Buck did not finish. He watched the two shoot past the tower. Banking left, they each came in for their landings. Conner put his down first as smooth as always. He taxied to the hangar and whipped the *Dragon's Heart* around. The elf climbed out and sat on the wing to watch his trainee's approach.

Isabelle lined up on the runway and deployed the landing gear. She throttled back.

"Okay, Rookie," *Amy* giggled. "Slowly now, that's it. Now keep the nose up and ease it down." Concentrating on every movement, Isabelle followed *Amy's* instructions to the letter.

"I guess flying was the easy part. I never thought about getting down." Isabelle gave a nervous grin as the tires touched the pavement with a bump. Solid on the ground, she pulled the throttle back. The tail wheel settled down, and she continued to decelerate until she cruised up to the hangar doors, spun, and applied brakes next to the P40.

"I thought you never flew!" Ned was amazed as he and his uncle approached the planes.

"I'm a quick study." Isabelle was in full smile. She never had such an exciting time.

"I am also very impressed." Conner joined in. "Buck, do me a favor and make sure that these two are refueled and armed for tomorrow. In the morning, we are going to put holes in things." Conner gave an elfish grin as he slapped the side of his P40. "Right now, I believe I owe someone dinner."

Chapter 18

Ardenelle sat on the polished hangar floor. He scanned his well-organized tool bag for his 7/16-inch open-end wrench. His long dark hair was pulled back, revealing his elfish ears. He spent as much time with his German fighter as he could. When he was not wrenching on her, he was in the air. He had been working all morning on the landing gear of his BF 109 Messerschmitt. The hydraulics of the main shock strut needed servicing.

As most of the planes were housed in the hangar, the BF 109 retained most of its original colors, minus the insignia of the fallen fascist regime. The aircraft was chosen for its performance and reliability, not its history. Ardenelle loved his fighter. It was a shame that it had been an instrument used in an attempt at global domination. With what had taken place lately, the elf was hoping that the small fighter would get a chance to redeem itself.

The Daimler-Benz V12 had been tuned and was running the best it ever had. The wings and tail displayed a new insignia. Dragon wings with crossed swords signified the new squadron that would defend the Earth from the forces of darkness. Like the rest of the squadron, this plane was heavily modified. It had a more powerful engine, more responsive flight controls, as well as more updated avionics than its predecessor did. This plane had its differences, as did the others. Ardenelle, as all other elves had been a magic user. When the magic had returned, Ardenelle cast spells on his craft. The small German fighter had been given a magic barrier that deflected all small arms up to 50-caliber in size. It would help him live a bit longer on a dogfight. Ardenelle had also cloaked the small craft. Although it could be seen by the naked eye, no radar, laser, or magic could detect the plane's existence. Conner had designated him the Scout for the group.

The elf was sure of his skill as a pilot. He knew he was nowhere nearly as good as Conner was, but he could hold his own against any modern fighter jet. He was sure that speed was not everything. Many times, he honed his skills against Conner. He was never easily brought down in a mock dogfight.

He, along with the rest of the squadron, was briefed on the latest worldly developments. He knew that he had to be ready for anything. He would be. As Ardenelle closed the valve on the hydraulic reservoir, he pondered what would happen in the days to come. Lives would be lost. His was one of the possibilities. He knew that when asked to stay behind that it might come to such a sacrifice. He believed that humankind had a right to live and be free. He knew that magic would destroy all since it had been set free. Now it had been.

As he gathered his tools and cleaned up his work area, he knew that his life was doomed soon. He would die in the glory of battle. He would give his life protecting the innocent. His stomach grumbled for attention. His work here was now complete. He would find nourishment. Like his Messerschmitt, he also needed to be in top form for the trials that lie ahead.

The busy streets were filled with those going about their own affairs. The entire city was in preparation. Ardenelle was no different. Every elf in the city had tasks in which to tend. The dark-haired elf had a meeting with the council. He did not want to be late. Winding through the streets, he took the quickest route. Salt air breezed through the tall spires of stone and brightly-colored coral. The smell of the sea was tranquil, but not in the least bit calming.

Today, the council was to announce their decision on a number of things. Dwarf diplomats had been in Atlantis for several months. They had been meeting in silence to discuss the turn of the age. All that Ardenelle had known was rumor and speculation. Some spoke of new magic. Others were talking about new technologies. One thing certainly known was that a small island outside the ocean city housed a secret project that had been labored on by both elves and dwarves. Times were changing.

Ardenelle reached the auditorium where he was to meet with the Elfin and Dwarf councils. To his surprise, he was far from the only guest invited. He looked around at over one-hundred elves and heads of dwarf families. As he scanned the crowd, his eyes stopped at the Rider. He was dressed in emerald green trousers and a white tunic. The sword that hung on his hip had large emeralds that gave the white-gold inlays of the handle a shiny green tint. The Rider was well known. Many a song and verse were written of Anthriel. His deeds were known farther than the Dwarf city of Shangri-La, to the east, and the nomadic men who lived on the continent to the west.

The council sat arranged at a table on the main floor of the auditorium. It consisted of six dwarves and six elves. Each known for wisdom and honesty, the elves had served on the council for thousands of years. Dwarves selected the members of the council in their own way. They were honored to be chosen. Each member would give their life for the people whom they served. They were the ones who kept order in Atlantis and promoted harmony between all races.

The council did not control the Riders, and most of these Riders swore individual allegiances to the *council. The council of the twelve settled many differences. Not by law, but by the trust of the people. Even wise men seeking answers presented their queries to the council of dwarves and elves.*

The auditorium quickly settled as the proceeding was called order. A tall regal elf dressed in the gray robes of council stood to address the large assembly. "You were summoned before us for a purpose," the elder began. He did not look any older than the others did, but his wisdom far outweighed that of anyone else. "The time has come. Change is inevitable. A new age is upon us. It is the age of man.

"We have watched man rise up from where The Creator has sent his people. Humankind has learned to become self-sufficient and social. These people are above all others on this planet," the wise elf continued.

"We are far more advanced than they are." a bitter dwarf interrupted.

"You forget, my long-bearded friend. We are not of this world." the councilman reminded his fellow member. "Since before time, The Creator has sent us here to nurture and watch over humankind. This we have done. It is time to leave these children to learn and watch for themselves." The High Elf continued with the council's decision.

"In one year, dwarf and elf will be ready to continue our journeys through the stars. We will be taking with us a new friend. Dragons have

grown strong with a magic that we cannot begin to fathom. Our friendship has grown into a fellowship. They have asked us to take them with us as we continue to explore that which The Creator has forged for us to see. Descendants of the dinosaurs wish for knowledge of their place. This we cannot deny. They will join us."
Throughout the auditorium came whispered questions and comments from the dwarves and elves seated.

"My brothers and sisters, we have one small matter in which to tend. The magic that we have brought with us has flourished on this world. It is what has caused our dragon brothers to survive the ice ages that had taken their ancestors. It is agreed that this magic would be harmful and dangerous to humankind once we have left.."

"Why not let man deal with it on their own? Whatever they do, let them deal with their own consequences!" another voice shouted from the crowded auditorium.

"We have brought the magic to this planet, Terra. Would you let your child play with your sword while you were attending your duties? I should hope not." A woman from the council answered the question before the eldest elf could open his mouth.

"Thank you, Isadelianna. You are more than correct. We brought magic to this world. Before we seek the stars once again, it has been decided to

lock it away, and out of the reach of humankind,"
The head of the council continued.

"And if it is discovered and released?" the voice
spat out. "The human race would be no better off
than if had not gone through all the trouble."

"Aw, that is a very astute observation and of
legitimate concern." The wise elf was ready for this
question as well. "That is why we have summoned
you here. You are the best of the families of
dwarves and each elf here has made a name for
her or himself." The council elder bowed his head
in deep regret. "We have summoned you here to
ask of you that which we cannot ask. You have
been selected, each according to her or his own
gifts. We ask that you stay behind to watch and
protect humankind from the magic which we have
hidden from them."

"You ask us to babysit an entire race of half-
evolved apes?" The voice had been of a dwarf
blacksmith. Ardenelle recognized him
immediately. The blades and tools that he
constructed rivaled anything ever created with
elfin magic. "What about our brothers, the
dragons? Where are their representatives?" The
suit covered dwarf protested.

"The sacrifice of the dragons has already been
made. It was the sacrifice of the great emerald,
which has hidden the magic deep within this
planet's crust. The dragons have sacrificed blood.
We cannot ask for more." The council head looked

sullenly at the Rider. "We will always remember our comrades and brothers, Emorthra." After a brief moment of silence, the council lifted their heads and the Head Council continued.

"Now we ask each of you to give for a race who has become our brothers. Humankind will not survive if the magic is found and released in the future. That is why I ask you," he swept his arm toward the crowd, "to be our eyes, ears, and our hearts. We ask you to stay behind and watch humankind. We hope that one day they too can sit with us at this council."

The crowd burst into talk. Many did not know what to think. Many knew what they had to do. The blacksmith fell silent. He stroked his knotted beard in contemplation. Matters weighed heavily on his mind. The blacksmith would be letting his family and friends go on without him, but this world was all he knew. Silence had blanketed the audience.

"I will stay! Who else can behold the mounts left behind?"

The Rider turned toward the dwarf. With a smile growing on his sullen face, the Rider took the hand of the dwarf and shook it. "Your family will sing of your sacrifice as well as your glory to come. You and your decedents, I will always call friends."

Chapter 19

The night sky over the nation's capital was starless. The city had ground to a screeching halt with the imposition of the dusk curfew. Due to the worldwide emergency, the entire nation was put under martial law. Similar scenarios played out around the world. Americans waited in their homes, wondering what their elected leaders would do to save them. They wondered what was being done about the current state of emergency. There was no electricity; food was a precious commodity; money was useless. People of the world were suffering a second Dark Age.

He sat in his office with the weight of his nation and the world pressing upon his shoulders. Being the leader of the most powerful nation was not the best job to have now. It seemed that the oak and leather chair in the office was the only thing holding him up. This recent terrorist attack was like nothing of which he had ever heard. His nation - *every nation in the world* - was totally crippled and defenseless. After a week and a half, no one came forward to claim responsibility. Above all his troubles, he had no one with whom to retaliate. This worried him the most.

Every computer in the world that had access to the Internet became a victim of the virus. Not all computers shut down. Some had been known to cause a comatose state in anyone who had been on them at the time of the strike. Documents and reports from the Center for Disease Control had confirmed this. Along with this waking coma, all experienced genetic changes and deformities, which resulted in massive and grotesque muscle growth and loss of brain function. Most of the lucky victims died within hours of the attack. This was the first known computer virus that actually affected humankind physically.

Casualty numbers were astronomical; over half the world's population had fallen victim. All satellites and other communications were down indefinitely. Top minds were working on a solution, though there were no possibilities in sight. The only communications that could be had took days or weeks in each direction. Messages had to be delivered by hand, and responses took just as long. He had read about these times in stories of medieval knights and of the Wild West. It did not occur to the world leader that martial law would need to be implemented again in this modern day.

He could not appear on the television screens to assure millions of his voters that all was being done to rectify the situation. He had distributed pamphlets and papers telling all citizens whatever he could. Those who had survived resorted to looting and violence to continue their survival. He could see the fires that burned in the city from the window in his office.

With a deep and heavy sigh, he stood. He was elected for his people, by his people. He remembered throughout his campaign that he would stamp out all political injustices and return the government to the people. He promised to bring this nation back from the ashes of the rich man's fires. Now his country was burning. There was no metaphor here. He would make sure that this nation was great again. He drew in a breath of assurance and walked toward the window. He had called for an emergency session of Congress. He had sent his messages and waited for all to arrive. As he watched the eerie orange glow on the horizon, he stood surer than ever. He would rebuild this country and unite all the people of the world under one flag; one financial institution with a diversity of all.

As he watched, something caught his eye. A small shadow appeared before the glow of death. It spread into a small cloud of winged creatures flying toward the city from across the river. He watched in curiosity, as the shadows grew larger.

"Mr. President, we have incoming. Lookout and listening posts have confirmed flying creatures with riders," a heavily armed marine reported.

"How many, and can we take them out with what we have?" President Robert Williams asked.

"We count a dozen creatures, sir. It's most likely that we can take them out, Mr. President. Small arms fire, as well as hand-held rockets, should be able to do the trick. Right now, we need to get you underground to safety. Your safety is my job, Sir. All precautions must be taken." The guard held the door for his Commander-in-Chief as he motioned for him to seek shelter.

"Quite right, Sergeant. We must carry on." Robert Williams let himself be led by the Marines in full battle gear.

The units deployed throughout the city. The streets of the District of Columbia were already deserted. The nationally-imposed curfew had already seen to that. Soldiers were scrambling in ordered chaos. Platoon leaders shouted orders and placed their men in the exact locations they needed to be. Sectors of fire were assigned, and each soldier waited nervously under cover.

This had been Private Gomez's first duty station. He had only been with the unit for a month. When he had gotten his orders, all his buddies in the Advanced Individual Training class had told him that Washington would be a sham job. He wondered what they were all doing now.

Gomez was a wiry Latino youth from Chicago. He chose to join the *Few and the Proud* to get away from the inner city. He wanted to make something of himself. All of his homies back on the block had to deal with minimum wage jobs at the Burger Palace or would be killed while playing Monty Hall. The game of *Let's Make a Dope Deal* was too popular back home. Books had not been his favorite toys growing up, so college was not an option for him. He longed for the adventure that the Marines promised.

Lance Corporal Rose was teamed up with the Chicago youth. His year and a half experience calmed Gomez. Rosie, as they called him, took the Gomez under his wing as soon as he had arrived at the unit. They had been assigned as bunkmates in the barracks from that point. Now they would fight for the nation's capital together.

They took positions near a checkpoint on Pennsylvania Avenue, just up the street from the White House. They used sandbags to fortify their position. They knew the rest of their unit had been deployed around them, but none could be seen. Their orders were to neutralize any air threats that would try to get into a set perimeter around the White House.

Gomez and Rosie scanned their sectors in search of aircraft that might make a run at the president. In the failing light, Rosie was the first to spot the attackers. He shook his head in disbelief. Through his night vision goggles, he saw a dozen winged creatures flying toward their position. Guided by pig-faced beasts on their backs, they flew in groups of four.

The groups split up. Four of the beasts flew toward their fortified position. The two Marines both thought it was a ploy to wreak as much havoc on the city as possible. They were correct. As they watched, the monsters dove low to the ground, grabbing whatever they could in their steely talons. Putrid liquid shot from the mouths of the dragon-like creatures.

Dragons were the only thing they had ever seen that looked like the beasts they were seeing now, but they were not the mythical creatures that had been in the storybooks of their youth. These creatures were twisted forms of the pictures they had seen in the movies and in fairy tales.

Nedloh watched the satellite feed intently. It was the only one still operational. The virus had shut down every other satellite in orbit. Built and operated by the elves and dwarves, the satellite was shielded by magic and had been disconnected from all other systems before the virus spread. Conner had ordered it shut down temporarily. No human programming could decrypt the elfin algorithms that could bring it back online. He had just brought the orbiting station back to life and was making certain the system was safe from the bug that killed all human technology.

Ned's eyes grew in horror as he watched what unfolded before him at the nation's capital. "Conner, you need to see this!" He stopped the elf as he passed by his monitoring station.

"What's up?" Conner leaned down to take a gander over the young dwarf's shoulder.

"I just brought the orbiting satellite up. It was over D. C. This is what I got." Ned looked back over his right shoulder to gauge Conner's reaction.

"The capital is under attack. This can't happen. This is the strongest nation. We need to keep it together if we are going to keep mankind safe." he said with a look of deep thought draped across his elfin face. "Get Buck to put together a group to get the president out of there and get him to safety. Bring him to Estal if you have too."

"Do you think that is a good idea?" Ned asked.

"Have any better?" Conner countered.

"Good point."

"Ardenelle and I will fly cover. We will see what these things are made of." Conner stormed out and into the hangar.

Ardenelle was just wiping down his tools and closing up the Messerschmitt.

"Ardy!" Conner called from halfway across the hangar. "Are you up to a mission?"

Chapter 20

Two teams of ground crew towed separate aircraft out onto the flight line. Two warbirds that would have flown against one another in a distant past now sat side by side on the same mission. Conner briefed his elfin brother as they stood between the two planes.

"Ardenelle, you will be my wing," Conner started. "I didn't plan on jumping into the thick of it so soon, but I guess we were forced. We swore to protect mankind, and we got caught with our pants down."

Conner pulled out his map to go over the route. "We will keep the airspeed under 200 knots to conserve fuel. I don't know what we'll need for combat, if anything."

"We'll never get there in time," the younger elf countered.

"No problem. Use the old words to slow time. We will make it. We have to." Conner scribbled the language of his ancestors on a sticky note and handed it to Ardenelle. Only on my mark, so we can stay in the same time."

"Got it," Ardenelle confirmed with a nod.

"Let's mount up and see what we are up against."
Conner began climbing into the *Dragon's Heart*.

As before, Clouds were almost motionless as the
elves came upon the outskirts of the capital. The
time around them came almost to a complete
standstill. To anyone watching, the trip would have
been instantaneous. Radios were silent on the
flight. Conner did not know what to expect with
these creatures. He had to be ready for anything.

Isabelle pulled up to the diner. What was once
busy and full of life now lay dark and deserted. Her
attention was drawn to the bus station and the few
buildings surrounding the diner. They, too, looked
as if they belonged to a culture long past.

She tried the door anyway. She jumped as the
small bell that hung above the door rang through
the silence. Her presence was announced to no one.
The counters and tables were still spotless.
Condiments remained neatly arranged around the
chrome napkin boxes and salt and pepper shakers.

Isabelle had been craving a double cheeseburger
and fries. She had hoped that the diner had been
spared from the disaster that had befallen the rest
of the world. She wandered over to the booth that
she'd shared with Conner on their first date. She
stared out the window in remembrance. Isabelle

could even smell the hot fries and meat patties. Her nostrils also sensed the smells of hot apple pie.

The daydream was so vivid she snapped out of her gaze into the past. Before her, was a plate with a fresh cheeseburger and fries and a hot apple pie with a scoop of vanilla iced cream. "Things have changed." She heard a voice say. She looked around. The voice was soothing and strangely familiar. A light suddenly appeared in the seat in front of her and began to take form. Isabelle sat in awe as she watched.

"Didn't your mother ever tell you that it was impolite to stare?" The woman had appeared from nowhere. She still glowed with a brilliance Isabelle had never seen.

"That's okay, dear. You are probably not used to things like this happening."

"Who are you?" Isabelle finally got her mouth working again.

"I am Joy." The woman smiled. "I know you have lots of questions. They will be answered in time."

"Are you an elf too?" Isabelle's mind raced.

"To the elves and dwarves, I am only an oracle. You may know persons like me as angels. Now listen. What I have to say is very important and only for you. You were given a gift from the time you were conceived. Even while in the womb, you were destined for this task. You must learn magic.

"When you return to the elves this evening, seek out the eldest in Estal. You know the elfin woman as Maggie. She is the eldest elf remaining on the planet. She will teach you what you need to know." Isabelle was confused. Maggie looked barely out of her teens. "Do not let looks confuse you. Elves do not age once they hit maturity. I am sure you know that already." Isabelle nodded her head slowly.

"Have no fear. You will do well. There are some things you must prevent and others you cannot. That is all I have for you now. We will meet again. I am needed elsewhere. Be brave, child, and you will prevail." Joy began to fade from her sight. "Eat your sandwich before it gets cold and don't worry about the bill." She was gone as quickly as she'd appeared.

Ravenous hunger made its presence known from Isabelle's stomach. She dug into her meal with zeal. She'd never had a better double cheeseburger and fries. *Heavenly* was the only description for the dessert.

"Illith dué Mellinathia" Two World War II fighter planes rippled back into the present time just as they entered the city. Everyone knew that the District of Columbia was a restricted airspace. Conner was no exception.

"Heads up Ardy. We are now entering restricted airspace. I doubt the Federal Aviation Administration is still around to enforce it, but keep your eyes and ears open." Conner told his wingman.

"Roger that, Lead," Ardenelle confirmed over his radio.

"Unidentified craft! You are in restricted airspace. Land immediately or be shot down." Conner heard another voice come over his radio. Looking around, he quickly spotted a formation of a half dozen Apache attack helicopters on his six o'clock.

"Apache gunships! We are here to lend a hand. I don't think you quite know what you are dealing with." As soon as the words left his mouth, the goblin and beast grabbed the lead AH-64 from underneath. It spun as it impacted with the helicopter's belly. Grabbing the landing gear as it spun, it threw the army chopper into an uncontrolled spin.

The pilot could not recover before the Apache's tail rotor slammed into the cockpit of the helicopter to its left and rear. They merged into one twisted hulk of fiberglass and aluminum, then plummeted toward the ground. Munitions and fuel caused a brilliant fireball and plume of black smoke as it struck the ground. The Necrogull and its rider watched with satisfaction.

"Crap! What are these things?" Conner heard one of the remaining pilots over the radio. There was no way there could have been any survivors.

"I have no idea. I count minus two for the good guys. Are you sure you don't need the help?" Conner reminded.

Without waiting for a reply, Conner banked his Warhawk down and to the right. Ardenelle followed so precisely, the maneuver looked rehearsed. Looking about, he quickly picked out a target. Conner pushed up the throttle and jockeyed behind beast and rider. He immediately realized it had a goblin on its back. He filed the information for later. It took no time at all to put it in his sights. He reached up under the safety and pulled the trigger.

The fighter shuddered as it released its guns. Several rounds hit their marks. Many glanced off the flying behemoth leaving only small scratches on its mottled hide. One lucky shot entered the wing and into its heart. The monster screamed as gravity took over and pulled it down.

The gunships quickly reassessed the situation and fell into formation with Conner in the lead. "Warhawk, it seems that you know what's going on more than we do." a new helicopter crew took the lead.

"Break into pairs. Lead will target the kill while the wing watches your six." Conner probably knew less than the Apache crews did, but he did not intend to let them in on his secret. "Ardy, you still have my wing." Flipping on his recording equipment, Conner pushed his P40 forward into the small swarm of winged creatures.

"No problem, Fighter Lead." His fellow elf confirmed, adding to the call sign hoping to resolve possible confusion between fixed and rotary winged aircraft.

From the ground, two marines watched as the army's finest attack helicopters were rushed by the monsters. They marveled at the destruction the beast could do. The fireball and black smoke set the two in awe. Quick to recover, Gomez pointed at the newcomers to the game. They watched as two fighters from an old war movie took down the first creature.

Engrossed in what was happening in the sky, they failed to see behind. A goblin rider quickly saw that his enemy was unaware and went in for easy prey. Swiftly and almost without a sound, the Necrogull swooped in for the kill.

Gomez turned around just in time to see Rosie swallowed completely. The creature tossed his head sideways as it devoured the young marine, sending Gomez through the air. The second marine went limp upon impact with a nearby building. On all fours, the beast came to where Gomez lay limp and disoriented. The remaining marine took aim with his M16's grenade launcher. Acid sprayed his body. He choked as his lungs failed. With his last bit of strength, he pulled the trigger. He did not see the headless body of the monster fall.

Conner banked his warbird hard right. Looking down toward the streets, he caught a glimpse of another monster on the ground. He afforded himself a second glance as its head exploded. Two down—ten left to go. His attention quickly came back to the task.

He quickly reassessed the situation, ten bogies, and six good guys. The gunships were not quite as fast, but were more maneuverable and had much more firepower. Hydra-rockets had taken out two more.

"Apache Lead, you have one on your six. Where is your wingman?" Conner shouted into his headset.

"I think he got munched. He had to auto-rotate. The bird hit hard, but I think they walked away." Well, scratch one more chopper. Conner was getting more than a bit irritated. He could not let it show. The lead helicopter did a pedal turn, rotated one hundred and eighty degrees, and let loose with a stream of thirty-millimeter rounds from its belly cannon. They exploded at the collarbone, severing the monster's neck at its base.

"Messerschmitt, you have an ugly on your tail. I can't get to you," the lead gunship warned.

"Thanks. I got it." Ardenelle pushed his throttle forward and pulled back on the stick. The loop was faster than the Necrogull could follow. The goblin rider's head followed the maneuver and quickly saw that he no longer had the advantage. Ardenelle swiftly remembered how thick the monsters hide was. The elf lined up his crosshairs on the rider. The fifty-caliber guns exploded the goblin torso. Without a rider, the beast was confused. It rolled over on its back and plummeted head first into the ground.

"Not bad Ardy." the ex-dragon rider tried to subdue his excitement, but he had to say something. Conner was glad to see another one downed. Even with the goblins inexperience in the air, their ferocity and strength of the Necrogulls more than made up for it.

They came from everywhere. The two fighter planes were doing all they could in the fray. It had been a while since Conner had been in a dogfight. This was the first time for his elfin brother. Conner was happy and a bit surprised that Ardenelle was holding his own so well. It did not take long for Conner's wingman to catch on.

"They are getting closer to the White House." The elves did not know which helicopter the voice came from. Conner knew he had to respond. With the right rudder and throwing the stick hard to his left, he made a steep bank. Just above the light poles and trees, Conner headed down Pennsylvania Avenue. Ardenelle followed close behind. To Conner's right, the remaining AH-64s banked and dove as well. They were so low they could almost fit between the buildings.

An army Black Hawk took the place of the usual UH-60. It was armed and ready to defend the leader of the most powerful nation on the planet. It did not have a chance to fulfill its duty. As the President entered the UH-60, the remaining six monsters split into two groups of three. The first stayed on the aircraft. Slashing at the deadly but slower helicopters with steel-like talons. Acid sprayed from one's massive lower jaw, instantly dissolving one of the remaining helicopters. As an answer to the fall of his fellow gunship, Hellfire missiles flew from the rails of its wingman, exploding with a rain of fire and flesh.

"Nice shot, Apache. You need to get down there and cover your President." Conner urged his new brothers-in-arms. It was too late. The Necrogulls pounced on the Black Hawk. The door gunners of the UH-60 made a valiant effort in protecting the Head of State. Secret Service emptied clip after clip into rider and beast. The attempts were futile. The beasts crushed, dissolved and devoured all.

Conner's heart sank. The crew of the remaining gunships saw their Commander In Chief die before their eyes. Anger quickly replaced the heart-wrenching confusion caused by what they had just witnessed.

"I have missile tone and lock, Raptor." All radio etiquette was now out the window.

"Roger that, Wiley, I have the same." With that, fifteen Hellfire missiles flew from the wing pylons of the two remaining gunships. The creatures and their keepers did not have time to react. The total destruction of the missiles wiped them from existence. A massive crater was all that remained.

Conner was amazed at the destruction. One of the last three beasts rolled and dove to avenge its comrades. Conner was faster. Lining up his crosshairs on the rider, he let go his guns. The hail of rounds streaked through the evening sky, exploding the torso and severing the winged beast's neck at the shoulders.

The remaining two bogies knew they were outmatched, and began their retreat. "This is done. We need to finish this, but we are empty. Can you take them with your antiques?" Raptor queried.

"That's a negative, Raptor," Conner answered. "Our fifties have a hard time getting under their skin. Let them go. I think they have done what they needed to do." Conner lined up on the trailing beast. Reaching up to his right on his instrument panel, he flipped a small switch. He pulled his trigger again, and several small, high-velocity darts shot from his wings, another brainchild of Nedloh's. A green LED just above the switch glowed. It was indicating that at least one of the darts had hit its mark and was tracking. Conner prayed to The Creator that it went unnoticed.

"P40, this is Raptor and Tex. My wing is Snuff and Taz. To whom do we owe the pleasure?" the lead helicopter asked.

"You can call me Conner, and my wing in the Messerschmitt is Ardy." The Apache pilots had been through enough. Conner decided to keep it simple. They would make great allies possibly in the future. Now was not the time.

"Well, Conner, we greatly appreciate the assist. We owe you a big one. Just name it." Conner finally got a look at the remaining Apaches' tail numbers as he settled into formation next to him, 24-019 and 84-290. He smiled at his new friends.

"Apache 019, Raptor, to start we could use some gas to get home." Conner and Ardenelle slowed their airspeed to keep pace with the helicopters. "By the way, good tail numbers." Conner saw thumbs up coming from the back seat of the lead AH-64.

"Standby, Conner." There were a few seconds of silence over the radio before Raptor's voice returned, "I think we can manage that. Stay with us. We are heading for Fort Eustis. Can you make it?"

"I think we can squeak by. We can talk more when we get there." Conner switched to an internal frequency.

"Ardenelle, you really did a great job." Conner praised.

"Thanks, Conner."

"I think I know how we can we can spend those favors. I just hope that the United States Army will agree."

"You can always turn on that elfin charm." Ardenelle could see Conner smile and give the thumbs-up in return.

Chapter 21

Isabelle pulled her old Chevy into the hangar. She began to make a habit of parking it right next to *Amy*. They were her two most prized accomplishments. As she put her street rod into "Park", implications of her visit to the diner slowly washed over her.

It had been weeks since she first came to Wyoming. It seemed like yesterday, but a lifetime as well. Isabelle had found where she belonged. She had a purpose. The fairytale seemed to grow stranger with each passing day. She was just a simple woman from Kansas City who was better-than-average in a few areas. They may have been areas that most women did not share an interest, but she had pride in her meager accomplishments. First, there was her car, then her achievements in the military, and now *this*. What was *this* anyway?

She had found herself down on her luck. Her faith had told her that no matter what, care would be provided. Now her faith has brought her to this point. The world as she knew it was in ruin. She did not even know if Kansas City still existed. She liked to believe that the Royals still played at Kauffman Stadium and that there was still a morning rush hour and construction in the Grandview Triangle.

The words of the angel, Joy, slowly seeped into her thoughts. *There are some things you must prevent and others you cannot.* What did that mean? *I know you have many questions. They will be answered in time.* Were the voices of memory inside her head? Her muscles relaxed as a wave of calm washed over her. Soft laughter came to her lips from nowhere. Isabelle knew why. *Joy.* She knew what she had to do. She opened the door and stepped out of the car.

In the last few weeks, she had found a new family. Conner had seen something in her that others could not. Buck had been a mechanical guide and mentor. Nedloh... Ned was the brother she never had. Thinking of him made her laugh even harder, in spite of herself.

She quickly turned her attention to the amethyst-colored Corsair to her left. She had taken a museum piece and made it into a working, flying piece of deadly art. Her masterpiece was faster and more lethal than it had been when it was part of the Pacific Fleet over sixty years ago. She ran her hand down the brightly colored skin. She felt every rivet and divot on the surface. Starting from the tail, she finished at the Pratt and Whitney radial engine that she had modified and put in herself. Her feeling of euphoria expanded with the feeling that she could accomplish anything.

Her adrenaline grew and she became happily restless. She had to get started. There was no time to waste. Conner would need her. The rest of humankind depended on her. *Rest now, my child.* These words came to her from nowhere. Were they her thoughts? *Tomorrow is another day. Start then.* She stopped and stared at nothing.

Stranger each day. She knew that those were her thoughts this time. She turned and walked across the hangar toward the elevator.

Tomorrow is another day.

Amanda walked by the rancid pools. Looking down, she saw wicked fish with excessively large fins devouring each other. There were hundreds. No...thousands. She knew they had a purpose. The strong preyed upon the weak by biting and chewing. They were submerged beneath the putrid liquid, but she still heard the screams of the lesser fish as they perished. She watched in horror and awe. She could not keep her eyes off the frenzy.

Massive pig-like brutes tended the pools— goblins. They did not harm her. She watched. Amanda would not let herself become one of the weak. She would be strong. The elves would help her. Conner would help. She could not see the elves. She could not see Isabelle. Although not harmed by the goblins, she could feel their contempt for her.

They feared her. She was frightened. She was strong.

Amanda reached into the pool. The ugly fish with large lower jaws bit her. She killed it.

She awoke gasping for air. Amanda looked down at her hand to see no blood. Cold sweat covered her body. She had remembered having nightmares about her parents' deaths. This had confused the young woman. She had never dreamt of a place she had never been. It was all too real in her mind. She never wanted to be there. She never wanted to return to that place.

There was a knock on her door. It slowly swung open. Fear paralyzed her. She let out a sigh of relief as she saw Isabelle's head peer around the edge of the elegantly carved door.

"Are you ok? I heard a scream." Isabelle was dressed and ready for bed. Her hair was wet. It was obvious that she had just gotten out of the shower. Amanda was relieved that she had awakened her.

"I'm okay. I guess had a bad dream." Amanda was glad that the older woman was there. Since she had lost her parents, no one had ever looked in on her when she had bad dreams.

"Do you want to talk about it?" Isabelle walked over and sat next to her on her bed. "Talking about it may help." Amanda shook her head as Isabelle held her hand through the silken comforter. "Okay, I won't push." Isabelle looked thoughtfully at the younger woman. She could see the fear in her eyes. She brushed a tassel of sweat-soaked hair from her face. "Things are getting pretty weird. I know elves, dwarves, and angels—I don't know what to expect. You know if a little wooden puppet walked in here and told us he wanted to be a real boy, I would not be surprised," Amanda smiled.

"Will we be okay?" Amanda quietly asked.

"You know, something tells me we are in for a rough ride, but we will be just fine. We will be stronger when it's all over and done." Isabelle gave Amanda a comforting squeeze of her hand.

Stronger...

"I believe you," Amanda assured Isabelle.

"About what?" Isabelle asked.

"Angels."

"What do you mean?"

"The woman at the diner... you know... the one with the bright lipstick?"

How did Amanda know about Joy?

"I saw her too, you know," Amanda answered as if she read her mind.

Did she?

"She told me to come here. She told me to get on the bus and find the elves. She told me that she would keep us safe."

"Her name is Joy." Isabelle was relieved to have someone she could confide in about tonight's events.

"That's a pretty name. You saw her tonight at the diner, didn't you?" The young woman was adding to Isabelle's confusion.

"How did you know?"

Stranger by the day.

"I don't know, but I just do. I know *things* sometimes. Do you think I am weird?" Amanda looked concerned. She did not want her new best friend thinking she was a freak or something.

"You know, Amanda, after all, that has happened these past weeks, nothing surprises me. It may take a little getting used to, but it doesn't surprise me at all." Isabelle gave Amanda a warm and comforting smile. "It's nice to know that I am not going crazy."

Isabelle began tucking the young woman in. "Now try to get some sleep. Tomorrow is another day." She gently kissed Amanda on the forehead.

"Thanks, Izzy. You helped a lot." Amanda returned the smile and snuggled into her pillow.

"Sleep tight." Isabelle got up and headed to the door. Before she closed it, she looked back at the young woman in bed. She was asleep.

Nedloh was working on equipment in a small conference room that had unofficially become command central. A few of his elfin brothers had helped him merge magic with technology. Spells had helped increase the range and clarity of his satellite surveillance and radios. The project had been all he had concentrated on since Conner and Ardenelle left for the capital.

Elfin magic had shielded the hard drives and wiring from magic attacks and the virus that crippled the rest of the world.

It's not just for baking cookies anymore. Nedloh smiled at his own joke.

Crystals were used to record massive amounts of information. He had engineered them into small discs to make them compatible with computers.

"You know, when this is all over, I may be able to mass produce these and put Bill Gates out of business," Nedloh said to no one in particular.

"I dannot think you have to worry 'bout him anymore, lad." Buck's voice startled the young dwarf.

"Ouch! Don't do that Buck." Nedloh rubbed the sore spot on his head that he smacked. "Dwarves aren't supposed to be so quiet." He slid from beneath the table, out from the tangle of wires.

"What mischief are ya gettin' ta now, m'lad?" Buck was aghast at the entire ruckus that one dwarf and a couple elves could stir up is such a small conference room.

"Well, where do I start?" Nedloh had crawled out from under the table and untangled himself from the jungle of different colored wires and cables. "Um, I have satellite feed going into these two monitors," Nedloh stated as he pointed to the high-definition television monitors on the wall. "These over here record and can be used to clean up and bring more detail to any image that comes in," He turned around and pointed to three more sets behind them. "These, dearest uncle, will be able to show us anything that Conner can see, providing that he has his cameras on. The more info we can get, the better," Nedloh's pride soon vanished as he continued. "The only problem is that we can't quite get the signals from Conner or Ardenelle yet. The satellite can be used, but with too much delay. What if there are clouds?" Nedloh sighed with frustration as he explained to his uncle.

"Well, lad, I am sure you will figure out something. You always had your father's brains and mother's tenacity. You'll figure out how to use crystals to boost the signal or something."

"You are a genius, Buck!" Nedloh's eyes lit up. He did all he could to keep from giving the older dwarf a hug. "I normally would have to wait until they get back to retrofit the planes, but I can start on what we have here in the hangar. Sheer genius!" he yelled as he hurried away.

"You're welcome," Buck said to the empty space where his nephew once stood.

Isabelle woke with a purpose. Her life was getting stranger each day. She had to accept that. Part of her was not letting that happen. She donned a clean pair of jeans and hotrod T-shirt and went to breakfast.

"May I join you?" Maggie came up to her with a piping hot cup of tea.

"Sure. I was going to find you after I finished." Isabelle motioned the elf woman to sit. The small table was one of about half a dozen set here and there in a small group. If they had not been underground, Isabelle had the feeling she was at a small outdoor café.

"I know. I thought it would be easier to find you," Maggie smiled at Isabelle's look of surprise. "Don't think angels only visit humans." She placed a comforting hand on Isabelle as she sat down. "Don't worry, you are in good hands."

Isabelle sat in silence for a moment trying to figure out what to say. She had no idea where to start. She just knew what she was supposed to do. "Okay, let's get straight to the point. Where and when do we start?"

"I am glad you are so forward. Most people would tiptoe and beat around the bush. It's not quite as easy as that," The look in Maggie's' eye became serious, but she never lost her comforting smile. "It's been over four thousand years since one of your people studied magic. Without the right tutelage, it often ends in disaster," Isabelle flinched inwardly. "Magic is like fire. It has to start small, like with a match or a flick of a lighter. Magic can be kindled and useful. It can warm us, heal, or sustain us like a cooking fire. If it is not tended to carefully or it's left unchecked, it will consume and destroy, leaving twisted and charred versions of our former selves."

Isabelle did not know what to think or say. She remained quiet and absorbed in what the elf woman was telling her.

"First, we have to learn to make the fire. That gives us an understanding of its power and abilities. In the days of old, humans used a flint and tinder to kindle a small flame. That is what we must do. If it is given to you fully and completely, you will not appreciate its power nor fear its own need to consume the soul." Isabelle sat transfixed. "Plain and simple, magic surrounds everything, living and non-living. It exists in a balance—positive and negative. I am sure that you know the law of physics that states 'for every action, there is an equal and opposite reaction'?'"

"Yeah, that's one of Newton's laws." Isabelle's mind slowly opened like a rosebud.

"Magic is no different."

Isabelle listened steadfastly as she poured sugar into her second cup of coffee. She stirred and placed the spoon down on her napkin.

"Magic can be controlled by words, or with the right person, sheer will." Maggie gently glanced at the spoon. Isabelle stared as it rose and slipped back into her cup of steaming caffeine and began to stir on its own. After three revolutions around the rim of the cup, it returned itself to the napkin. "You have a rare gift. It will do your will without the words of old. You try."

"This all sounds like one of my favorite sci-fi movies!" Isabelle smiled in slight disbelief.

"Just because the magic was not there does not mean that the wisdom or ability to use it was not. Now, go ahead and try."

Isabelle closed her eyes and pictured the spoon as it rested on the napkin. She could feel it sitting there. As she opened them in a slight daze, she continued the scenario in her mind. She pictured herself picking up the spoon. The spoon began to shake. Isabelle felt as if she could not grasp it. It was slippery and felt semi-solid in her mind. The daydream quickly melted away and was gone. "You are strong." Maggie could barely contain her amazement. "That was done extremely well for someone who has never touched anything with magic."

"All I did was cause it to shake." Isabelle felt disappointed.

"You don't understand the feat you just accomplished." Maggie's voice had a reassuring tone. The elf's face brightened as she had an idea. "Do you like horses?"

"They're okay. I had a bad experience once when I was little."

"You'll like these horses. They're not your average quarter horses. Finish your coffee and we will go for a ride." Isabelle tried to sip the nervousness away. It was slowly replaced with curiosity and excitement.

"Whatcha doin'?" Amanda found her way into the conference room. She was amazed and curious about all the boxes, monitors and wires strung out throughout the room.

"Why does everyone do that?" Nedloh slid from under the console rubbing his head. "Does everyone insist on scaring the genius out of me?"

"Sorry." Amanda stifled a giggle. "I just was bored and wondered if I could lend a hand."

"If you know anything about servers, hard drives and—never mind. You probably don't." Nedloh easily forgot his injury and returned to his task.

"Do you mind if I watch?"

"Just sit down and be quiet. This is way too important to mess up." Amanda pretended to be hurt by Nedloh's curt response.

"It looks like you are having an issue."

"Not really. This has just been more challenging that I first thought. I love a challenge!" The dwarf gave a mischievous smile.

"Well, maybe I can help."

"I doubt it."

"Okay, then talk it through to me and maybe the solution will present itself." Amanda hoped that she could be a good sounding board for the dwarf.

"Well..." Nedloh stood, scratching his beard. He looked about the room as a monarch surveys his kingdom. "I had this working earlier. I don't understand. The radios have the new crystals wired into the receiver to boost and clean up weaker signals. They are interfaced with the server..." Nedloh began to go into detail, talking himself through all he had done. "Satellite feed is through its receiver and into the server. Recorders and monitors are linked and backed up by the server... I am thinking that the motherboard or the hard drive in the server is bad."

Amanda looked through all the wires and cables and smiled. In one swift movement, without a word, the boxes and monitors hummed to life. She smiled at her accomplishment.

"What did you do?" Nedloh stood aghast and wide-eyed.

"I just plugged the surge protector into the outlet."

"Oh. I knew that. I was going to check that next."

"I bet you were." Amanda patronized.

"I think I may be able to use you a bit if ya got time," Nedloh rethought the idea of accepting the young woman's help.

"I don't know. I have a lot to do today." Amanda teased, "I was going to the library, maybe see the horses. I think I can pencil you in." Amanda said with a mocking smile.

"Okay, smartly-pants. What would you do next?"

"Well the next thing I would do would do is route all your wires and cables in the convoluted tubing.

Use colors and a numbering system so it will be easy to fix." She remembered Nedloh's ego. "Just in case," she added.

"Hey! That's not a bad idea. We have some tubing in the hangar and some numbered marking tapes that we use for wiring. What about the coaxial cables?"

"We'll just zip-tie those into bundles to keep them straight and off the floor." Amanda was happy to lend a hand. She had felt useless the past few weeks. "I think I know where they are. Isabelle showed me when I was helping her." Amanda turned and slipped through the door.

"So, how's it goin', lad?" A much older dwarf had replaced the young woman.

"Well, Buck. I thought I could put her to work since she helped me solve a very challenging problem." Nedloh's ego would not let him admit his simple mistake.

"What. Did you forget to plug it back in when you finished?" Buck smiled.

"Um, yeah... something like that." Nedloh just looked at the floor.

"You did a great job, lad." Buck was proud of his brother's son. "Don't let one mistake dishearten you like that. Wisdom and solutions to even the biggest problems can come from the strangest places. No matter how smart ya are, ya cannot do it all by yourself, lad." Buck let his advice sink into the younger dwarf. He turned and walked away.

Isabelle and Maggie talked on their way to the stables. It was just idle chat. Maggie seemed to be very impressed with the woman's mechanical ability.

"…and my father bought me the car for my sixteenth birthday. It was a mess…" Isabelle lost her train of thought as they walked into the stable.

"Here we are." Maggie embellished the hand movement of the game show girls. "These horses, until a few weeks ago, were just like any well-bred Arabian." The elf woman walked up to the closest of the elfin steeds and kissed its nose.

"When the magic was released, it returned to the steeds of the elves."

Isabelle was reluctant to touch the beautiful white mare.

Do not be afraid. This thought came to her mind. *I do not fear, so you should not fear.* Whatever apprehension Isabelle had toward these creatures melted instantly.

"Do they always talk to you in your head?" Isabelle smiled as she asked.

"Only to those pure of heart. You should feel honored." Maggie assured her.

"Oh, I do." Isabelle began to stroke the mare's nose. "They are so intelligent."

"Yes, they are. They are also very proud and easily offended." Maggie tried to give the woman a hint about etiquette.

"I am sorry. I forgot my manners. I am Isabelle."
The woman quickly picked up the hints that the elf
woman dropped. "Please forgive me."

*There is nothing to forgive, Isabelle, Daughter
of Man. I sense your greatness ahead. I am
honored. I am called Lathiéna. In the language of
the elves, it means 'Mother of Horses'. Again, I am
honored to make your acquaintance.* Isabelle
smiled and gave a sideways glance to Maggie.

"Animals speak to us in different ways. Many
animals have the ability to speak if you only have
the ability to listen. These are magical creatures.
They have been born of unicorns. You will meet
many more such creatures in the times to come."
Maggie turned to her horse friend. "Will you and a
friend carry us into the forest?"

"Isabelle has much to learn," the mother of
horses agreed. With a painted mare, they set out,
bareback, to the seclusion of the forest.

"I don't remember seeing these woods before,"
Isabelle remarked.

"That is because you haven't. No one has, in
thousands of years." Maggie explained.

"Where did it come from?" Isabelle's curiosity
overwhelmed her.

"Nowhere. They have always been there." Maggie
tried to sate Isabelle's curiosity and thirst for
knowledge. "It is a magical forest. Because it is
magical, the magic was locked away, and became
invisible to all non-magic users."

The mares carried the women toward the forest at a walk. "You have a unique gift, Isabelle. This is proof to you. Before, you had never used magic. Ever since you gave movement to the spoon, you had the ability to see." Maggie explained. "This gift will not be without price. With this gift of sight, you will see things that you may not want, nor be able to change." Maggie continued. "I am afraid that our young friend may have already experienced this." Isabelle wondered to what degree Amanda could use magic. She wondered if she would be taught and when.

Nedloh and Amanda spent hours organizing, zip-tying and sorting out wiring and cables in the control room. They engaged in idle chat as they took a spider web of cables and wires and sorted them into organized bundles that could be hidden from sight. Both the dwarf and the young woman were amazed at their accomplishments.

"Now that this is finished, a small team of elves and dwarves will monitor it, and we can use this information to figure out what in all that comes from stone, is going on."

"Sounds like a good time to take a break and get something to eat," Amanda commented.

"That, young lady, is the best idea you have come up with yet. I can't remember the last time I had a bite. Would you care to dine with me, my young friend?" Nedloh smiled and exaggerated all the manners he could.

"Why, young master dwarf, I would be delighted," Amanda giggled as she bent down to hook her arm through the dwarfs. "As long as we don't have to eat seed cakes and vegetables."

"Ah. Elfin food. What you need is a good dwarf meal. You need lots of meat, a loaf of bread and a tall glass of mead!" Nedloh assured her. "It will put meat on your bones."

"Well, I don't know if I need more meat on my bones, but I could use something more than a salad and honey cakes." The two talked all the way down to the city of Estal.

"So, have you ever wondered what would happen if Estal was ever discovered?" Amanda was extremely curious.

"This city has been here for thousands of years." Nedloh started to explain. "It was discovered once."

"Really?" Amanda's attention peaked.

"Yeah, in the early 1800s, a young man, and his new bride settled on this land. They acquired it during the big land rush." Nedloh and Amanda had arrived at a small pub in the city that obviously had a dwarf as a proprietor.

The establishment was dark, although lit with a luminescent crystal quarried from the rock in which the dwarves had worked. They were lead to their table by a small, but stout dwarf woman. The table was hewn from solid granite and polished to a highly reflective luster.

Amanda was amazed at the difference between the dwarf and elf. It was more than apparent in this pub. Dwarves preferred not to use electricity to brighten their way. Amanda looked around with excitement and curiosity.

"It has been quite an age since I have seen ya, Master Nedloh." The stout dwarf woman returned. "What brings you to my humble establishment?" She regarded Amanda with curiosity.

"Food and mead, my good woman. The world is changing above us. Times of old have returned. It brings ravenous appetites upon people who work above ground." Both the dwarf woman and Amanda smiled at Nedloh's dramatic production.

"My most humble apologies my fair maidens. Millicent, this is Amanda, fairest of human maidens." Even in the darkness of the tavern, Amanda blushed. "Bring us a feast worthy of warriors of this new age, for we have bolstered our computerized fortress." Amanda was doing all she could to stay in the wooden chair. "Now go, woman. Return with only full platters of your most succulent meats and with bottles of your finest ales." Nedloh was in rare form. Millicent walked away shaking her head and smiling.

"I've read that dwarf women have beards."

"No. That is a myth. Actually, you and Isabelle are the first humans to ever see a dwarf woman." Nedloh informed the young woman.

"Now, young lady, what were we speaking of?" Nedloh continued

"Oh, stop," Amanda said between breaths. She was laughing hard now.

"Okay. Where were we?" Nedloh finally decided to calm down.

"You were telling me how Estal was almost discovered," Amanda reminded.

"That's right. It was during the land rush of the 1800s," Nedloh began again.

"'Twas a man barely in his twenties and his young bride—they settled on these lands and staked their claims. Little did they know that the land was already occupied. They had fallen on hard times when they discovered the entrance to Estal.

The young man started a cattle ranch that struggled. One winter, it was bitter cold. The young man lost several head of cattle and his wife became deathly ill. There was not a town, city or doctor for miles. He desperately tried to make it to Fort Laramie to get her the medicine she needed. During his journey, not far from his homestead the young man became disoriented in a blizzard. They were both near death when the elves found them just outside the entrance to our city.

Against the advice of the dwarves, they brought them to our city to be healed. The elves always had a soft spot for humans. I guess they felt a kinship with them, I don't know. Anyway, the couple weathered out the winter in the city. They knew that the couple was kind and pure of heart. The elves taught them all they needed to know about ranching and raising cattle. They even helped them from time to time during drives. The elves even asked the natives to leave the couple alone so that they could prosper. As thanks to us for what we shared, they gave us dwarves all the beef we could handle and they signed over the deed, making the land a private sanctuary for us. It was their fortune in beef that gave us a foothold and security in the government. We owe the family our existence." Amanda sat wide-eyed as Nedloh recounted their history.

"That is a wonderful story," the young woman smiled. "It was kind of like the elves and the shoemaker, only in the western days."

"I don't know that one. I bet Conner or Maggie could tell you how that went." Nedloh's mouth watered as the food came. Millicent and two other dwarf women brought a large turkey with all the fixings. Several pitchers of thick dwarf mead had also been set on the table. "You see, every fairytale that you have been told as a child, even some of the ones that have been made into animated movies, have some truth to them. Your people sometimes change them to give them happy endings."

"So, Snow White was true?" Amanda asked.

"Yes, but there were ten dwarves and no poisoned apple," Nedloh smiled as he dove into his meal.

Chapter 22

Conner did not know what to think as he and Ardenelle stepped out of their cockpits. As they met their new allies face to face; both sides were unsure of what to expect but glad they had met.

"I'm Colonel Thomas Davies; you may know me as *Raptor*." Conner grasped a strong and honest handshake. "This is my front seat, Snuff Jones." He pointed to the other two men in olive-drab flight suits. "This is my wing and his front seat, Taz and Wiley. Just like the cartoon characters."

"Nice to meet you, I am Bob Conner and this is my wing Ardy." Conner politely introduced the two of them.

"I am so glad you two showed up. I don't know where you came from or where you got your ammo, but I am glad you did." the tall Colonel told him. Conner could tell that although a down-to-earth man, the colonel had been in the military for his entire adult life. Just by his demeanor, he could tell that the man started as an enlisted soldier and worked his way up from there.

"Well, we are glad to be of help," Conner replied without trying to give away anything he knew.

"Look…" Colonel Davies turned toward Conner and all pleasantries were gone. "I don't know where you came from, but I need answers. I am a man of my word, and I will make sure you get gas and whatever you need, but I have questions that I think you have the answers to." Strength seemed to melt away from the Apache pilot, leaving years of troubles and worries weighing him down. "I am sorry Conner. I don't mean to seem ungrateful for saving our butts out there."

"I'll tell you what, is there a place we can go and talk in private? I think a cup of coffee and long talk is what we need." Conner tried to set the aged pilot at ease.

"Sure, let's go to my office. I'll get a pot brewing."

The tall Apache pilot motioned to his new acquaintances to have a seat. "I'll tell ya something I am not supposed to talk about. What is said here cannot leave this room," Colonel Davies started.

"You look like an honest man and a man of honor. I will hold you to that." Conner replied. Colonel Davies gave the elf a curious look.

"As you know, a couple of weeks ago a virus hit us like nothing ever had. The entire world was crippled instantly. The US military was no exception. On top of that, eighty percent of the world population has been affected. They have either died, are dying, or are altered genetically. We think this is some sort of terrorist attack." The pilot poured two cups of coffee and handed them to the elves.

"I can assure you, Colonel, that this is not a terrorist attack." The man looked at Conner waiting for him to tell more. "Colonel Davies, you are an honorable and a noble man. What I am going say, you have to tell no one until I deem it necessary."

"Now you just wait one dang minute. I only take orders from my chain of command. From the best I can tell, you aren't wearing any stars and you sure the heck don't look like the president!" Colonel Davies began to protest.

"No, I'm not a general, and the last I checked the president's life was just snuffed out by those things we took on." Conner mounted his counter assault.

"Okay, you're right. I will agree. Nothing spoken here will leave this room." Davies surrendered quickly.

"Look, there is really no easy way of saying, this so I will try to get to the point." Conner poured sugar into his steaming cup. "Do you remember hearing and reading stories about elves?"

"Yeah. When I was a boy, Tolkien was my favorite. What does a fantasy book have to do with a terrorist attack?"

"It is not an attack like you are used to, Tom. This is not technology. This is magic. We are elves." Conner and Ardy pulled their hair back to show their ears.

"Yeah, right... You are just a couple of guys who had some genetic defect that gave you both pointed ears," Tom Davies tried to rationalize.

"No, Tom. I flew that fighter plane over the Burmese jungle with the Flying Tigers. I am sure you are familiar with them."

"Yes, I know my military history, but there is no way you are an elf and there is no way that magic..." The tall man stopped in mid-sentence as he watched a spoon stirring Conner's coffee by itself. He fell and landed in his chair almost missing.

"That's okay. It's hard to get used to," Conner smiled.

"That must be some sort of trick, an optical illusion."

"Yeah just like the shorts and T-shirt you are wearing," Conner smiled. The man felt breezy. He looked down to find himself in his boxers and brown T-shirt.

"Okay, you got me, but how?"

Conner began to explain as he returned the pilot's clothes.

"...this is bigger than all of us." Conner finished telling the story of the elves and dwarves that stayed behind to protect humankind.

"So, you are saying that somehow this magic has been released and someone has total control?"

"No. This magic has been released but has control of someone, or maybe a group of people.

We just don't know much yet. What we do know is that we are outgunned. With the goblins helping and this virus killing humankind, we are also outnumbered." Conner definitely had control of the bargaining table.

Colonel Davies stood up, began pacing and rubbed his lower face. "I can pull some strings. We are at war but don't know who against. I will get you all the resources I can. My brother is actually one of the Joint Chiefs. He won't ask questions if I tell him not to."

"Thank you. We do have a small air force, but our weapons need upgrading..." Conner started.

"I can do that. Let me know what you need. I will send it."

"...and we will need fuel." Conner continued.

"No problem."

"But most importantly, we need all the Intel you have," Conner challenged.

"That's a doozy!" Tom Davies assured Conner. "I think I can do it," Conner smiled and offered his hand to seal the deal. "I have one personal stipulation."

"Fair enough..."

"I want to see this city of stone personally. I am curious how close the books and fairytales were to the real thing." Colonel Davies smiled.

"No problem. When you come, come alone. You are a friend of elves and you will be a friend of dwarves." Conner grasped the man's hand. As he did so, Colonel Davies's eyes closed involuntarily. He saw in his mind's eye the hangar, the farmhouse, as well as the route to take. The man opened his eyes and smiled. It was done.

As Maggie and Isabelle sat in the forest, the horses grazed quietly nearby. They were surrounded by life. To Isabelle, the flowers were brighter and more vivid; the grass was greener and the trees were taller. Even the butterflies were bigger and had bolder colors of oranges, yellows, blues and purples. There were creatures that Isabelle had never before seen. Maggie introduced her to many creatures: sprites, pixies, fairies, and gnomes.

"I am honored to meet you, Elijah." Isabelle bowed to the little man in the red pointed hat and shook his little hand.

"Likewise, m'lady." The little man smiled.

Isabelle was amazed at all the creatures she had seen. Maggie felt it was important for the young woman to understand all the creatures that depended on magic for their very existence.

"Even the most magical and sacred of all creatures resides in this forest. Once abundant throughout the world, the unicorn had been ravaged by man and hunted to near extinction. Evil mages used the horn of the unicorn for the magic that cannot be spoken of and its blood to live an unnaturally long life," Maggie explained to Isabelle.

"The magical creatures here are the last of their kind. Hopefully, they will be able to once again be abundant and thrive."

"I feel that life is strong here. I can feel the energy given off by all the creatures." Isabelle noticed.

"That is the magic. As I had said before, it thrives on life. It is present in the rocks and the water. It exists between even the smallest specks of dust. How it is used is important. If not cared for and used properly, it will consume you like a fire," Maggie began to smile. "Fear not my pupil. You are pure of heart. You will be fine if you heed my words."

Before long Isabelle had realized that they had spent all afternoon and part of the evening in the forest. The sound of two aircraft overhead brought the elf and woman back to the real world.

"That is all for today. I will talk to Conner. Every spare moment you have, I must school you in the ways of magic. It is imperative to the survival of your race. You will be given access to the library. There, you will find books to further your knowledge." Maggie informed Isabelle. "Some books, you will not have access to until, and only if, I deem you ready."

"How will you know if and when I will be ready?" Isabelle asked.

"You will be challenged and I will know." Maggie gave Isabelle a stern look. "This is an undertaking like you have never experienced. Open your mind and heart, and it will come to you. If you do not, it will grab you, pull you down and devour you."

Maggie whistled for the horses. "That is all for today. Let's dine and find what news Conner brings." She smiled and mounted the elfin steed. They trotted back to the stables. Isabelle noticed that a hunger stirred within her. Was it for knowledge or was it because she had not eaten since the morning? She was not sure which.

"Glad to see ya back, m'lad." As usual, Buck was the first to greet the returning elf."

"Glad to be back, Buck. We need these refueled." Conner turned to Ardenelle.

"You did great on my wing, brother. Do a post-flight inspection on both these, and join us for a meal in about an hour and a half."

"Thanks. I am honored to have helped, Anthriel. I would be happy to dine with you tonight!" Ardenelle clapped his hand on Conner's shoulder as he turned to the fighters and got to work.

"We have much to talk about, my dwarfish friend!" Conner was closing a panel in the belly of the *Dragon's Heart*. "I think this footage will be valuable. We will look at it after we eat. I am starved."

As Conner handed Buck the disc from the flight recorder, Isabelle and Maggie entered the hangar.

"I think we should have our meal in the conference room," Conner suggested.

"I don't think that would be a good idea," Buck tried to warn Conner as he opened the door. It was too late.

What in Tolkien's name happened here?" Conner exclaimed.

"Well, my brother's son had gotten a wee bit creative while you were gone." Buck tried to head off any emotion that Conner might have.

"Okay, have him join us as well." Conner nodded as he surveyed the equipment. "You might as well have Amanda join, also. Bring the whole famn damily!" Conner closed the door and headed to the elevator.

The shower before dinner had done him well. The pure spring water that ran through the stone city had washed all the tension in his muscles from the battle away. Instead of the flight suit that he usually wore, Conner decided on an ordinary pair of jeans and dark, emerald green sweater. Dressing quickly, he headed toward the Great Hall where it was decided beforehand that all would meet for dinner.

A large table sat alone in the vast hall. There were seven place settings at the lonely table. Unlike the cold surroundings, the table and seven chairs were made of a warm, dark oak. Wine and pitchers of water were set about the table. Conner was not the first to arrive.

Buck and Nedloh were already on their fourth pints of ale. In their jeans and T-shirts, the dwarves' dress was a great improvement from the dirty coveralls they normally wore. Conner smiled and remembered how the dwarves liked their alcohol. As Conner sat at the head of the table, the women entered the room. Both Buck and Nedloh dropped and spilled their drinks as they caught sight.

Maggie was dressed in a bright yellow tunic and khaki slacks. The combination of the two showed every curve on her perpetually youthful body. Isabelle and Amanda were in dresses. Isabelle's was small and black. Conner was amazed at its simplicity and its elegance. Amanda's dress was a short, teal formal gown. Its elegance brought maturity to the young girl's blossoming body. All four men stood and waited until the women sat. Both Isabelle and Amanda blushed at the chivalry displayed.

As soon as they had all been seated, food began to arrive on platters. Great portions of cakes, breads and cheeses were brought by elves. Dwarves brought platters of meats. Pork and beef were steaming and neatly sliced on jeweled platters of dwarven craftsmanship.

Conner prayed to The Creator for a blessing upon the food and those seated at the table. Buck stood with his mug.

"My elfin brothers and sisters, and the son of my brother, and to our newest friends of humankind," He nodded at Isabelle and Amanda. "In these troubled times, may fortune smile upon all of us. May we get through these times to once again add to the songs and legends of old with new tales of heroic valor. May our courses be straight and our adventures take us to happy endings." Buck pulled long and hard on his mug of ale. The other six surrounding him drank in kind.

"Tonight we feast for several reasons," Conner stood midway through the meal. "We feast in the victory of the battle of the nation's capital. By feasting in this victory, we must mourn the dead. We mourn the loss of the nation's leader. We also mourn the blood of the warriors spilled on the battlefield." Conner lifted his glass and waited for the others to do the same. They all stood and drank together.

"Could you please pass the peas?" Amanda asked Buck.

"Let me try, Buck." Isabelle closed her eyes. After a few seconds, the silver bowl of steaming vegetables lifted and floated along the table. All were amazed when the bowl settled in front of Amanda.

"You are strong and learn quickly," Conner said. "Congratulations on your first step into a larger world. We have more to feast for." They finished their meal in idle conversations.

"As you are all aware, a great evil has fallen on this planet," Conner began after the meal had been cleared away. Only pitchers of wine, water, and dwarf ale remained. "We have fought an enemy of whom we know nothing. That will soon change. I have made a deal to get information from what is left of the military. Furthermore, I would like to ready Estal for any possible attacks." Conner turned to Nedloh.

"I have set up a command center in the conference room. I will need to finish modifying the aircraft. I have come up with a system that will greatly increase the range of communications and help keep the enemy, whoever it may be, from eavesdropping." Nedloh looks at Conner and around the table as he informed everyone of his accomplishments. "I would like to publicly recognize and thank Amanda for all she has done to assist me." Nedloh knew this would help Amanda feel part of the family. He wanted his young friend to have a sense of worth.

"Thank you, Amanda." Conner gave a nod of gratitude to the young woman.

"What about these creatures? Where did they come from and what are their weaknesses?" Buck asked.

"We don't know what they are or where they come from, but they are heavily armored." Ardenelle joined the conversation. "Apache gunships had no problems with their explosive rounds or rockets, but they took very skilled shots just under the armpit with our 50-cals to bring them down. The only other weakness is the goblin rider. It seems without them they become confused."

"They are called *Necrogulls*," Amanda said as she stared off into nothing. "They were grown in pools by the goblins."

"How do you know this, sweetie?" Isabelle gave Amanda's hand a firm squeeze.

"I had a dream. I was standing near the pools. I reached in and grabbed one of the babies. It bit me, so I killed it." This vision disturbed Conner. He could see the concern in Maggie's eyes as well.

"There is no way goblins could create such creatures," Buck interjected.

"No, it was the bad man. He did it. He created other very bad things." Amanda grew quiet.

"Obviously, an evil mage or sorcerer is upon us," Ardenelle added. Conner pondered briefly.

"With Isabelle's new found skills and our new friends, we may be able to use magic to bolster our resources. We can use magic to shield our aircraft from attack. Fuel and a few special goodies from our new military friends will give us a slight advantage in weaponry, but we will still be greatly outnumbered." Conner was somber.

"My country's forefathers fought against great numbers for their freedom. We can look for others to help in the battle." Isabelle stood up. "I have fought before to preserve peace and democracy. I thought there was no greater cause. Now I am fighting for the existence of all humankind. I have been proven wrong. You can count me in."

"You may not know what you are saying. You also do not know what is before you if you do this." Conner wanted to make sure she knew what she was getting into. "We elves, along with our dwarf brothers are here specifically for this purpose. We were ready to lay down our lives, hundreds and even thousands of years before you were born." Conner became quiet and gave a look of concern to Amanda. "What do you think of all of this, young woman?"

Amanda slowly raised her head. She suddenly realized everyone was looking at her. She straightened in her chair.

"I am where I belong. I saw the elves in my dreams. I also saw the winged tiger. This is where I was sent. Whatever I can do to help, just ask. I don't know anything 'bout magic or fighting, but I will do what I can. It's my world too, and I ain't gonna let anyone take that from me. I spent too much of my life getting a beating from bad people. No more!" Amanda seemed to change before everyone's eyes. Before them, she changed from a timid and shy girl into a strong and sure woman. It seemed that a light glowed from behind her, illuminating her. Afterward, she shrank back into her chair and became quiet. She once again returned to that shy timid young woman they all knew. This disturbed Conner and Maggie. Isabelle also had noticed and did not know quite what to think.

When the meal was over, Isabelle walked with Amanda to her room. The woman wanted to make sure that her younger friend was all right with whatever was going on. Isabelle thought it was time to have a heart-to-heart. She just did not have any idea where to begin.

"That was quite a meal." Isabelle took a stab at it.

"Yeah, I am incredibly stuffed." Amanda forced a smile. "I don't think I could eat for a week."

"Yep. Kind of like Thanksgiving and Christmas combined." Isabelle felt the tension ease.

"Well, most of my foster parents didn't do much on those days." *Ouch.*

"I am so sorry, Amanda. Look, we both know that things are going to be different from now on." Isabelle decided to go for broke and let it all out. "There is no way of getting around it. Well, the fact of the matter is...you scared me back there when you gave your speech; you changed for a little while."

"Really? How?" Amanda was surprised.

"I don't know. When you gave your speech, something bad came out. I don't think I was the only one who noticed," Isabelle continued.

"I am sorry. Do you think everyone else is mad at me?" Amanda began to look worried.

"No, I don't think anyone is mad." Isabelle held Amanda's hand. "Look, this magic stuff is weird, I know. Maggie is trying to teach me to use it. It's hard to even believe it exists. You are young and going through many changes yourself. I don't know how this manifests itself in different people. I think you should try to learn what you can." Isabelle tried to be the role model. She knew by the look on the younger woman's face that she was failing.

"I see what you are trying to say. You are telling me that I need to watch my step or something bad is going to happen." Amanda began to get angry. "I have been looking out for myself since my parents died. I can take care of myself!"

"No! We are in this together." Isabelle tried to salvage what she could. "If you need someone to talk to there are plenty here to help."

"Whatever!" Amanda turned around and went into her room, slamming the door.

How dare she talk to me that way! Who did she think she was, my mother? Amanda was extremely angry.

She is not your mother. She is trying to help. Isabelle knows that this cannot be easy for you. The voice inside her head was not hers. It was soothing. It was also right. She felt her anger melt away. Tears welled in her eyes as she cried on her bed.

Isabelle is a strong woman. You should look up to her. My sweet Amanda—these will be troubled times for all. You will be no exception. Listen to all you can. Do not turn away the hand that helps. If she does not understand, talk with her. Show her so that she may. You are special. You are being tested, and in your darkest hour do not turn her away. The voice was soothing and yet wise. *Rest and speak with her upon the 'morrow.* With that, Amanda cried herself to sleep. She dreamt of her mother and father. She smiled as she slumbered.

Isabelle's mind was racing. As she got ready for bed, she wished she could have someone to talk to about her discourse with Amanda. No sooner did the thought go through her mind, there was a knock on the door. Isabelle stopped for a split second. She thought that reasoning was playing tricks on her. Then it happened again. She slid into her robe of elfin silk and answered the door.

"I hope I didn't wake you," Conner's smile showed through his look of concern.

"No, that's okay. I was just getting ready to lie down. Come in." Isabelle opened the door to let in her elfin friend.

"Thanks. I promise I won't be long. Tomorrow is a busy day." Conner stepped in and Isabelle shut the door. "I know Amanda is under a lot of pressure. She is trying to deal with all that has happened. On top of all this, she is trying to find her place here." Conner really did not know where to go with this conversation. "I am glad you are here to be like a big sister to her. Obviously, she knows things that we don't. She has a second sight. I think I will have Maggie help her channel it better if you don't mind sharing for a while." A genuine smile came across the elf's face.

"No, I don't." Isabelle could not help but return the infectious smile. "Something tells me she will need her to have her wits about her. We also need to protect her. From what, I don't know."

"I agree. I will talk with Maggie to see where we go from here. She will know." Conner looked into Isabelle's eyes. "Something happened to her tonight. I don't know what, but it has me worried."

"Me too," the woman agreed.

"Uh, one more thing..." Conner changed the subject. "I hope you don't think I am avoiding you."

"I know you are busy." The thought actually did not cross Isabelle's mind. She was far too busy even to consider Conner as of late.

"I mean, I really want to try to spend time with you." Conner looked distracted. Isabelle noticed. She smiled inwardly. "I have not felt like this about anyone in hundreds of years. What I am trying to say is that... well, please be careful. I don't want anything to happen to you, that's all." With that, Conner turned around and left.

Isabelle stared a moment at the door that was closed behind him and smiled. She felt giddy. *He does like me*. She slipped into bed and fell asleep.

Chapter 23

Two goblin riders returned to the grottos and rancid pools. The dark mage waited impatiently for their reports. As they dismounted, goblin handlers soothed the beasts, and technicians hooked cables and wires into a port on the side of the beasts' heads. They downloaded information of the previous battle.

"Report, swine!" Esuorts wanted information immediately.

"We took heavy casualties but we were successful. The enemy's leader was destroyed." The goblin reported in broken English accented with grunts and squeals.

"And their forces?" The mage prodded for more.

"The insect-like craft was easy to defeat. They did not know of combat with flying beasts. But..." The rider averted the dark magician's stare.

"But what? What are you not telling me?"

"There were two other craft, an ancient craft that came from nowhere. They flew like birds, not like insects." Lord Esuorts knew that the rider was talking about fighter planes.

"We are ready, my lord." The technicians informed their master that they had retrieved the information from the storage within the mind of the Necrogull. He motioned to a small monitor next to one of the rancid pools used for breeding.

"Show me," Esuorts turned to watch the monitor. He was not surprised at what he saw. The air rippled and where there was nothing, two ancient warplanes appeared. *Magic!* One of the planes he recognized. As he watched, he clearly understood that the P40 Warhawk was the leader. He had an enemy. Someone was there to try to stop him. Before he could take his place as leader of this world, he had to kill this menace.

"Where did this come from?" Lord Esuorts pointed to the planes on the monitor.

"That we do not know," the technicians informed their master. "But we do know where they went."

"Track them down. I want to stop this at the source." The dark lord waited for action. "Now!" The technicians scrambled into action.

Brett "Taz" Elliot stepped out of the smoky bar into the muggy Newport News night. The yellow glow of the streetlights shown dimly on the empty pavement. On a weeknight such as this, not many people ventured out. Being single, he could keep whatever company he pleased. After yesterday, he wished to keep no company at all. Taz was ordered not to discuss what he saw over the nation's capital.

He was doing the best he could to forget the World War II fighter planes and the huge monsters that had the ugly riders. Too many shots of tequila made it all seem like a bad dream.

He was proud to be an Apache pilot. He used the glory of driving his gunships to attract many one-night stands. Tonight, he was pushing them away. He fumbled for the keys of his 1969 Corvette Stingray. More than his love for flying, this was his baby. He pushed in on the clutch and started it up.

Minutes later, he was in front of his apartment complex with annoying blue, red and white lights flashing in his rearview mirror. He had no idea from where the lights had come or how he ended up in front of his home. He just wished the lights would stop.

"License and registration please!" He heard these words all too often. Now was not a good time, but whatever it would take to get the lights to stop... He looked up to see a police officer in full riot gear.

"Yes officer, I was just on my way home." He looked slowly around. "I think I am here. Thanks so much for your help."

"I am going to have to ask you to step out of the car, sir." The officer said in a typical monotone voice.

"You like this car, officer? I got it six months ago, I think. Ain't it a sweet ride?" Brett was doing all he could do to stand. He was thankful that the car was there to help. "It rides like crap, but boy is it fast."

"Yes, sir. It is a nice car. I need you to breathe into this tube." The officer affixed a sterile plastic tube on top of a small black box. "That's good. Try again." The officer was doing all he could not get too close. He waited for half a second as the numbers told the story and made it official.

"That's a cool gadget. What does it do, check your bad breath?"

"Something like that. Mr. Elliot, I'm afraid that I am going to have to take you downtown."

"Why? I just got home."

"It seems you have been driving under the influence." As they spoke, another patrol car arrived. More lights. The two officers spoke a few feet from Brett. The young pilot waited patiently with his hands cuffed behind his back. He just wanted the lights to stop.

"Okay, Mr. Elliot, we are going to take you in. We are citing you with driving under the influence and being out after curfew. Tomorrow morning you can call your commanding officer and have someone post bond. You know, if you were not in the military, these penalties would be extremely severe. Tomorrow we will let your chain of command take care of it." The two police officers skillfully led him to the back of the second patrol car. Holding his head, they placed him in the backseat. Within a few minutes, the officer in the front made a few radio calls and they were on their way. Brett was thankful that there were no more lights.

The cell was typical. He was alone in the middle of the week. Security was on high alert because of the curfew. Most citizens had been compliant. A few had been protesting or preaching judgment day. Brett vomited several times in the stainless-steel toilet and just lay down on the thin green plastic mattress and passed out.

"Awake, Mr. Elliot!" In the bright light of his cell, he saw an elderly man in strange black robes. The lapel of the robes had purple embroidery. Brett had no idea why he noticed.

"Who are you... some kind of special judge?" That was the only way that Brett could explain the robes.

"No, my friend," the man smiled. Brett felt no warmth in the man's gesture. "I am in need of your help."

"Look around, pal. I'm really not in a position to lend a helping hand." Brett squinted in the bright light.

"Ah, that, I can see," the older man looked him analytically. "I could fix it so that it never happened and you wouldn't even see a court martial..." Obviously, this was not a common kind of judge.

"Yeah, that would be great, your honor." Things were looking up for the young pilot. "I would do whatever it took to make this all go away. This could end my career."

"I have one thing to ask of you, my young pilot friend." The smile on the older man's face made Brett feel uneasy.

"Sure, anything..."

"I have an ongoing need for information. If you can give it to me when I need it, none of this will have happened."

"Sure, what do you need?" Brett half sat up on his bunk.

"I want to know who flew with you yesterday, and where they went after they left here." Eagerness appeared in the old man's eyes replacing the imitation friendliness.

"They are two guys from Wyoming. One guy's name is Bob Conner, and his buddy's name is Ardy, I think," Brett started.

"Where?" The stranger became very impatient.

"I don't know exactly." Brett ran his fingers through his hair, doing the military's high-and-tight little good.

"You must find out."

"I suppose I could, but it will take a couple of days. Why are you so pushy?"

"That is my business. Do you want my assistance or not?" The man shot back.

"Yeah, sure, I'll get it for you."

"I will give you until this time tomorrow to give me answers." The older man grabbed Brett's wrist. "To make sure you know that this is not just a bad dream, I will give you something to remember me by." Brett's skin began to burn where the man had touched him. He could smell the searing flesh. "There! It is done! We have made our bargain." With the tequila still in his system and the pain in his burning flesh, Brett passed out.

Brett Elliot woke the next morning in his bed. He had never felt more refreshed. The aroma from his automatic coffeepot smelt wonderful.

Last night must have been a terrible dream. With that thought, pain shot up his arm from his right wrist. He looked down to see a strange symbol branded in his skin. It looked like a three-pronged fork with three tiny dots at the end of each prong. A circle went through what would be the middle of the handle, and each prong with the three dots on the outside of the circle. It was not a dream. Something told him that he had made a deal with the devil and he needed to get some information.

His 1969 Corvette Stingray waited for Brett in its assigned parking spot. In a clean flight suit, he got in and drove off. Today was beautiful, but he did not bother to put the top down. He had to get to the tower and see if his new fighter buddies filed a flight plan.

The gate was heavily guarded, as it had been since the virus sent the world into a dark age. Chief Warrant Officer 2, Brett Elliot, had to maintain a room at the officers' barracks in this time crisis. He had never stayed there. He showed his military ID and driver's license to the private at the gate and he was waved in.

As Brett parked his car, he saw Colonel Davies walking into the flight office.

"Excuse me, Sir." Brett caught his commanding officer just as he entered the door.

"Good morning, Mr. Elliot." The colonel was exceptionally cheerful. Brett thought it odd considering all that happened the past two days.

"Sir, uh, I was wondering..." Brett did not know quite what to say.

"Go ahead, Brett, get it out."

"Well those guys really saved our butts the other day, and I have a really good bottle of scotch that I had been saving for a special occasion." Brett was working well on the fly. "I was wondering if there was an address I could get to send it to them."

"Actually, I promised not to disclose that information." Brett's heart sank at the colonel's words. "But, I do have a few things I am going to take to them personally. They know you already. You could ride shotgun with me. You can give it to them yourself." Brett's mind whirled. This may be able to work. He would have to talk to the curious dark lord.

"Uh, sure, that would be great. Where and when?"

"0400 tomorrow morning. Meet me at my place. I'll have coffee ready for us."

"Great. I'll be there." *Now I have to talk with the curious old man and buy a bottle of scotch.*

Good booze was getting hard to come by in the past few weeks. Brett had to part with half a month's food rations just for a bottle of ten-year-old scotch. He walked into his apartment and set the bottle on the counter. Brett had begun hoarding and trading as soon as the virus hit. He had a small stockpile of whatever he needed. This was the main reason for keeping his off-post accommodations.

"I see you have not learned your lesson from last night," the old man said. Brett jumped at the words, almost knocking over the bottle. "What do you have for me?"

"I don't know where, but I am going to find out tomorrow. I am going there with Colonel Davies." Brett flinched, waiting for something terrible to happen.

"You are going there? Why?" Anger flashed in the man's eyes but quickly dissipated. Curiosity welled up in its place.

"I told Colonel Davies that I wanted to thank them for their help." The anger that flashed in the old man's eyes and was quickly dissipated. "He said that he had a few things that he wanted to give them in appreciation and wanted me to go along." The old man smiled.

"This might work even better." The old man walked over to the bottle of scotch and picked it up.

"A bottle of twenty-year-old scotch is a fine gift," the man said as he read the label.

"I couldn't find anything that old. I did manage a bottle ten..." Brett looked again at the date. He was amazed that the date had changed. It indeed was twenty-years old.

"Young Master Elliot..." The older man sat the bottle back down and walked to the window. I see that have a knack for procuring things and brokering them. Since money is useless now," a smile of self-satisfaction grew on the old man's face, "I can make you a very wealthy man."

"How can you do that?" Elliot asked.

"We may have an agreeable arrangement here. If it continues, and you help me with more that I need, I can make sure that you get things that can be easily brokered or exchanged for anything you may desire."

"I can only hold so much in this apartment. I'm afraid I can only help you so much."

"That can be remedied. To show my good faith I will leave a case of the same scotch that you have here on the counter." A dusty crate appeared on the floor next to him. Brett's eyes had widened in surprise.

"Young man, I am not to be trifled with. This arrangement may be profitable for you or it could be a fate worse than death." The old man put his fingers on Brett's chin. "Find out all you can about this place and this Conner." The old man said the name as if he were spitting out a bad piece of fruit. "I will see you in two days. Do not fail me." Brett turned toward the old man, but he was gone.

What was he getting himself into? He looked down at the dusty wooden crate. He smiled to himself. Just a little information was all. He was going to want for nothing.

Chapter 24

Matt Timble had a family for which to care-a young wife and two-week-old baby boy. He was used to doing without. Making do was a full-time occupation for the young father. He had a hard time finding a decent paying job. A career was a fairytale to him. He had worked construction, washed dishes and flipped burgers almost everywhere in Kansas City.

For the last two weeks, he had no telephone, water, or electricity. He had already done without. He knew how to make it. A lot of others did not. Gas was in short supply. Fuel for transportation was conserved for city busses. Most of them were overcrowded. Lines for them lasted for days.

Matt saw this as an opportunity. He was skilled with tools and he had many clever ideas. He was not afraid to put forth some effort. He knew he needed water and food for little Scotty. Emily was still nursing. Matt needed to make sure they were cared for. He had a clever idea.

Matt and Emily packed as much as they could into their well-worn 1988 Dodge minivan. With few clothes, a tent, camping supplies, and his tools, he knew he had to get out of the inner city. The violence had escalated since the virus hit. It was only a matter of time before he and his family would be murdered in their sleep for just a few morsels of food. He had half a tank of gas, which would hopefully get him where he needed to go.

He drove down Van Brunt and hopped onto Interstate 70 going east. There was money near Lee's Summit and Blue Springs, Missouri. If he had the gas, he may make it as far as Grain Valley or Pleasant Hill. He seriously doubted it. He turned off at Lee's Summit Road and past the Home Depot. All was quiet and dark.

The home improvement store still had a few scraps of lumber left and one small trailer. He reached into the back of the van for a large pair of bolt cutters. He was glad he had not pawned them as he had most of his power tools. He laughed to himself. *Power tools*. What good were they now? He cut the padlock on the trailer and hooked it up to the ball mount on the back of the van.

Cautiously, he went inside to see what hadn't been looted. He found a few power saw blades. He thought about their uselessness but decided to pick them up anyway. A couple of handsaws, some plywood and two-by-fours were all that remained on one end of the store. As he searched the rest of the building, he was able to pick up an assortment of hardware: nuts and bolts of various sizes; some pipe and pieces of threaded rod in different lengths and sizes; a hacksaw and blades; and a number of spools of electrical wire. He had a few ideas.

He loaded everything in the trailer. The young man tied everything down with plenty of rope. He knew he could never have too much of it.

He continued driving down Lee's Summit Road. The road ran over a stream. He pulled to a side street that followed that same small stream. Houses of the affluent were only a few miles away. It was a secluded spot. He would stop there.

Emily was curious to what her husband had in mind. She watched him as he went to work without a word. Matt had not spoken with her in almost a day. This worried her. As she held the baby, Matt began to empty the van.

"Doesn't someone own this land?" She asked.

"No one owns anything anymore," Matt said as he began to set up his two-room Coleman tent. "Don't you see that, Em? Since the virus hit, if you ain't dead, you don't have anything. We are on our own. We are used to being without. Now everyone has to learn survival skills. The difference between us and them is that we know how to do it. They don't." Matt said nothing else. He just continued to work.

It was getting late as he finished setting up the makeshift camp. He had a small fire with an oven rack, and a few pots and pans. As he laid out the bed for his family, he made plans for the next day.

By noon the following day, Matt had set up a full outdoor kitchen. He had set out a fishing line in the stream and several small traps in the woods that bordered the little camp. He was proud of his accomplishments but had no time to rest.

"I am going to take a look around and see what we have to work with. I'll be back in a few hours. Stay close." With that, Matt set off with a walking stick and empty duffel bag.

He walked up the road a few miles and cut into a neighboring wood. Here he found plenty of dead wood for their cooking fire. He located several wild mushrooms and a blackberry bramble. The berries still had not ripened. They would in a week or so, and there were plenty. Making do would be hard work, but so was any nine-to-five job. Putting in the overtime would be no problem.

As the afternoon passed, Matt returned to his family. He was not empty handed. He had snared two rabbits in his traps and the fishing line had been abundant as well. For the first time in months, they ate well.

The next few days had not been as easy. The snares had been empty and the fishing lines were bare. The Timble family had dined on ramen noodles and canned beans. On the fifth day, he went to check his traps.

As he neared one of his traps in the woods, he heard a little voice struggling. There was a little man in blue trousers and a green shirt with red suspenders. Matt looked curiously at the little man.

"I am so sorry," Matt said. "I didn't think anyone else was out here."

"Is this your work?" The little man was furious.

"Yeah, I'm afraid it is." Matt felt very badly for snagging the little man. "I hope you're all right. I didn't mean to hurt anyone." Matt walked over and began to let the little man down. He was extremely curious about the miniature old man.

"These are my woods. You should ask before you start placing traps about willy-nilly." There was something appealing about the little man. All the stress he was under to take care of his family broke him at that point. Like a floodgate, it washed over him.

"Again, I'm very sorry. I came out here to take care of my family. My little boy is only a few weeks old," Matt began. "Let me make it up to you. We don't have much, but you are welcome to join us for dinner. Our camp is just outside these woods." As the little man watched the larger man try everything in his power to keep himself from losing his composure, his anger melted.

"I suppose I ain't hurt none," The little man said. "My name is Jacob and these are my woods."

"My name is Matt Timble. I am very glad to meet you." Matt squatted down to shake the little man's hand.

"I could use a bit of a bite. I will take you up on your offer," little Jacob agreed.

Emily watched her husband emerge from the wood. Her hopes quickly sank when she realized that he had brought nothing from his traps. She was curious about the little man propped on her husband's shoulder.

"Em, we have our first guest for dinner." Matt returned the little man to the ground. "This is Jacob. He kind of found his way into one of my snares. I thought we might have him join us for dinner. It's the least we can do."

"We barely have enough to feed ourselves, let alone another mouth," Emily told her husband off to the side.

"He can't eat much, and after all, I did accidentally snare him." Emily reluctantly agreed. "Emily Timble, this is Jacob. These are his woods." Matt smiled as he introduced the two.

"Nice to meet you, um, Mr. Jacob." Emily did not quite know what to think.

"Likewise, Mrs. Timble. You can call me Jacob." Emily could not help but warm up to the little man. Beans were in the pot and Emily dished out an extra plate for their guest.

"These are wonderful, Em. What did you put in them?"

"They are the same beans we had last night, nothing special." Emily realized that her husband was right. They were exceptionally good.

"Well," Matt smiled. "Maybe it's the company we have."

"Perhaps, so," Jacob smiled back

After the meal, they sat around the small campfire. Emily got up and went into the tent to feed little Scotty.

"This is all we have," Matt told his new friend

"Don't you miss all the gadgets and 'lectricity?" Jacob asked.

"We are used to doing without," Matt answered. "We'll get by."

Emily returned with a little bundle in her arms. She fed Scotty and he was cooing contently. The baby was happily blowing little bubbles.

"You are good people, Timble. I will help you as much as I can." Jacob pulled out a pipe, filled it from a pouch on his belt and lit it, blowing fragrant smoke rings. "There is an abandoned stone farmhouse up the road about two miles. There is a well out back and an orchard." Jacob closed one eye and looked at Matt with the other. "If a man were clever enough, he just might make a home for his family. It's on the border of my woods, so you know you would have good neighbors."

"Thanks, Jacob, I will check it out tomorrow," Matt assured him.

"No, not tomorrow. Tomorrow you need to pack up your things and move into it. There will be a flood through this valley upon morn after."

Jacob got up and walked over to see the baby. "Interesting creatures, these babies..." Jacob watched in wonder. "I can tell this one's future. Do you wish to know?"

"Sure." Matt did not know if someone could see the future, but this man was like no one he had ever met.

"He is a gifted child. The child will have great choices to make in his future. He will find friends in strange folk and they will not harm her. She will achieve greatness there. She will have one friend with whom she will bond for life. You will be proud," Jacob told them.

"No Scotty is all boy." Emily reminded their guest. Don't let the hand-me-down clothes fool you." She smiled and brushed off the little man's use of pronouns.

"I am sorry. I did not wish to offend—my mistake." Jacob apologized, but he did not correct himself. "I see the future, and I am never wrong."

The sun had set and it was getting late. Fireflies began to twinkle in the fading light. A chorus of frogs and crickets began to sing their evening songs. A whippoorwill joined the choir.

"If you'll have me tonight, I will take you to the house in the morn," Jacob bargained.

"Sure, I don't see why not," Matt agreed. "Like I said before, we don't have much, but we are willing to share." Matt brought him a blanket and small pillow and made him a pallet by the fire. In no time, the strange little man was asleep.

As soon as little Scotty was asleep Emily and Matt curled up on a comforter and old sleeping bag.

"What an odd little man," Emily whispered.

"In these odd times it's nice to find a friendly face and a helping hand," Matt told his wife.

"What if he's some kind of ax murderer?" Emily instantly looked worried.

"For some reason, I don't get that feeling," Matt reassured her. "I don't think you do either."

"If you say so..." Emily reluctantly answered. Emily felt the same way. As odd as the little man was, he gave them a safety net in a mixed up and turned around the world. They quickly fell asleep.

The next morning the sun came through the colored nylon of the tent. Matt and Emily woke to the smell of eggs and bacon.

"Good morning, neighbors. I trust you slept well." Jacob was cooking on a small fire twenty feet from the tent.

"Yeah, I actually did." Matt ran his hand through his bed-ruffled hair and surveyed his surroundings. The camp was no longer by the stream. It sat behind a three-story stone house. "Where are we?" Matt managed to mutter.

"We are in what you would call the backyard of the abandoned farmhouse I spoke of," Jacob smiled. "I told you I would help you move."

"But how?"

"That's my secret," Jacob winked. "You are to take care of your family in this house, as well as take care of these woods. Only your family has permission to enter. No one else will receive the kindness I have shown the Timble family."

Matt's mouth could only open and close. No sound could escape. "Yes, it is magic. I will teach you some useful tricks with it. Now let's eat, before it gets cold."

Emily slipped out of the tent with the baby in her arms. She smiled at her husband. For once, they had their own home. It was not much, but they were used to doing a lot with a little. Matt began to laugh aloud with joy.

"Look, honey, magic."

"I know," Emily smiled and answered. She did not know how, but she knew. She bent down and kissed the little man's forehead. "Jacob, you are always welcome in our home. You have given us gifts we cannot repay."

"You may not, but one day your daughter..." He stopped himself before he gave away too much of the child's future. "I mean your *child* will. I cannot tell you everything about your child's future. Things that you do not know cannot be changed. Your child is blessed." Jacob finished serving up breakfast. "Relax today, Mr. Timble. Enjoy the sunshine. It will rain on the morrow. You have enough in the cellar to get you by for a few months. When I return, I will teach you to hunt for your family."

Dragon Squadron

After they finished their meal, Matt and Emily
Timble watched their new neighbor disappear into
the woods.

Chapter 25

Brett Elliot rang the doorbell at 3:45 am holding an aged bottle of scotch. Colonel Davies' wife Joan answered the door with a smile.

"Good morning, Brett." She showed the young pilot in. "He's in the kitchen drinking coffee."

"Thanks," Brett replied nervously.

"Morning, Brett!" Tom Davies smiled up from a cup of coffee at the kitchen table.

"Hey, sir," Brett's nervousness almost took over. "Um...what's with the rental truck outside?"

"Well, that's one of the favors I promised our friends," Tom explained.

"Oh, Okay." Brett looked around nervously. "So, where are we going? It must be ways from here if you had me pack an overnight bag."

"Correct you are. They are making you pilots smart these days," The colonel smiled. "We are going to Wyoming."

"I see." *Now we are getting somewhere.* "Cool. I guess we should do a map recon so we can switch off driving." Brett's excitement replaced his nervousness.

"You two need to get going. The sun will be up soon." Brett did not know if Joan was being motherly, or just trying to get rid of them. "I packed some sandwiches and snacks. Here, you each have a Thermos of coffee for the trip." The two Apache pilots were quickly out the door.

Nedloh spent the better part of the morning working on the radios of both the Messerschmitt and the *Dragon's Heart*. The young dwarf actually enjoyed the small spaces in the aircraft. His diminutive frame made him perfect for fitting in the tail boom or under the instrument panel.

He worked diligently and, aside from a few choice metaphors, he was silent. Amanda watched intently. She was standing by, willing to lend a hand wherever she could. Within hours, Ned and Amanda had both aircraft retrofitted and ready to go.

"I still dannot like you going up against those hell beasts with what we have," Buck argued with Conner as they walked across the hangar. "That hide is much thicker than what our guns can handle."

"Don't worry yourself, my stout little friend," Conner tried to calm his dwarf friend. "I've made a few friends and called in some favors. We're getting a few new toys to add to our bag of tricks. With a little magic, we will have no problem shooting those slimy perversions down." This seemed to work.

"I'll feel better when I know what's comin'."

"Don't worry. It's on its way and we should see it in a couple of days." Conner always knew that Buck had to have the last word. This was no different from any of the millions of times before.

"We'll see lad, we'll see."

Conner and Buck found themselves just outside the newly commissioned control room. Conner wanted to see where these monsters came from. He was hoping that he could get something from the tracking dart he left in the hide of one of the retreating foes.

Conner was still amazed at what Nedloh had done to the room. Every time he came to the room, something was added. This time, he noticed two world maps. One was part of a new conference table that showed the world countries, terrain and states backlit in the console. Ned had made the tabletop into a giant flat screen monitor that was covered in thick glass.

A large monitor also took up the back wall, displaying a similar map. Overlays marked different cities and various patterns of information as it became available to the center.

Conner concentrated on a red dot that was shown on the table. It glowed from what looked like the middle of Arizona.

"Is that my dart?" Conner asked Ardenelle, who had been monitoring the information.

"Yes, it is," Ardy replied. "The batteries just died in it, but it had been transmitting up 'til five minutes ago."

"Well, what do you know about it?"

"The last time this area came upon the government radar, the Senate approved a geological study, by the University of Kansas, of a gravitational anomaly in the area." Ardenelle waited for Conner's response but only got a raised eyebrow.

"Go on," Conner finally said after an awkward silence.

"Um, we do have a few of the reports that the team sent back to the University." Ardenelle handed a thick manila folder to Conner. Conner began to flip through the pages, skimming the information. After several seconds, he stopped. Buck watched curiously, as Conner almost dropped the report.

"What is it, lad?" Buck lead Conner to a leather chair around the table.

"It seems that not only did they find a major geological discovery, but a paleontological find as well," Conner handed Buck a small stack of papers that had black and white photos paper clipped to it.

"A dragon?" Buck looked at the photos in wide-eyed amazement. "It could just as easily be a new dinosaur, lad." Buck tried to put the elf at ease.

"No, look. The report stated that the bones were partially mummified and no fossilization had yet occurred. To top it all off, a piece of emerald green skin was found at the site."

"I'm sorry lad. The final resting place of a friend and comrade-in-arms should not have been desecrated. That is a sacred place."

"Well, we know where the idea for the Necrogulls came from," Conner swallowed back his grief. He had never known where Emorthra had laid. Conner knew of the task and sacrifice that the dragons had made to save the planet. All this time Conner had never had a chance to say good-bye to his Skymate. Now the bones of Emorthra were used to create an evil perversion that he soon would have to battle. Rage began to burn inside the elf. "Emorthra deserved better than that. I will see that whoever created these monsters atones for his actions."

"Now that we have decided that we are going to do something, we need to figure out what and when." Buck changed the subject.

"Right, we know where they are. We have to figure out who they are and what to do with them," Conner moved on, "Any suggestions?"

"We could launch an assault." Buck was pulling ideas from thin air.

"True." Conner liked it. "We need more info and lots of planning. Plus we need to wait for the goodies to get here."

"What goodies?" Buck was curious.

"I think you'll like what I have coming." Conner gave his dwarf friend a grin full of mischief.

"Here's an idea you may not like," Buck stopped and changed subjects again. "If we know where they are, what's ta say that they dannot know where we be. Have ya thought on that one, laddie?"

Terror flickered in Conner's eyes. Magic was involved, and Buck was right. They did know the location of this new evil. Who is to say that their enemy did not know or would soon find their location? This new line of thinking bothered Conner. He had much to consider.

"Okay, Buck, you could be right," Conner thought more deeply on the subject. "We have lived in the shelter of Estal for thousands of years. We need a plan in the case that shelter is breached. I'll have to think on it. In the meantime, we are going to need help. I think you need to send a message. Have it repeating on the homing beacon. Bring our kin home. Attach all that we know about it." Conner sighed, "I don't know if they will come in time, or if they'll come at all."

"Don't fret none, laddie," Buck reached up and placed his hand firmly on Conner's shoulders. "We ain't goin' down without a fight. That's if we go down at all." Buck's gesture and words were a great comfort to the elf.

"You betcha, Buck! You betcha!"

"So when do I get to try?" The young woman wanted to do what Isabelle was doing. Amanda had been spending more time with Maggie and Isabelle. She enjoyed time in the forest most.

"You have a slightly different gift, my child," Maggie tried to explain to the younger woman. "You may be able to wield the power as Isabelle, but it will not be nearly as strong. Your skill lies in a second sight."

"Oh!" Amanda did not even try to hide her disappointment.

"Now, Amanda, the *sight* comes to those not trained to use it in dreams," The young woman remembered the nightmare of the evil fish and the goblins. "But if we are relaxed and open to it, it can come to us while we are awake."

"What if we don't want to see it?" Amanda asked.

"Amanda, the sight is a very important gift," Maggie started to explain. "In these times, it would be beneficial to glimpse the future or see things that may give us information. This may be just what we need to defeat the evil that has been released. You may save the lives of your kind as well as elf and dwarf."

"I understand," Amanda was slowly beginning to see her piece of the puzzle fit in. She calmed herself as Maggie had told her. She sat on a large stone, made soft by thick green moss. With her eyes closed, she heard birds, insects and the music made by other magical creatures of the forest. She was able to feel their presence.

She was back in the city of Estal. Elves and dwarves hurried frantically about. Amanda could see the desperation in each of their faces. She turned around. Goblins! In another flash, she saw a human in an army flight suit. His smile was evil.

The young woman's eyes snapped open. Her heart raced as she tried to catch her breath. Cold sweat beaded upon her brow. She quickly looked around. Amanda jumped into Isabelle's arms as soon as she realized that she was no longer in the stone city. Amanda held on for dear life. Isabelle calmed her.

"What did you see?" The older woman asked.

"I saw the city being overrun with goblins." She burst into tears, as Amanda thought about the safety of Estal overtaken by the evil hordes. She had come all this way to find safety with the elves, and her vision told her that it would be short lived.

"The possible future you have seen may not come to pass," Maggie consoled the younger woman. "There are some things that we may prevent and others we cannot," The elf woman took both of Amanda's hands in her own. "With your gift, we may or may not be able to do this. Without it, we would definitely fail."

Amanda sat with renewed hope. She once again felt important. The young woman had something to offer in exchange for her safety. She often felt that her new friends only let her stay out of pity. Now she could be just as important to them as the elves and dwarves were to her. Maggie smiled as she read this revelation on the young woman's face.

"We will tell Conner when we return. Do not worry," Maggie calmed the young woman. "You are finished for today. Go and explore the forest. Make new friends. Do not wander far. You will know when it is time to leave."

Amanda's face changed as the little girl inside her smiled. For the first time since she had come to Estal, she had the chance to play and explore. The young woman immediately took the opportunity to catch up on her missing childhood. Amanda got up from the mossy rock, brushed off her blue jeans and was gone.

"It is good to see her smile again," Isabelle said.

"Yes. She needs a chance to play as children do," Maggie agreed. "She will be forced to grow up soon enough."

"Kids these days grow up too fast as it is," Isabelle continued. "I wish I had spent more time with my Hot Wheels."

"Did you not play with the Barbie Doll?" Maggie queried.

"I had them, but would rather play with cars and build models," Isabelle relished in her childhood. "I do remember receiving the '57 Chevy that you could get for the dolls for Christmas one year. As soon as I opened it, I ran off to my model sets and found a blower to glue on the hood. I painted it black and

put flames on it. I didn't care for the pink at all."
Maggie and Isabelle laughed long and hard.

"We have work to do." Maggie's laughter
changed to a business-like smile.

"I guess so." Isabelle knew the elf woman was
right. She had much to learn and it seemed that she
had little time left to study.

"There is much more to magic than moving
objects or making them disappear." Maggie jumped
in without losing a step. "Magic depends on life.
Life consists of beginning, middle, and end. We all
know there is magic in birth. We forget that magic
is with us when things grow. Magic provides growth
or helps growth in other ways. By simply opening
your mind to something new, you are growing.
Magic is very much a part of this."

"I can very much see the magic in birth, and now
I understand how magic affects our growth and
everyday life, but how can magic be a part of
something as horrible as death?" Isabelle was truly
stumped.

"That is not as difficult as it seems," Maggie
began to explain. "There are many ways that magic
is a part of death. When we pass from this world to
the next, according to our love for each other and
our accomplishments, our souls make a
wonderfully magical journey. If we have loved in
this life, we will be rewarded with eternal love in
the next. If we were bigoted and craved only money
and material possessions in this life, our souls will

be doomed to an eternity of anguish," Maggie continued her philosophy lesson. "Not only that, our loved ones we leave behind receive part of the magic that had been with us throughout our lives."

"How so?"

"Death is very painful for most, as a cut to the skin. When a wound opens, magic helps it to heal by the growth of new cells. These cells eventually close the wounds. The pain of the loss of a loved one is no different. We cannot see the wound, but we know it's there because we can feel the pain. When we lose a loved one, we must learn to accept the loss and move on with our own lives, to make them as prosperous as we can. This is growth also."

"But, how do we receive the magic of those who go before us?" Isabelle quietly asked.

"When we remember those we have loved and lost, their deeds and knowledge continue to live on. They continue to grow and flourish."

A light seemed to go on as this knowledge glowed inside her. Maggie saw it on her face. "I want you to practice listening to the forest. Tomorrow, I will ask you what it has said to you." Maggie got up, leaving the woman to herself and the forest.

Amanda began to wander through the mystical forest. It was hard for her to believe that up until a few weeks ago, she would not have been able to see the forest. After a short while, she found herself by a small brook. She found a place on a smooth stone on its banks. She sailed leaves in its gentle currents downstream. She wondered where it would end up. She began watching the little leaf-boat bouncing down the rapids and bumping into the stones that stuck out of the water.

She closed her eyes, and could easily see her boat as it danced its way downstream. It spun and rocked in the gentle current until a small branch reaching across the water caught the little leaf-boat in its twiggy fingers.

Her eyes snapped opened. She immediately jumped up and ran down stream looking for her little leaf boat. Across the brook, she found it. Her boat was in the grasp of the branch that she had seen in her mind's eye. It held gently, as the current washed under it. Amanda smiled; her gift was good after all. Moreover, if the tree wished to play with her boat, that was fine with her. There were many more leaves. She quietly walked back up to where she put it in the water.

Maggie walked through the forest giving great thought to what Amanda had seen. "*What you feel is correct, Magnethella.*" The familiar guiding voice told the elf woman. "*This is one of the things you cannot prevent.*"

"Why, Oracle, can we not stop this?" Maggie pleaded.

"*In order to appreciate and celebrate victory, one must know loss,*" Joy explained. "*I cannot tell you if you will succeed and become victorious overall. There are too many choices ahead. Some of you will choose unwisely. There will be consequences, but growth will happen. Mistakes will be opportunities from which to learn. One must fall in order to rise above and overcome. You cannot appreciate what you have unless you lose it. Nevertheless, remember this—what you gain will be greater than what you lose.*

"*You know it to be true. The world will never go back to the way it was. It will not be as it was in the days of the Riders, nor will it be as it was in the days of man. Both worlds have been propelled together. Some that are with you now will not be with you as victory is celebrated. Those that remain will be changed - even your leader.*"

"They are afraid. They do not show it but they fear the change that has come to the world." Maggie tried to help her human friends.

"*As are you,*" Joy made her aware.

"What do I have to be afraid of? I have seen changes like this before." Maggie argued.

"*You are afraid that you may not be able to stop disaster this time. You fear that your kin will not arrive in time to save this Earth,*" Joy countered. "*You are old and wise, yes. Even you, young elf are not as old as the Earth or Heavens. You too have room to grow. As the schoolteacher tutors her pupils, so must she continue to learn. For one day, her students may have a question that she may not be able to answer."*

As Maggie stared at the grass, she knew that Joy was right. The elf woman swallowed her pride and looked up. "Thank you for opening my eyes." The woman that had been standing there was gone. Maggie also had much to learn.

Amanda had seated herself once again next to the small stream. She continued sailing ships of leaves but no longer followed them with her gift.

"Hello!" Amanda was startled by a small voice. "It has been a while since a human has come to visit."

Amanda looked around only to see a badger sitting next to her on the bank of the stream. "Hello to you, badger!" Amanda quickly regained her composure and her heartbeat settled back into its normal rhythms.

"You may call me *Ms.* Badger if you don't mind; I would rather not be confused for a boy badger."

"I suppose not," Amanda giggled. "My name is Amanda."

"It is very nice to meet you, Amanda." The female badger reached out her paw. Amanda gently shook it.

"These are very odd woods, Ms. Badger."

"Why do you say that? Do badgers not talk where you come from?" the badger asked.

"Well, we see so few of them. Most simply run away. I suppose they may speak, but humans just don't take the time to listen."

"Maybe badgers, where you are from, don't have much to say."

"I think they would if they could. Mankind has taken a lot of the land in which they live." Amanda had remembered what she learned about endangered species from her science class.

"That's too bad. It would be better if we could all get along. Sometimes people can be greedy. So many people need a place to live also. I guess since they think they are on top of the food chain, they can do as they please without regard to anyone else's feelings."

"I don't think you have to worry about that anymore. A lot of mankind is dead." Amanda took a small twig and started playing with it.

"Did a forest fire wipe out their burrows?" Ms. Badger looked very concerned.

"We really didn't live in burrows. We lived in houses. But it wasn't a fire. It was kind of a sickness." Amanda tried to explain what she could of what had occurred in the past few weeks.

"I hope you are feeling all right dear."

"I am fine. An angel sent me to stay with the elves and dwarves." She began to break the twig into small pieces and toss them into the clear spring.

"Elves are wonderful people. I don't know much about the dwarves, but anyone who loves to dig and tunnel in the ground cannot be all bad." Amanda could almost see a smile on the little badger's face.

"They told me I had a gift."

"Yes, you do. You have a second sight."

"How do you know?" Amanda asked her little furry friend.

"Magical creatures, in magical forests have ways of knowing things that others do not." Ms. Badger explained.

"That makes sense," Amanda agreed. The young woman talked to the badger woman for quite some time.

"It's getting late. You should be getting back to your friends. Not all magic is good. After dark is not a good time to be in a wooded area such as this." the female badger explained.

"I guess you're right. It was very nice to meet you." Amanda told her new friend.

"Likewise, my dear."

"Will I ever see you again?" Amanda asked. She did not want to lose to a good new friend.

"I am here, this time, every day to get a drink from this brook." the badger explained.

"Good. When I return I will come here and look for you." Amanda got up and began to walk back to Isabelle and Maggie.

"Do come back soon." Ms. Badger waved as she watched her new friend walk toward the edge of the forest.

Maggie knew what she had to do. Soon they would have to leave the safety of Estal. The elf woman found herself deep within the forest. The trees were extremely tall and wide in girth. They grew fifteen stories or taller. Most of them were bigger around than a house. She missed the trees.

For thousands of years, elves called trees home. Trees had a kinship with the elves. The elves had asked the trees for shelter. In exchange for growing shelter for the elves high in their branches, elves sang songs and told them stories of those who could move around. They heard of heroes and legends. The trees always longed to move freely, but this was not The Creator's way. Therefore, the elves told them such stories.

"Your mothers and fathers have sheltered us in the past, my brothers and sisters." Maggie began to speak to the forest in the elfin tongue of old. "Yes, there were boy trees and girl trees. Some trees even chose to be both. Although very confusing at times, the elves accepted and loved the trees just the same."

"We are once again in need of shelter. The evil and those who are not pure of heart cannot see you. Will you loan us your branches to shelter the Earth's last hope?" Maggie waited for some time in

silence, but the trees tended to take their time responding to these kinds of matters.

"Elf, you are a friend to tree and leaf, but you ally yourselves with the dwarf and their axes." Maggie heard the whispering leaves reply.

"But they only cut and burn the dead wood, leaving room and sunlight for new growth," Maggie argued.

"This will be taken into consideration. Return tomorrow and you will have our final answer."

With that, Maggie turned and left. She had to return to Isabelle and Amanda. It was getting late.

Isabelle sat, hearing the whispering of the tree leaves and the rustling of grass blades. She calmed herself and let musical tunes of nature sweep over her. Soon, the gentle rhythm joined a stringed quartet of insects. The chirping was a wonderful addition to the orchestra. Soon after, the symphony had the bass of frogs added from a stream nearby. Isabelle was slowly engrossed by the melodic sounds surrounding her.

"*We know why you are here,*" a voice began to whisper to her from out of the music. It almost sang to her. *"Do not be afraid. We can guide you. Do not speak, just listen."* The voices were soothing. It calmed Isabelle from all the stresses that had built up over the weeks. *"That is good. Give us your worries and frets. Your stresses will blow away on the summer breezes, as do our voices. We have been sent to calm you. We are guided to free your troubled heart from that which clouds your mind and judgment."* Isabelle sat entranced by Mother Nature's opera.

As she sat listening, Isabelle did feel as if a dreadful weight lifted from her shoulders. In a few moments of attention, and actually hearing what nature had to say, she sensed a freedom in her soul that she never before felt. It was like looking through a dirty window to the world that diligently cleansed itself.

"For now, we see through a glass darkly..." This had passed. An era of cleansing was part of her awakening.

For the first time, Isabelle was truly seeing her place in the new world. Fear and anticipation slowly dissolved and replaced themselves with courage and enthusiasm to take on whatever challenges that could come her way. Like a wave washing the sands of a beach clean, Isabelle felt nature's song washing her soul clean. She actually felt crisp and whole. A smile grew on her face. Joy, the heavenly messenger, seemed to kindle warmth deep inside.

"Hey, are we ready to head back?" Isabelle came back to Earth by Amanda's voice. The crispness of a clean soul and joy remained, burning deep within the older woman.

"Yeah, I guess it is getting late." Isabelle looked at the younger woman. She seemed to stare, as the younger woman looked more vibrant. To Isabelle, it seemed like a difference between black and white television and high definition.

"Are you okay, Izzy?" Amanda asked.

"Yeah, actually I've never felt better."

"It's amazing how an afternoon in the fresh air can change a person," Amanda said, hinting at her own experiences.

"You'll have to tell me all about it when we get back." Isabelle was almost glowing.

"Oh, I will. You too..."

"Are we ready to head back, ladies?" Maggie came out of the brush in a different light as well.

"We were waiting on you." the women said almost simultaneously. Maggie smiled. She whistled and the elfin steeds returned from their unseen pastures. They mounted and trotted off back to Estal. All three women knew that their time in the forest today had been spiritual. It was unspoken but known by all. They spent their return trip in silence.

Chapter 26

The drive was long and boring from Newport News to Wyoming. Colonel Davies kept off the major highways to avoid looters and robbers. It was definitely a difficult time for the world. It had shown in the evidence of crime and destruction in the major cities. The closer they got to a metropolis, the more burned out cars, bodies and other signs of violence appeared.

Brett was very surprised how well the small towns pulled together and kept their own order. When they drove through one, they saw that shops were open as merchants continued trying to make a living. With all the death and violence, Brett was astonished by how small-town America had picked up and continued on with their lives. Most of his crew chiefs came from these towns. They were extremely hard workers. Brett had a strong conviction that all aircraft maintained by his crews would always be safe in the skies.

It was safer when they only traveled during the day. When they had to stop for the night, Colonel Davies would stop just outside of the town. With

Brett standing guard on the front of the truck with an M16, the colonel would bring out two cases of Meals Ready to Eat [M.R.E.]. They were not Brett's first choice in the field, but when you had nothing else, you could almost make a gourmet meal out of them. If not, the tiny bottle of Tabasco would kill the flavor of anything offensive or bland inside.

After they put the two boxes of M.R.E.s in the front of the truck, they continued into town. They would trade the food for a room and the security of the truck. When times were hard, people grabbed what food they could get. Brett and the colonel had no problems with the bargain. Many asked about the contents of the truck. Colonel Davies made sure that it all appreciated that the contents were a private matter. On more than one occasion, rounds from the M16 fired.

On the fifth day of their travels, Colonel Davies began to slow down in the middle of nowhere. Brett noticed a small green sign with an airplane stenciled on it. *This must be the place.* The Colonel smiled. He signaled and turned right onto a long private drive.

Conner, Isabelle, and Buck had been working all morning on *Amy*. Both Buck and Conner were impressed with Isabelle's skill and talent for aircraft restoration.

"I'm still not sure 'bout the color, lass," Buck commented.

"Well, if you wanted a different color, you should have had overhauled her yourself," Isabelle replied smartly.

"Ouch." Conner stifled a laugh. He looked up to see Nedloh running across the hangar floor.

"Hey, Conner!" Nedloh yelled. His voice rang in the enormous hangar. "We have company. Do we need to call to arms?"

"That won't be necessary, Ned," Conner told Nedloh as he jogged up to the Corsair panting. "I did not expect them 'til tomorrow, though."

Conner and Buck both hopped off the wing and started toward the open hangar doors. "You are puttin' far too much trust in strangers, laddie," Buck warned as they headed toward the massive doors.

"You could be right, but Colonel Davies is an honorable and trustworthy man," Conner countered.

"He'd be a fool to come all this way, alone. His friends may not be as honorable," Buck continued.

Conner knew that the dwarf was right. It was better to be cautious than to be caught with one's trousers down. Conner whistled. Four elves and three dwarves appeared with side arms. There were two shotguns and five nine-millimeter Berettas between then.

The dwarves and their elfin brothers took positions around the truck as it led them into the hangar. The rental truck stopped just inside the door. Colonel Davies was the first to exit the vehicle with his hands held up. Brett followed suit.

"Is this how you greet a friend?" Davies asked.

"One can't be too careful these days," Conner replied with a smile. The weapons were lowered and the two shook hands like old war buddies. "Good to see you again, my friend."

"Likewise," Colonel Davies returned. "We have come bearing gifts."

"You don't say?" Conner smiled. "You two must be tired and hungry. Be our guests. Dine with us."

"We could use a bite to eat and a nap before we leave," The Colonel agreed. They walked across the hangar together. The armed guards disappeared, and returned to their previous activities. "Although, it is quite an operation you have, this isn't quite what I expected."

"Don't worry, Tom. You haven't seen anything yet," Conner only smiled as he led them to the tower elevator. "Tomorrow I will give you a tour of the hangar if you'd like."

"That would be great," Brett piped up. He was so excited; he almost forgot what he came here for. "I hope you don't mind, I brought you all a little something for saving our butts over DC." Brett handed Conner the aged bottle of liquor as they reached the elevator door and stepped in.

"Twenty-year-old scotch? This is a hard find in these times!" Conner said as he read the label.

"Maybe your friends aren't so bad after all, laddie." Buck snatched the bottle from Conner's eyes.

"Down?" Tom Davies noticed Conner's finger on the button and was extremely curious.

"We have many secrets that have kept us safe over the centuries." Conner tried to explain.

"How long have you people been on this land?" Tom was flabbergasted.

"Well, that's a long tale that should be shared over a good meal," Conner smiled.

"What is this place?" Brett was aghast as the doors opened up onto the city.

"My friends, welcome to Estal!" Conner led them down the steps and into the main courtyard. "Buck and a small guard will show you around. The meal will be ready within the hour. Please enjoy our hospitality." Buck gave Conner a scornful eye. He could not wait to get his hands on the bottle of scotch.

"You brought them here; you should be their tour guide," Buck told Conner under his breath.

"I have a bad feeling. I am going to check on something. Keep an eye on the young one." Conner told the dwarf brother in the stone language of the dwarves.

"Him? With gifts like this, he can't be all that bad." Buck replied.

"Just watch him." Conner left.

Isabelle joined Conner and his guests for dinner. She was dressed in jeans and black silk blouse.

"Have we met before, Miss Thompson?" Brett asked as the platters of food were offered.

"Actually, I crewed your bird in Germany," Isabelle said scornfully.

"Yes, I remember. It was Illeshiem, correct? B-Troop?"

"Yes, sir. Mr. Elliot. I was a crew chief in Shock Troop. If I remember right, you threw a fit because you didn't want your bird crewed by a woman!" Brett Elliot suddenly felt uncomfortable at the unpleasant memory.

"That bird was a piece." Brett shot back.

"I find that hard to believe, lass," Buck stuck up for one of his best mechanics.

"That's okay, Buck, I can handle an ass. This time, I don't have to worry about rank." Isabelle gave a grin that would have made a piranha jealous. "That was the best bird in the fleet. She just always seemed to dance when you wanted to fly her. You ever wonder why you scored so high at gunnery?" Isabelle did not wait for a reply. "I spent the weekend before on rotor smoothing so your sorry ass could shoot straight." Brett seemed to cower before the woman.

"I see we have some history." Conner tried to douse the fire.

"One-hundred-and-ninety-one accident- and incident-free hours with that bird—she shot best out of the entire fleet at gunnery. I have that award to prove it!" Isabelle felt relieved. That had been something she had been holding onto for years.

"Now, shall we eat, Brett?" she spat his name out like poison.

"I hear you are great with a wrench," Tom Davies tried to change the subject. "Actually, I had heard of you a few years back. I am sorry I didn't have the fortune of serving with you."

"Likewise, sir. You seem to be an honorable man. I would have been proud to serve under you, Colonel, sir."

"Just Tom, please..." Davies smiled. "You have done your time, and we're not here in an official capacity. In fact, no one but my wife knows we are here. To the rest of my chain, Brett and I are fishing off the coast."

"Tell us about the city." Brett grew tired of waiting.

"Uh, sure." Conner was not quite ready to tell the tale.

"It all started about four-thousand years ago..." Conner's guests were instantly intrigued as he began.

They shared tales and went through many pitchers of dwarf ale. They shared stories until early morning. The humans were amazed to hear the tales of elves and dwarves and the magic that had been released.

"I can't believe that this magic stuff is real," Brett argued.

"You always were a jerk, Elliot." Isabelle stared intently at Brett's mug resting on the table. With a thought, the mug floated into the air and emptied its contents onto the Apache pilot's head.

"I hope that's proof enough for you," Conner said as everyone had a laugh at Brett's expense.

"If you'll excuse me, I think I am ready for bed. Conner motioned for one of the elf women who had been serving Conner and his guests.

"Show these gentlemen to their rooms," Conner motioned the woman close and said something that no one else could hear. "Make sure they have everything they need," Conner said once again out loud. "And gentlemen, you are guests here. Please do not wander around. It's a big place. We wouldn't want you getting lost." With that, the men were led to their rooms.

"So, what do you think of our friends?" Conner asked Isabelle and Buck.

"Any man that can afford twenty-year-old scotch can't be all that bad," Buck said as he poured himself another drink from the aged bottle.

"Davies seems like a great guy, but I have never trusted Elliot. I worked with him a long time. Conner, watch your back. He's a snake. He is only out for himself. The booze only says that he wants something." Isabelle was firm in her opinion.

"I agree with you on all points. I like Davies. He is pure of heart. He is a great ally. I will have my eye on the other." Conner agreed.

"Is it really smart letting him down here? And what do they have in the truck, me lad?" Buck asked.

"Don't worry my friend. Their rooms will have a guard posted in the corridor," Conner calmed his dwarf friend. "The truck was unloaded while we dined. You can begin installing upgraded weapons tomorrow. I also want the new ammo loaded into all the planes. Get them ready."

"What new ammo and weapons?" Buck was as giddy as a schoolchild.

"For starters, I have a Vulcan cannon for the Griffon Claw and depleted uranium rounds for the rest of the fighters. This is only the first delivery." Conner explained. A twinkle lit in Buck's eye. The dwarf could not wait to play with his new toys.

"Conner, I know it's not my place, but I think you should put a tail on them for their return trip," Isabelle suggested.

"That would not be very trustworthy," Conner answered.

"Do you want to be trusted as much as you want to be safe?" Isabelle asked the elf. "Besides, wouldn't an elf be able to follow without being seen?"

"You have two good points. I will make it happen." With that, Isabelle went off to bed leaving the elf and dwarf to talk.

"So what do you think of our new friends?" Davies asked his fellow pilot.

"I think this magic stuff is a load," Brett told the Colonel. He played it off. Brett knew better. The magic that Isabelle showed explained a lot. He now knew how the old man got into his cell and how the ten-year-old bottle of booze became twenty.

"I don't know where these 'Gull things came from nor their ugly riders, but I think these guys can help," Tom was sure of it. "This place does feel safe. I feel calm like I haven't felt since all this started. The salvation of our people rests here."

"That's just the scotch talking. Twenty years of aging can make you feel warm and fuzzy," Brett said with distaste. "I think I am going to turn in." With that, he went through the door adjoining the rooms and went to bed. Tomorrow he could get a better look around for the old man.

The next morning Tom Davies was awakened by a knock at the door. "Conner asked me to invite you to breakfast, sir." Isabelle was standing there in a purple flight suit.

"That would be great. We'll be ready in about half an hour." Tom told the Isabelle.

"I'll be back for you then. Make sure your friend is ready." Isabelle turned and left.

"She is such a witch," Brett said through the adjoining door. He was already showered and dressed in civilian attire.

"You were being an ass and she called you on it. That's why you don't like her. I think she will be important to human and elf relations."

"Elf, dwarf, whatever..." Brett went back into his room to let his commanding officer get dressed.

Isabelle returned as promised to escort their new friends to breakfast. As they went, she showed them a few of the finer points of Estal. She felt like she had been there all her life. It was hard to believe that she had only arrived a month ago. *Had it been that long already? Where did the time go?*

"So, how did you find yourself here, Ms. Thompson?" Tom asked.

"I found my way here just before the virus hit, and you don't have to be so formal. My friends call me Izzy."

"Likewise Izzy, please call me Tom."

"I was drawn to this place. I couldn't get a decent job after the service. I guess Kansas City doesn't have much use for a female airframe and power mechanic. So, I packed up my old Chevy and started driving and here is where I wound up." Isabelle explained.

"So how do did you do that trick, Izzy," Brett asked.

"First off, it was no trick. Second, you can call me Ms. Thompson." Isabelle corrected.

Before long, the trio had arrived at one of Estal's outdoor-style cafes. "Good morning gentlemen. I hope you slept well." Conner sat behind a cup of coffee, smiling.

"We slept like babies." Tom Davies did not give his fellow pilot a chance to open his mouth. Brett Elliot took the hint and said nothing.

"Good to hear. Coffee?" Conner offered.

"That would be great," Tom said as the two sat down. Tom took everything in stride. The night before he had discovered that most of the fairytales he had read as a child had some truth to them. He had learned that there were ten dwarves with Snow White and no poisoned apple. He handled it very well. Magic answered many questions. Being a Colonel in the United States Army, he tried to find it hard to believe. It was just too hard not to.

"Sorry guys. I have to get to work. I need to help Ned and Buck before I go for a ride this afternoon with Maggie." Isabelle excused herself from the testosterone fest.

"Are you sure you can't stay?" Conner knew she had to go but tried to be polite.

"No, boss. I gotta get crackin'." Isabelle smiled and left.

"You didn't tell me she works for you," Elliot said.

"You didn't ask. You let the greatest mechanic in aviation go, so I snatched her up." Conner was most proud of her.

"She's not bad looking either," Brett said as he watched her walk away.

"Out of your league, chopper boy," Conner laughed. "Besides, I don't think you made a very good first impression."

After breakfast, Conner took his guests back up top for a tour of the flying museum in the hangar. Colonel Davies was fascinated by the military history surrounding them. As always, the P40 drew the most attention. As usual, Conner proudly showed off his favorite plane in the collection.

"You kept the pilot's name, I see," Tom noticed.

"Of course, I did. It was mine," Conner explained. "You see, with your government, I had to pretend to be dead for a while then resurface with a new identity. That's the price for being an elf. I guess with no more government, I no longer have to worry about it."

"True," Tom said. "What are we going to do about that?"

"First, we have to stop the threat, whoever he is," Conner answered. "And after this threat is over, maybe we can reassess the situation; see who remains, and start over."

"I always thought the end of the world would happen with nukes. This is just too weird." Brett tried to join the conversation.

"One end is another beginning. It is a continuing circle, Brett. This is far from over," Conner explained. "We will pick ourselves up, dust ourselves off, and begin again."

Brett did not like Conner's philosophy. He decided to wander around on his own.

"So, you put this scrap heap together yourself?" Brett wandered over to the Corsair. He could not help but be attracted to the bright amethyst fighter.

"I beg your pardon," Isabelle shouted from underneath the fighter as she was loading the armor-piercing rounds. "This *heap* will do 475 miles per hour without so much as a vibration. I'll take it up against that whirly bird of yours any day."

"Do you fly, Izz... I mean Ms. Thompson?" Brett asked.

"Yes, that is one of the hobbies I have taken up since I've been here." Isabelle shot back.

"You know, if you are ever on the east coast, maybe we could have dinner sometime." Brett could not help saying as he watched only the bottom half of her flight suit on the hangar floor.

"You know, Elliot, just because I am having a conversation with you, does not mean that I wish to have your babies. I would be happy to answer any questions, but let's keep this professional."

"You were always like that." Brett reminded her.

"And I always will be. I never dated up the chain of command, or in this case beneath me." Isabelle did not like where this was going. Once before, Brett had tried to take advantage of her when she had first arrived in Germany. She was alone and thought he was just being nice. Then there was the night when he would not leave her barracks room. She tried to report the harassment, but no one believed her. This was a common thing in the military. It was also the reason that she did not reenlist.

"Sounds like you have someone else who spins your blades," Brett continued taking shots. "Funny thing is I don't see any nice human guys to choose from. Maybe you have a thing for midgets." Brett had an evil grin.

"What I do with my personal life is my business, and they are dwarves, not midgets," Isabelle was doing all she could to keep control. "And, Mr. Elliot, if you wish to continue to have a personal life for yourself, I suggest you walk away." Isabelle had come up from under the fighter to stand directly behind the Apache pilot.

"And if I don't?" Brett turned around pinning the woman against the plane.

"If you don't, I will make a little wish and you won't have anything but a hole that will connect your bladder to the outside world," Isabelle looked him straight in the eyes.

"There is no way you would be able to do anything like that." Brett tried to call her bluff.

"Wanna try me?" Isabelle smiled. "Your *tighty whities* could have a whole lot more room." Brett swallowed hard and walked away.

"Are you okay, Izzy?" Nedloh had heard most of the commotion. Brett did not see him in the ammo bay reworking the uploading assist.

"Yeah, I think I am," Isabelle looked relieved. "I think I like being able to use magic. It's kind of like having a big stick. You don't necessarily have to use it if others see that you can." Isabelle smiled and went back to her work.

"I really enjoyed the tour," Colonel Davies told his host. "Your hospitality has been wonderful."

"We have enjoyed having you," Conner added to the pleasantries.

"And thanks for the new toys, Colonel," Buck added. The smile had not left his face all day.

"Don't worry, Master Dwarf, you shall receive more in the future," Davies assured the stout little man, "I do plan on coming back to this marvelous place again. Maybe I'll buy some land down the road and retire."

"Colonel Davies," Conner took the elder man's hand and looked him in the eyes. "You are pure of heart and a natural leader. You are now a friend to elf and dwarf. You are welcome here always."

"I really enjoyed the tour." Brett hoped for a return invitation.

"Mr. Elliot, I wish things had gone better for your stay," Conner tried not hurting the man's feelings. "My employees are like my family. You scorn them, you scorn me. I hope that I may be able to fly with you again soon." Brett Elliot knew what Conner had said. Conner had wished no ill will toward him, but at the same time offered no further hospitality.

"I think we will be headed back. Our fishing trip is almost over. Joan, my wife, is probably missing me and we have to think up stories about the one that got away." Tom Davies chuckled as they loaded back up in the rental truck.

The two army pilots drove past the wind turbines. Both were quiet for the moment, not knowing what to think about the past events. Elves, dwarves, and magic; it was all very confusing for the both of them. Brett knew that Conner and his little group of elves and dwarves were weak. The old man was far stronger than any parlor tricks that Isabelle could do. As they drove away, neither of the pilots noticed the eyes following them. There was no cloud of dust nor were there any visual signs in their mirrors.

"What was that all about, Izzy?" Conner was upset at Isabelle for being rude to his guests. He also understood that there were ill feelings between Brett Elliot and his best mechanic.

"It's in the past. I really don't want to talk about it." Isabelle tried to end the conversation.

"Look, our allies are very few. As a matter of fact, they are the only ones we have." Conner would not let it end without an explanation.

"Okay, do you want to know what happened?" Isabelle gave in. Weariness washed over her as she leaned against *Amy*. "When I got to my first duty station in Germany, I was the only female mechanic. I spent a month in a maintenance troop before I was sent to a line unit. In the line unit, I was made a crew chief and assigned my own bird.

"The front seater, also known as the gunner, was Elliot. He was just a warrant officer then. We talked a lot and he was very nice to me. I thought he was kind of cute. I thought he was trying to welcome me into the family.

"One night he stopped by my room. He had a few beers with him so I invited him in. After a couple, he decided that he would try to get into my pants. I thought of him no more than a friend or brother. He was an officer. I was enlisted. He was a very persistent officer. He wouldn't take *no* for an answer. After he ripped one of my best shirts, I lost my head. Luckily, a half-empty beer bottle was within reach. I broke it over his left eye, knocked him out, and drag him down the hall and propped him up against the bathroom door. No one paid attention to him. There were always people passed out in the halls on Friday night. Heck, it was Germany. They invented beer."

Conner could see the tears well up in Isabelle's eyes. "Did you report it?"

"Yes I did," Tears flowed. "Elliot paid someone to lie for him. Since no one remembered seeing him in the hall, I didn't have any witnesses, and he had an alibi." Conner put his arms around Isabelle and pulled her close. What was happening? He tried very hard to keep himself apart from this one. This human woman was drawing him in. Before, he had been with women for fear of loneliness or boredom. This one had his heart.

Isabelle felt secure in his arms, like being cradled in a warm comfortable blanket. It felt like the warm sun on a cool spring morning. It warmed her from within. Nations would be born and fall. It did not matter. This feeling he had for her, here and now; this was what life was about. This small measurement of time, this was what was worth fighting for.

Chapter 27

Tom Davies read quietly on his twin bed. The hotel was cozy but clean. He bartered for two singles, but could only get a double room. He had no problem sharing with Brett. The M.R.E.'s were getting old. There were a lot of others doing without, so he was glad to have them. He also would be happy when he got home to Joan and a home cooked meal.

The drive had been long and tedious. It was the first of many, Tom felt. He just wanted to unwind. Brett, on the other hand, paced the room like a caged tiger. He could not stand still. There was no more television, and the younger pilot was not much for reading. "I'm going for a walk. I need to get out."

"Be careful out there." Tom would prefer to have his friend stay in, but he knew he could not keep him. Brett was a grown man with military survival training. He could handle himself.

"I'll be back in a bit," Brett said as he closed the door behind him.

The young pilot did not know what to think. The world had changed so much. Things he had thought were only fairytales were true. He did know one thing. The elves and dwarves did not have a chance against the old man. They did not know what kind of foe they faced. He was glad he was on a side where he could potentially be in a position of power. If he played his cards right, the old man would see to that.

"What did you learn?" The old man appeared from behind a darkened street lamp. "Do you know where my adversary is?"

"Yes, I found out what you wanted." Brett knew that all he could ever want was about to happen, although the old man made him uneasy. Brett told him about the stone city under the hangar. He spared no detail. The old man sat intrigued. A crooked smile grew on the magician's face. As the magician heard the words, he formulated a plan.

"You serve me well. I will grant your request for riches and power." the old man promised.

"Thank you, kind sir." Brett felt that *Easy Street* was just around the corner.

"You must stay where you are at the moment. You may be needed for further updates. If need be, you will be altered to serve my purpose."

"As long as you hold up your end of the bargain, I will do whatever you ask," Brett confirmed. He knew he was getting himself in further with each passing moment.

"When you arrive back in Virginia tomorrow, you will be dropped off at your residence. I am sure you will find it acceptable," The old man told him. "But remember: if you fail or cross me in any way, no one will save you. You now belong to me." The old man turned and disappeared into the darkness. Brett felt a growing unease.

Buck sat in the hangar surrounded by olive drab wooden crates. Their sizes varied. With a crowbar, almost as long as he was tall, the dwarf tore into the largest. It stood as tall as he and was twice as long. His muscles barely strained as his stout arms pried the top off the crate. Wood creaked as the nails that held the box together let go. The dwarf's eyes lit up as he saw what lay inside.

He moved molded foam from the top to reveal a large Vulcan cannon. An evil grin grew across his face. A twinkle sparkled in his eye. He could not wait until he opened the rest of the wooden crates.

As Nedloh walked across the hangar, he heard his uncle giggling with glee amongst several wooden crates. "What's up, Buck?" chewing on a carrot, Nedloh asked as he approached the pile of opened crates. His eyes bulged as he saw the contents. "Are these from our new friends?"

"Aye! That they are, m'lad!" Buck confirmed. "Conner said that we'd be getting some things to help us, but I didn't think they would be this good."

"This would be great on the top turret of the *Griffon Claw*," Nedloh suggested.

"I was thinking the same thing, lad. We have ammo and tracking computers." Buck informed him.

"Computers?" Nedloh began to smile. "Can I play?"

"I insist."

"Well, I hope you approve," Conner said from behind.

"How did you pull this off, lad?" Buck asked the elf. The dwarf looked Conner in the eyes and stroked his beard.

"The world is changing, my friend. The humans need all the help they can get, even if it means bending their own rules." Conner told the older dwarf.

"You used that elf charm-thingy again, didn't you?" Isabelle joined in as she followed Conner.

"Every little bit helps." Conner shot back a mischievous smile.

"Oh, my!" Isabelle finally saw what had been in the crates. "I think we could mount the Hell Fire missiles in the bomb bay of the *Griffon Claw*."

"I was thinking we could mount them to the bellies of the fighters," Conner suggested.

"Good idea in theory, but they would rip the pylons off during launch." Isabelle countered.

"Point taken," Conner replied. "I'm glad we have someone here with experience," Conner turned to the dwarves. "How long would it take to get them installed?"

"With this lass's help? A day, maybe two." Buck looked thoughtfully at the woman.

"I'd be happy to help," Isabelle smiled. "You know, Conner, if we could get some Stingers, I think we could manage to mount those under the wings," Isabelle suggested. "It would do the same thing and be a little lighter. They don't have the same punch, but would be more effective in air-to-air combat."

Conner gave this some thought. "I'll see what I can do. This is just the first gift from the military we will be getting."

Isabelle cocked an eyebrow. "We're getting more?" she inquired.

"Colonel Davies promised ammunition as well. We are going to need something in our 50-cals to punch through that armor of those creatures. We have some already in this shipment, but I am afraid that we are going to need a lot more." Conner said.

"Great, I am in the army all over again." Isabelle's sarcasm was blatant as she walked away.

"It's not like that, Izzy." Conner followed. "This is not a volunteer situation. Evil is loose in this world and it's up to us to stop it." Conner gently grabbed the woman's arm and turned her around to look her in the eyes.

"I know. It's just so hard with everything that has happened all at once!" Tears began to flow down Isabelle's cheek.

"Hey, it's okay. You are not alone. Remember, Izzy, you and Amanda are lucky to be here. Kind of like that insurance commercial; you are in good hands!" Conner tried to calm the woman.

"I know, it's just all the others who are not here. What has the rest of the world come to? Does Kansas City still exist? What about my parents? Are they alive or dead? There is so much we don't know." Isabelle was sobbing now.

"You know what? You still need some flight time as well as a few more lessons in magic. How about tomorrow we do a bit of both. Let's take a trip to KC and see what's up. Maybe we can find your parents. If we can find them, we will come back for them in the *Griffon Claw*. You can learn how to fly something a bit bigger."

"Okay. I think I'd like that." Isabelle sniffed and wiped her eyes. "I think I should help Buck and Ned get the new hardware installed."

"Are you sure?" Conner asked with concern.

"I need to get my mind off things and work is a good way to do it."

"Okay, but don't get too worked up. Take it easy. Would you join me for dinner later?" Conner gave her a half smile.

"Now you're using that elf charm-thingy again." She smiled. "I don't think that works anymore."

"That depends if you join me or not." The elf grinned.

"All you have to do is ask." she said.

"I just did and I didn't use my charming spell." Conner walked toward the makeshift command room as Isabelle went back to work with the dwarves.

Isabelle met Conner at one of the outdoor-style cafes for the evening meal. She was excited about spending time with the elf. The woman had never felt so close to anyone. It was strange to her, especially in such a short time.

Isabelle and Conner both ordered a salad. The only difference between the two meals was that Isabelle requested fried chicken strips with honey mustard dressing. Conner ate his plain. "I know this isn't quite the dinner that we are used to, but I hope you like it."

"No, this is nice. I like the ambiance," Isabelle was once again envious. "Those weapons upgrades are coming along well."

"That's good to hear," Conner sat stirring his lettuce. "Izzy, I know I have made it more that perfectly clear that I need your help. I just want you to know that you are also under our protection." A grim look of concern came over the elf's face.

Isabelle picked up his stern tone. "I know. I don't know where I would be if I hadn't found you and this place."

"You didn't find us, Isabelle. You were brought here. When will you realize this?" Conner pleaded. "Like I said earlier, tomorrow we will go check on Kansas City. Maybe we can hear the word of your parents." Isabelle became quiet. She did not know what to expect. Neither of them did.

Conner taught Isabelle the words that slowed time. Even though only seconds passed for the rest of the world, the two pilots spent several hours in their small planes. Isabelle took, this time, to read up on elfin history and work on the vocabulary of ancient words. She let *Amy* do the flying. She also thought deeply about what Conner said the previous night.

No matter what she faced, she could not get past the idea of being in a fairytale. The surreal feelings that she had would not go away. Amanda was an anchor for her, but it only had a thin rope. The friendships she had made were indestructible, almost too good to be true. "Maybe you are thinking too much on this." She heard *Amy's* too perfect female voice tell her.

"I didn't realize I was talking out loud," Isabelle told the artificial intelligence device that Ned had installed.

"You weren't." The box on the gauge panel answered. "Remember that I was designed to read the thoughts of my pilot as well."

"I appreciate your concern, but I wish you wouldn't unless I ask."

"I'm sorry," the plane's personality answered. "It must be difficult for you to get used to the nuances of the magic and technology."

"It is," Isabelle admitted.

"Remember, it may be hard to adjust, but you will miss them if they ever leave you."

"I guess you are right," Isabelle had received another realization. "Thanks, Amy, that's food for thought. I guess I'll be able to wrap my mind around it eventually."

"Sure you will, Izzy," Isabelle could almost feel a smile coming from the voice in front of her. "Besides, what are girlfriends for?" Isabelle smiled in return.

"Dragon-two, this is Lead," Conner's voice interrupted the conversation.

"Lead, this is Two. I copy," Isabelle responded appropriately.

"Revert to real time on my mark... three, two, and mark." On Conner's mark, Isabelle spoke the words that he had taught her. She rippled back into normal time a fraction of a second after the P40.

Isabelle was amazed at the devastation that she saw as she looped the downtown airport. It looked as if World War III had settled into Kansas City. She could see burned out warehouses along Burlington Street that ran parallel with the runway. She could also see abandoned lofts and apartment buildings downtown. Smashed buildings and burned out husks of cars that she could no longer recognize also littered the streets.

"I get no answer from the tower," The elf told his wingman. "I guess there is no one home. Izzy, you go in first and taxi over to the Executive Beechcraft building."

"Roger that, Lead," Isabelle confirmed.

"Just stay in the cockpit and keep your sidearm handy," Conner instructed.

Isabelle was amazed when Conner had given her a nickel-plated .45 caliber handgun. She checked the Colt in its shoulder holster as she slid the canopy back and waited for Conner.

It was not long before the P40 taxied up next to the gull-winged Corsair. Isabelle stepped out as Conner shut down.

"It looks like World War III happened here," Isabelle commented.

"Well, this *could* be part of it. There are always civilian casualties. It looks like they paid the highest price," Conner looked around with his hand on his sidearm. The elf believed that they should always be protected. In the days of old, he would have carried his bow and quiver and his elegant elfin blade. In this twenty-first century, the blade and bow had been replaced with his Leatherman utility tool and a .50 caliber Desert Eagle pistol in his hip holster. "Stay close. We have no idea what we are in for."

Conner said as he grabbed a small digital camera. The two set out through the gates.

Isabelle stopped just past the gates and turned around to look at the planes. "*Tedium silent.*" The two fighters shimmered into nothing.

"An invisibility spell. I am impressed. You are a powerful magic user. You may even make a fair sorceress someday." Conner smiled.

"I am learning. I have been studying in the library in my spare time." Isabelle beamed with pride.

"Since when do you have spare time?" Conner asked.

"You're not the only one who can bend time," Isabelle smiled as they walked down the street.

"Maggie has taught you well." Conner was more than impressed. The only thing that would make her more powerful would be a dragon. He knew that would not happen anytime soon.

They walked down the street to the north. They passed several burned out warehouses. He could still read the *Apache Belt and Hose Company* on one of them. A fluttering thought of irony passed through him... thoughts of Colonel Davies and Brett slipped by.

They walked toward North Kansas City, past the *Save-A-Lot* grocery. Both Conner and Isabelle were surprised that looters had not emptied the store. With no power, they pushed through the automatic doors. There had been people shopping at the time the virus had struck. There were a few bodies up and down the aisles. Even though Isabelle had been in the military, she had never smelled death. Conner, in his infinite years, had smelled it plenty of times. "Maybe you should wait outside." the elf suggested. After a nose full of rotting flesh that made the woman's stomach heave, she easily agreed.

Conner continued through the store alone. He quickly traversed the aisles, stopping to pick a few items from the shelves that might make a snack or meal later. He stuffed them into his backpack. As he rounded the paper goods aisle, he found a source of the heavy and rancid odor. A young man lay dead. Conner found part of his face and right arm grotesquely enlarged. The elf took out his digital camera and began to snap a few shots. Muscles of the jaw and arms had quickly enlarged causing disfiguring stretch marks. In some places, the skin split apart.

Conner left the man and found what looked like a woman in the pet aisle, her entire body grossly mutated. The only thing that indicated the gender of the human lying on the tile floor were ripped shreds of pink and purple fabric draped loosely across the hulking shape. *Who would have done this? No one should die like this...* Conner thought to himself as he took notes and photographs of the misshapen woman. He put away his notepad and returned to Isabelle waiting outside.

"Well, what do you think?" Isabelle was waiting on the hood of a new Jeep Grand Cherokee.

"Whoever did this showed no mercy. It also looks like the virus affected people differently." Conner tried to explain without getting too graphic.

"I kind of saw it when I went to find us a ride. There is something extremely wrong. At first, I thought it had to do with the virus and the decomposition. I soon realized that these people had been changed," Isabelle told the elf what she had noticed. "Do you think this was created in some evil lab somewhere?"

"No. The tissue growth happened too fast. Magic is involved here," Conner explained. "Someone really wanted to either totally wipe out mankind or alter them to their own design."

"I guess that makes sense," Isabelle decided. "I feel like I am in some kind of warped science fiction movie. This is getting extremely weird." They climbed into the Jeep with Isabelle at the wheel.

"Hey, where did you get this?" Conner asked.

"Oh, this... I borrowed it from the dealership across the street. I figured no one else would need it. There is no one out here," Isabelle explained. "I did have to step over a dead salesman to get the keys."

"Was he changed too?" Conner queried.

"Um, yeah..." the woman answered. "It was extremely gross," Isabelle remembered the hulking mass of flesh on the floor of the showroom. Bodies had littered the dealership here and there. They had dropped when the virus hit. It was obvious that the changes were instantaneous.

"We should be careful. It affected each one differently," Conner stated. "There may be a possibility that there are survivors. There is no way to tell what shape they could be in. We know how it affected the body, but not the mind."

Isabelle decided to drive south into the city. Much was the same. She saw devastation everywhere. From time to time, she caught a glance of shapes looking out the windows or around the corners of the buildings. The more that came to her eyes, the more her heart sank. She began to wonder if there was anything left of humankind to save.

"Do not give up hope, little one." A thought came to her mind. *"All is not lost. Humankind is out there. You must believe. When it is safe, they will come."* The thoughts and feelings were familiar... *Joy.*

Chapter 28

As the weeks played on, Esuorts' armies grew. The heavies multiplied at an alarming rate. They rapidly grew to adulthood, all according to the dark lord's design. Trained by the goblin troops, the sorcerer quickly had a force large enough to dominate the new world.

While they were raiding military bases across the continent, they struck a blow to the armed forces of the old nation of the United States of America. With these raids, they plundered weapons and supplies. These goblins were rewarded with an abundant source of human flesh. The goblin species became a mainstay in the world. From city to city, their armies marched. They slaughtered anything in their paths, claiming the land in the name of the Dark Lord.

Small villages of humans popped up out of the devastation. Survivors lived in fear. Pockets of resistance held on to thoughts of freedom. Military officers that strived for the survival of the human race led most of the resistance. Some were survivalists that had stockpiled weapons and munitions for the nuclear holocaust that never came. Instead, they witnessed a holocaust of a different nature. Magic and might overcame those who survived the virus.

The homeless knew how to survive on the streets more than anyone did. They battled the elements with the barest of essentials. They foraged for food throughout the city. Now that food was short, many stockpiled what they could wherever they could lay claim. The poor and wretched on the streets forgot by society were now were all who were left of humankind.

Jimmy had seen many things on the streets of Kansas City. He had run away from home at the age of thirteen and did what he could to survive. He had witnessed robberies and murders. No sight was as horrible as the sight of grotesque armies marching down Eighteenth and Vine, claiming the city in the name of a Dark Lord. He watched as children and entire families were rounded up and carted away in big trucks. Ugly brutes, once human, were the collectors. Even more hideous were the pig-like creatures presiding over them.

Where the others were going, no one knew. There were rumors that they were biologically restructured into other mutant humans. There was even talk that they were being rounded up for slave labor and farmed as food. To the heavies and the pig-like creatures, the people who had survived the sickness were nothing more than cattle.

Jimmy was now sixteen. His short thin frame gave him a very boyish look. His hair was long and tangled and kept under a dirty baseball hat. Being malnourished stunted his growth considerably. He did not care, nor did he care if he became a big strong man. The only men he had ever known were abusive. When he had reached the end of his tolerance, he left.

From under the bill of his dirty ball cap, he watched the columns of monsters march down the street. He hid in the alleys among the dumpsters and garbage. Soon the beasts quickly began looking there as well. They searched in groups of four, one goblin to three of the transformed human heavies. Rummaging among the garbage, they found tweakers and winos sleeping off the night. They collected the dregs of society as if they were wild animals. The goblin officers hunted many just for sport.

In an effort to escape, he found himself in North Kansas City. He had hoped that things would be different away from the inner city. He was wrong. Staying in the shadows, Jimmy slipped from building to building. What had once been furniture warehouses and auto shops were now abandoned, leaving everything behind. If he could wait it out here, he might be able to make a decent life for himself with what he could find.

At home, he could not fit in. His father pushed him to play sports in school. He was never happy. He did well and practiced hard just so that his father would not beat him. He was bold enough once to try out for the school play. All his life, he'd pretended to be something he was not. When he landed the lead, he had never been happier. This was short lived. When his father found out that he quit the football team in favor of the school musical he was furious. His father's anger had put Jimmy in the hospital. The police were told that he was in a dirt bike accident and no more questions were asked. As soon as Jimmy was sufficiently healed, he left the hospital and had not seen his family since.

As he slipped down the alleys, he noticed a man and a woman talking outside of a grocery store. The woman had been sitting on a brand new SUV. They were in a bad place at a very bad time. The goblin and heavy forces would be here at any moment.

Isabelle pulled out of the parking lot and headed south on Burlington. Before she could reach the bridge over the Missouri River, Conner spoke up. "Turn this thing around, Izzy!" He could see the armies marching across. They had been sighted. Trucks and squads on foot ran ahead of the rest.

Isabelle took a quick right on Atlantic and gunned it. She knew that they needed to head back to the planes. Her heart raced as she watched their pursuers in her rear-view mirror. The small truck was closing in.

"Where are you going?" Conner asked frantically.

"Back to the planes," Isabelle managed to say between watching the road and her mirror.

"They are too close! We would never get the planes started in time, let alone off the ground!" Conner tried to calm himself. He could tell he had spent too much time with the humans. He was letting his emotions get away. "Get some distance from them so we can hide. We will come back for the planes later." Isabelle did not like the idea, and it showed on her face.

She turned and retraced their moves to Burlington. With all possible speed, she parked the Jeep back in the parking lot where they found it. They opened the doors and ran. Both hoped that they had not been seen. For the moment, they had lost their pursuers, but they were still being hunted.

Heavies and goblins had been sniffing the air, trying to pick up a scent. The brutes were making no attempt at stealth. They overturned dumpsters and burned cars as they searched. "With all the noise they're making, we should be able to stay one step ahead," Isabelle whispered.

"Not if that is what they want us to do," Conner countered. "Goblins are skilled hunters. They are not nearly as dumb as they look. They are trying to flush us out."

"Well, got any bright ideas, boss?" Isabelle asked.

Conner pulled out his pistol and chambered a round. "It may get nasty. I hope you can shoot that thing as well as you can fly." Conner motioned to Isabelle's Colt.

"It's been a while, but I am sure I will remember quickly." Isabelle forced a smile. Her heart was racing and she began to perspire. Every ounce of her being told her to run for her life, yet she was calm. Part of her soul told her to stay with Conner. Everything would work out just fine.

Jimmy tried to follow the couple. He had to stay one-step ahead of the hunting squads. Something told him that these people could help him get out. That same voice also told him that they were in trouble. He watched for a moment. He could hear the racket as the hunters searched the dumpsters and overturned cars. He was a step ahead of them. He could hear them in the alley behind. It was time for him to move.

He jumped out of his hiding place and sprinted across Burlington towards the car dealership. He made it unseen. He crouched down behind a pile of garbage. The stench of the bag seemed to grow stronger. The smell of fetid meat seemed to seep into his nostrils. Without turning around, he sprinted back out into the street. The goblin missed the grab but gave chase. He let out a squeal of victory as he snatched the boy from the pavement.

From behind a silver Jeep Liberty, Conner heard the goblin squeal. He pulled his pistol from its place on his hip, thumbed the safety and took aim. One shot rang from the handgun and the goblin fell. The boy hit first and screamed in pain. He could not get up.

Conner darted out from his hiding spot and waved Isabelle to follow. "We can't stay here. They must have heard the shot. They will be on top of us in moments. We've got to get the boy." Isabelle pooled her courage and followed.

"Are you alright?" Conner asked as he reached the sixteen-year-old boy.

"My ankle—it popped when I landed on it and I can't move it!" The kid replied almost hysterically. Tears of pain flowed from his eyes.

"It could be broken but we don't have time to look at it here in the street." Conner motioned for Isabelle to help. They scooped up the kid and ran toward an empty building.

They slipped around back undetected. Isabelle reached for the doorknob and whispered something that Jimmy could not hear. There was a click and the door opened. They slipped into the darkness and locked the door behind them.

Conner's eyesight easily adjusted to his dim surroundings. He could tell that the building was undergoing renovations. Wall studs were neatly stacked in the corner. The elf found a hammer and barricaded the door. "We are safe for the moment," Conner assured the two.

"Who are you people?" Jimmy asked in-between the seething pain of his ankle.

"We just flew in from out of town," Isabelle answered. "Now let's look at that ankle," She pulled a small flashlight from her backpack and began to investigate. It was extremely swollen. "It looks broken," Isabelle looked up at Conner. "We can't leave him here alone. He won't make it with those monsters out there."

"True. By the looks of things we aren't going anywhere either." Conner looked through torn paper on the windows. "Even if we could get out to the planes, they are only one-man fighters. A second person will not fit in either of them."

Isabelle knew Conner spoke the truth, yet she was still determined to find a way to take the kid back to Estal. She could tell that he was about the same age as Amanda. Conner came over and took off his jacket. He gave it to the kid as he knelt down beside the wounded boy.

"I'm Conner and this is Isabelle," The boy found the man's voice soothing. All his fears eased as Conner spoke. "And who might you be?"

"I'm Jimmy." the boy answered.

"It's nice to meet you, Jimmy," Isabelle smiled as she laid his head in her lap and covered him with Conner's jacket. She noticed the boy's dirty Royals hat and thought of Buck. "Where do you live?" the woman asked.

"Here, there, everywhere," the boy answered. Jimmy felt very relaxed.

"So you live on the streets?" Isabelle looked worried.

"Yeah, you can say that." Jimmy never felt as much like a second-class citizen as he did just then.

Conner looked around and found a couple of two-by-four scraps. Taking off the boy's shoe, he began rubbing his ankle. Jimmy's pain began to dull as he relaxed. As Conner rubbed the ankle, the pain almost went away completely. "So, do you believe in elves?" Conner asked trying to distract the injured boy.

"What?" Confusion washed over Jimmy's face. An explosion went off in Jimmy's brain as Conner set the broken ankle. It was too much; the boy lost consciousness. Conner handily splinted the ankle as the boy lie quietly.

"Poor kid," Isabelle said as she brushed his unkempt hair out of his face.

"I agree with you in more ways than one," Conner said.

"Meaning that we need to take him out of here?"

"Yes, and there is more to him that can be seen," Conner told her. "But let's get some rest for a while. I am going to try to get to the planes at nightfall and radio back to Buck. He can come in the *Griffon Claw* to take him back. Our meeting him was not by accident."

"You are doing it again," Isabelle said.

"What?" Conner asked.

"We all have a purpose and there is something special about this kid," Isabelle stated. "Just like Amanda and me. Are you going to tell me that he is needed to save humankind too?"

"Yes he is, but not as a warrior or hero, but as a survivor," Conner told him. "Don't worry about that now. Let's just try to get out of here alive. You need to rest."

Isabelle took off her jacket and slid it under the boy's head. She curled up on the sawdust floor and quickly dozed off. As she dreamed, she saw a young girl about Amanda's age lying next to her in a field. She had the same dirty baseball cap as Jimmy did.

Conner woke Isabelle from her dream with a gentle shake. "I am going to try to get to the planes soon."

"What about us?" Isabelle asked as she watched Jimmy sleep. She noticed the baseball hat again and thought of her dream.

"I can see better in the dark and can run faster. You will be much safer here," Conner assured her. "Goblins can see better than humans in the dark. You would be in more danger if you moved now. Stay here and rest, but stay awake and listen to everything. I will reach out to you before you can hear me." Before Isabelle could lodge a complaint, Conner slipped into the darkness and was gone. Now she was terrified and felt alone.

Conner sprinted down Armour Boulevard. His feet hitting the ground made no sound. He stopped and peered down Burlington from behind an automotive wheel and muffler shop. He saw fires set by goblins and heavies who roasted what human flesh they could find. Conner sprinted quietly across the road.

As he traveled parallel to Burlington, he was sure he was behind any enemy activity. He watched and waited at every corner for movement. When there was none, he knew it was safe to go. As he watched, he knew this was the face of his new enemy. Through magic, some of mankind had been warped and twisted into something grotesque. Joined and trained by goblins this was a force that would not be easy to defeat. The question was; who held the leashes? Where did he get his magic? The thing that bothered Conner most was the fact that if one could control the goblins and set forth such a devastating virus, what more was he or she capable of?

Conner pushed these thoughts out of his head as he concentrated on reaching the *Dragon's Heart*. No matter how fast the elf went it still took him several hours to reach the fighters. Whispering the old words, the *Dragon's Heart* shimmered back into view. The elf glanced around to make sure he had not been seen. All was clear. From behind a refueling truck, he sprinted toward the plane. He jumped onto the wing and ducked into the cockpit.

Another quick word and he were invisible again and safe.

The elf reached down and toggled the battery switch. His instruments came to life with the flood of electricity to their circuits. He reached forward and to the left, and switched on the radio. It had already been tuned to Estal Tower's frequency.

"Estal Tower, this is Delta-Hotel-019-Alpha." Conner began his call and waited. After a few seconds, he called again. "Estal Tower this is Delta-Hotel-019-Alpha, over."

"Go ahead 019." Conner heard Buck's voice answer. "Where have ya been lad?"

"Estal, we are in Kansas City and in need of some help, over." Conner was glad to hear the dwarf's voice.

"Roger that, lad. Are you and the lass alright?"

"We are fine. We have a civilian with a broken ankle. He won't make it without help. Things are pretty bad down here."

"There ya go again, lad. Ya always be pickin' up strays." Buck answered. Conner could hear the smile in the old dwarf's voice.

"Well, you know me. I'm not happy until I have collected them all." He smiled back even though he knew that Buck could not see.

"I guess we will be bringin' the *Griffon's Claw* to ya. She needs a shakedown anyway." Buck confirmed.

"You need to make sure she is armed and has a squad on board. This place is crawling with unfriendlies." Conner warned.

"Aye, lad. That we can do. We should be there in a couple of hours."

"Thanks, old friend. *Dragon's Heart* out." Conner switched off the radio and killed the battery power.

Isabelle had started to worry. Conner had only been gone for two hours, but she still let her imagination run away with her. Many times, she thought she heard noises outside only to find a rat scurrying in a corner. The only thing she could hear was Jimmy's breathing as he slept and her own heartbeat. *I'm on my way.* Isabelle could feel Conner's presence in her mind. This calmed her greatly. She tried to relay a sense of urgency to him, but he was gone.

Just outside, she could hear something. It was not like the skittering and scurrying of the rats. Something big was rummaging through the back alley. Isabelle reached for her Colt. She could hear grunts and heavy breathing as the beast clumsily dug through debris and garbage. It was definitely looking for something or someone. Isabelle's heart raced.

Could it hear her heart as well? Could it smell them?

Conner remembered where he skirted the goblins. He memorized a route that could get them quickly to the airport without being seen. Buck was hopeful that he would not have to wait long to see them.

It was much quicker for Conner to get back to Isabelle and the boy, but it would not be so easy for the three of them to trek back to the flight line. The boy would slow them down immensely. He would have to carry him.

As he rounded the corner to the vacant building in which they were hiding, a sound made him stop. He could hear grunting and heavy breathing. A goblin was looking for them. The elf listened more intently. By the sounds of things, there was just one. The beast was probably out hunting alone and looking for the glory of the kill for himself. His elfin ears also told him that the goblin had not yet found what it was looking for.

Conner reached into the pocket of left thigh of his flight suit and slid out his Leatherman multi-tool. Without a sound, he opened the razor-sharp blade. Its polished steel shimmered with the dark reflections of the alley. The creature's back was turned to Conner. *Too bad...* With elfin speed, stealth and strength the goblin toppled over. It gargled and grasped its throat as rancid black blood flowed through the slit carved by the small, sharp blade. It fell with a loud humph.

Isabelle could hear the struggling outside. The grunts became gurgles and rasping sounds. *Were there more goblins?* She held up her Colt, pointed at the door. Terror shook her entire body. She had to protect the boy.

Calm wafted through her as the door opened. She could not see the elf but could feel his presence. Tears filled her eyes and she began to sob. Conner rushed in, bent down, and grabbed Isabelle. He shushed and rocked her as she sobbed. He could feel her warm tears soaking through the fabric on his shoulder. For a moment, he could feel her fear and her relief.

As he calmed her, the woman's sobbing subsided. The tears ceased and her breathing once again became light and normal.

"What took you so long?" Isabelle finally asked with all the sarcasm she could muster.

"I ran into an old friend who tried to crash the party," Conner told her. "After we finished talking all he could do was smile."

"I am glad you talked to him first." Isabelle looked at Conner sternly. "Don't you ever leave me alone like that again!"

Conner smiled and looked deeply into Isabelle's eyes. "I promise I will never leave you again. Ever."

Chapter 29

"We got to get out of here," Conner told Isabelle. "Buck will be here in about an hour and a half."

"How?" Isabelle asked. The change of subject helped her gather her composure. The fear had been pushed back to be dealt with later.

"He's coming in the *Griffon's Claw*. He is also bringing a squad of elves for support. It's pretty nasty up by the airport. I think they have a feeling we flew in, but they can't find the planes." Conner gave a grin. "It's a good thing you had the idea to make them invisible. Unless they run into them, they will never know they are here."

"I suppose we should get moving," Isabelle was more than nervous. She patted Jimmy's cheeks gently. "Wake up sleepy head."

The boy stretched and quickly assessed his surroundings. He blinked and looked at Conner and Isabelle in the coming daylight. He remembered what transpired the prior night. "What's going on?" he asked. He did not survive the streets this long without being aware of his surroundings.

"We have to get moving," Conner told him.

"Where do you think we are going, some magical city where it's safe?" Jimmy said facetiously.

"Actually, yeah." Isabelle got up and smiled down at the boy who just looked at her in bewilderment.

"There isn't enough room in the planes we came in, so we are having some friends stop by to pick you up," Conner told him.

"You have to be kidding me, right?" Jimmy was more than annoyed. "So what, you flew in here in some cramped World War II fighter planes, and don't have enough room for me?" Jimmy asked sarcastically. "Bet your friends are coming in some old bomber to get me out."

"I'm impressed," Isabelle said to Conner.

"Me too! Let's go. The goblins can't see very well this time of day." With that, they gathered up their things and left.

They all squinted as they stepped out into the bright summer Kansas City morning. Remembering the route he took the previous night, Conner led them back to the downtown airport. Even with Isabelle following, and Jimmy on Conner's shoulder, they made decent time. It took them just over two and a half hours to reach the gates. They were not alone.

The *Griffon Claw* was circling the hangars waiting on Conner and Isabelle to arrive. The engines of the B17 attracted an unwanted party. A small group of heavies and goblins were firing into the air with small arms. Shotguns, assault rifles, and handguns were being fired at the bomber.

The Flying Fortress answered back with its fifty calibers in its nose and tail as well as the newly installed Vulcans that were added to its top and belly turrets. They swiftly mowed down Esuorts' forces, giving time for the bomber to make its approach and land.

As the last goblin fell, the two fighters shimmered back into existence. The bomber came down the tarmac with landing gear down. It touched down and taxied up to the fighters. The bottom opened up and a squad of elves jumped down and formed a perimeter around the three planes just as unfriendly reinforcements arrived. Bullets ricocheted off the enchanted metal skin of the Fortress. Conner and Isabelle settled into their cockpits as Buck and Ned helped Jimmy into the *Griffon's Claw*.

The Corsair and P40 chugged to life with ease. Both Conner and Isabelle taxied and took off at the same time. The birds of prey banked together as they came around to lay cover for the bomber. Fire rained down from the fighters. The squad of elves on the ground answered round for round as the goblins and heavies attacked. The elves had no casualties for the early morning sun blinded the goblins that were directing fire for their slower, altered human brothers.

Within minutes, the elfin protectors were back in the Flying Fortress. Ardenelle had kept the props turning. He released the brakes and taxied down the runway. More reinforcements rapidly appeared on the scene. This wave of goblins and heavies were too late. The bomber had already left the ground before they could get into position.

They were not out of the woods yet. The elves were not the only ones to have an air force. Six Necrogulls quickly appeared behind them. "Dragon Leader, you have flying uglies on your six," Ardenelle informed Conner hastily.

"Roger that, Three, and thanks for the heads up," Conner answered the bomber. "Two, this is Lead. You're with me. I'm going to take them out. Your job is to keep them off of me." Conner informed Isabelle. He hoped that she would not break as she did the prior night.

"Roger, Lead." Conner could not discern the emotion in Isabelle's voice. "I got your back. Remember, I owe you one." Conner and Isabelle broke formation to the left. Conner throttled up and Isabelle followed almost instantly.

"They broke in twos. They're trying for the *Claw*. Don't let them make it." Conner ordered.

"I got it." Isabelle allowed fear and anger mix within her heart. She broke from Conner and lined her sites on the nearest monster. Almost without thinking, she flipped up her safety and pulled the trigger. Without waiting to see if she hit her mark, she pulled back on the stick and spotted a second. She pulled the trigger. The instant she squeezed, the Necrogull seemed to sidestep in midair. She missed. Jerking her flight stick to the right she followed. Conner appeared with the sun behind him shredding the beast in flight.

"You can't have them all, Two. Great shot on the first." Conner quickly realized that Isabelle did not know that she had brought down the first.

"Thanks, Lead." That was the only answer Conner got.

"Lead, this is Three. I think they had enough," It was Ned's voice this time. "They are turning tail."

"Let them go. We don't have the fuel to pursue," Conner sounded confident and sure. "Form up and let's go home. I owe you a drink, Two."

Isabelle smiled to herself and took her place on the right wing of the *Griffon Claw*.

Captain Rawl realized that his life was forfeited. He knew that he must answer to the Dark Lord. His death would not be easy or quick. His failure would bring him dishonor. He had lost troops and now two of the master's beloved flying beasts. The enemy was stronger than the master had hoped.

The goblin captain sniffed the air in hopes that he could bring some information to his master. As he observed the scents, he picked up something familiar. He shut out the smells of death and battle. He pushed aside the smell of aircraft fuel and exhaust. A scent struck terror in the goblin's heart. The *awful goodness* filled his senses. He would take this information to his master. After sifting through all the scents and odors, he smelled the elves.

In *Amy's* cockpit, Isabelle felt safe. She was no longer in danger from those massive brutes. Conner had given her the ability to soar into the clouds to safety. *Amy* had become an extension of her. The woman remembered how focused she had been when she first pulled the trigger. Somehow, she knew that she had scored a hit. She never saw the beast fall, but she knew that it had. It had been her first kill. Something told her that it would not be her last. That thought left a sick feeling in the pit of her stomach. No matter where she went, they could find her. At least in the air, she had a fighting chance.

As time slowed to a standstill around the three warbirds, Conner thought about the skirmish. Whoever led those forces was not happy with the resistance. Were the goblins and altered humans in search of food? With the virus that wiped out most of mankind, food would be in short supply within a few months. Things were not looking good.

It was obvious that the goblins knew of the elves. Their secret was no longer safe. Conner was just thankful that Estal was. For how long, he could not imagine. When he returned, he would prepare for the worst and pray that it would not happen.

Amanda waited patiently in the tower for news of her friends' return. It had been two days since she had heard from Isabelle and Conner. She missed them. She had seen their trials in Kansas City. Her skills with sight had grown considerably, but she could not see the outcome of the battle. She did see that they were not coming home alone.

The thought of someone her age in the city was exciting. She saw Jimmy. Her talents let her see the streetwise kid who was returning with them. It also let her see something more. She could not see exactly what it was, but Jimmy was more than just a homeless runaway. There was much more.

"Estal Tower, this is Dragon Lead. Do you copy?" Conner's voice came in loud and clear over the tower radio. Amanda's heart leaped with joy.

"Dragon Lead this is Estal Tower. We read you Lima-Charley." Maggie had been waiting for their return as anxiously as the young woman had. "I do have you on radar."

"Tower, we have three tired birds that will need to be fed and put to bed as soon as we set down." Conner's voice came back.

"Roger that Lead, there is a crew on standby to rearm and refuel you as soon as you shut down," Maggie informed. "The nest is clear. Welcome home." Maggie smiled as she saw the aircraft come into view. Even as old as the warbirds were, it still was an impressive sight to see three of the Allies' most dangerous aircraft in a formation. They buzzed the tower and circled the airfield. The two fighters in the most need of fuel touched down first and taxied to the hangar doors. The *Griffon Claw* followed suit.

Amanda was down and out the hangar doors before the propellers stopped turning. "I'm so glad you're back." Her arms were around Isabelle as soon as the older woman's feet hit the ground.

"I missed you too." Isabelle hugged her in return.

"So tell me about your new friend," Amanda asked.

"We brought this kid back from KC. I think he broke his ankle. He helped us out a lot. We couldn't leave him behind."

"Are you forgetting someone?" Conner asked. Amanda turned and wrapped her arms around the elf and squeezed.

"Never," she assured him. "I am so glad you are back." Conner could see maturity in Amanda's eyes. With a look, he could see that she had learned much in just the two days he'd been gone. There was still the confusion of a child lying hidden just beneath the surface, however.

"Go and meet him. You two are about the same age. Maybe you will have something in common." Isabelle suggested. Amanda smiled and ran off to the *Griffon Claw*.

"Hi, I'm Amanda." The young woman introduced herself to the wounded young man as a group of elves brought him out of the plane on a stretcher.

"I'm..."

"...Jimmy, I know," Amanda finished his sentence. "I saw you when you were helping Izzy and Conner."

"How could you? You weren't even there." Jimmy shook his head in disbelief.

"You can say I have superpowers," Amanda giggled. "Don't worry, you'll understand soon enough. The elves and dwarves will keep us safe." Amanda tried to calm the boy's curiosity, but only brought forth more questions.

"So, Jimmy, have you ever read any fantasy books?" Conner fell into step next to the stretcher that carried the injured young man. The elf's smile could calm the furious storms.

"Yeah, I used to have a copy of *The Hobbit* stashed. I've read it five times. Why?" Jimmy gave Conner an inquisitive look.

Conner smiled as he looped the hair behind his pointed ears and began to explain. Amanda smiled as she watched the different facial expressions flash across the young man's face.

Esuorts was furious at the loss of his forces at the airport. The only thing that spared Rawl's life was the information about the elves that had defeated them.

"So it is elves that I am dealing with. That human pilot was correct." Esuorts began to pace. The goblin captain still cowered before the sorcerer. "I know where they are and I will crush them in their own home. Their stone city will not be their safe haven for long," Esuorts smiled. "Captain Rawl, you have one more chance to prove your loyalty to me. I will send you to them and you will destroy them in their hole, like the rodents they are. I want you to plan and execute an attack. In one week, I want you to destroy our enemy in its lair."

"My lord, I will gather a team to take down our enemies." The goblin groveled.

"No. Take an army. These elves are stronger than you think," the sorcerer commanded. "What they lack in brute strength, they make up for in speed and cunning. Do not underestimate them, Captain. That is not a mistake you can afford to make twice," The sorcerer looked deep into the goblin's eyes. "Take two flights of Necrogulls. I want those aircraft wiped out as well the entire city of Estal. When that is done, nothing will stand in my way!" The mage returned to his throne of cold stone and motioned for the goblin to go. "Prepare, and do not disappoint me again."

Chapter 30

Amanda awoke with a start. Once, her dreams frightened her. She had learned that the dreams were a tool to keep her and her friends safe. They were no less frightening, but she could control her fear. This dream was alarming as well as disturbing. Conner must be notified at once.

She spared no time donning a flight suit and heading out the door. She had never been to where Conner stayed, but she somehow knew the way. Amanda twisted, turned, and went deep into the city of Estal to an ornate wooden door. Here she stopped and knocked.

Conner quickly answered. His face looked refreshed and he was dressed. Amanda remembered that elves did not require the sleep that humans did.

"Amanda, it's late. Shouldn't you be in bed?" Conner knew that something was wrong. He tried his best to make everything sound as normal as possible.

"Sorry to bother you at this time of night, but I really need to talk to you." Amanda insisted. She fidgeted with her hands and rocked back and forth on the sides of her feet.

"By all means, come in," Conner opened the door and motioned her inside. Conner's room looked more like the inside of a large hollow tree than a hole in the rock. The walls almost looked organic with their browns and greens. The floor was carpeted with a thick soft moss that made the multi-roomed suite feel warm and cozy. "What seems to be the problem?" Conner asked.

"I had a dream." Amanda began.

"Dreams can mean different things." Conner tried to calm the young woman.

"Not this one," Amanda continued. "The dark sorcerer who is responsible for everything was in it," Conner sat the young woman in a chair as she spoke. He tried to make her as comfortable as he could without missing a word. "I know I am new to using my gifts and they aren't always reliable. This time, I'm scared. Conner, he knows where Estal is. The Apache pilot told him. The one that Isabelle doesn't like. The goblins are going to attack."

"I know that is a chance and we are taking precautions. We will be able to defend the city from anything within a couple of weeks."

"Anthriel, we don't have time. They will be here in one week. They are coming with an army and those hideous flying beasts."

Conner sat in a chair next to the young woman. He felt dread rise from inside. There is no way he could get everything ready in time. The only hope he would have in saving the population of Estal would be to hide them in the forest. Conner pondered for a brief moment. "Go wake Izzy and have her meet me in the conference room up top. I will bring Buck and Ned. I think Maggie already knows to be there. Hurry, Amanda. Be quick. Tell Isabelle to be there in half an hour." Amanda nodded and left the room with a sense of urgency.

Isabelle jumped when she heard Amanda's small fist pounding on her door. She swiftly opened it in her silk housecoat. "What's wrong?" Isabelle was startled, but that passed quickly.

"Conner wants us in the conference room in half an hour!" Amanda blurted out.

"Okay..." Isabelle blinked the sleep from her eyes and opened the door to let in the woman. "Give me just a minute." Amanda seated herself at the small table in the corner and watched Isabelle go into the bathroom.

The older woman quickly returned wearing a fresh pair of jeans and black tank top. She was pulling her hair back into a ponytail as she walked toward the door. "Let's not keep the men waiting too long." Isabelle let the younger woman open the door as she finished her hair.

Buck was much less happy to be brought out of a dwarf slumber than Ned. The younger dwarf was used to pulling all-nighters working. Conner smiled as he could hear the older dwarf mumble under his breath about the time of night. Ned tried to console his uncle as they twisted down the corridors toward Estal's main entrance. As Nedloh looked back, Conner was gone. "I guess he will meet us up there," Ned commented and continued toward the elevators.

Jimmy could not sleep. He was amazed at how fast his ankle was healed and even more astonished with the room that he had been given. The bed was too soft. He preferred the floor. The stone reminded him of the streets of Kansas City. They were much smoother than the concrete sidewalks but were just as soft. He did not want to get accustomed to living in such luxury, nor did he want to get used to being in one place.

The knock on the door startled the young man. It had been too quiet anyway. He got up to answer it.

Conner stood there in the doorway smiling. "I'm sorry to wake you, but we could use your help."

"Yeah, sure, I wasn't asleep anyway. I was kind of bored, though." Jimmy went directly into the hall. He was already dressed. Conner peeked into the room to see his bed on the floor.

"Is there something wrong with the bed?" Conner asked.

"Naw, I just didn't want to get used to it." The young man was quick and to the point. It did not take long for Conner to notice that Jimmy was dressed in blue jeans and a pastel-blue T-shirt that barely covered his navel.

"So where did you get those clothes?" Conner asked.

Jimmy looked down and blushed. "Amanda let me borrow them. She didn't have anything more manly to wear. I am supposed to get new clothes tomorrow. These are okay and better than nothing at all. I was just amazed I could fit in them." The boy tried to be as macho as he could. He did not want Conner to know that he actually liked them. It was too weird, even for him. "Don't worry, I'm not in her underwear," Jimmy assured him. "So you're a real elf?" Jimmy quickly changed the subject.

"Yes, I am," Conner assured the young man. It was obvious that the boy's small frame was a result of living on the streets and being malnourished. With the kid's long uncut hair and Amanda's clothes, he did remind Conner of a young woman. Conner knew that Jimmy was different. He would come out when he was ready. "I bet if you ask Amanda, she would be happy to tell you the story. But first, we have to save the world." Conner gave Jimmy a calming smile.

"Sounds like fun," Jimmy shot back a smile. "Let's get 'er done." They continued their walk in silence.

Jimmy knew everyone who had gathered around the table. He was amazed at all the monitors and maps. If he did not know better, he would have thought that he was in a sci-fi movie's control room. "Are you getting ready for war?" Jimmy said flippantly.

"No, we are just trying to monitor it." Isabelle shot back directly, as Jimmy took a seat next to Amanda.

"Okay, we have a problem," Conner jumped in without waiting to see all that was there. "Our lovely little Amanda had a dream." Jimmy looked sideways at Amanda. "Her gift has let us see what our enemy is up to. In addition, it has shown us that we are in grave danger. We have less than a week to prepare."

"So, lad, you are saying that we are acting on a child's nightmare?" Buck scoffed.

"Yes, I am," Conner shot back. "Young lady, could you tell us what you saw?"

Amanda grimaced and took a deep breath. "I saw the sorcerer in his dark place. I saw the one that controls the goblins and created monstrous flying creatures known as the Necrogulls. He also warped and twisted people into hideous forms to serve him," Amanda started. "I saw armies of goblins and what he calls heavies getting ready for battle. The Apache pilot told him where we are and now he is preparing to overrun Estal, the only place where we are safe."

"That snake!" Isabelle whispered under her breath.

"Although this city is a fine work of dwarf craftsmanship, it is not the only place we are safe. There is a place where we would be safer." Maggie chimed in as she entered the room behind Conner.

"There cannot be a safer place than this stone city!" Buck was quick to defend his kin.

"I mean no disrespect, Master Dwarf," Maggie calmed the older dwarf. "There is one place that only the noble and pure of heart can see. No evil can penetrate it."

"The forest..." Amanda thought aloud.

"Correct, young lady," Maggie smiled.

"You know. Everyone talks about hiding. I think that's bogus," Jimmy could not keep quiet. "You are elves and dwarves, and I have seen what you can do in those old beaten up fighters," Isabelle shot the boy a look of disgust. "No offense, they look great and really kick goblin tail, but we need to be ready for them and take them out."

"Jimmy has a point," Conner stepped up. "We cannot run and hide forever. We do have friends. A few, but friends nonetheless. We should be able to keep them at bay until our kin return."

"From where?" Jimmy asked.

"We have sent word to our kin amongst the cosmos that we are in dire need. We cannot defeat this foe without them." Conner explained.

"So we just hide and wait? No way! Not this kid. I'd rather take my chances on the streets of KC." Jimmy said adamantly.

"Jimmy has a point. We can't just sit here. If they come into our homes, we should kick the stuffing out of them." Isabelle joined. The table nodded and spoke words of agreement simultaneously.

"Okay. We fight, but we cannot do it from here. We need a place we can fall back on and take the planes."

"There is a meadow within the forest that would be big enough to hold the aircraft and is long and straight enough to launch them. I will go and speak with the forest and ask for its help." Maggie said.

"Then it is settled. We fight for Estal. The forest is where we will fall back to." Conner reaffirmed.

"You know, lad, that dwarves dannot belong in trees," Buck argued.

"We have enjoyed your hospitality for more than an eon, friend dwarf. Now you shall enjoy that of the elves." Conner smiled. Buck sat quietly with his arms folded.

"I will return in the evening with word from the forest," Maggie assured the group as she turned and left.

"Good. Now we all have much work to do. Time is of the essence," Conner prioritized in his head. "Izzy, you and Ned are in charge making sure all the aircraft are ready. Buck, you will move all the support equipment in the hangar to the meadow as soon as we have clearance. I will get everyone else ready for the fight of their lives."

Everyone got up from their seats and went about their business. The two youngsters stayed put, looking at each other. "Hey, um, Conner, I owe you a lot. I hate to sit around while everyone is getting ready for Armageddon. Is there anything we can do?" Jimmy asked.

"Well, now that you mention it," Conner stopped in his tracks and turned around. "Amanda knows her way around the hangar pretty well. You can stick with her and help Izzy and Buck wherever you can. I think you two will probably do well loading up tools and spare parts. I need Amanda close, in case, she has another vision."

"Sure." the kids both said together.

"So, you can see things," Jimmy asked as they got up to head out to the hangar.

"Yeah, you could say that," Amanda answered.

"Can you see anything about me?" Jimmy queried.

Amanda closed her eyes and let the magic flow. She was soon outside herself. She was standing by a girl her age who was wearing the same clothes that she lent Jimmy. The girl was Jimmy's height. Amanda smiled as the girl filled out the T-shirt better than she did.

"Well, what do you see?" Jimmy saw the smile grow on Amanda's face.

You will know when you are ready to know." Amanda giggled.

"What a cop out! Are you sure you can see things?" Jimmy prodded.

"Let's just say you can keep the clothes. You look better in them than I do anyway." Amanda turned and walked into the hangar.

"What is that supposed to mean?" Jimmy ran after Amanda.

"You'll know when you are ready," Amanda stopped and looked into her new friend's eyes. "Know this. When you are ready, you have friends who will not judge you. We will accept you for who you are and love you just the same, maybe more." Amanda smiled with a twinkle in her eyes and she continued walking onto the hangar floor.

The kids found Isabelle with a legal pad talking to Ned. It was obvious she was making a list of priorities. "I'm glad you two decided to join us." Isabelle noticed the smile on Amanda's face and the bewilderment on Jimmy's. "What's up with you two?"

"Ask me later," Amanda told Isabelle.

"Hey, isn't that some breach of confidence or somethin'?" Jimmy pleaded

"Only in the world that used to be and not if you want help later. Trust me; it will be for your own good." Amanda was strong as she spoke to Jimmy. This was a new side of the young woman that Isabelle had never seen. It suited her.

"Okay. Just fill me in some time," Jimmy conceded. "So, what do you have for us to do, boss?"

"You're gonna love this." Isabelle handed the kids a couple of old binders. This is an inventory of parts. I need you to go into the stock room, count it, and make sure it is accurate. Make any changes in pencil. If we have time we will put it into the computer and update everything."

The kids looked at each other in disgust. "This is gonna take forever," Amanda said.

"Only if you keep whining about it. The sooner you get started, the sooner you get it done." Isabelle did not say anything else but went back to her previous task. The two knew they had no argument. They turned and went into the parts room and went to work.

Magnethella walked barefoot through the forest. Soft grass caressed her toes with each step. An elfin steed had taken her deep into the magical wood, but she dismounted before she reached the heart. The elfin woman could feel every living thing: blades of grass, birds, insects, the tallest trees...she felt life.

She soon reached a great oak. Wisest of all trees, it stood several stories high with branches that were big enough to hold large trucks. The wise old oak had been in the forest since time began. Long said in songs and tales of yore, the old oak was the first tree to take root on the Earth.

As she neared the master of the wood, she disrobed, baring herself as a tree sheds its leaves in autumn. She bared herself to the oak as she prepared to ask for the wood's assistance.

"It is so good to see you, Magnethella, daughter of elves." A booming gruff voice came from the ancient tree.

"As it is for me, Master Oak." The elfin woman waited for the tree to respond. Trees were easily offended.

"It has been too many seasons since your last visit, my friend." The tree noticed.

"My most humble apologies. You have been hidden from sight for thousands of years."

"Is that so, child?" The old oak had just a hint of sarcasm in his ancient voice. "I have known of the release of magic. I also know that humankind has been violated. Their evil slashing and burning of my kin will not go unpunished."

"How do you know of these things?" The elfin woman queried.

"My roots go deep. They touch those of other trees and even the grasses," A breeze blew through the branches with something that almost sounded like a sigh. "I also know why you have come. There is a great evil that has fallen upon Mother Earth."

"That is not why I have come, but if you wish to share what you can, the elves would be most grateful, father of all trees," Maggie bowed deeply. "I have come to ask for shelter in your wood for my kin and their friends."

"This I know. You may use the meadow as you wish. The grass has already decided to make their sacrifices," The tree told the elf woman with sadness. "We will shelter you in our branches. The larger trees are already preparing to produce shelters for you as in the days of old."

"We will owe you a great debt." A breeze blew through the elfin woman's fiery red hair.

"You will owe us nothing," The oak gruffly shot back. "Filthy man has unlocked the magic that should have been left to slumber. You must understand, Magnethella, the magic has changed in its sleep. It has separated from its rudimentary state. As all living creatures, it has evolved." Maggie sat in the grass with her legs tucked underneath her. Her hair fluttered in the breeze. She listened intently. The wise oak continued. "As the magic lie dormant, its essence separated into their purest forms of good and evil. I have felt it in my roots. Evil has festered and has become aware of itself. It has taken a man who has become the sorcerer in which you now face. He used to be a mild-mannered teacher of Mother Earth. This I tell you as a favor. When you have defeated your enemy, I will ask for it to be returned."

"I thank you, oh wise father of trees," Magnethella spoke with sincerity.

"Go now and share the safety of our wood. We once again welcome the elves back to our branches." The elf woman could hear the smile in the tree father's voice.

Amanda and Jimmy worked quietly for almost an hour. Amanda read off part numbers with their quantities as Jimmy checked and marked the binders. They listed the parts in numerical order. Jimmy flipped from page to page looking, checking and adjusting quantities.

"This is going to take forever!" Jimmy was frustrated with the tedium.

"Do you have a better idea?" Amanda asked. "This is the best system I can come up with."

"Well, you said you have a gift of seeing." Jimmy hinted. "Could you look at the numbers and see the parts?"

"I never thought about that!" Amanda was almost excited about the suggestion.

"I haven't tried to do something like that." She flipped through the book and picked a number. Closing her eyes, she tried to find the part. To her surprise, numbers came rushing into her mind. Her eyes snapped open. As she scanned the parts numbers on the pages, quantities of the parts came rushing to her. The young woman scribbled numbers in pencil next to the part.

It amazed Jimmy of the speed in which his friend went through the list. He watched her intently. For the first time, he actually saw her. Her auburn hair framed her face perfectly as it cascaded across her shoulders. The face was flawless to him. The young woman showed strength and innocence in her bright blue eyes. She moved with grace and power that she did not even know she possessed. As the boy watched, he was smitten by the young woman and he envied her. He coveted her female body. He wondered what it would be like to be her, or like her.

Amanda looked up and noticed Jimmy staring. She smiled as she looped her reddish hair behind her ear. "What?" she asked.

"Um, nothing..." Jimmy knew Amanda caught him. He wanted to tell her but could not. He thought she would probably think him a freak.

"It must be something. You have been staring for the past five minutes," She closed the last binder with a loud clap. "The numbers aren't the only things I can see. What are you thinking?"

"Really, it's nothing," Jimmy insisted. Amanda knew he was lying. She looked around to make sure there was no one else in the parts room.

"Look, it's okay." Amanda reached out and held his hand. The touch was like electricity to the both of them.

"It's okay?" Jimmy started. "I am supposed to be a guy. I'm not supposed to have thoughts like this."

"Like what?" Amanda asked. "If you like me, that's okay. I like you too."

"No, that's not it at all." Jimmy tried to explain.

"What? You don't like me?" Amanda jabbed.

"Yes, I do." Jimmy could not imagine that those words came out of his mouth. "There is something more."

Amanda smiled and squeezed his hand. "I know."

"Know what? Do you know what I am thinking?" Jimmy was very confused.

"Okay. Stop for just a second. This place is full of magic. Close your eyes." Amanda closed hers and saw Jimmy as she had seen before. She projected the image of the young woman in Jimmy's dirty ball cap into the boy's mind. Jimmy could see the young woman also. He knew it was him. His eyes snapped open and he quickly let go of Amanda's hand and ran out of the room.

"I'm sorry, Jimmy!" Amanda yelled after him. She tried to follow as tears filled her eyes and spilled over. It was too late. He was gone.

Chapter 31

The city was buzzing. Dwarves and elves prepared to defend the city with everything they had. Strengthened doors and stone battlements were placed outside the main gates as well as in other strategic locations within the city. Where it was practical, the dwarf masons made the openings as small as possible. The fewer of the enemies that could get through at a time, the easier it would be to defend. Eventually, the city had become a fortress buried under layers of rock. The only thing that remained was to make certain the back door was not visible. They knew that they would need an escape route.

Conner was in the library talking with the elders. It was his priority to keep all of the books and scrolls safe, but there was not enough time to move the entire library. He had called Ned down to help.

"Yeah, we could put them all on crystal storage, but that would take years to get everything." the young dwarf explained.

"Well, do you have any other ideas?" Conner was at his wit's end.

"We can't take them with us, but we can't let the sorcerer have all the elfin secrets," Ned started. "We are dwarves. The only thing I can say is that we seal them in and come for them later." Conner's heart sank. He knew that the young dwarf was correct. It was the only option.

"That can be part of the solution." Maggie entered through the huge wooden library door. "We can take what is feasible with us to the forest. What we cannot get out, we can seal in," The elf woman placed her hand on Conner's shoulder. "There is a time where we may have to let go. It is a new age with new things to learn. Some of what is here, we no longer need. Magic has evolved and now, so shall we."

"Did you beseech the wood?" Conner asked.

"Yes, I did. The trees will welcome us home." Maggie smiled warmly at the younger elf.

"Then what are we waiting for? You heard the woman. Let's get these books out of here!" Conner turned to the Keeper of the Books. "Prioritize: most important first, then oldest. Make sure our history goes as well." With a nod, the keeper turned and began directing other librarians.

Buck expeditiously got the approval for the move. They assembled large tents to serve as headquarters and maintenance operations. Buck thought of Burma in 1940. He had green tents in the jungles. They removed trees to make a sod landing strip and taxiway to park the aircraft. This was very similar to Burma in so many ways and just as different in much more.

This time, he could not use jeeps and trucks to transport what he needed. Everything had to be moved by horse and wagon. He did not have technology on his side this time. Wagons were constructed of lightweight aluminum and magnesium. Tools and parts were put into shelters built onto the aluminum frames. These would serve as rooms and shelters by themselves. The elves and dwarves worked quickly and efficiently. Buck oversaw it all.

Isabelle had her nose buried in aircraft logbooks. She had been busy computing the weight and balance after the modifications to the *Griffon Claw*. She was startled as Jimmy slammed into the desk in which she was working. She noticed that tears were in his eyes.

"What's wrong, Jimmy?" she asked as she began to straighten the fallen books.

"Nothing..." Jimmy was trying to avoid a conversation.

"Let's see, tears, not looking where you are going and running into things—I think I'm going to have to disagree with you," Isabelle tried to calm the young man. Putting away her work, she gave him her complete attention. "Okay, spill it."

"I really don't want to talk about it," Jimmy lied. He really wanted to talk to someone, but he really did not know these people. Jimmy liked being in Estal. He enjoyed all of his new friends. He was afraid that if he talked about what he and Amanda saw, they would think him a freak and he would lose the friendships that he just acquired.

"Look, I know this is not easy to get used to. A kid like you should be playing football and video games. No one should have to go through what you are going through right now," Isabelle tried to understand the best she could. "I know that your whole world has been turned upside down. Everyone's has."

"That's not it at all." Jimmy wanted to talk but did not know what to say.

"I tell you what. I can tell you want to talk. It's a little busy around here. What would you say if I took you out for a burger?" It dawned on the woman where to take him for a talk.

"I guess, but where?" Jimmy asked.

"I know the perfect place," Isabelle smiled. "Do you like hotrods?"

"Yeah. They're okay." Jimmy shrugged.

"Come with me!" Isabelle grabbed Jimmy's hand and led him to the other side of the hangar. "Hey, Ned!" Isabelle paused at the bomber.

"What's up, Izzy?" Ned asked from the cockpit.

"Can you cover for me for a while? I have some business to take care of." Isabelle asked.

"Sure, I guess. Conner won't be too happy." Ned reminded.

"Tell him I'm on my lunch break and let him know that Jimmy's with me." Isabelle continued across the hangar floor.

"Bring me back a Rueben and fries!" Ned hollered to her back. Isabelle just waved an acknowledgment.

Jimmy was amazed when Isabelle led him to her old Chevy. "Wow, this is cool!"

"Thanks, I built her myself. Well, alongside my dad." Isabelle beamed with pride.

"This is really nice," Jimmy said as he slipped inside. Jimmy was so amazed by the car he was afraid to touch anything. The chrome trim and every detail dazzled him. "It's amazing. This looks like a brand new car."

"She's my baby," Isabelle said as she started the engine and headed to the hangar doors.

"Where is she going?" Conner asked as he came up to check on the progress.

"Where she needs to go..." Maggie placed her hand on Conner's shoulder. "She has taken him to see the oracle."

"Oh. I wish I would have caught her. I'd have her bring back a piece of pie." Conner turned and walked through the hangar.

"This place looks like it hasn't had a customer in years," Jimmy commented on the deserted diner as he stepped out of the car.

"Trust me, you'll be absolutely amazed," Isabelle answered.

As before, everything was in its place. A small layer of dust covered everything. Jimmy panned the diner. A small booth in the corner caught his eyes. It was clean and set for two. All he could do was look at Isabelle. She smiled in return.

"Here we are," she said as she led the boy over to the table. Jimmy and Isabelle sat. Isabelle picked up the menu as if she were ready to order. After a few seconds, she put it down.

"I have to use the ladies room. Be right back." She smiled.

"Are you nuts? There is nobody here. We won't get anything to eat. I doubt the plumbing even works." It was no use. Jimmy was alone.

As Jimmy sat waiting, a bright light appeared in the seat across from him. It shimmered and began to take shape. A woman appeared from the flickering bright light. She was more beautiful than anyone Jimmy had ever seen. Her hair was flowing like spun gold. The woman's face was young but showed a wisdom of ages. Her smile warmed Jimmy's heart and melted all his fears.

"Who are...? Where did...?" Jimmy couldn't finish a sentence.

"*May peace be with you, little one. I am Joy. I know you have questions. I am here to help,*" The woman told him. Her voice was soothing and melodious. "*I know your fears. You should not be afraid of who you are.*"

"But I don't know who I am. Not anymore..." Jimmy said as he remembered the vision that Amanda had shown him.

"*A friend has shown you a vision. Ever since you were small, you knew you were different. You did not like regular boy things. You always wanted clothes for Christmas and you never played with the trucks and cars you got. Your father pushed you into sports and you went out for the school plays instead. That is when you ran away. Do not deny the signs. They are a gift to you.*"

"How do you know?" Jimmy asked in amazement.

"*I know many things.*" the woman replied.

"Why am I so confused?" Jimmy asked.

"*Because you allow yourself to be unclear,*" she said with a smile. "*You are who you are. There is no way you can deny that. I know what Amanda showed you. It scared you, but were you afraid of what you saw or were you afraid because Amanda now knows how you feel?*"

Jimmy thought about the woman's words. He knew she was right. He was afraid that Amanda knew. "In just a couple of days, I feel like I have known Amanda for a lifetime. I really like her. I'm afraid that if she knew me that way, she wouldn't like me anymore. I'm afraid no one would."

"You are with friends. They did not judge you when they took you off the streets. They will not judge you now. Remember with whom you are living. The elves and dwarves are the most loyal beings on this planet. Once they have pledged their friendship and protection, almost nothing can break that bond. And don't be surprised if Amanda likes you as well, no matter what you look like."

"Why am I cursed with being like this?" Jimmy stammered.

"Who said anything about a curse? My child, you have received a great gift. You should cherish it." Joy explained.

"How can this be a gift?" Jimmy's questions seemed almost never-ending.

"Little one, when the time comes you will know. Just remember you will be able to see things in a perspective that few can." Joy smiled.

Jimmy paused and stared at his menu for a moment. "Okay, but how can I change?" Jimmy asked. "I have met girls on the streets who took hormones that helped them, but that is all out the door now. I have no money and I doubt there are even doctors anymore."

"Don't worry, little one. With magic, doctors are not needed. As we speak the changes are already starting, but to complete the changes you must perform a selfless act. You have a good heart. It

will happen when you are ready. Be patient in the meantime. Even for innate women, it doesn't happen overnight. Great women are not born. They become great through great deeds. Trust me when I say, one day you will reach that greatness."

Jimmy sat in awe as Isabelle returned. "Hello, Joy," Isabelle smiled at the woman in her seat. The woman got up so that Isabelle could sit.

*"It is good to see you again, Isabelle. You have done the right thing in bringing this little one to visit with me. I think **she** has much to say. Please listen with an open heart and mind. Jimmy needs your help and guidance."*

Jimmy blushed at Joy's words. *"I must go now. Remember it is a time of magic. Miracles can happen to those that are true of heart and virtuous of the soul. Enjoy your meal."* As she shimmered and faded back into the nothing as she had arrived, two double cheeseburgers appeared with drinks in front of them. *"Both sodas are diet. I think someone has to watch their figure from now on."* The woman's body had faded, but her voice echoed as she vanished. Two white Styrofoam boxes appeared on the side, one with Conner's name and the other was Nedloh's. Both were in handwritten script. *"I didn't forget Conner and the young dwarf."*

Isabelle looked at Jimmy thoughtfully. "You don't have to talk about it if you don't want too. What Joy has to say is usually just for you."

"That's okay. I think I would like to talk about it now." Jimmy smiled at Isabelle as he dove into his burger.

"Okay, first and foremost, why did Joy call you *she*?" Isabelle asked.

"I think that's a good place to start," Jimmy squeezed some ketchup onto his plate. He began to tell Isabelle about the vision that Amanda had shown him. He also told her about how he agreed with it. "The more I think about it, the more I feel I should have been a girl. I think that maybe God just made a mistake."

"Actually, I don't think so. I believe that God is perfect and is incapable of making mistakes. I think you are the way you are for a reason. You will be who you will be, who Amanda and I both saw, for that same reason."

"What do you think that reason is?" Jimmy asked.

"I don't know. We have yet to understand. Would you be offended if I called you girlfriend about now?" Isabelle asked.

Jimmy smiled. "No. It will take a little getting used to, but I would appreciate it a lot." Jimmy smiled and they both finished their meals talking about several different subjects.

The drive home was quiet. Jimmy had a lot to consider. His life had changed so much, and more changes were yet to come. The changes ahead of him were unlike anything he could ever imagine.

Looking over at Isabelle, he felt a calm wash over him. He knew he now lived with friends.

Amanda did not know what to think as she watched Jimmy run out the door. She did not intend to hurt his feelings. She had just hoped that she could help her new friend. From the moment they met yesterday, she knew that there was more to the boy than could be seen with the eye.

Amanda had hoped that her gift could help him. Now she had wished she had never shown him. She wished even more that she had never seen the vision in the first place.

"Do not worry, little one. All will be well. Your heart has guided you correctly." Amanda had heard Joy's voice in her own thoughts.

"I hurt him," Amanda said aloud to no one.

"Your friend will heal. You have helped start that healing process. You will be needed further. Talk with Isabelle when she returns. She knows as well."

"Thank you," Amanda said to the unseen angel.

"Who are you talking to?" Nedloh asked the young woman.

"Oh, no one," Amanda answered with a smile

"Well, as soon as you are finished with your conversation, would you mind giving me a hand?" He had a feeling that he had walked in on Amanda and an angel. Nedloh never knew what to think about human's angels or the elves' oracles. Dwarves always relied on themselves and their breed. Sometimes they would call on their kin on the other side to aid them in need or give them guidance. He had felt the presence of his late father guiding him.

"I would love to," Amanda said with pure enthusiasm. She was thrilled anytime she had a chance to sit inside an aircraft. She would always remember when she flew with her father. "Whatcha doing?" she asked as she climbed the ladder up into the cockpit.

"We have mounted the new hardware and now I am installing the new fire control computers." Nedloh began to explain.

"I thought they were manned like the old turrets," Amanda started. "Or should I say, dwarfed to be more politically correct?" She giggled.

"Either way," Nedloh caught the joke and laughed. "Actually, they can also be controlled from the cockpit by either the co-pilot or navigator through the computers." Nedloh always enjoyed working with Amanda. He knew she was the youngest human in Estal. He knew what that was like. He was also glad to have met Jimmy. He sensed that they would be good for each other.

Ned started to show Amanda where to install the new black boxes. They mounted on vibration-free mounts. Four screws, a couple of cannon plugs, and they were set. Amanda started to run the diagnostics at the copilot's console. She loved to sit behind the yoke of any aircraft.

"So what happened to Jimmy? I thought you two had something from the beginning." Nedloh tried to start a conversation as the computer tested the circuits of the new system.

"I think I scared him off," Amanda said. The conversation hurt. It was something she really did not want to discuss. She did not feel right about telling Ned Jimmy's secret.

"How could a girl, with a personality that could charm an elf and the looks to match, scare anyone off?" Nedloh asked.

"I showed him something that I don't think he liked," Amanda said through her blushed cheeks.

"Anything that you have to show anyone can't be bad." Ned was trying to make her feel better.

"I shared my gift and I don't think he liked the vision," Amanda explained.

"Did it bother you? I mean it must not have been too bad for you to show him."

"I didn't think it was bad. I actually kind of liked it." Amanda blushed again at the thought of Jimmy actually being a girl in a boy's body. "Why aren't you asking about the vision I showed him?" she asked.

"I would, but it's none of my business. I learned a long time ago that if I'm supposed to know something or someone wants me to know, then I would be told." The young dwarf explained.

"Good philosophy." Amanda agreed with him completely. She never considered that Ned would have such a profound statement. They continued working a while in silence.

"Well, do you like him?" Nedloh finally asked, breaking the long quiet between them.

"Jimmy?" Amanda tried to pretend she did not know what Ned was talking about.

"Yes, silly!" Nedloh shook his head. "Sometimes humans are kind of slow," Ned smiled.

"Actually, I think I do," Amanda thought about it. "It's weird. I saw something in Jimmy that no one else had, not even him."

"Really?" Ned gave a mischievous grin. "So you think there are wedding bells in the future?"

"I don't know about that. I can't see that far," Amanda smiled and gave Ned an elbow to the ribs. "There is definitely something, or at least I thought there was. I hope I didn't screw it up."

"You know, I don't think you could screw anything up, even if you tried," Nedloh told her.

"Yeah right..." Another elbow hit Ned's ribs.

"Seriously, you are smart, funny, and very attractive, even for a human. To top it all off, you have a great heart," Nedloh could see that he had the young girl's attention. "Just give it time. It will work out. No one could stay mad at you if they tried," Amanda blushed. A tear rolled down her face. She wrapped her arms around her dwarf friend and squeezed with all her might. "Now I don't think there is cause for all of that!"

"Thank you, Ned," Amanda whispered into the dwarf's ear.

"There are no thanks necessary," Ned pulled away from the girl's embrace and looked her in the eyes. "I was just being honest," He smiled. "Call it a character flaw."

Amanda quickly returned the smile without even knowing. She wiped the tear from her cheek. Before anything else interrupted her thoughts, the computer screen at the copilot's console blinked ready. 'Diagnostics complete. All systems ready. ' scrolled across the screen.

"Diagnostics are concluded, and all systems green," Amanda changed the subject. "All we have to do now is test it."

"Well, I have a feeling we will be running it through a full combat field test soon enough. Let's see if it tracks." Nedloh suggested. With a flip of a switch, the two new Vulcan cannons began to articulate on their own. They searched for unseen foes.

"Lemme check..." Amanda hurried out of the cockpit and down the ladder. She stepped to the side of the aircraft, far enough to see the top and bottom turrets. Nedloh stuck his head out the window to track Amanda. When Amanda knew that Ned was watching she gave him the thumbs up and ran back into the airplane.

"That's a job well done, I think," Nedloh told his young partner.

An engine could be heard pulling into the hangar. Nedloh stuck his head outside once again to see Isabelle pulling up next to the amethyst corsair.

"Isabelle and Jimmy are back," Ned informed Amanda. "I think you should go talk to him."

"What if he's still mad at me?" Amanda worried.

"I doubt anyone could be mad at you. Besides, you'll never know unless you find out." Ned gave Amanda a gentle shove out of the cockpit. Amanda took the blatant hint and continued down the ladder on her own accord.

She was nervous as she walked over to the purple street rod. Part of her wanted to run and hide in shame, but a bigger part pulled her in the direction of the old car.

"Hey, Amanda!" Isabelle spotted the girl first.

"Hey." was all that Amanda could manage.

"Well, I got a lot of work to do. It's going to be a late night, so I better get cracking." Isabelle took her leave.

Jimmy and Amanda sat in silence that seemed to last perpetually. "Jimmy, I'm really sorry for showing..." Amanda started.

"No, it's okay. Really!" Jimmy interrupted. He took Amanda's hands in his and looked deep into her eyes. "Look. I don't know what all is going to happen or how, but I do know that there are a lot of big changes ahead for me and I don't think I can handle them alone. I could if I had to, but it would be great if I had someone to lean on from time to time."

"I was way out of line for pushing you. I'm sorry. I like you a lot, Jimmy, no matter what happens. I want to be there for you whenever I can."

"Don't worry. You will be as long as you want to be." Jimmy did not know what else to say.

"Look, I don't know when it will happen, or if it will happen, but when it does, I want you to know that I will always be there for you." Amanda pledged to Jimmy. They were both amazed. They had known each other for fewer than forty-eight hours and already felt like lifelong friends, maybe more.

"Amanda, it will happen," Jimmy assured her.

"When? Is it what you want?" Amanda's heart leaped.

"It is what I want and it has already started. I don't have any clue about what to expect, but I guess we'll find out." Jimmy's eyes filled with tears of joy. He smiled at Amanda for what seemed like forever. Amanda grabbed Jimmy and held him in her arms. Jimmy returned the embrace.

"I guess we have a wardrobe to plan," Amanda said. "Are you scared?"

"Yes and no. I don't know anything about what's going on. I have no idea what is happening to me, but I do know as long as I am here with my friends I'll have nothing to fear."

"Hey, have you ever seen the inside of a B17 Flying Fortress?" Amanda tried to lighten the conversation.

"No." Jimmy returned.

"Come on. I'll give you a tour." Amanda took Jimmy's hand and led him across the hangar toward the bomber.

"Tight!" was all he could say in his excitement. It could have been a pile of dung. He did not care as long as he was with the present company. The fact that he was about to see a vintage World War II bomber was a bonus.

Chapter 32

Buck stood in the meadow as the caravan of tents and maintenance support equipment arrived. Once again, he thought of fighting the Japanese in the jungles of Burma. He orchestrated the maintenance crew's set up. Tents stood away from the flight line. Small lights and little brightly colored flags were set to mark a makeshift runway. He stood with his arms folded in gruff satisfaction as everything came together.

Amanda and Jimmy waved at the older dwarf as they arrived on one of the carts. Although the dwarf was busy with the logistics, the teens noticed the battle ax across his back. The younger humans hopped down from the carts and gave the horses their thanks with a gentle stroke of their muzzles.

"Welcome to your home." the dwarf said in his gruff voice. Buck had only known the boy for a short time, but he noticed a something different about him. He was still dressing in Amanda's clothes, but he did seem much happier. To the dwarf, happiness was an oddity in these troubling times.

"This is beautiful," Jimmy was in awe of the forest and all its grandeur. "The trees are huge!" Jimmy craned his neck back to see the canopy. His mouth was agape in awe.

"We used to call these trees *home*, eons ago." Ardenelle joined the conversation from behind the youngsters.

"Only apes and elves could ever call the trees their home," Buck said shaking his head. "The tool shed goes over by the operations tent!" the dwarf bellowed at his helpers as he walked away.

"Pay no attention to him. Most dwarves can't stand being out of their mines, let alone open spaces," Ardenelle looked down at the kids with a smile. "Don't worry. He'll get used to things. He knows it's for the best."

"Is there anything we can do to help?" Jimmy asked.

"Everything is almost set," The younger elf assured them. "Why don't you go ask the trees where you'll be staying? They are wise and have provided a place for everyone according to their varying needs."

Jimmy and Amanda looked into the trees and saw extremely large pods hanging from the branches. Some seemed to grow out of the bark on the tree trunks. Vines and branches were woven together to form walkways between them. Stairs formed from large pieces of bark and smaller branches that wound up into the canopy. The kids were off to explore the woodland city.

"This is amazing!" Amanda beamed. "Within a couple of days, the trees have grown this way."

"This happened on only a few days?" Jimmy was bewildered.

"The last time I was here, it wasn't like this," Amanda assured him. "It was like any other forest, except for the talking animals."

"Animals don't talk," Jimmy argued.

"Jimmy, this is a magical forest," Amanda tried to explain. "I think almost anything can happen here. You should be figuring that out by now." Amanda smiled at her friend, as they continued to explore.

Pod after pod lined their way. Branches beneath their feet were woven so tightly together to make a floor, they could not see the ground. They paused to see how high they had climbed. The two stopped and looked over a railing that had grown in place. The tents and people working in the meadow seemed like tiny insects from their perch.

They continued deeper into the city. Every pod they had passed seemed to be a home. Some were small, and would only hold a single person. Others were larger. They may have been family dwellings. Some were larger still. Water trickled down from branches into small pools and fountains. This added an elegance matched by nothing ever before seen. They did not have a clue why the larger pods were created. Eventually, they stopped at one particular pod that stood among many. It was not small, nor was it one of the largest. Both of the teenagers felt compelled to investigate.

"This looks cozy," Jimmy told Amanda as they looked around. "I feel very drawn to this place, almost welcome here."

Amanda closed her eyes and let herself feel the trees. "This place was grown for us." She smiled

"Don't you think we should be in separate rooms or pods, or whatever these things are?" Jimmy asked.

"No, the trees feel that we need to be together," Amanda informed with a smile.

"Are you sure you're not making it up?" Jimmy asked suspiciously.

"No. I don't make things up." Amanda said sternly.

"Great, even the trees know more than I do," Jimmy did not know what to think. "So, where do we put the couch?"

"How about over there along that wall?" Amanda answered with a smile.

"That would be a great view out the window." Jimmy agreed. As soon as the words came from Jimmy's mouth, small branches formed at the wall—a perfect place for the kids to sit. The couch looked just like it attached to the wall. Before their eyes, a bright green moss budded and grew to make the living bench more comfortable. Both were amazed.

"The trees are tending to our needs," Amanda observed. "Thank you!" She looked up and spoke aloud to the trees.

"This is way too weird," Jimmy said.

"You should be getting used to it by now," Amanda told him as she sat down, pulling Jimmy down with her. The new couch was amazingly soft and comfortable.

"I don't know if I can ever get used to it." Jimmy looked at the home that sprouted for them. It was sparsely furnished but had many possibilities.

"Jimmy, you are here for a reason. We all are." Amanda put a comforting hand on Jimmy's, waiting for an argument.

"I know that now." Jimmy started. He was still trying to get himself to believe all that had happened and was happening to him.

"You just didn't talk with Izzy, did you?" Amanda's face lit up. "You saw her, didn't you? You met Joy." Amanda's face beamed with happiness.

"Well, I saw someone. She was so beautiful. She told me what you showed me. She comes from a higher place. How can I argue with someone that comes from Heaven?"

"So, me showing you wasn't good enough?" Amanda got defensive.

"No, that's not it," Jimmy backpedaled. "I believed you. I just didn't know what to think. Joy put things in perspective for me," Jimmy paused and looked seriously at the young woman.

"Amanda, I'm really scared," Jimmy felt a lump form in his throat. "We are all about to be in great danger, possibly killed. I have seen what these things can do. It's not pretty. I just found a friend, and I don't want to lose any of this all in the same week."

"You'll never lose me, Jimmy." Brushing the hair from Jimmy's eyes, Amanda tried to calm his fears.

"Can you see it? Can you show me?" Jimmy pleaded, trying to hold back the tears.

"I'm not that attuned yet," Amanda squeezed Jimmy's hand. "I'm sorry."

"Everyone has superpowers but me," Jimmy smiled sarcastically.

"Don't worry, you have gifts," Amanda assured her friend. "I have a feeling there is more to come after all is said and done."

"Is this a private party?" Conner appeared in the doorway.

"No, Conner," Amanda smiled. Jimmy was relieved to have a change of conversation.

"Isn't this place wonderful?" Amanda asked.

"Well, I'm glad you like it," Conner said. Conner turned toward Jimmy. "You've had a busy last couple of days, haven't you?"

"I guess you can say that." Jimmy did not attempt to cover the sarcasm.

"You know, I think I will go see if Buck or Ardy need any help." Amanda knew Jimmy needed to talk with Conner. She did not want to intrude.

"No. Please stay, Amanda. This is one of those tough times." Jimmy entreated, squeezing his friend's hand.

"Okay." Amanda sat back down, returning the grip.

"Isabelle told me about what happened at the diner. Joy told me the rest," Conner started. "Don't worry. You are fine. You are with friends. We do not judge, nor do we question what The Creator has in store for us," Conner smiled. Jimmy immediately felt calm. All fear seemed to melt away. "You feel extremely calm now, don't you?"

"Actually, yeah, I feel pretty good," Jimmy told him.

"Let me fill you in on a little secret," Conner smiled. "That is an elfin charming spell. That specific spell only works on human females.

"Really?" Jimmy smiled. "I feel weird." Jimmy's head began to swim. The world went dark all around him.

Jimmy awoke in a soft comfortable bed. He felt enveloped in soft satin and silk. A familiar soothing scent filled his nostrils. It was lavender. The room was dark as Jimmy opened his eyes. He could feel that someone was in the room. He slowly began to realize that he was back in his room in Estal.

"Hey. Are you ok?" It was Amanda's voice.

"Yeah, where am I?" Jimmy was trying to focus. He still felt light headed. "How did I get back here?"

"Conner thought that you'd be more comfortable if we brought you back to more familiar surroundings," Amanda told him.

"What happened?" Jimmy was trying to regain his composure.

"You are still in shock." Amanda began to explain, trying not to laugh out loud.

"Your body is ready to be female, but your mind is still tussling. You are still fighting it. It may be conscious or subconscious, but you are sparring nonetheless. Don't. The less you fight, the sooner you can enjoy being you," Jimmy sat there in silence. "Maggie talked with Conner. There is going to be one final dinner in the city. You are the special guest. Proper dress is required."

"What do you mean *proper dress*? I don't have a thing to wear." Jimmy was already getting nervous.

"Spoken like a true woman," Amanda laughed. "I had a feeling you would say that, so I laid some things out for you. There a few things I think you'll look nice in. Run through the shower. It will help you clear your head. I'll be back in a few minutes. There is a robe for you to wear hanging on the door. I think you'll like it." With that, Amanda got up and joyfully bounced out the door.

Jimmy walked over to the bed where Amanda left the clothes. Jimmy picked up the hangers, one by one. The first was a black dress with lace and spaghetti straps. A white satin button-down blouse with a long black skirt lay next to it. A black camisole with a red overshirt and a medium length blue denim skirt rounded out the choices, with appropriate undergarments.

"Wow!" Jimmy said aloud as he shook his head. "This is too weird." It felt a bit overwhelming, but at the same time, it seemed to fit. Jimmy turned and went into the small bathroom just off his main bedroom.

The shower seemed to melt away the stress. Jimmy could not get the thought of the clothes out of his mind. The thought of them excited him but still made him a bit uneasy. He thought about the clothing options as the warm water cleansed his body. Nerve endings all over seemed to be more awake. Maybe it was just an over-active imagination.

Jimmy toweled off and returned to the main bedroom. Making his choice, he set the other outfits aside. Dressing in the camisole and denim skirt felt odd. The camisole fit snugly on the torso but was very comfortable. The skirt went on like a normal pair of shorts but hung down to the knees. The red overshirt and matching flats finished off the ensemble. With his hair still wet, he looked at the reflection in a full-length mirror. For the first time, he looked different. It was a strange but familiar view. A shiver went down his spine. There was a knock at the door.

Amanda was waiting in the doorway with a smile. "You look good. Excellent choice. You may have an eye for fashion yet," She said as she let herself in. Amanda was dressed in a black denim skirt and white silk blouse. Jimmy was amazed at how beautiful the young woman looked. He was envious. She was carrying a small case she sat on the small table in the room. "Now, for the finishing touches!" Amanda smiled.

"What finishing touches?" Jimmy got more nervous as Amanda pulled out a blow dryer, curling iron and plugged them in.

"I borrowed a few things from Isabelle. Let's get to work." Amanda started Jimmy's makeover. "When it comes to makeup, remember a little goes a long way. Don't worry, you'll catch on." Amanda could tell that Jimmy was nervous.

Within forty-five minutes, hair, makeup, and nails were completed. "Take a look." Amanda was pleased with her work. As Jimmy once again looked in the mirror, amazement grew a smile on his – no, *her* face. It was excessively confusing. He no longer saw his own reflection. Instead, a beautiful young woman stared back from the looking glass at Jimmy. Jimmy also felt sad. He felt like it was only an illusion.

"What?" was all that could be muttered as a hand went up to touch the young woman's face.

"It's you, Jimmy. This is who you are meant to be," Amanda smiled at the young woman. Jimmy realized that this was the young woman seen in Amanda's vision, except for the boyish figure. "Just a few more things and we'll be ready to go." Amanda produced a beautiful silver necklace with a winged tiger pendant and a pair of diamond earrings.

As Jimmy faced the mirror, Amanda placed the silver chain around Jimmy's neck. Reaching under Jimmy's hair she clasped the chain. The pendant rested on the collarbone. Amanda placed the earrings on Jimmy's lobes. The diamonds seemed to sit there magically. A quick prick of pain in both ears made Jimmy wince. "Maggie sent those as a gift. They are self-piercing earrings," Amanda stepped back to look at Jimmy's refection. "You are beautiful," Jimmy smiled in agreement. "I think we are ready." Jimmy noticed that Amanda wore a matching necklace.

Conner was again seated at the head of the table in all his elfin finery. He was dressed in an emerald green tunic and tan britches. A band of emerald thread and silver adorned his head. His elfin blade hung to his side and a bow and quiver hung on the back of his chair.

Maggie sat opposite of him in a long flowing dress of silver-woven thread. It shimmered with every movement. Maggie looked angelic with a headband of the purest silver holding back her red locks. A silver sash adorned her waist that held an elegant, but deadly, elfin blade.

Buck sat to Conner's right, and Nedloh to Bucks. Both were in proper dwarf battle dress. They wore tan tunics with their family crest embroidered in silver and gold. Their heads, adorned with ceremonial helms wrought of gold and silver presented a noble sight. They were fashioned by the finest dwarf artisans. Their dwarf battle axes sat at their sides with broadswords at their waists.

Isabelle was the first of the human women to arrive. A simple black flight suit that was unzipped to just above the naval covered an amethyst camisole. It may not have been red-carpet attire, but it was elegant and battle ready. The flight suit still illustrated her shapely figure. She took her seat at Conner's left. Two empty seats to Isabelle's left awaited their occupants. The five did not wait long.

Amanda entered the dining hall first. She paused at the doorway with a smile. The young woman looked back to motion in her unseen friend. "Please don't laugh. Jimmy is kind of nervous." She said looking down at the ground and teetering on the side of her foot. She stepped to the side of the door. Making the motion of a game show model, she held out her hands in presentation. Jimmy peered in around the edge of the door. Jimmy was more than a little nervous.

"Please join us, little ones." Conner motioned the two to have a seat at the feasting table. Amanda reached out and took Jimmy's hand, leading Jimmy to the table. Amanda even pulled the chair out for her friend and waited for Jimmy to sit before seating herself. Conner smiled. Jimmy felt a familiar calm rush over. This time, Jimmy did not faint.

"You look absolutely beautiful, my dear." Maggie reached out and gave Jimmy's hand a comforting squeeze. Maggie's smile warmed Jimmy's heart.

"Thank you," Jimmy said as a blush warmed his face.

"Tonight we dine on this possible eve of battle." Conner broke the silence.

"These are troubled times, and our fair city may be in lethal danger. We have found friends of honor and purity among humanity. To protect our newfound friends, I present these gifts!" With a wave of his hand, a table appeared with four bundles wrapped in elfin silk—three bundles were for each of the humans seated. The first was a long and narrow bundle, wrapped in silk the color of amethyst. There was a second gift wrapped in scarlet while the third offered the deepest purple. "These gifts are not given lightly. They are presented to you in the hope that they serve you well." Conner stood and handed the amethyst bundle to Isabelle. Amanda accepted the purple bundle while Jimmy received the scarlet.

After all, bundles had been handed out, all present waited for the packages to be opened.

Isabelle was first. Her bundle was close to six feet long. She removed the elfin silk to reveal a long wooden staff. One end gilt and the top adorned with an amethyst crystal. The wood of the staff had grown around it. "This staff is of great power. A wise hickory of the forest donated it. It is strong enough for defense and its crystal will focus your magical energies." Conner informed the woman and nodded to Amanda.

Amanda's bundle was long, but not close to the length of Isabelle's. She pulled back the violet silk to reveal a golden bow and a white leather quiver full of beautiful, but deadly, elfin arrows. "This bow and quiver are magical weapons that have been in elfin possession for eons. It was the last bow made before the magic was locked away. To the pure of heart, any arrow shot from this bow will always hit its mark. It has an ease of pull but multiplies the power of its archer's arm one-hundred fold. The quiver is also magical in nature. In a time of need, it will never empty. The bolts multiply with a power of their own."

Jimmy opened the last bundle. The removal of the bright red silk revealed a long elfin blade. The elfin steel had an elegant blue sheen. Its pommel was of purest gold with a flawless ruby set at its end. The pommel's handle was wrapped tightly in leather to give it a comfortable, firm grip. "This sword was the last blade made by elfin smiths. It is called *Nathra*, "Evil's Bane". It was forged from the hottest fires, deep within the Earth. It, too, contains great power. It is light in weight but stronger than any other weapon ever forged. Its edge will never dull. If lost or dropped, simply speak its name. It will return to you."

Conner opened the fourth bundle himself. The plain white silk bundle contained three undergarments of elfin silver. Each one was of feminine cut and had room in the chest for womanly curves. The elf handed the garments to the three humans seated at the table. Jimmy looked at the gift with confusion. It had the most room. Conner just smiled.

"These undergarments are of a magical cloth. No blade, arrow, nor spear shall penetrate this cloth. These are given in the hope that they may protect you from a fatal blow," Conner took his seat at the table. "Now that the gifts have been received, let us feast!" The elf waved his hand once again. This time, the table filled with food and drink. Tankards of ale for the dwarves, and fine elfin wine for the rest.

"I would like to propose a toast!" Maggie stood in all her elfin radiance and raised her glass. "To Estal, the city that has protected us for these past eons. May she hold fast and her walls be strong." The rest of the table raised their glasses and tankards with cheers of agreement. All drank deeply. Amanda and Jimmy felt the warmth well from inside. Jimmy also felt something unfamiliar.

"I think another toast is called for," Conner stood as Maggie sat. He looked directly at Jimmy. "We have a new friend with us who is in need of our help in a special way. Jimmy, you are beginning a journey few take. Since you have come to us, you have found yourself a new. Deep in a male's body lies a female soul. Confusing as it may be for you, we are here to help you through this," Jimmy felt a lump well up. "This is a special meal that not only honors our beloved city but you," Conner continued. "Not many have the courage to undertake such a journey. I believe you have that valor. I am sure that I speak for everyone here as we offer you our strength as well," Conner paused and raised his glass in Jimmy's direction. "From this moment forth, I bid you release your male labels and grasp your new found womanhood!" Jimmy felt very odd as well as a strange calm. "Though your journey is just beginning, I decree that you will no longer hold any male titles. Now, do you wish to take a new name? If so, one will be offered to you." Conner waited for Jimmy's response. The newly proclaimed young woman contemplated.

"I don't wish to confuse everyone more than I have to, but I think I would like something similar," Jimmy said sheepishly with her hands folded in her lap.

"We are all family here," Conner looked around the table. "Is there anyone here who wishes to rename this beautiful young lady?" Conner smiled as the teen blushed.

"I do!" Amanda quickly spoke up. "I think *she* should be called *Jamie*." She smiled at her friend as they held hands.

"Are there any objections?" Conner looked about the table once again and stopped at the young woman in question. The table agreed. "Then, from this moment forward, I proclaim you..." Conner looked at the teen seated between Amanda and Maggie. "...a young woman in the eyes of all seated here, and in the eyes of the cities in which we seek shelter. I can grant you that status no further than those boundaries. I also name you, with all seated here and in the cities in which we seek shelter, *Jamie*.

"Now, I don't know about you all, but I'm famished. Let's eat." Conner lifted his glass as the table cheered. The teen, newly named Jamie, began to shed tears of joy as Amanda embraced her and kissed her cheek gently. All drank from their glasses and tankards, sealing the words with a bond of friendship.

As the meal progressed, Jamie felt more at ease with her new status. The conversation was light and cheerful. Every time she heard her new name spoken, she easily responded. She felt it odd how quickly she began to shed her old self. Her new name seemed to feel right. This true self newly discovered easily began to envelop her sweetheart.

The meal came to an end too soon. As the candles on the table burned low and the platters of food were emptied, Conner once again stood and addressed the table. "This meal has ended. Let us all get some rest," Conner looked at the three women seated to his left. "Cherish your gifts, for they may save your life. Tomorrow is a new day, possibly one of loss and danger. Sleep lightly, but rest. If you'll excuse me, I bid you good night." With that, he got up and left the table. All watched him leave.

Jamie sat quietly in her room with the elfin blade on her lap and the undershirt at her side. The events of the meal replayed in her thoughts. She looked at the blade for a moment before grasping the handle and drawing it out of its leather sheath. Jamie felt the power surge from the blade. She also felt strength build in her right arm. The ruby glowed shortly. The sword had found its new mistress.

While she was sheathing the sword, she picked up the undergarments. She was awed at their delicate beauty. How could something so beautiful stop a blade or spear? She undressed to her waist and donned the undershirt. It fit sufficiently well except in the chest. She checked herself in the mirror. It felt so odd to her, but she figured that it had been tailored for changes to come. She also tried to replay the conversation at dinner. *She, womanhood, female, her, Jamie.* All these words swam in her thoughts. It was hard to refer to oneself in the opposite gender after being used to being male for so long. Jamie may still be anatomically male, but she knew that mentally, emotionally and spiritually, she was female. She took a moment for everything to sink in.

You are on your way, little one. She could hear Joy's voice in her thoughts. *You are who you are. You are a young woman.*

"How can this be?" Jamie said to her reflection. Joy's transparent image appeared in the reflection just behind her. "I still have all the outdoor plumbing. I don't even look much different."

*But you **do** look different, do you not?* Joy asked.

"Yes. I am just having a hard time grasping the concept. Does this not make me a freak of nature? Is this some kind of blasphemous sin?" Jamie questioned the morality of it all.

In time, you will understand the meaning of your gift. As for The Creator, he does not make mistakes, so how can this make you a freak of nature? He does not see this as a sin, but as a blessing and a challenge for you. Joy tried to explain.

"I still have feelings for Amanda. Is it wrong? Shouldn't I start to have a thing for guys? I am so confused!" Jamie felt the frustration build inside her.

The Creator has brought you together. Do you not feel that you and Amanda have gotten close in a short period of time?"

"Yes. I feel like we have known each other forever." Jamie told the angelic reflection.

The Creator has created you two for each other. You are soul mates. She feels drawn to you as well. Fret not! As for the outdoor plumbing, that, too, will change in time.

Jamie was startled by a knock at the door. When she looked back in the mirror the image of Joy was gone. She turned to answer the door.

Amanda wandered the corridor. She knew she should return to her room and get some rest. She could not get Jamie off her mind. She began to care deeply for her almost immediately upon meeting. Amanda knew that all of this was hard for her friend. Learning about elves, dwarves and magic were extremely hard to fathom. Jamie had to deal with an identity crisis as well. Her heart went out to the newly proclaimed young woman.

Wandering in deep thought, she found herself in front of Jamie's door. She stopped. Amanda hesitated a moment before knocking. She hoped that Jamie was still up.

Opening the door, Jamie's heart leaped at the sight of her friend. "Hey." was all she could manage to say.

"Hey, I was hoping you hadn't gone to bed yet." Amanda was glad Jamie was still up.

"Naw, I really can't sleep too well. I have many things to try to figure out." Jamie fidgeted. She really did not know what to say. Jamie wanted to say many things but she did not know if she should. There was a short silence.

"If you want, we could talk." Amanda looked thoughtfully into Jamie's eyes.

"Um, yeah, sure, come in." Jamie opened the door wider to let Amanda in.

"It's been quite a night, hasn't it?" Amanda tried to get the conversation started as she seated herself on Jamie's bed.

"Yeah, crazy..." Jamie felt her heart racing in her chest.

"That shirt looks kind of strange on you." Amanda noticed Jamie wearing the silver undershirt.

"Yeah, it fits in most places." Jamie looked down and pulled the undergarment, trying to stretch the looseness out.

"It looks like you have been given room in the cups," Amanda explained.

"Cups? I don't get it." Jamie looked even more confused.

"The cups are where your boobies go, silly!" Amanda giggled.

"Oh!" The confusion quickly left. She did feel silly. "Sorry." Jamie felt embarrassment well up inside her.

"Hey, it's okay. You haven't been a girl for long. You have a lot to learn. Don't worry, you'll be okay," Amanda assured her. She grabbed Jamie's hand and sat her on the bed. They looked at each other in an uncomfortable silence. "I wonder how mine fits?" Amanda stepped into the bathroom to change.

"I hope yours fits better," Jamie commented.

"Well if it's anything like yours, I hope it fits just as badly," Amanda said an insincere tone. Jamie could not help but giggle. Amanda quickly joined her.

"It's not too bad," Jamie commented as Amanda showed off her new clothes.

"You still have room." Jamie tried to help.

"Yeah, but I think you'll have me beat." Amanda giggled hysterically. Both laughed together like the teenage girls they were. After several moments, they both began to compose themselves.

"I guess I better get to bed. Tomorrow is probably going to be busy. You should get some sleep too." Amanda got up and headed for the door

"Amanda," Jamie called to her friend as she reached for the doorknob. "Please don't go. I don't want to be alone. Could you stay with me tonight?" Jamie had tears forming in her eyes.

"Sure. I think I could do that," Amanda turned around to face Jamie. The tears in Jamie's eyes had spilled over causing her eyeliner and mascara to run. Amanda wiped the colored tear from Jamie's cheek. "Go wash your face first." Amanda gave Jamie a warm smile.

"Okay." was all Jamie could manage to say as she sniffed back the tears. She went into the bathroom. She blew her nose and washed all the makeup off. Her face felt clean and refreshed. Knowing that Amanda was staying calmed her fears. When she returned, Jamie found Amanda curled up asleep on the far side of her bed. She was still dressed, but fast asleep. Jamie pulled back the covers and crawled in beside her. Sleep overtook her as quickly as it did Amanda. Both dozed in each other's arms.

Chapter 33

Aanor sat outside the huge wooden gates. Stone had been fitted before him in an oddly definable placement. The dwarf had the comfortable warmth of stone surrounding him. A small slit built into the wall allowed anyone coming down the large corridor to be seen. To his side sat his trusty ax and short broadsword. Situated in front of him stood a machine gun, ready to be used to cut down multiple targets without leaving his safe place. Cans of ammunition for this modern weapon were stacked all around him. Floodlights also stood at the ready. His brother, Aaron, sat opposite of him in similar conditions.

Aanor was the eldest son of Aador. Aaron was fifty years younger. Aanor had been a master mason all his life. Stone was all he knew until recent weeks. His family had sworn to help protect humanity and magic thousands of years ago. They were a proud clan. Pride in the family duties passed down through the generations.

Tonight, there was no peace at all, just an eerie quiet. For the past week, he had sat here as part of a guard detail of dwarves that changed every four hours. He watched and waited patiently alongside his brother. The corridor was well lit. Nothing would get by them.

Felthig busied himself in the armory. Along with many other elves and dwarves, they readied weapons for battle. The master swordsman polished every blade to a razor sharp edge. He had seen many battles through time. This one was not only for the sake of the city but for all who lived on this planet.

Conner had put him in charge of the task of readying the weapons. Dwarves hammered armor; elves strung bows, fletched arrows, and polished blades. There were also modern weapons added. M60 machine guns and a myriad of small arms ammunition were stored here. The modern weapons were well oiled and maintained. The elf saw to this. It was his passion.

General Rawl waited outside the hangar until nightfall. His troops were growing restless. They were three thousand strong. Heavies and goblins waited for battle in separate camps. As dusk grew near, the Necrogulls took flight. Twenty-four armored beasts and their goblin riders searched the ground for the enemy. They were ready to capture or kill anything that may escape.

He was not surprised by the quiet in the air. "They are hiding in their holes like vermin," he said to the setting sun. Dark sunglasses made the sunlight bearable. He would be glad when the bright light shut away for the night.

As the goblin watched the sun sink beyond the horizon, he called the troops together. A blast of a horn made from a long defeated dragon summoned them to arms. Fires sprung up from around the camps. Heavy and goblin alike began to form ranks. Row after row of grotesque brutes could be seen. In the same valley where the Seventh Cavalry was slaughtered by savages, the army of evil gathered to slaughter once again.

"Attack!" Rawl bellowed with a crude battle ax in his left hand and sawed off shotgun in his right. Both were high over his head in a battle frenzy.

Quickly, the masses flowed over the hangar like a tidal wave, crushing and destroying everything in their path. Thunder rose from the ground at the advancing horde. The massive doors to the hangar were peeled away like aluminum foil. The surge of flesh rushed through.

It was faint at first, like a gentle rain on an old barn roof. The quiet of the night slowly left Aanor. The gentle rustling in the distance grew steadily louder into a distant roar, which grew louder still. The dwarf picked up the handset to his right. The intercom was connected to a small but heavily fortified command room within the city.

"Conner here." The elf was on the other end.

"We have incoming," Aanor informed. "They are coming through the front gates."

"Roger that. Hold steady. Give us as much time as you can." Conner told the dwarf.

"My brother and I will do our best. Remember us in song." The dwarf knew that this would be his last act, as did Conner.

"It will be done. You will not be forgotten, my friend." He hung up the receiver knowing that they would be the first to die in this battle.

The sound of the horde grew to a defining roar. He pulled his weapons charging handle to the rear and looked down the sight of his M60. The darkness seemed to bloom from the corridor. It came like a cloud, absorbing the light that emitted from the fluorescence in the ceiling. His dwarf eyesight quickly adjusted. In the darkness, he saw the misshapen human hulks.

Muzzle flashes were quickly extinguished in the magical darkness. This did not make the enchanted ammunition any less effective. Bodies fell as soon as they came into view. Putrid flesh began to pile up in the main corridor. For every goblin and heavy that fell, twenty more took their places. Without a word, Aaron would cover as Aanor would change ammunition belts and vice versa. Empty brass shells fully covered the stone floor. Soon, the dwarves were up to their waists in spent rounds. Aanor realized he was on his last belt and it was growing short. Until this point, nothing had gotten through.

Click! The belt was empty. With their last rounds spent, the brothers jumped from behind the safety of the stone. Standing back to back, they began defending with their axes. They cut, hacked and slashed, but it was only seconds until they were defeated. Each had brought down a dozen by the blade before they met their ends in glory.

Conner sprinted down the corridor. He wove his way through the elves and dwarves coming to the protection of Estal. In the chaos, there was order. He had to make sure of it. He quickly ran into Isabelle. He grabbed the woman and held her firmly by her upper arms.

"Get the kids. It's time to get out of here. Go out the back way. It comes out into the forest. We don't have much time." Isabelle nodded an acknowledgment and then ran in the opposite direction. In the distance, Conner could hear the pounding on the massive wooden doors.

Conner raced to the main promenade. The sounds were deafening. Each impact was punctuated by a faint crack, which grew louder with every strike. Archers and gunners stood their ground as they watched the wood, several feet thick, flex inward.

Several minutes went by until the door finally gave in. With massive splinters of wood flying through the air, Estal was breached. Lines of archers welcomed their guests with volley after volley. Small arms quickly rang out from both sides. Elves and dwarves used the stone tree columns as shields. The clang of steel on steel added to the symphony of destruction. Goblins and heavies poured through the gaping maw like hot pitch. The promenade filled with destruction.

"Pull back! We can't hold them." Conner bellowed. "Everyone to the forest!" With the order, explosions burst from the ceiling. Large stones rained from above the intruders. Many of the hordes were crushed by boulders the size of small cars. The confusion allowed the defenders to flee.

Some brave souls only retreated as far as the library. A small band of elves, which consisted mostly of the keepers of the knowledge, defended the remaining volumes with their lives. With the onslaught, they lasted only a few minutes.

The horde began to break into smaller parties, chasing the survivors as they retreated. They had orders to kill all dwarves and decapitate all captured elves on sight. Elves and dwarves alike made sure that their individual deaths were worthy of song.

Isabelle ran ahead of those retreating. She came to Jamie's room first. Without knocking, she barged in. "It's time to leave. Grab what you can carry and let's go." She was not surprised that Amanda was in bed with Jamie.

The teens quickly put their tops back on over the elfin clothing and grabbed their gifts. Isabelle checked the corridor. It was empty but would not remain so. She could hear the battle approaching. With her sidearm drawn, she waved the two into the hall.

The three humans ran as quickly as they could. Jamie had her blade drawn and Amanda had notched an arrow. As they turned the first corner, they met a half dozen of the horde.

"Two to one, not too bad..." Jamie said. Jamie felt a surge of strength as she swung. A goblin parried and answered with a crude battle-axe. Jamie easily blocked the beast that was close to twice her size. Before Jamie could swing, again an arrow pierced the beast's eye.

"You don't need to impress me," Amanda said. "I already love you." Jamie was distracted by the girl's words. A heavy raised a homemade mace. Isabelle dropped it with a shot through the head. Before the others could avenge the deaths of their comrades, they fell at the hands of Amanda's bow and Isabelle's Colt.

"We don't have time to plan a wedding, girls. We have to move now!" Adrenaline pumped through her veins. The three quickly returned to a sprint down the winding halls of Estal. They were far from safe. The pursuit was relentless.

"I never had any idea this place was so big. Are we lost?" Jamie asked in between breaths.

"No. The exit is just up ahead." Isabelle assured the teens.

"I have to catch my breath," Amanda informed Isabelle.

"I think we have lost them. We can't stop long. We have to keep moving." Isabelle was also gasping to fill her lungs, as she replaced the empty magazine in her pistol, they swiftly returned to their escape. This time, they had a slower, but steady, pace.

Amanda screamed and fell as a bullet sliced through her shoulder. Their pursuers were gaining. Jamie was immediately at her side.

"I'm okay. It's just the shoulder. We can take care of it when we get to the wood." Jamie could see the pain Amanda made a futile attempt to cover.

Jamie helped Amanda to her feet, carrying her on the opposite shoulder. "How can you love me?" Jamie asked.

"I'll tell you later," Amanda answered.

"There may not be a later."

"Don't say that. You know there will be." Amanda gave Jamie a stern look. "Shut up, and let's go!"

Jamie picked up the wounded girl with a strength she did not know she possessed. As they moved forward, a pinprick of sunlight appeared before them. With renewed energy, they ran toward it.

The small remnants of the horde were closing quickly. Isabelle turned around periodically in the hopes of lengthening their lead squeezing off several shots. Her rounds were rapidly spent. They ran toward a flight of stone steps with goblins immediately behind. They could smell the goblins rank odor as they started up the stairs.

In a frantic attempt to move her feet faster Jamie missed a step. Falling, she landed on the now unconscious Amanda. She could feel the monsters pawing at her ankles, pulling both of them back into the darkness.

Jamie was lifted up and pulled into the light. "*Vearnul masrieneth!*" Isabelle recited ancient words as the crystal glowed instantly into a blinding light. Jamie could see nothing. Conner rushed back into the tunnel, firing round after round as he chased the blinded goblins back into the depths of Estal.

"*Demaruth hasthbreth.*" Conner invoked words, sealing the tunnel in which they just exited with a massive cave in.

"Where's Amanda?" Jamie demanded frantically as she blinked away the green spots before her eyes.

"She's gone," Conner tried to calm the girl.

"What do you mean, *gone*? I just had her in my arms," Jamie insisted.

"You fell on top of her and when I picked you up the goblins grabbed her. I'm sorry." Conner knew that not all the elfin magic in the world could calm the ache of lost love.

"We have to go back! We have to save her!" Hysterical tears flowed down Jamie's cheeks.

"There are too many of them, sweetie. She's gone. I'm sorry." Isabelle stood the young woman up and embraced her. Holding her as tight as she could, the embrace was keeping Jamie from trying to dig her way back in, as well as letting her know that she was not alone.

The dark lord surveyed the spoils of his victory. Heavies escorted him up the stone steps that led to the library. He marveled over the remaining volumes. A thin smile formed on his lips.

"You have done well, General. We have the city as well as elfin knowledge. Whatever escaped can be hunted down with the information left behind."

"Thank you, my lord." The goblin general had followed his master. He remained at a constant three steps behind as homage to his dark lord.

Maggie knew of the battle. She had spent the entire evening preparing to receive wounded. She now had a more pressing task. She searched the volumes of magic that brought in from the city in hopes of saving the texts that had remained behind. Evil could not be allowed to possess it. The evil could eventually possess the elves.

"Necthar remount." As the words were spoken, a large volume floated from the huge stacks. It was bound in the large breast scales of a dragon. The book gently floated to her hands and opened to the pages in which she sought. She scanned the page for the incantation

"Emeleth pem adule es mereanné alane." the elfin woman began to chant. As she repeated them, the wind blew her hair into fiery wisps from all directions. Her voice boomed louder with every refrain. As her chanting came to its climax, powerful elfin magic brought the remaining texts into the meadow with a blinding flash of blue-green lightning. The elfin woman collapsed.

Esuorts was proud of his captured knowledge. He knew that with it, evil could corrupt the good that lay within the bindings before him. From there he could corrupt and bend the entire world to his bidding.

As he perused the pages of a nearby text, he felt the power surge around him. A gust fluttered the pages within the library. In a blinding flash, all was gone.

"Elves!" He blinked the vision back into his eyes. With one stroke of his hand, the head of his general burst and the body fell to the floor. His black life's fluid poured from the opening. "You have failed me for the last time, Rawl!"

Amanda could barely breathe from the stench. The pig-like brute had her slung over its shoulder. If it had not been for the goblin, she would have been crushed by the cave in. She wondered if she would have been better off.

Why was she still alive? Would she be a meal? Every possibility ran through her mind all at once. Thoughts of torture and a slow, painful death brought a terror she had never previously felt. Panic caused her heart to race. The rancid air made it difficult to fill her lungs. Spots flickered before her eyes just before total blackness overtook her.

Esuorts sat in the now empty library contemplating his next conquest. It was obvious the elves had not been destroyed, only weakened. They no longer had a home. Wandering around the countryside, his enemy could be slowly crushed like dying embers.

The cold stone of the city was elegantly carved. He admired the dwarf artisanship. Maybe he would enslave what was left of them and have them build him a stone empire. He relished his victory and mourned his loss.

"My lord, I bring a gift." A smaller goblin entered the empty library with a limp body slung over his shoulder.

"Who is it who bothers me during my musings?" Esuorts was irritated with the interruption.

"I am Corporal Theck, Sire." The servant of the dark lord genuflected and did not raise his head. "I bring you a prisoner."

"I ordered no prisoners, Theck." Anger flashed in the sorcerer's eyes. "Why have you disobeyed me?"

"Forgive me, my lord," Theck cowered before the sorcerer. "It is human." The goblin placed the young woman down before his master.

"Human you say?" Esuorts inspected the unconscious girl. "This one has great power. You have done well by bringing it to me," The sorcerer reached down and drew the goblins jagged sword. With one clean swipe, he cleaved the brute's right ear. Theck squealed and grabbed his head where his ear used to be. "I cannot have disobedience go unpunished. Consider yourself fortunate that you have brought me such a prize. Let this serve as a reminder for the future, General Theck."

Chapter 34

Conner found Maggie barely hanging to life. To the side of the meadow, amongst a massive pile of books and scrolls, she lay. The magic she had used was great, almost too great for her to handle. Conner knew immediately what had happened.

"We need a stretcher over here!" Conner called. What able bodies could be seen were tending those that were not so able. Wounded were scattered about on tables, stretchers, or anything that could be used. Moans of the wounded and wailing for the dead were all that was heard.

Two elves came with a stretcher for the elfin woman. Gently picking her up off the grass, they quickly took her to a healer. Conner knew that the only thing that could be done was to watch and wait. The healers knew what herbs could be used to strengthen her magic. As the elf watched her being taken away, anger boiled up from deep within.

"Isabelle, meet me in the operations tent in ten minutes and be ready to fly!" Conner demanded as he walked off alongside Maggie. "Call in Ned, Buck and Ardy." Isabelle choked back her grief for Amanda. She had an idea what the elf had in mind.

An evil smile formed on her face as thoughts of revenge came to mind.

The woman quickly rounded up the two dwarves and elf. They waited patiently for Conner. The four sat in silence. Losses had been great for all, but there was no time for mourning. The battle was not over.

"Are the aircraft ready to fly?" Conner came into the tent and wasted no time getting down to business.

"Aye, lad. That they are. We could only get the vintage planes to the meadow in time." Buck tried to explain. "I believe that anything else left back was destroyed."

Isabelle's heart sank as she thought of her car being smashed by goblins and heavies. She dispelled the thought. The loss of the car was nothing compared to losing Amanda. Material things could be replaced, but Amanda could not.

"This is the deal. We all knew what was at stake when we decided to stay behind, but we are not going to just take this lying down," Conner started pacing in front. The rest of the pilots sat in the rows of folding chairs set up inside the tent. "I saw two flights of Esuorts' precious flying beasts over the hangar. I know I do my best in the air, so I say we bring the fight back to him."

Buck stroked his beard as he listened to the elf. "It could be used as a diversion to send a team of elves to see if Estal can be retaken. We can see if anyone was left behind and..."

"See if they can find Amanda." Isabelle interrupted.

"If they can find her alive, and bring her back," Conner finished. "I think knowing what happened to the girl would help all of us a lot. Agreed?" The room nodded and mumbled in tired concurrence. "Isabelle, you'll fly with me again, and Ardy, you fly wing for the *Griffon Claw.*"

"Who is going to fly the bomber?" Ned asked.

"You know her best. Have you still been playing with your simulators?" Conner looked at the young dwarf.

"Yeah, but computers and the real thing aren't quite the same." Nedloh reminded the elf.

"We don't have time for lessons, lad," Buck stated the obvious. "I'm just wonderin' who ya gonna get to work the targeting computers."

"Good question, Buck," Conner smiled. "And to answer it: You will."

Buck's eyes grew as large as saucers. "You don't think I'm goin' up in an untested plane, with untested systems and a pilot that has never flown before, do ya, lad?"

"You just survived a goblin horde, how bad can it be?" Conner raised a brow at the dwarf. "Now, let's get in the air."

"If ya kill me, lad, I'll never speak to ya again." Buck gave his nephew a gruff look.

"You promise?" The younger dwarf smiled as they left the tent.

Within minutes, all blades were turning. The fighters were first to leave the ground. The B17 took up the rear. It took mere seconds to reach what was left of the airfield. The massive beasts instantly saw that they were not alone.

"Dragon Squadron, this is Lead. We have twenty-four bogies. Take them down and watch each other's backs." Conner gave orders over the radio.

"Acknowledge."

"Two copies!" Isabelle was the first to pipe up.

"Roger, that!" Ardy took his turn. "Three copies!"

"Aye, lad." Buck made no attempt at radio etiquette.

"Buck, if you get your chance, take out ground troops with hellfire," Conner interjected. "We want to clear them out as much as possible."

Conner set the *Dragon's Heart* into a steep dive. Isabelle followed. They rushed in on the swarming monsters from above. Lining up his crosshairs, Conner was the first to take a shot. He missed. Breaking left, he leveled off. Shooting past his target, he realized his mistake. He just made himself the prey.

Conner looked in his rear view and saw the beast slash at his rudder. "I got ya, Lead." Isabelle was still behind Conner. She flipped the safety switch up on her flight stick. The woman waited patiently to line up her target. When she could, she gently squeezed the trigger. The small craft shook as her machine guns spit enchanted rounds. A fraction of a second after impact with the beast, the monster was shredded.

Conner was glad that Maggie had taken the time to put spells on the ammunition. Just as they had done to arrows in the days of old, the spells had turned ordinary lead rounds into armor-piercing, high explosive rounds. One down. They were only getting started.

Ned was still getting the feel for the bomber. He was a quick study. "Lad, we are surrounded by those infernal beasts. Do somethin' ta get them away." Buck was being too much of a side seat driver.

"Shooting them down is your job! I'm just trying to keep this thing in the air!" Ned was more than frustrated. "There are the computers, so get busy shooting those damned things down!" Ned banked the bomber right and put it into a dive.

Buck targeted the first monster manually. This enabled the computer to identify future targets based on size, shape, and temperature. Watching the screen, Buck squeezed the trigger. Red brackets formed around the Necrogull silhouette, locking the information into the computer. As the brackets flashed red, the cannons spat enchanted fire. The top turret purred as rounds spewed forth, and the second monster fell. The bottom turret then came alive and sang its song of death.

Ardy watched as two more of the flying amphibians fell by the might of the *Griffon Claw*. He was in awe at the destruction that the cannons brought forth.

"Four, this is Three. You are dropping everything that comes close to you," Ardy informed. "Whatever you did worked great."

"Thanks, Three," Ned answered. "I could never have done it without Amand..." The dwarf stopped short. "Never mind."

"I know what you mean," Ardy could hear the pain in the dwarf's voice. "Don't worry. We'll get her back."

"Give the radios a break you two. Stay focused. We'll mourn our losses after we even things out a bit." Conner cut in.

"Roger that, Lead," Ned answered. Pulling back on the yoke, the dwarf pulled the nose of the bomber up. The beasts quickly followed. The goblin riders realized that the larger plane was their greatest threat. They began to team up and systematically attack.

"They are going after the *Griffon Claw*!" Conner warned the others. "Watch your back, Four. We're on our way." Conner squeezed his trigger. His plane shook as fire spat from its wings. Breaking right, he pushed his throttle forward. Reaching the bomber would be imperative. He had to keep the monsters busy.

Conner and Isabelle reached the bomber almost at the same time. Isabelle picked off one of the creatures as it hit the nose and began to tear through the bomber's nose turret. It fell, but not without ripping the glass from the front of the B17.

Ned could feel the difference in the handling of the bomber almost instantly. With the lack of aerodynamics, he lost speed. She may not have been as fast, but the *Griffon Claw* was just as deadly.

The fighters were careful not to hit the bomber. They also did what they could to avoid the clouds of acid that the monsters emitted from their lower jaws.

The beasts quickly fell. Their numbers dwindled, but they were not running. It was better for the beasts to die in battle than to fail their dark lord.

It took some time, but the Dragon Squadron emptied the skies above Estal. They turned their attention to the hangar. The hordes still clambered over it like ants on spilled sugar.

"How's our ammo looking?" Conner asked as they all formed up.

"I'm at the half with six kills, Lead," Isabelle answered.

"Great work, Ace." Conner returned.

"I have three-quarters. I have four kills." Ardy answered.

"We are almost empty, but we still have the big guns, Lead," Ned answered.

"Three, you and two go in first, side by side."

Isabelle fell into formation next to the Messerschmitt. She pulled her charging handle and placed her finger on the trigger. As the two planes came in on the deck, she noticed goblins and heavies celebrating their victory. Her eyes burned in anger as she saw a group ripping her Chevy apart. She pulled the trigger.

The sound of the fighter planes startled the mob on the ground. All heads turned just in time to see fire shoot from the wings of the modern raptors. Many did not get to cover in time. They were cut down before they could move.

The mob parted like the Red Sea. Goblins and heavies ran for cover. The battle was no longer on their terms. Confusion was rampant.

Felthig followed his dwarf brother to another exit. He was thankful that it had not been covered. It was away from the forest so that if the enemy did find the exit, they still could not find the forest. At the same time, he thought that it was careless to have exits so close the forest. He would not be surprised if there more ways than this one back to Estal.

The master swordsman nodded his thanks to his guide. It was imperative that no sound be made. Along with the blade, he was a master of stealth.

Elves had a natural way of going about undetected. Felthig had taken this natural ability and made it an art form. He was dressed in a dark gray tunic and trousers. The same cloth covered his face, except for his eyes. The elfin cloth blended well with all stone and shadows.

Keeping to the nooks and crannies of the corridor, he made his way to the city. He was always vigilant for anything that could be on patrol in the tunnels. The corridor he was traversing was thought to have been known only by dwarf-kind. So far, it remained a well-kept secret. His footsteps were still silent as caution was the better part of valor.

Before long, he came to a crossroads in the tunnel. This is where he had to be on his toes. His elfin ears detected the faint squeals and grunts of the goblins. He could sense the others were getting frustrated. He surmised that they were the heavies. Being of human origin, they could not understand the goblin speech.

Squabbles broke out among the groups. Felthig utilized this distraction to advance his position. As quickly as the elf passed, commanding fiends squashed the arguments.

Goblins had set up camp within the stone city. The elf's art form was tested more than once as he slipped from stone to crevasse within the shadows.

The trek took several times as long as it should have. He waited patiently for opportunities to move. When that window opened, he quietly slipped through, unseen. Many times, he had to stop until the coast was clear.

The elf entered the promenade. The encampment was thickest here. Sticking to the outer walls, he made his way around to his right. He soon found himself outside the library doors. As a spider, he scaled the ornate pillars and slid into a hole in the elaborate carvings above the massive wooden door.

He watched an elder human male speak to a minor goblin. He knew that this was the dark sorcerer. He saw the goblin place an unconscious human girl at the sorcerer's feet. Felthig's keen elfin eyesight brought the girl's face to him immediately. He recognized Amanda.

The elf waited and watched, making less noise than the growing grass. Perched amongst the complex stone carvings, he was undetected. He waited for hours until the sorcerer left with the girl. He needed proof to take back to the woodland city. The only thing left behind was a bow and quiver. He slithered down to retrieve it.

Felthig pulled a small, lightweight bag of the same material out of a cargo pocket on the side of his left leg, and placed the weapons inside. As he was strapping the bag to his back, he could hear clumsy footsteps returning. He was sure they were looking for his position. Once again, he waited in the shadows.

A different goblin returned looking for the bow and quiver. As the goblin searched in vain for the weapon, the elf sprang from the shadows. With no more than a breath, he slid his blade across the throat of the creature. He held his hand over its putrid mouth to stifle the gurgling last breaths.

Isabelle banked right as she came within sight of the burning hangar. Goblins and heavies were already tearing it apart to make access to the city underneath. She hoped to discourage anyone wishing to stay.

The beasts were already returning fire. Machine-gun rounds whizzed by her canopy. She completed her first run and swiftly moved out of range of the small arms.

Conner brought the *Dragon's Heart* in front of the B17. He made more of the detestable creatures run for their lives with a squeeze of his finger. As the planes before, he rained fire down on the unwelcome monsters. He cleared the way for the *Griffon Claw*. The B17 flew just behind the P40 with its bomb-bay doors open. A heavily modified missile rack extended out of it holding, providing twenty-four of the self-propelled projectiles. The damage done by just one served its namesake well: *Hellfire.*

Conner flew just off the deck with the bomber behind. He was amazed at how quickly the young dwarf took to flying. "Steady, Four. On my mark..."

Conner let the hangar get closer, scattering the enemy as he came. "Now!"

Missiles flew from their racks as Conner pulled up into a lazy spiral. As each impacted in the hangar, they caused massive explosive damage.

Conner brought the *Dragon's Heart* around to survey the damage and choked at the sight. The smoke cleared a path. Esuorts stepped forward through the smoke and death. Hundreds of bodies lay scattered about the sorcerer. That did not matter. The only thing that did was the girl standing with him. He had Amanda.

The sorcerer raised his hand. A fireball shot from it directly at the P40. Conner banked left and dove. He could feel the heat as it barely missed him. Before he could think, the sorcerer and the girl blinked out of sight.

Chapter 35

Jamie sat in bewilderment. The babbling of the brook was the only comfort she had. Jamie could not believe that Amanda was gone. She should have saved her friend. The trickling rapids bounced and twirled the little leaf-boats that she had sent downstream. She paid no attention. Tears fell as easily as the stream danced upon the rocks, but her sobbing was not falling on deaf ears.

"Hello," a small voice said from behind her. Jamie jumped at the interruption. She just turned to see a badger standing behind her. "I'm sorry. I thought you were someone else."

"That's okay." Jamie did not say anything more.

"I'm Ms. Badger." The woodland creature tried to make conversation. "You look like you could use a friend."

"I had one, but I got her killed," Jamie said as she stared at the ground.

"I am so sorry. That sounds dreadful." Ms. Badger was honestly sympathetic. "Do you know this for certain?"

"The goblins took her just as the opening of the cave collapsed. They will eat her just like they eat everyone else." Her tears started fresh.

"I have met your friend. She is very special. Those who you do not know are watching her. Her destiny is not yet completed. Her light has not yet gone out."

"How do you know? I have seen what those things can do." Jamie felt anger well up inside.

"Do not worry. Just as you are here for reasons not yet known, so is Amanda." Miss Badger placed a warm furry paw on Jamie's hand. The gesture calmed the girl.

"Why are you even here? I'm sure you have other things to do besides spending time with a freak like me." Jamie pulled away from the soothing touch of the female badger.

"Actually, I was sent by another mutual friend to help you through this rough time. I am here to remind you that not all is lost. There is yet hope for Amanda." Jamie saw a smile form on the badger's face. Warmth glowed in the dark brown eyes of her furry friend. "The rest need you. They need your strength." Ms. Badger offered Jamie a tiny handkerchief.

"I don't feel very strong anymore." Taking the little hanky and drying her eyes. "It's not like it used to be."

"Fear not. What you lack now in the physical strength of a male, you make up for in the emotional and mental strength of a young woman." The smile grew wider and a sparkle shown in the badger's eye. "Yes, I know of your past. I too have a purpose."

"I should have saved her." Jamie choked back more tears.

"Could you have taken on the entire evil army? I think not. If you had, you would also have been lost. Two lights would have been foolishly extinguished. Instead, there is a chance to save our friend, Amanda. Conner and Isabelle will know not what to do. You need to point them in the right direction. You will suggest a rescue mission."

"I have no idea where they have taken her. How can I? I barely know who I am and what I'm doing." Jamie shook her head.

"In searching, you will find more than Amanda. It will lead you to where you are supposed to be." Ms. Badger assured her. Jamie could sense the wisdom in the badger's words.

"Thank you very much." The young woman dried her eyes. She embraced the woodland creature in an affectionate display of gratitude. "Forgive me, please. Being emotional is new to me."

Ms. Badger smiled. "You are fine, dear. Welcome to a whole new world." The badger returned the gesture. "Now run along. I think you have a lot to do to get our Amanda back. This will not be an easy task."

"You're right. I need to get back and see what we can do." Jamie got up and dropped her last leaf-boat into the stream. She did not watch it dance away. As she waved one last time to her new friend, she heard a buzzing overhead of returning aircraft. She looked up and dashed back into the forest.

Maggie rested comfortably. There was little that she could do to help. The best elfin healers had been watching over her since she was brought to the makeshift city. She had regained much of her strength but still had a long way to go before she could use her magic again. The trees had helped her as much as they could.

The Oak and otherwise trees had lent their strength so she did not have to recover unassisted. The elfin woman flowed deeply in the magic of the trees. This magic was related to that which held the Earth itself together.

Jamie knew that Conner and Isabelle would be busy with the aircraft. She was not quite ready to plan a rescue mission, anyway. She sat quietly next to the elfin woman. She watched her sleep in the hospital bed that grew right out of the wall of the massive pod. The Great Oak itself looked after the wounded.

"I had a dream about you," Maggie said in a soft tired voice as her eyes fluttered open. "I saw how bravely you fought. Womanhood has made you stronger and love has made that strength ferocious." Maggie's voice was barely a whisper. She motioned for Jamie to come closer.

Reaching out, Maggie gently touched Jamie's hand. Jamie felt a rush of warmth surge through her. It pulsed like a heartbeat. She felt the rhythm start with the elfin woman and race through her blood. She could gently hear it in her ears and soon her own heart was coordinated with it.

"Do you feel that?" Maggie asked.

"Yes, it's weird," Jamie informed her friend.

"How so?" The elf queried.

"At first, I could feel it in my heartbeat. It was as if they were in competition, but soon they fell into the same rhythm. It was as if they were beating as one."

"Good." Maggie let a warm but feeble smile form on her face. "You have been given power that most people can only be born with. Your love for Amanda has granted you friendship with all that grows."

"I don't understand." Jamie looked puzzled.

"The trees rule over all that is green and blooms. They feel your loss and pain. They also know of how selflessly you acted in trying to save her. They have pledged their friendship and loyalty. This has not been done for one of your kind since before the Son of The Creator walked the Earth."

"I don't understand how." Jamie was still puzzled, though somewhat less.

"All plants have roots that gather nourishment. This is common knowledge. What many humans do not know is that they also communicate through this massive system. You have been seen and heard, and it has been passed on to the king of trees. This Great Oak that you are in now rules over all that grows buds and blooms.

He has asked me to connect him to you so that he could bestow the gift of friendship upon you. Every plant throughout the world will do as you request of it. All you have to do is ask." Maggie's eyes closed in exhaustion. The conversation had taken a lot out of the elf woman.

"How do I do that?" The young woman asked.

"I must rest now. I can tell you more when I am well. As for knowing how? You will know when the time comes." Maggie drifted off to sleep.

"She's getting better. I think the trees are helping somehow" Jamie said. She really did not understand any of what was going on.

"Yes. This is a place of healing. The branches of the Great Oak cradle us and lend strength to those who need to heal. This speeds up the process. Maggie should be up and about tomorrow. She will be one hundred percent in a day or two." Conner explained.

"Excuse me, Anthriel." An elf dressed in dark gray appeared behind Conner and Isabelle. Together, Conner and the other elf stepped outside the door.

"Are you okay?" Isabelle asked. Concern radiated from the woman's body.

"I'm fine." Jamie lied.

"You don't have to be tough anymore," Isabelle started. "You're a chick now. You can let go. It's okay to hurt." Isabelle smiled at her own words. The expression on the woman's face was infectious. Jamie followed suit.

"I miss Amanda, but I already found a couple of friends to talk with while I was waiting for you to get back. Really, I'm fine for now. Maybe later?" Jamie asked.

"Sure. I need to clean up and rest. Maybe we can explore a bit after dinner."

"Amanda and..." Jamie started, but a lump in her throat quickly stopped her. "I saw most of it already." Jamie choked the lump back. "I can show you around a bit if you would like."

"I would like that." Isabelle turned and started to leave.

"Izzy?" Jamie got up as she saw Isabelle begin to leave.

"Yes?" Isabelle asked as she turned to see what the young woman needed. Without a word, Jamie ran up and put her arms around the tall woman. She began sobbing at Isabelle's bosom. The older woman felt Jamie's pain as she returned the embrace. "There, there. Go ahead and let it out. It's okay." Isabelle ran her fingers through Jamie's hair as she held her tight. With Isabelle's chin resting on the top of the young woman's head, she held her. She afforded a tear of her own to fall.

As Isabelle prepared for bed, the day's events had played out like a B movie. Her nightly rituals were tainted with death and destruction. To her astonishment, Isabelle slept peacefully. Although much had weighed her mind down when she closed her eyes, the gentle swaying of the trees seemed to lull her to rest almost instantly.

She awoke refreshed and ready to start the day. The events of yesterday seemed only a nightmare, but she still felt emptiness with Amanda gone. Her little place among the trees brought that reality rushing painfully back. The woman knew that the first order of business for today was to find Conner and see what needed to be done. Isabelle knew that Amanda had been taken. She just did not know where or if she could be rescued.

She dressed quickly. Donning a clean pair of jeans and tank top, she put her hair up in a ponytail. She did not have time for anything else. Time was a luxury that Amanda did not have, so why should she squander it? She stepped out of her home onto the walkway and into the warm summer morning.

"Good morning." A young voice greeted Isabelle. Jamie was perched on the sturdy handrail right outside Isabelle's pod.

"You're up early." Isabelle tried to make the conversation as casual as possible.

"I know. I have been up since before sunrise," Jamie answered. "The birds woke me."

"It's pretty up here." Isabelle took the time to soak in the wonder of the city hoping to keep Jamie distracted from the obvious.

"Yes, it is," Jamie was reaching for the strength she did not know she had. "No matter what, I can't deny that fact. I just wish I could have someone with whom to share it." Isabelle winced inwardly.

"I'm sorry." The older woman choked back returning tears.

"Don't be. We'll get her back and then I will enjoy the sunrise with Amanda." Isabelle saw the pain melt from Jamie's face. She had never before seen the strength.

"You are determined, aren't you?"

"I just know some things for a change that no one else does," Jamie smiled as she hopped off the railing.

"Really?" Isabelle saw the strength in the young woman. "Like what?" She prodded.

"If I told you, then I wouldn't be the only one that knows them." Jamie's smile grew broader. "What I can tell you is that Conner sent me down to get you. They are having a discussion about Amanda in the new meeting hall. He didn't think you knew the way."

"So he sent you to show me?"

"Kind of like that..." Jamie smiled.

Isabelle fell into step next to the young woman. There was something different about her young friend. Isabelle knew that loss can cause someone to grow up fast but that was not it. "So, why didn't you knock?" She asked.

"I knew you were almost ready, so I just waited until you came out," Jamie answered.

"How did you know?" Isabelle asked.

"The trees told me." Jamie's smile turned into a giggle. "They know everything."

"You talk with them?" Isabelle was curious.

"You can say that I have a special relationship with all things that grow." Jamie cupped her hand and whispered to a branch. She smiled as two beautiful white blossoms with petals tipped in pink budded and opened before their eyes. "These are a gift from the trees. They say that since we can't have blossoms of our own that we could have a couple of theirs." Jamie smiled as they dropped off into her hands.

"Tell them, thank you," Isabelle said as Jamie put one of the flowers into Isabelle's hair.

"They can hear you. They said you are most welcome." Jamie giggled as she put the other bloom in her own hair.

Isabelle was amazed. Just a week ago, the person walking next to her had been just a frightened homeless boy. The woman was astonished at who her friend had become in such a short time. Before her eyes, that scared little boy was becoming a beautiful young woman in mind, body, and soul.

Isabelle noticed the changes even in how Jamie looked and presented herself. As Jimmy, he acted like a tough street kid. Now Jamie was giggling. She still did not doubt how strong and tough Jamie was. As a woman, Isabelle was sure that her friend was even stronger in heart and mind.

She was amazed at how pretty the young woman had become. Her hair had definitely gotten longer. She noticed the curves in the young woman's waist. She was even sure that Jamie was getting breasts. Isabelle remembered how scary puberty was for her. She knew Jamie must be terrified. This was something completely new and unexpected for the younger woman. As long as Jamie was happy, Isabelle was happy for her. If Jamie needed anything, Isabelle vowed to herself that she would be there for her.

Chapter 36

Conner was waiting for Isabelle in the meeting hall. He was not alone. Around the large table in the center gathered several elves and dwarves. Maps were strung across the glossy living room table. Conner pored over them with Buck and Ardy. Murmurs of voices echoed, but no individual conversations could be singled out.

Looking up from the maps, Conner motioned everyone to their seats as soon as he saw Isabelle and Jamie enter the room. There was quiet almost instantly.

"You are probably wondering why I have asked you here after such a long and grueling day yesterday," he paused and heard only silence. "I know you are ready to mourn our losses, but it is still not the time. We have one loss that can still be retrieved." He motioned to the shadows. A darker elf emerged with a parcel. Isabelle recognized the elf from the night before in Maggie's wellness room.

"This is Felthig. He is a master swordsman and a master of stealth," Conner began to introduce the elf. "Not only is there no match for him with a blade, he can walk anywhere without being detected. Yesterday, he returned to Estal to gather information on our enemy. We provided cover in the form of an air offensive as a distraction. What we learned is grim. All our elfin brothers were decapitated and dwarf brothers enslaved."

Murmurs and whispers flowed around the room. "All is not lost. We had thought the one that I had sworn to protect was among the lost. Master Felthig proved us wrong. When he returned, he brought me this," Conner unwrapped a package. Jamie gasped as she watched him uncover Amanda's bow and quiver. "I personally watched as Esuorts, the evil sorcerer who brings these wretched times among us, take Amanda with him."

"Where did he take her?" Jamie asked as a tear rolled down her face.

"I do not know for certain, but I have an idea," Conner started as he handed the bow and quiver to Jamie. "You should watch after these until Amanda's return," Conner said to the younger woman.

"As I said, I have an idea where she is," Conner said as he unrolled a large map of the former United States of America and set it on the table. "I have seen his fortress here," Conner pointed to a place in the southwest portion of the map. "In the desert of what used to be Arizona, he has made himself a stronghold. Now I know we are all tired, but I propose a counter-offensive to return our brother dwarves and our sister to us," Conner looked straight at Jamie when he said this. He watched as the young woman's eyes lit up at the thought of reuniting with her friend. "Does anyone else agree?"

Whispers and talk went out amongst the group. Opinions varied. "We should cut our losses." a female elf said from the crowd.

"Our brothers have given much for our survival," Buck stated. "They dannot need to be left behind." More murmuring began.

"Look..." Jamie stood up. "We can leave no one behind!" She shouted. The room fell silent. "I know I have not been here long. I do know that the dwarves have given the elves a place to stay for thousands of years. Is this the way you reward hospitality? Amanda was the one who gave you warning of the attack. Without her, you would all be dead in your sleep. Is this how you say thanks?" Elf and dwarf hung their heads in shame. "If we know where they are, I say we go get them! Bring them home, or die to try!"

Isabelle was amazed at the words that just came out of the young woman's mouth. She knew she was right. By the looks of the crowd, they also knew it. Isabelle smiled.

"From the mouths of babes," Isabelle said aloud. She began to clap. Conner followed suit as he felt the strength and leadership flow from the young woman. Soon, the entire room roared with applause.

The elfin woman with dark flowing hair and bright eyes of sapphire was the first to answer. "I must apologize. I was wrong. You, young child, are correct. We owe a lot to our brother dwarves as well as your friend. I, Canthriel, pledge myself to your quest of bringing home our brothers and sister."

"I am honored," Jamie tried to show as much graciousness as she could. "All I ask is to help with whatever Conner has come up with. I trust him implicitly."

"Thank you," Conner smiled. Jamie could have sworn she saw the elf blush.

"I believe that if we strike within two days, Esuorts will not be prepared. We will strike him from the air and have a team of elves leads by Master Felthig bring out our brothers and sister." The table agreed in silence.

"Felthig, will you be ready within two days?" Conner asked.

"I will. My team will, but I will have to give our special member a crash course in techniques—one day with me, and the other day to rest. Yes, we can do it." the elf answered.

"Good," Conner stated. "Jamie, I know this is a lot to ask, but I need you to help Felthig find Amanda. Can you be a part of his team? I can personally promise your safety. He is the best."

"Whatever I need to do to get Amanda back, I will." Jamie was sure of herself.

"Then it is done. Buck, ready the aircraft. We will take all that we have. Isabelle, I need you to use your magic to add protection to them. When it is done, you will need to rest. Get with me and I will help you with the spells. You probably could use the practice," Conner started dividing assignments to everyone at the table. "Same time tomorrow we will meet here with aircraft and wingman assignments. I also want to go over how and why we will fly the routes. Am I clear?" The table acknowledged. "Good. Let us not sit here, ladies and gentlemen. Let's get to work!" With that, everyone got up from the tables and went about their tasks.

"Jamie, may I speak with you before you go?" Conner asked, stopping the young woman before she went out the door.

"Sure," Jamie started. "Conner I want to thank you for going after Amanda. She means a lot to me."

"I know she does. I know she means a lot more than you think I know. What I want to know is, are you okay with this?" Conner looked concerned for Jamie. "This is a lot to ask of you."

"Conner, I would do anything for Amanda. I would lay down my life for her."

"Jamie, this is serious. What you are saying may be a possibility." Conner was blunt.

"I understand, Anthriel. If this does not kill me, I know it will cause me to grow in ways I cannot even imagine." Conner knew that with the use of his given name, Jamie was serious.

"Alright, then. Go, but use the gifts given to you wisely. They will protect you." Jamie could say nothing. She just looked the elf in his eyes. Reaching up she grabbed his neck and hugged him. Tears of joy fell from her face. She did not know why.

"Thank you." was all she could say.

Isabelle met Buck at the airfield. With her staff in hand, she waited for Conner. She did not have to wait long. Conner came into the meadow holding a large, leather-bound book under his arm.

"I thought this may help." he said, handing the book to Isabelle.

"What is that?" the woman asked.

"It is an elfin book of protection spells. See if there are any in there that you can use."

"I can't read the elfin language." Isabelle tried not to sound frustrated.

"You won't have to. When you look at it with your staff in hand, it will translate for you. When you speak it, you words will come out in elfish." Conner explained.

"Sure, whatever..." Isabelle looked at him with one cocked eyebrow. "You've been doing this longer than I have." She took the book and went to work.

"So, Buck, how are things coming?" Conner asked the dwarf.

"Things are better that they look, lad," Buck started. "All of the birds are repaired, fueled and ready. We do have enough ammo for one skirmish. I dannot know how long that'll hold ya, but I think it'll be long enough ta get yer point across."

"Good. That's all we need to do."

"One more thing, lad..." Buck pulled at Conner's arm as the elf started walking away. "Do ya think the lad, I mean lass, is up to it? I'm sorry, lad. This whole thing with the child from the city has me confused."

"To answer your first question, yes, *she* is up to it," Conner started. "To help you out with the second issue is actually quite simple. The boy we brought back from Kansas City was actually born with a female mind and soul in a male body. *She* has been given a gift. This gift is a chance to correct the body to match the rest of her. You wouldn't like to have been born a dwarf with pointy ears would you?"

"No offense lad, but heavens no!" Buck was blunt and to the point.

"If you were, you would want a way to correct it, wouldn't you?" Conner asked with a smile.

"You betcha I would! No offense..." Buck slid his fingers up to feel his ears.

"Well then, that is how Jamie feels." Conner began to chuckle as he noticed Buck's hand. "I hope you understand better. Jamie is no less a person for being different. Actually, these experiences may make her stronger than you and I. Therefore, if you respect her, she will do the same. She is still the same person."

"Aye. That does explain a lot, lad." Conner left Buck to finish his tasks and think about what was just said. The elf knew that he just made a breakthrough with the dwarf. Conner knew that as a rule, dwarves are hard headed and not open to new ideas.

"Good. I'm glad we had this talk. I think Jamie will be happy also. It's hard enough for her to be going through this and not understanding it, herself. Knowing others are making an attempt to understand as well will help her a lot," Conner smiled. "Keep up the good work with the aircraft. Make sure all inspections are up to date. You may want to give all the birds a once over before we launch. We do not have much. We need to be sure that what we do have is one hundred percent."

"Aye, lad," the dwarf assured Conner. "Have I let you down before?"

"Good point," Conner smiled.

Jamie slid *Nathra* from its sheath. She felt its power surge through her. Her arm buzzed with the blade's magic. She was amazed at the weapon's beauty and grace. The elfin letters burned brightly just above the indentation that ran along the length of the blade. She wondered about its purpose.

"I have not seen that blade in a very long time." Felthig stepped out of the corner of her room.

"Oh." Jamie's heart jumped in her chest. "Don't you know it's rude to come into someone's house without being invited?" Jamie was more embarrassed about being frightened than of the intrusion.

"Forgive me, my lady. I only did so to prove a point." The elf bowed his head slightly.

"What point was that, that you could scare the jeepers out of a girl?" Jamie paused as she heard herself use the female pronoun. She smiled inwardly.

"No. The point I made was that I could enter any room undetected." Felthig defended.

"I'm sorry. I don't know what came over me. I have been a little moody lately," Jamie's apology was sincere. "Please, have a seat."

Felthig looked around, but no seat was to be found. "I'm sorry, I haven't had time to decorate." Jamie closed her eyes and vines sprouted from the floor and wove themselves into a comfortable chair. As soon as the chair formed, the vines detached themselves from the floor so that the chair could be moved about the room.

"Thank you. Your hospitality is most generous," Felthig seated himself. "As you know, I am not here on a social call," Jamie nodded her head. "I am here so that I may keep you alive long enough to rescue our friends."

"So you have seen my sword before?" Jamie asked, quickly changing the subject. She was not looking forward to meeting those monsters again.

"Of course, I was the one who forged it," Felthig told the young woman without expressing his pride.

"Really?" Jamie's amazement was more than obvious. "So you know what this writing is?"

"Yes. *True power lies within. Only the true of heart will find it.*" Felthig translated.

"What does that mean?" Jamie looked puzzled.

"You will know when you are ready," Felthig smiled.

"More riddles." Jamie crossed her arms.

"I am truly sorry. Telling you the answers would take away the lessons that need to be learned as you find them. Now, shall we continue our lessons?"

"I'm sorry. Was I keeping us?" Jamie flushed with embarrassment.

"No, my lady. Knowing the origin of one's blade is a good place to start. Questions are always welcome." Felthig smiled.

"Okay. What is this thing?" Jamie pointed to the indentation that went down the back of the elegantly curved blade.

"I guess you should learn the anatomy of your blade." Felthig drew his sword as an illustration. "The indentation you asked about is called the *bloodletting groove.*"

"Ew, gross!" Jamie's face clearly showed her displeasure.

"Sorry. War is neither pleasant nor pretty."
Felthig gave her a stern look.

"You're right, I'm sorry."

"Now back to the lesson," the master swordsman
brushed it off without skipping a beat. "The handle
is called the hilt or pommel. It is weighted to
provide balance to the blade. This makes it easier to
control," the elf quickly twirled his blade in a circle
to his side. Jamie could feel and hear the blade
cutting through the air. "Along with the blade, there
is not much to it. Simplicity, and elegance."

"That makes sense," Jamie stated. "So will you
show me how to use it?"

"Rumor has it you already have done quite well,
but I can show you how to improve. That is why I
came here. If you would like, after we have returned
from our mission, I can take you on as an
apprentice until you become a master swordsman."

"That would be great, but I think it's *mistress
swordswoman*," Jamie smiled.

"Very funny."

The elf and Jamie spent the rest of the day
together. The swordmaster showed her as much as
he could in that little time. He showed her how to
hold her sword and the proper stance during the
melee. Jamie listened to everything her master had
to say. She learned quickly.

Several hours went by. At sunset, Felthig ended
the lesson. Soaked with perspiration, Jamie stood
as she attempted o catch her breath. "That will be

enough," Felthig stated without as much as a bead of sweat on his brow. "You learn quickly and show great potential. I hope that what I have shown you will save you on the day after the 'morrow."

Crews of elves and dwarves went over the aircraft with fine-toothed combs. They inspected and fixed everything they could. Isabelle went through the book of elfin spells. It did not take long to find something she could use. She was amazed. With every turn of the page, the elfin letters rearranged themselves into words that she could read. The book was indeed magical.

With staff in hand, Isabelle read the spell for protection. She felt the hickory wood pulse in her hand. This was it. Her eyes skimmed the words on the page. "All magic that is good, answer my plea. Protect these things which I ask from all the evil that be."

"Elieth melthina dem, relital zem tulleth. Verno dríes belanem elieth drednel tue." These words came from her mouth as she read aloud in English. As the words were spoken, a light flashed from her staff-mounted crystal and leaped onto her Corsair. For a split instant, *Amy* was bathed in brilliant light before it faded into the plane.

The woman stopped to catch her breath. The instant the light leaped from her staff, she felt the energy drain from her body. She felt as if she had run a marathon.

"This is going to take a while," Isabelle whispered to herself as she sat on the left tire.

"Maybe this will help," Conner leaned against the left horizontal stabilizer holding a leather wineskin. He unstopped the leather bag and handed it to the exhausted woman. "You only need a sip. It will not give you any more power, but it will refresh you and give you the strength to finish your task."

Isabelle let a bit of the liquid slide past her tongue. The excessively sweet drink contorted her face briefly. She felt the exhaustion wash away as the fluid slid down her throat.

"Just a sip after every spell you cast should keep you going," Conner informed her. "You must have a large meal and rest after you have finished. I would love to join you if you'll have me." A twinkle flashed in the elf's eye.

"That would be great," Isabelle said as she stood up. "I would really like that also. Thank you." Isabelle looped the wineskin over her shoulder and around her neck. She gave Conner a warm smile and went back to work. *Maybe today won't be so long, after all*, she thought.

As she continued, she found spells for accuracy and agility. She used them as well. The task she had to perform took her about four hours, after which she was truly exhausted. The elfin drink could no longer hide that fact.

Conner returned as she rested on the wing of the *Dragon's Heart*. With her arm covering her eyes, she drifted off for a moment.

"Are you ready to eat?" Isabelle's eyes snapped open and she quickly sat up. "Are you rested?" Conner asked. "You have been asleep there for twenty minutes."

"I just closed my eyes," Isabelle argued.

"You must be tired." Conner laughed gently to himself. "Come on, sleepyhead. Let's get some food in you and put you to bed."

"It's only early afternoon!" Isabelle argued again.

"You'll need as much time as you can to recharge," Conner told her as he lifted her down from the wing. Although she was slightly taller than the elf, he was stronger than he appeared. Her feet settled on the ground lightly.

"You did a great job today. You are strong with magic." Conner told Isabelle as they climbed the walkway into the trees.

"I hope it holds up," Isabelle answered. "I'm still new to all of this."

"I am sure it will. You never cease to amaze me," Conner reached for her hand. She let him take it and give it a squeeze. "Never doubt yourself. If you begin to doubt, that is when you will fail."

"Okay." Isabelle could think of nothing else to say.

They arrived in an outside café high in the trees. She realized that it was not far from her pod, though she had never seen it. Tables had been grown in place and vines had woven themselves into elegant chairs that had been decorated with bright green leaves and red moss-covered seats.

"I don't remember this before," Isabelle commented as Conner pulled out a chair for her to sit.

"Now that we have moved into the city, the trees are tending to our needs. They are always growing things that would make our stay here pleasant and enjoyable. They wish us to be comfortable and stay indefinitely." Conner explained.

As soon as Isabelle sat down, a beautifully decorated silver tray was brought to her. Conner had received a similar one. A silver cover hid its contents from her. A familiar scent wafted from under the lid. Isabelle lifted the cover to reveal a large double cheeseburger and fries. A side dish of ketchup sat off to the side.

"How did you find a cheeseburger in the trees?" Isabelle asked. "Or is this something other than beef?"

"Don't worry. It's real beef. It is Angus, I believe," Conner smiled as he watched his friend's eyes light up. "You forget, my dear. It's magic. Now eat up and save room for dessert." Conner watched the woman dig in. Her chores had left her famished. He lifted his lid to reveal a large, lush salad. He poured a little oil over it and joined Isabelle in the feast.

"Isabelle, I have something to tell you," Isabelle stopped and looked at her massive, half-eaten sandwich. "This is not easy for me, but I want you to know that within these last few months I really appreciate what you have done."

Isabelle swallowed a mouthful. "It's good to be noticed. Thank you, boss."

"Actually, I wish you would not think of me as a boss," Conner winced inwardly. "I really like you, more than any other woman I have known for a long time," Conner paused. Isabelle stared wide-eyed at the elf. "I would like to think of you as a friend."

"Conner, I do. You are the best friend I have ever had." For some reason, a tear-choked Isabelle's throat.

"I would like to be able to one day, possibly, take this relationship further than a friendship," Conner let his thoughts fall out of his mouth. "I may not show it much, but I care for you deeply," Isabelle put down the remainder of her sandwich. She did not know what to say. "I'm sorry. I should have kept my mouth shut."

"No, it's okay. It's kind of like this burger - great, but hard to swallow all at once." Isabelle gave Conner a warm and inviting smile and finished her meal.

After hot apple pie and ice cream for dessert, Isabelle felt content and had a bit more energy. She also felt the need for another nap. A yawn escaped her lips, and tears of sleep blurred her vision.

"You look as if you could use some sleep. Can I walk you home?" Conner asked.

"That would be great. Thank you. It's been a hard day." Isabelle and Conner got up from the table. Conner led her down the wooden pathway to Isabelle's home amongst the trees.

"Well, here you are," Conner said as stopped in front of the door. "Look... I'm sorry if I scared you during lunch. I just needed to get it off my chest. We don't know what the day after tomorrow will bring."

Isabelle wrapped her arms around the elf's neck and kissed him on the lips. Reaching behind her, she opened the door and drug Conner in. The door closed behind them.

Chapter 37

Conner woke before the sun. He still had much to do. He rolled over and watched Isabelle sleep for a moment. Sliding out of the elfin silk sheets, he got dressed. He tried not to wake the woman.

"Do you think we are more than just friends?" Isabelle rolled over and smiled sleepily at Conner.

"Yes, I think so." Conner stepped into the flight suit, which he had worn the previous day. Looking back at the woman, he smiled. Her glowing face returned the gesture.

"Today, I have a lot to do. I'm sorry for running out like this," Conner apologized.

"Maybe I can come with you and help," Isabelle suggested.

"You, my little sorceress, need to get some rest. You need to recharge your batteries." Conner watched her heart sink at his comment. "Maybe you can join me for lunch again. Same place?"

"Do they have more than cheeseburgers?" Isabelle perked up instantly.

"I think they have a larger menu than that, yes," Conner smiled as he laced his boots.

"Then I think we can work something out," Isabelle said flirtatiously.

"Good. It's a date. I'll see you at noon." Conner smiled like a little boy. He grabbed his bag of papers and lists and went out the door. Isabelle curled back up in her sheets basking in the warm glow. She was still smiling as she fell back to sleep.

Conner closed the door behind him gently. Last night had been wonderful. It had been too long since he had been in the company of a beautiful woman, and Isabelle was the most beautiful woman with whom he had ever been. Maybe all the previous women's beauty faded with time.

Time... He had all he needed but Isabelle's supply was painfully limited. Dread burned its way through his soul. He knew she would age and he would stay forever youthful. Was this relationship fair to her? Was it wise to put himself through the pain of losing another lover to the gnashing teeth of age? These thoughts distracted the elf from where he was needed.

"Good morning!" Jamie sang to him from the railing outside Isabelle's door. Conner was so deep within himself he did not see her there.

"Well, hello," Conner returned as he regained his composure. "How long have you been there?"

"Just a few seconds. I got here as you were leaning on Isabelle's door. I guess you have come to ask her to breakfast too."

"Actually, Isabelle has used a lot of magic and is still sleeping," Conner explained.

"Wait a minute!" a lightbulb flashed in Jamie's mind. "You didn't just get here, you are just leaving!" Jamie put her hand up to her mouth to stifle a giggle. "No wonder she needs to rest. I bet there was magic going on." Jamie began to laugh so hard she nearly fell forward. Conner's face turned bright red.

"We were up all night talking about tomorrow." Conner fibbed.

"Don't worry. I'm not stupid. Remember, I grew up on the streets. Some of my best friends were prostitutes. I know what can go on between two people behind closed doors," Jamie winked. Conner knew he was busted. "If you want to tell the world, go for it. If you want me to keep quiet, it will cost you breakfast." Jamie smiled as she grabbed Conner's hand and led him down the walkway. Conner shook his head as he followed.

Conner and Jamie sat in the open air café. Sunlight filtered through the treetops as shadows danced across every surface. The trees put on their own shadow puppet show as the summer breeze played through the branches. Conner sipped his tea as he watched the young girl nibble on a honey-glazed cake. He was lost in the thoughts about last night, amazed how quickly the girl's demeanor had changed.

"Look. I know you are upset about Amanda. We all are." Conner tried to help.

"No. It's not that. I don't know..." Jamie tried to sort out her emotions, but only got more confused. "I'm sorry, I know I'm moody. I just don't know why. Amanda is one of my best friends. I will be up and down until she gets back, but I think it's more than that."

"You are probably right. I may not be able to help you with the girly things, but I have good ears." Conner smiled as he pulled back his hair to let his elfish ears show. Jamie laughed, almost spitting orange juice through her nose.

"Thanks, I needed that," Jamie said as she wiped her face with her napkin. "Maybe I'll have lunch with Isabelle. I could use a little girl talk."

Conner's heart sank. He knew that the young woman was right. "That's a good idea. I can listen too, you know."

"I know, and I appreciate it." Jamie tried to think about what she could talk to Conner about. She knew he was only trying to help. He was very helpful. It was weird, but there were some things that she didn't feel comfortable talking about with him.

"The thing is, it's more than missing Amanda. Only a couple of weeks ago I was living on the streets. I was a boy. Now look at me!" Jamie puffed up her chest and held her arms out to her sides in a motion for Conner to see. Conner did see. The changes in Jamie were more than obvious. "I guess this is a little overwhelming sometimes."

"I know it can be," Conner said as he brought his gaze back to the young woman's eyes. "You have to understand that the changes you are going through are more than just physical. We all go through something like you. Most of us never go through anything nearly as intense, but something similar. It's called puberty. For you, it changed halfway through. More than that, you are growing up. You are becoming who you are supposed to be. You are becoming the person you are going to be for the rest of your life. Do you understand?" Conner was trying to give as much wisdom as he could. He had very little experience dealing with younger persons.

"I think so." Jamie let the elf's words sink in. A light slowly came on in her mind.

"You are who you are. You can't change that. You are going to be someone other than who you are some day. You cannot stop that. You can only learn from it and take in what you can. The right choices will lead you to the right path. From there you will be who you are to be. Happiness is the only thing that can come from that." From Jamie's facial expression, Conner could tell he hit home. He was as proud as any father could be.

There was a pause in their conversation. "So, what did you two do last night?" Jamie was the first to break the silence.

"That is none of your business, young lady. If that's not just like a woman. It didn't take you long to jump the gossip train." Conner commented with a smile.

"What can I say? We girls have to get the scoop before we hear it from another place first. Trust me, I will hear it from someplace else." Jamie flashed Conner an evil grin.

"Let's get going. Maybe I can put you to work for a few hours to keep you out of trouble." Conner helped Jamie from her seat.

"Me? Trouble? Never!" Jamie began to laugh as they walked down the pathway toward the meadow.

Lunch came quickly for Jamie. She almost ran up to Isabelle's place to get her.

"Hello!" Isabelle greeted Jamie after she knocked on the door.

"I was wondering if you wanted to get some lunch." Jamie's eyes sparkled with anticipation. "Conner said it would be a good idea if we talked and had some girl time."

"He did, did he?" Isabelle did not know what to think about Conner giving up his lunch date to Jamie. The elf must have known that Jamie needed her more than he did. "Okay, I'm ready if you are."

They stopped at the little café and picked up a picnic lunch. With basket in hand, they wandered into the forest until they reached a particular little brook.

"This is where I met Ms. Badger," Jamie stated.

"Really? Who is she?" Isabelle once heard the name but was still curious.

"She is a talking badger and is friends with Amanda. We had a good talk," Jamie fondly reminisced. It was hard to believe that it had only been a couple of days ago. "I thought that this would be a good place to talk."

"It looks like a beautiful spot. The stream is a nice touch." Isabelle said as she laid out the blanket and began to set out sandwiches and fruit.

"I think Amanda likes it, too." Jamie thought of her friend.

"I can tell you have had a lot on your mind lately." Isabelle sat down on the blanket and motioned for Jamie to join her.

"Yeah, I talked a little about it with Conner. He helped a lot, but there are a few things I didn't feel comfortable talking to him about." Jamie started nibbling on her sandwich. She remembered a time when she would have inhaled it. Life on the street was hard.

"Let me guess, you have been extremely moody lately? You have been going from happy to depressed or angry in the blink of an eye, right?" Isabelle started.

"Yeah, how did you know?" Jamie looked baffled.

"Welcome to womanhood, girl," Isabelle smiled. "You are feeling the wonderful effects of what are called hormones."

"Is there anything I can do?" Jamie looked worried.

"Not unless you want to go back to being a guy. All women have them and the only thing you can do is enjoy it. You definitely can't fight the changes. There is hope, though."

"Really? What?" Jamie asked.

"Eventually, you'll get used to them and it won't be so bad." It felt good for Isabelle to be helping Jamie get through these rough times. Since her mother had passed away from cancer when she was little, it had only been her and her father. She wished she had someone to help her when she went through it.

"So it will eventually go away?"

"Oh, no, girl, unless you go back to the way you were, you're stuck with it."

"I definitely don't want to be a boy. It's weird. I know I used to be one. In some ways I still am, but it doesn't feel right." This added to Jamie's confusion. Isabelle could see it in her young friend's face.

"Don't worry. You'll be fine. You look great and I don't think anyone here would want you any other way. Amanda would feel the same way." Isabelle knew she could head off emotional disaster.

"That's another mess altogether," Jamie said as she finished her sandwich. "I think I have feelings for her."

"She is a good friend. We all do." Isabelle had a feeling what was coming next.

"No. I have feelings for Amanda like you have for Conner." Jamie had said it. She was glad to get it out.

"Don't worry. It was weird world and getting weirder by the day," Isabelle told her. "Remember what she told you in the tunnels?"

"Yeah..."

"I think she feels the same way." Isabelle started on an apple with a juicy crunch. "As long as two people love each other, nothing can go wrong. Love is a weird thing. It can't be stopped by anyone. It can be faked, but true love cannot be stopped. I think it's something that is meant to be. Like I said, don't worry. We'll get her back and you two can see where it goes." Jamie sat in silence thinking about spending her life with Amanda. She felt warm all over. The two women continued their conversation well into the afternoon. They talked and gossiped about everything.

"It's getting late. We better get back." Isabelle waved her hand and the basket and blanket disappeared. Jamie looked at her in amazement. "I've been practicing," Isabelle smiled. "We have a meeting to get to."

"Right. Tomorrow's the big day." Jamie smiled at the thought of bringing Amanda home.

In the meeting hall, Jamie and Isabelle were the last to arrive. Everyone else was again seated around the large living table in the middle of the room. Elves and dwarves filled the room.

"I see you two are fashionably late." Conner looked up from a map and smiled."

"You know how girls like to make an entrance." The two women looked at each other and stifled a giggle.

"If you would take your seats, we can get started." Conner did not wait for Jamie and Isabelle to find their places. He pulled down a large map from the ceiling. This was a new addition to the room. With a laser pointer, he began his briefing.

"This is our objective. It is a fortress in the middle of the Arizona desert. We know little about it. It would be safe to assume that the horde has not returned in full force. I would also feel safe to say that there will be plenty of those flying salamanders keeping a close watch. How many, I don't know.

"We will have two teams. The air team will be led by me, and the ground extraction team will be led by Master Felthig. The air team will be known as *Dragon Squadron*. I will have the call sign of Dragon Leader. Isabelle will be *Dragon* Two. Canthriel will be Three, and Sonieth will be Four. Ned and Buck will be *Dragon Mother*. You'll be higher up and will be watching out for all of us. Ardy, you will be *Dragon Scout*. Since you are the fastest, you will fly ahead and get our bearings," Conner handed maps and radio frequencies to all the pilots. "Everyone knows their planes, except for Canthriel and Sonieth. Canthriel will fly the Mitsubishi Zero and Sonieth the P51 Mustang. I wish we had more, but we have to do with what we have.

"As we're mixing it up in the air, the ground team will sneak into Esuorts' stronghold and search for Amanda and our dwarf brothers. I will turn it over to you, Felthig, to explain the rest." Conner gave the floor over to the master swordsman.

"Thank you, Anthriel. My team and I don't have much to go on. Getting in may take a while. We are prepared to spend as much time as we have to find a way into the fortress. I think the easiest way is through the front gates." All jaws dropped around the table. "Once we are in, we will find our targets and retrieve them. Are there any questions?" Jamie's hand went up. "Yes?"

"How do you intend to get that far, that fast?" Jamie asked.

"Have you not learned anything, child?" Felthig smiled. "We will use magic of course."

"Oh," Jamie felt stupid but quickly recovered. "Master Felthig, Do you have any specifics on the layout of the fortress?"

"No." The elf was blunt.

"How do you think we can find her and get out without being captured ourselves?" Jamie's heart sank as she asked.

"Faith, child. You don't think you are along for pleasant conversation, do you? I believe that your bond with Amanda will help us quickly locate and rescue her. Logically, wherever she is, the dwarves can't be far away."

In some strange way, the elf made sense. "Any more questions?" The room was silent.

"Okay, people. We start at 0500. Get plenty of rest. We need to be on our toes." Conner dismissed the room. They scattered and went their separate ways.

Jamie woke with an eerie feeling. The summer sun was just starting to bring the darkness to a light gray. She saw a shadow resting on the table across from her bed. As she slipped out from between the sheets, the lights in the room brightened. The shadow became a stack of clothes with a note.

"This is a gift to you. I know that you enjoy the one-piece flight suit, so I have tailored these clothes after it. The flight suit will make you appear as a shadow anytime you wish to not be seen. The cap will cover all but your eyes. I have also given you shoes that make you as light as a feather and will make no sound. I regret not having had the time to teach you true stealth. With these gifts, you will be

*as invisible as me. They will serve you well. I will
see you when you wake.*
Master Felthig.

Jamie was amazed at how light the fabric was.
She donned her elfin undershirt before sliding into
the flight suit. The fabric hugged her body. She was
thankful that it held her sore chest comfortably,
keeping movement to a minimum.

The shoes were also quite comfortable. Every
step was like walking on air. She made no sound.
She strapped *Nathra* to her back and was ready.
She was meeting with Conner and Isabelle for
breakfast.

Talk at the table was idle. No one wanted to talk
or think about what was about to happen. Jamie ate
in silence the entire meal. She knew it was
important to eat. Her stomach protested, but she
forced herself. She didn't know when she would eat
next. She would need all the strength she could get
to save Amanda.

The crews met in the meadow. The *Dragon
Squadron* was checking their flight gear one last
time. Jamie watched as they climbed in, and
engines chugged to life effortlessly.

"Here, you will need this," Felthig caught Jamie's
attention by surprise. "There is some elfin food
designed for long journeys as well as a few sweets.
There are also some matches, and a multi-tool to

help you out of jams. Remember what I have told you, and you'll be okay. Stick with me, and we will find Amanda together." Felthig placed his hand on her shoulder. She nodded her head in thanks and turned to watch the aircraft.

One by one, the planes took off. Each circled around the forest and fell into formation. One by one, each plane blinked out of sight.

"Are you ready?" Felthig asked.

"Is it going to hurt?" Jamie asked.

"It may feel a little weird at first, but it won't hurt a bit." the elf told her.

"That is what my dentist always said."

Before Jamie could look back at where the planes were, she felt disoriented. She stuck her hands out for balance. It was no use. She fell. Jamie quickly discovered that the lush green grass of the meadow was replaced with coarse, hot sand.

Chapter 38

Blinking back into time over the Painted Desert, Conner led the formation of antique fighter craft to meet the hordes of Necrogulls. "*Dragon Squadron*, this is Dragon Leader. Form up on me and let's come in on the high side. Buck, I don't want any surprises from above." The vintage warcraft staggered their formation at different altitudes.

"Roger that, lad. You have more experience with these abominations than anyone else." Buck acknowledged from the *Griffin Claw*. Ned piloted the B17 like an ace. All his attention was on his task. The time he spent in the flight simulators in which he built had paid off. Combined with the previous mission, Ned picked up plenty of flight experience. His kin would have been proud of the young dwarf.

"You bet, Dragon Leader!" Isabelle confirmed from her bright-colored Corsair. The woman once again felt the extension of herself that *Amy* had become. She felt safe in the cockpit of the fighter from the famous Black Sheep Squadron. Her skills, along with her newly found magical abilities, had made her almost as good as Conner in a dogfight. This was not her first battle. It did seem like no other battle mattered but the one about to unfold. She knew that the squadron was on the enemy's turf. The only thing that was on her mind was getting Amanda back.

She dropped in next to Conner. She was going to do everything within her power to make sure the elf came out alive. Everything she had learned all her life had completely changed in a matter of seconds. It had taken her the past months to realize that she was actually living in a fairytale. Elves and magic did exist. With all this, only one thing scared her: she was in love with Conner. Even if she survived today, Isabelle knew that her lifetime was but seconds to what Conner had already lived. That did not matter. She would spend every second she could with him. This very second was no different. Isabelle pushed the remainder of these thoughts out of her head. She focused on her flight.

"I have a visual, Dragon Leader. Radar counts fifty bogies." Ardenelle, the dark haired elf that was scouting ahead in the faster and smaller Messerschmitt reported. "Hold one, Leader. I stand corrected. Radar counts one-hundred bogies."

"Copy that, Dragon Scout. Fall back with the rest of the flight and get ready for a bumpy ride." Conner knew that without a miracle, there was no way to win this. He had no governments to count on for support. Esuorts made sure there were no governments left. Thanks to the virus, the human population was not one-tenth of what it had been before this started. The devastation unforgivable. He was sure that one way or another, it was going to stop here and now. "Break off in pairs. Stay with your wingman and cover each other. We need to take out as many of these nasty things as we can. I don't think their goblin riders are as quick in thinking as we are. Good luck!"

Esuorts knew the elves would follow. Predicting the elfin loyalty to their friends was too easy. The sorcerer would be ready. One hundred of his pets would make quick work of the small group of outdated aircraft. The Dark Lord ordered everything he had into the air. Nothing would be left alive this time.

With the beasts engaging the fighters, he had a new friend of his own. The young woman he had brought back with him was resting comfortably. When he was finished, she would want to stay with him. He knew he could win her friendship and trust. He would teach her things she could never learn with the elves. He would then use her powers against her own friends. The young woman would be the undoing of the elves.

The flight of antique fighters broke apart and dove down to meet their destinies. Necrogulls banked and climbed to meet their mechanical foes. Their leather wings pushed them up into the fray. It had begun. Isabelle was the first to score a hit. Banking left she quickly lined up her visuals on a crowded gaggle of the evil beasts. The goblin screamed in horror as the 50-caliber rounds sliced through magic armor that was worn both by him and his putrid steed. The goblin general realized quickly that this was not going to be as easy as it was to conquer the other human forces.

The small band of elves, dwarves, and single human had the range and distance to their advantage. The flying goblin horde had sheer numbers. They had to get in close enough to spray their destructive saliva. Conner was all too aware of this. He had destroyed over half a dozen before he was caught in a cloud of the goblin air force. At close range, the Necrogulls took their toll. The acid spray from the glands under their tongues was doing considerable damage to the *Dragon Squadron.*

Isabelle thrust the nose of her corsair down to increase airspeed, diving away from the screaming beasts. The acid sprayed on her canopy. The layer of magic infused Lexan only fogged temporarily. She quickly outdistanced the monsters and looped into a barrel roll. As she did, her sites lined up on two and her guns cut them out of the sky.

Her attention was swiftly grabbed by a plume of smoke. She discovered that the Zero flown by one of

her new elfin friends was pointed towards the
ground. It was at the mercy of gravity. A colorful
cloud of a silken parachute blossomed as Canthriel
bailed from her dying aircraft. She was quickly
snatched out of the air by the enemy and consumed
in one bite.

The Mustang also fought valiantly. Sonieth
banked the P51 to the right and lined up his sites on
the beasts swarming around the Warhawk. His
machine guns sang a ballad of death to the
Necrogulls swarming around Conner. As one beast
fell, more entered the melee with the P40. The
numbers were unbelievable. Lost in his musings,
Sonieth was grabbed from behind by two of the
beasts. Flesh and metal spun downward as they
entangled. Steel-like claws ripped into the cockpit.
Like a nut being cracked for its meat, the fighter
was shelled. The elfin pilot was pulled from the
twisted metal and devoured. The deformed fighter
plummeted to the ground in a fireball.

Conner also watched the death of two good
friends. He did not have the time to think about
what had just happened. He had problems of his
own. Conner had five Necrogulls on him. The
titanium talons had already ripped through his left
wing and pierced his fuel cell. The time that the
Dragon's Heart had left in the air was limited. This
only made him more determined to take as many
with him as he possibly could. With a yank on his
stick, he rolled and lined up a monster and quickly

cut it down. Rockets locked and he let three loose in immediate succession. All three hit different marks.

"Dragon Mother, this is Dragon Leader. Buck, I am hit. My fuel cell is ripped wide open," Conner reported to the *Griffin Claw*. "I only have a few minutes, but I am taking as many of these beasts with me as I can."

"Bless you, lad. Good luck to ya. I will get someone to come and get ya once ya hit the ground." Buck was worried for the elf. The dwarf also had just seen what happened to the elfin pilot of the Mitsubishi. Conner and Buck had been friends all his life. The elf had even been there at his birth and had been such good friends of his family for several generations. He had faith in the elf, but he worried still.

The *Griffin Claw* did a lot of damage. The tail gun and the guns in the nose and top turrets had all been replaced with extremely rapid-firing Vulcan cannons. Conner's connections with the militaries of the world had been very beneficial. It was a shame that the virus had done so much devastation. Now they were no more. The firing of all the guns sent vibrations through the entire airframe of the *Griffin Claw*. Buck did not have much in the way of test firing the updated weaponry. This bird was going to need a going through when it got back... *if* it got back. The elfin and dwarf gunners were not letting any of the goblin riders get close to the aircraft.

Nedloh flew the bomber as nimbly as its fighter counterparts. Once again, updated flight controls made the old bomber extremely responsive; diving, rolling and looping almost as well as the *Dragon's Heart*. A spell on the airframe kept gravity at a constant, reducing inertia and centripetal forces. This allowed the gunners to better concentrate on their targets. Computers also aided in the acquisition of targets. With the targeting and designation system now installed on every turret, the computer would easily acquire the next goblin rider as soon as the first had been downed.

With all the computer technology the young dwarf genius added to the bomber, sheer numbers of the enemy had begun to take their toll. The bomber's size also made it an easy target for the horde. Buck heard a teeth-wrenching scream of the aircraft's metal flesh being ripped from the fuselage. The dwarf mechanic quickly unfastened his safety belt and ran to investigate.

He could see that a Necrogull had ripped a hole in the tail section, big enough to fit its head. It had already been gnashing at the elfin gunner above it in the turret. Putrid saliva splattered everywhere. Buck rapidly planted his battle-axe on the beast's forehead. The 'Gull went cross-eyed and then immobile. The head slid through the gaping expanse in the belly of the bomber and spun downward toward the ground.

"Be more careful about lettin' 'em get a hold on us, lad. This 'un put a world o' hurt on us." Buck yelled up front over the whistling of the inward rushing air. The stout dwarf tried the best he could to push the twisted aircraft skin back into place. He knew a gaping hole would cause more drag and tax the fuel supply greatly. He did not want to consider the handling issues it brought. After spraying a sealant that Nedloh designed with the help of Conner's elfin magic, the fissures in the metal seemed to heal themselves within seconds. It once again could support the weight of its crew.

Time was of the essence. Conner knew he had to do as much damage to the swarm as he cold before his time was up. He kept one eye on his fuel gauge and one on his crosshairs. The computer painted and prioritized his targets. He dropped everyone. Quickly doing the math, he estimated at the current rate of fuel loss that he only had two minutes left in the air. Two minutes is a short lifetime for his enemies. It was not long before he racked up over fifteen kills. Goblins howled as their slimy winged steeds fell from the skies.

Conner's last seconds came upon him much too quickly. He spent his last few climbing to gain airspeed. He went through his mental checklist. He had his parachute strapped on tight and his fifty caliber handgun on his thigh. The *Dragon's Breath* was loaded with the safety on. The father's blade was sheathed to the back of his Kevlar seat.

Dragon Squadron

Leveling off the *Dragon's Heart*, Conner squeezed
the trigger on the stick one last time. Not even
looking to see if the rounds found their marks, he
slid the canopy open. "Dragon Squadron, this is
Dragon Lead. I am bailing. Cover me if you can, and
Godspeed. You have fought well. If it has to be, die
with honor."

Conner released the crash belts and stepped up.
Once again, he felt the wind rush around him like
the days of old. He instantly felt exhilarated. As he
stepped to the edge of the cockpit, a goblin flew in
to attack the wounded and dying Warhawk. Conner
drew his father's sword as he ducked the gaping
jaws. In one fluid movement, he came up and
swung the elfin steel blade. The sword found the
soft tissue of the neck and sliced the putrid gray
skin quickly. The head and body went in two
different directions. The rider howled with fear and
anger as it and its evil beast plummeted to the
earth.

Conner straddled the open cockpit as he cut two
more foes out of the sky as the mortally wounded
aircraft fell. He quickly realized he was out of time.
He released his parachute and separated from his
second home. The parachute bloomed into a
brilliant emerald green with a yellow crest and
green dragon in its center.

Isabelle could do nothing to help her companion.
Emotion welled up inside her. She realized for the
first time how deep her love for the elf went. As she

watched the speed and gleam of his sword and the swiftness of his actions she also felt something else. She watched Conner cleave two of the Necrogulls with just a sword. Following the love and amazement, attacked the most vicious of enemies— fear. She felt this not for her own life or welfare, but for his. Before her eyes, she had lost him. As she had watched the death of Canthriel, she was certain Conner's fate would be the same.

I am fine. She heard his voice comfort her. *Concentrate on your flying and you will be too. I will see you back in the wooded city.* Warmth washed over her and she snapped back to the task at hand. Pitching her amethyst-colored Corsair onto its left wing, she banked sharply to line up her crosshairs once again.

Conner drifted towards the ground. He felt like he was in the middle of a feeding frenzy. Hearing the scream of the 'Gull, he turned around to see the beast coming toward him. He took a quick assessment of the battle. Only half of the goblin air force had been vanquished, and only two members of the Dragon Squadron were left. *Amy* still fought strongly felling enemies left and right. The *Griffin Claw* still spewed enchanted lead and fire but it was not faring as well. It had lost two turrets and one engine.

Angry at the loss of his favorite aircraft, he drew his 50-caliber handgun. He lined up the sites on the fast approaching beast and goblin rider and squeezed off two rounds. Each found their marks. The rider grabbed its chest and let out its howl of death. The 'Gull's eyes snapped shut. Dark, putrid blood could be seen coming from its forehead before it went lifeless and fell to the earth. More attacked Conner's parachute. Conner cut down many more in the same manner. He had emptied two full clips before he hit the ground.

Buck watched his friend as he continued to battle even without his noble steed. He only took a fraction of a second to admire his gallantry. Buck had his own issues. One turret was dissolved, along with the dwarf gunner inside, by the enemy's putrid saliva. The top gun turret was ripped open and the gunner devoured before Buck was able to reach the monster and split its forehead with his battle-axe. "Not like the old days, lad." He yelled back to the cockpit at Nedloh.

The young dwarf flew the bulky bomber with an elfin grace. He was able to line up sites for the gunners with the help of the computer targeting system that he had devised. He was also able to assist with the diminishing of enemy forces with the missile payload that had been installed in the bomb bay. This had been exhausted along with much of the ammunition in the surviving turrets. Buck had busied himself with transferring remaining munitions from the destroyed turrets to the living. There was still much to be done. The battle was not looking good and was far from over.

"Buck!" Nedloh yelled. "I need you back in the flight cabin."

"You are doing great, lad," Buck retorted absentmindedly. He was engrossed with his own tasks. "Give me just a few more moments."

"You don't understand. You need to come and see this now!" The young pilot persisted. There was urgency in his voice that Buck quickly recognized. The dwarf mechanic feared the worst.

"What are ya losin' now, lassie?" He spoke to the bomber as if she was an old friend. To him, she was. He was doing all he could to keep the vintage bomber together. At the moment, duct tape and bailing wire seemed to be the two main choices for tools as well as spare parts.

Frustrated, Buck dropped the box of shells off in the nose and tapped the dwarf gunner on the shoulder. Without taking eyes off his targeting computer, the stout little gunner nodded confirmation. Within seconds, Buck had climbed back into the flight cabin.

"What now, lad?" Buck asked a very dumbstruck pilot staring out the pilot's window.

The only thing that Nedloh could do was point and utter one word. "Dragons!"

Conner gently glided to the ground. He rolled with his landing and quickly got to his feet. He did not want to be taken by surprise, but it was too late. The elf was surrounded by almost as many human heavies as there were goblins in the sky. He quickly brought the sites of his handgun to bear on the closest one and squeezed. One round hit its mark and the Heavy fell, then came the click of an empty magazine.

The remaining gaggle of heavies carried goblin swords as well as various large machine guns. Sword drawn, Conner dove into the fray. He had no hope of coming out of this alive. He moved with the speed of lighting. The elfin blade was stronger than any man-made steel. His smaller size definitely gave him the advantage over these larger, more lethargic blasphemous creatures.

Quickly they fell. For each one the elf cut down, it seemed that five more had taken its place. He dodged and parried blows. The elfin blade cut many a crudely made mace and sword in half. Many of the small arms that these beasts carried were rendered useless by the laser-sharp elfin edge. Ducking swings from his titanic opponents, he was overtaken. He felt a blow find its mark on the back of his head. All around him quickly faded to darkness.

Larissa Vitt was a child of the 80's. She joined the United States Army where she graduated top of my class and received distinguished honors upon completing the US army attack helicopter course and spent six years as a crew chief and mechanic.

Science fiction was still in her blood. From the first time she saw the science fiction explosion on the silver screen in the late 70's and read the works of J.R.R. Tolkien, she was hooked. She had worked several jobs and after not finding an aviation career, the pen called to her.

When not writing she spends her time painting and tinkering with old cars. These are some of the aspects of her life have found their way into the fabric of her stories. Her ability to see and paint a picture shines through from the beginning.

Today she enjoys life in Shawnee Kansas, married to her best friend while wielding her brushes and painting with words.

Made in the USA
Monee, IL
14 April 2023